ALSO BY MARGARET BROWNLEY

A Match Made in Texas
Left at the Altar
A Match Made in Texas
How the West Was Wed

Christmas in a Cowboy's Arms anthology

Cowboy
Charm School

MARGARET
BROWNLEY

sourcebooks
casablanca

Published by Sourcebooks Casablanca, an imprint of
Sourcebooks, Inc.
P.O. Box 4410, Naperville, Illinois 60567-4410
(630) 961-3900
Fax: (630) 961-2168
sourcebooks.com

Printed and bound in Canada.
MBP 10 9 8 7 6 5 4 3 2 1

With loving gratitude to my dear friends and guardian angels, Pat and Steve.

When buying a horse, don't consult a pedestrian, and when courting a woman, don't ask advice of a bachelor.

—NINETEENTH CENTURY WISDOM

1

Haywire, Texas
1885

BRETT TUCKER HUNKERED LOW IN THE SADDLE AND
urged his galloping horse to go even faster. With the
wind in his face and the sun at his back, he pressed his
boots hard in the stirrups. He didn't know her name
or anything about her; all he knew was that he had to
save her.

With a slap of his reins, he yelled, "Giddup!"

His mind raced along with his mount's pounding
hooves. *But what if he was too late?*

The ground shook beneath his hurtling horse, sending
squirrels and rabbits racing for cover. Frenzied blackbirds
shot from treetops, scorching the air with protesting
squawks. Deer took flight with leaping bounds.

A farmer pulled his wagon to the side of the road,
allowing Brett to race by unhampered. Mavericks
raised their tails and ran. A buffalo lifted its shaggy
head and bellowed.

Jaw tense, Brett narrowed his eyes against the dust

and the glare of the hot, white sun. The only things identifying him as a Texas Ranger were the Colt at his side and the shotgun slung from his saddle. That and maybe his grit.

It was his grit that had brought him to this moment. The moment he'd waited for. Waited too long for— three years, two months, and twenty-one days to be exact.

The road sloped upward, slowing his progress. Digging his heels into his horse's flanks, Brett urged him up the hill. "Come on, Soldier, come on."

His mount crested the hill, and the steeple of the white church came into view.

Behind him lay the town of Haywire, and before him the moment he'd hoped would forever define him as a man.

The horses and wagons parked outside the church gave Brett a small measure of comfort. In less than two minutes, the wait would be over, and he would have done a woman a favor in the process. That is, if he wasn't too late.

One minute. Anticipation coursed through his body.

Thirty seconds.

Twenty.

Reaching the church, he pulled hard on the reins, and Soldier's front legs rose in the air. Brett slid out of the saddle, boots hitting the ground hard. With one quick move, he wrapped the reins around the hitching rail and reached for his holstered Colt.

Surprise was on his side, and he dared not waste a minute. Taking the steps two at a time, he rushed through the double oak doors leading inside the hushed chapel and ran past the two startled ushers. He hated ruining a bride's wedding day, but better now than later. No woman in her right mind would knowingly marry an outlaw.

"Stop the wedding!" he yelled. A collective gasp greeted his outburst, and all heads swiveled in his direction. Sunlight slanted through stained-glass windows, bathing the church in a rainbow of colors.

Pausing a moment to gather his bearings, he raced down the center aisle, vaguely aware of the pews on either side packed with wide-eyed guests.

A heavyset man with a walrus mustache rose from the front pew. "What is the meaning of this?"

Brett halted. "I'm looking for Frank Foster."

All eyes turned toward the groom stepping forward, a puzzled frown on his face. "I'm Frank Foster."

The would-be groom looked nothing like the man who had ruined Brett's sister's life and was wanted for robbery. For one thing, he was shorter, leaner, lighter in complexion. He was also at least five years too young.

Brett had a bad feeling about this. "*You're* Frank Foster?"

The man glowered at him. "Yeah. So, what of it?"

"Frank J. Foster?"

"Franklin Thomas Foster, if you must know."

Brett sucked in his breath. *Good God!* What had he done?

Holstering his firearm, he gave the bride and groom a sheepish grin. "Sorry to bother you, folks. N-nice wedding." He tossed an apologetic glance at the stone-faced preacher. "Continue what you were doing."

As he turned to leave, he met the bride's gaze. Even

the veil couldn't hide her big, blue eyes or the look of dismay on her pretty, round face. He felt bad for disrupting her special day. Absolutely terrible. The worst. On impulse, he leaned forward and whispered in her ear. "Sorry, ma'am. Didn't mean to interrupt your wedding. Hope you find it in your heart to forgive me."

He backed away just as the groom grabbed hold of his arm. "What is this, eh?" He cast a narrow-eyed glance at his bride. "Who is this man?"

"I-I never saw him before in my life," the bride stammered.

"That's not what it looked like to me." Foster shoved Brett hard. "What are you doing here?"

Brett held out the palms of his hands to calm the man. "I'm a Texas Ranger—"

"How do you know my fiancée?"

"I don't, sir."

"Don't lie to me." The veins stood out on the groom's neck. "I saw the way you looked at her."

"I felt bad for her is all. I shouldn't have come here. My apologies. I'm leaving."

"Yeah, well, not without this, you aren't!" Foster let his fist fly, a steel-like knuckler that landed on Brett's jaw. Brett's head jerked back and parted company with his wide-brimmed hat. Guests gasped and jumped to their feet.

The bride's mouth dropped, and her eyes rounded in horror.

Shaking away the fog in his head, Brett reached for his sore jaw. For such a compact man, this Foster fella was strong as a bull. As mean as one, too, if the look on his red face was any indication.

Spectators were either too shocked or too dazed to move. The stunned silence was broken by the sudden frantic ringing of the church bell, signaling trouble.

"Frank, please," the bride cried, grabbing hold of the groom's arm.

Shaking her away, Foster advanced toward Brett, fists ready to strike again.

This time, Brett was ready for him. He grabbed the groom's swinging arm within inches of his own throbbing jaw. In the tussle that followed, a candle overturned. Flames shot across the altar cloth, and a woman screamed. The preacher spun around, grabbed the basin off the baptismal font, and tossed the contents.

The water missed the fire but not the bride. Crying out, she stared down at her soaked wedding gown and sputtered in shock and disbelief.

An usher slapped at the flames with his frock coat, startling the bride and snapping her out of her daze. Yanking off her veil, she glared at Brett, her chest heaving, before running up the aisle, her train dragging behind her. Several women, including the bridesmaid, followed her out the double doors.

The bride's absence only made the groom more furious. Lunging forward, he barreled into Brett headfirst. The air whooshed out of Brett with an *oomph*, and the two of them fell to the floor. The best man, ushers, and even some of the guests tried to separate them, but failing that, took swings at one another instead. Soon, all hell broke loose.

Fists flew in every direction. The sound of pounded flesh was followed by grunts and groans. A baby cried, a woman screamed, and the church bell kept pealing.

Breaking free from Foster, Brett jumped to his feet and pulled out his gun. When his order to stop failed to gain the hoped-for results, he aimed high. He fired a warning shot at the ceiling, and pieces of plaster rained down on the chaotic mass of bodies on the floor. Fists froze in midair. For a long moment, silence reigned.

"You shot Jesus," the minister finally said, sounding like a man announcing the end of the world.

Brett spun around. "What?"

The reverend pointed upward. All eyes lifted to the fresco painted on the ceiling.

Brett groaned. Not only had he ruined the wedding of two perfect strangers, but he'd also decapitated the Man on the donkey. Accusatory gazes lit into him, and a half dozen men moved forward.

The doors swung open, and the arrival of the sheriff stopped the men in their tracks.

Sheriff Keeler surveyed the damage and turned to Brett with a smirk. Rubbing his chin, Brett glared back. He'd sent a message for the sheriff to meet him at the church, but the lawman sure had taken his sweet time getting there.

"Looks like you got yourself in a heap o' trouble," the sheriff said in a mocking tone.

Brett holstered his gun but said nothing. He didn't know what to say. No doubt the sheriff would notify Brett's superior officer, and he'd have a lot of explaining to do. A heck of a lot. Grimacing at the thought, he bent to pick up his hat.

After the sheriff and his men rounded up a respectable number of citizens—including the groom—and carted them off to jail, Brett slipped the minister a gold eagle. He doubted that Jesus could be saved, but surely the money would help pay for the rest of the property damage.

Dabbing at his sore jaw with a handkerchief, he then staggered outside. There was no sign of the bride, and the makeshift paddy wagon had already pulled away.

Brett threw himself onto his saddle and groaned. He'd always had a bad feeling about weddings. Now he knew why.

2

THE HAYWIRE BOOK AND SWEET SHOP WAS EMPTY except for Aunt Letty, and that was just fine and dandy with Kate Denver.

Normally, anyone entering the pink-and-white shop found a world far removed from the realities of life. The colorful sticks of candy and sweet-tasting gumdrops and sugarplums offered a momentary respite from one's troubles.

Today, however, not even the familiar smell of toffee and cinnamon could erase the pain and embarrassment Kate felt. It was Monday, only two days since her disastrous wedding. She'd been tempted to stay home and hide, but what good would that have done? Eventually, she would have to face the public. May as well get it over with.

Her aunt gazed down from atop a ladder, her well-lined face suffused with disapproval. "I thought you agreed to stay home this week."

"And I thought you agreed that your ladder days were over."

For answer, her aunt descended, feather duster in

hand. At sixty-five, she was as agile as a woman half her age, but Kate couldn't help but worry. Aunt Letty was the only family she had. If anything happened to her, Kate would be alone in the world, and she feared that more than anything. Not that she couldn't take care of herself. She also had many good friends, but that wasn't the same as having a family of her own, and no one knew that better than she did.

"So, what are you doing here?" Aunt Letty asked.

Kate shoved her purse on the shelf beneath the counter and swiped a strand of red hair away from her face. "It was either come here and work or stay home feeling sorry for myself." She reached for an apron and lifted it off a peg. "And we have orders to fill."

Mrs. Jenkins had been promised an array of sweets for her granddaughter's birthday party, and the school-marm, Miss Hopkins, wanted jelly beans for teaching her young pupils to add and subtract. Then there was the standing order of mixed candies for the weekly meeting of the Haywire Women's Club.

"I whipped up a fresh batch of lemon drops," Aunt Letty said. "Soon as it cools, we can box it up."

Kate sighed. Getting her aunt to slow down was like trying to herd a flock of chickens. She and Uncle Joe had started the shop thirty years ago, and it was the longest-running business in town. The small but well-stocked book section had been added during the war to meet the demands of soldiers.

Aunt Letty moved the ladder to the back room, which served as part kitchen and part storage. She returned moments later with a new shipment of dime novels that had arrived on the morning train.

"Have you spoken to Frank?" she asked, slitting the box open.

Kate donned her apron. Yanking the ties, she wrapped them around her waist. "No, and I don't intend to." Had it been left to her, Frank would still be in jail—and it would serve him right for the way he'd acted.

Aunt Letty studied her. "It wasn't his fault that your wedding got ruined."

Kate scoffed. "Then whose fault was it?"

"You know very well that the Texas Ranger was to blame." Her aunt gave a derisive snort. "He's the one who should be in jail."

"The ranger apologized."

"And you accepted his apology and not Frank's?"

"Oh?" Kate tied the apron strings into a bow. "Did Frank apologize? I must have missed it."

Her aunt pulled a book out of the box and studied the lurid cover. "Where men are concerned, you sometimes have to read between the lines. You know Frank's a very proud man."

"I can live with that." Kate reached for the box of dog cakes and dropped a handful into the treat bowl kept on hand for her furry friends. "What I can't live with is his jealousy."

"Now, Kate, you know what happened when Mabel Adams didn't forgive her husband. He shot himself in the foot to prove how sorry he was."

"I don't think we have to worry about Frank harming himself in any way. He can't stand the sight of blood."

"Maybe not, but then Ruth Bayer didn't think her

husband would run away with another woman. And I'll tell you another—"

Fortunately, Kate was saved from her aunt's long list of horror stories by the bell—or rather a riot of bells jingling on the front door. It was Mrs. Peters, right on time.

She appeared every day like clockwork. A creature of habit, she peered at the colorful candy displayed beneath the glass counter as if unable to make up her mind. After long and careful deliberation, she invariably purchased the same thing: one hickory-nut cup. It was basically how she'd lived her life—safe and careful, never venturing more than a block or two from home.

Today, she was all tutting sounds and sympathetic looks. "Oh, you poor, poor dear. To have your wedding ruined in such an awful way." She stared across the counter at Kate with faded blue eyes, her crinkled face framed by an old straw bonnet that had gone out of style long before the war. "I can't imagine how you must feel. What are you going to do?"

Her aunt answered with a meaningful look at Kate. "She's going to reschedule her wedding, that's what."

A look of relief floated across Mrs. Peters's face. "Oh, of course. I should have known."

After much consideration, she decided on the usual hickory-nut cup and slid a coin across the counter with a gloved hand.

Kate placed her order in the bottom of a paper sack and added a strip of paper with a handwritten prediction that was meant to be amusing. It was a tradition started by her uncle. As far as Kate knew, few customers took the fortunes seriously, but they were good for a laugh or two.

Mrs. Peters giggled like a young girl. "The last prediction said that I was about to meet a tall, handsome stranger, and he would sweep me off my feet."

Kate smiled. "Maybe you will." Though her husband had died long before the war, Mrs. Peters still wore widow's weeds.

"You know that's not going to happen. Men prefer younger women. For a man to be interested in me, he'd have to be a hundred."

Kate laughed. She felt better already. How she loved her job, loved bantering with her customers. Loved making them smile, even on days when it felt like her own heart was breaking. "Have a good day, Mrs. Peters."

"You too." Holding her purchase in one hand with the care one would give an injured bird, Mrs. Peters hobbled out of the store.

The moment their customer left, Aunt Letty started in again. "About your wedding…" She turned to the calendar on the wall. Having planned Kate's wedding with the care of a general plotting an attack, she looked no less determined this second time around. But then she'd always been a hopeless romantic.

Now she stabbed at the calendar with her finger. "I think we should reschedule it for a week from Saturday. That will give us time to get word out and—"

"Auntie, please." Kate felt a pang of guilt for having to disappoint her aunt, but it couldn't be helped. "I don't want to talk about this right now."

Aunt Letty turned, her expression a combination of surprise and disapproval. "But we have to talk about it, and there's no time like the present. You know what happened to Missy Gaylord when she put off her wedding. That awful war started, and she never saw her fiancé again."

Kate sighed. "I don't think we're in danger of another war."

"You never know." Her aunt's thin, gray eyebrows knitted. "So, when *can* we talk about it?"

Kate was tempted to say never, but she didn't have the heart to upset her aunt any more than necessary. Despite her aunt's best efforts at matchmaking, suitors had been few and far between through the years. Most men were put off by Kate's independent ways. Some even felt threatened by Kate's ability to match skills in just about any male endeavor. Aunt Letty had sworn that Kate was doomed to spinsterhood. That is, until Frank had walked back into Kate's life.

It never seemed to bother him that Kate was more adept at changing a wagon wheel and shoeing a horse than hosting a quilting bee or a tea party. Even candy making was considered a male occupation, and Kate excelled at that—or would once she mastered her uncle's prized cut rock-candy recipe.

"I remember a time when you and Uncle Joe didn't even like Frank," Kate said.

"Oh, we liked him all right. It's just that you and he were spending so much time together. It wasn't a problem when you were still children. But when you turned thirteen, people began to talk."

At the time, Kate couldn't understand what all the fuss was about. Why was it okay to run around with Frank one year and not the next?

Aunt Letty took another stab at the calendar. "What about two weeks from Saturday?"

Kate shook her head. "I need time to think. I want…to make sure my marriage is just as perfect as yours and Uncle Joe's was. If Frank continues to be jealous whenever a man so much as glances at me, I don't see that happening."

Aunt Letty scoffed. "If it's perfection you want, become a nun. Perfection has no place in a marriage."

"That's not true, Auntie. Why, no marriage was more perfect than yours." Her uncle had died more than two years ago, and they both still missed him dearly.

"Fiddlesticks. You need flint and steel to make a spark, and the same is true of a marriage. When things went wrong, your uncle and I talked about them." Aunt Letty tossed her head. "Sometimes in loud voices."

Kate reared back in surprise. "I don't ever remember you and Uncle Joe arguing."

"That's because we battled out our differences in the barn where you couldn't hear us." Aunt Letty pulled off her apron and hung it on a wooden peg. "Your uncle could be stubborn at times."

Kate gave her aunt a loving smile. "And you're not?"

"Certainly not." Aunt Letty sniffed. "I'm not stubborn. I'm persistent. Not the same thing."

Kate sighed. Arguing would get her nowhere. Once her aunt made up her mind, not even an act of Congress could change it. "All right. I'll talk to Frank."

The frown melted from Aunt Letty's face. "That's my girl." Apparently thinking her mission accomplished, she reached for her purse. "Since you're here, I'll go and pick up supplies." She pulled a glove over her hand. "We need cream of tartar. Anything else?"

Kate checked the notebook next to the cashbox. "We're running low on molasses."

With a nod and a wave, Aunt Letty was out the door, and Kate immediately set to work.

She picked up a spatula and started by scooping pralines for the afternoon quilting bee into a cardboard box. The ladies preferred chocolate to the nut-and-sugar confections, but despite her best efforts, Kate had yet to find a way of keeping it from melting in the Texas heat. Not even adding more sugar to the recipe helped. Chocolate was a luxury best kept for cooler weather.

Now that she was alone, she felt her spirits drop. For months, she had dreamed of the perfect wedding. The perfect marriage. The perfect life. She'd spent hours taking measurements and picking out wallpaper for the apartment over Frank's saddle and leather shop. She couldn't wait to turn it into a real home for the two of them. At least until they had saved enough money to build a house.

Staring down at the cardboard box, Kate bit back tears. She and Frank had a long history together. Though still angry, she missed him dearly. During her childhood, no one had been as much fun to be with as Frank. He'd taught her how to play poker and horseshoes and how to hit a ball with a stick. He figured she could do anything he could do, and that's what she had loved about him.

It had nearly broken her heart when her aunt and uncle insisted that she stop seeing Frank and act more ladylike when she became a teen. That meant tedious hours spent learning to embroider, play the piano, and carry on polite conversation. Though she and Frank had enjoyed arguing politics, no such talk was ever allowed to sully her aunt's parlor.

Despite Aunt Letty's best efforts, Kate had never given up her wild ways. After her uncle died, she'd started working at the shop full time and had less time to herself. Still, she never completely stopped doing the things she loved. It was at the old swimming hole where she and Frank got reacquainted on a whole different level, and the next thing she knew, the town seamstress was measuring her for a wedding gown.

She'd always known that Frank had a jealous streak, but she'd honestly thought that once they were wed, he would change his ways and learn to trust her. How foolish to think that such a deep-rooted problem could be so easily resolved!

She swiped away a tear just as the shop door flew open. Recognizing the rugged square face staring at her from beneath a pearl-gray Stetson hat, she dropped her spatula.

Oh! It was *him*.

Brett Tucker walked into the Haywire Book and Sweet Shop with more than a little dread.

Judging by the looks he'd received around town since Saturday's fiasco, he was probably the most despised man in Haywire. Not that he didn't deserve public scorn. If only he could think of a way to make amends.

Upon entering the shop, he paused to get his bearings. A strong but no-less-pleasing aroma that was all sweetness and light greeted him, taking him back to his childhood. He'd liked the scents of vanilla, cinnamon, and licorice then, and he found that he liked them just as much now.

What the pleasant scents did to his sense of smell, the burst of bright colors did for the eye. No shop in his memory had been so gaily decorated.

Paper whirligigs dangled from a pink-striped ceiling. Pink curtains fluttered at the open windows. Jars of colorful stick candy stood like soldiers on counters and shelves. Quilts hung on walls that were also plastered with neatly printed signs. *A Balanced Diet Is a Piece of Stick Candy in Each Hand*, read one sign. There were quotes from Shakespeare and Elizabeth Browning. Another sign read, *Candy Makes the World a Sweeter Place*.

His gaze zeroed in on the woman behind the counter, and his breath caught. Thanks to the morning paper, he now knew her name was Kate Denver. She looked just as fetching today as she'd looked in her wedding gown.

The eyes watching him flashed with blue fire. Her bright-red hair looked like it was in flames, too, thanks to the sun slanting through the transom over the door. She wore her hair pinned back in a snood, tendrils curling around her ears. Her long-lashed eyes looked even larger than he remembered. Freckles marched over her nose and rosy cheeks, all the way to the shiny balls twirling at her ears.

Somehow, the combination of red hair, freckles, and turned-up nose worked together to make a very pleasing whole. That Foster fella didn't know how lucky he was. What a dang fool.

Light shadows skirted her eyes, suggesting she'd gotten little sleep since her disastrous wedding. A wave of guilt washed over him as he tugged on the brim of his hat.

Ducking beneath a whirligig, he stepped closer to the counter. "Miss Denver. I'm afraid we didn't get properly introduced the other day. I'm Brett Tucker, Texas Ranger."

"I know who you are," she said, her voice as hard as the peanut brittle in the glass counter standing between them.

He sucked in his breath. If looks could kill, he'd be a goner for sure. Not that he could blame her. Thanks to him, not only was her interrupted wedding the talk of the town, but the *Haywire Dispatch* had planted the story on the front page beneath a bold headline: "Wedding Ends in Disaster."

Brett cleared his throat. "I…eh…came to apologize again for what happened. I had no idea that there were *two* Frank Fosters." Thinking that an explanation was in order, he continued, "The Foster I was looking for is a wanted man. I've been on his trail for a long while." Twice, Brett had almost caught him. Both times the man had slipped away. "When I heard that someone by that name was getting married, I immediately assumed it was the fugitive I've been chasing."

Miss Denver crossed her arms. "Next time, you might want to look before you leap."

"I hope to God there isn't a next time, ma'am. I never want to stop another wedding." He rubbed his still-sore chin. "All I could think about was saving you."

"Saving me?" She stared at him. "You don't even know me."

"Not personally, ma'am, that's true. But the Frank Foster I'm after is a danger to any woman." She said nothing, and he continued. "I hope you'll let me make it up to you. If there's anything I can do…"

"I believe you've done quite enough already, Mr. Tucker," she said.

He drew in his breath. She wasn't making it easy, but then, why should she? Still, he wasn't ready to give up. "There must be something. I tried bailing your fiancé out of jail, but he refused to accept my help."

Something flickered in the depths of her eyes. "If you're serious about wanting to do something, you'll leave town and not return."

Tilting his Stetson forward, he rubbed the back of his neck. "I'm afraid that will be a little hard to do, ma'am." A crime wave had hit the county, overwhelming local lawmen. The opportunity to serve as a special Texas Ranger couldn't have come at a more opportune time. Brett had been sent to Haywire to assist the sheriff in bringing the culprits to justice, but the reason he'd volunteered for the job was far more personal.

When he'd heard about the crime wave in Haywire, he was convinced that Foster—not her fiancé but the other Foster—was behind it. The methods were the same. Men dressed in black and wearing flour sacks over their heads robbed stages and an occasional bank and then vanished without a trace until the next holdup. Either it was the same gang who had wreaked havoc in San Antonio and other towns, or a copycat gang was on the loose.

"I'm here on special commission from Captain McMurray."

Miss Denver greeted his news with a look of disdain. "Then I suggest you attend to your business and stay away from the rest of us."

Attending to business was exactly what Brett planned on doing. "As you wish," he said.

She slanted him a look of curiosity. "What did this man…this second Mr. Foster…do?"

Brett hesitated. Even after all this time, it hurt to talk about it. "Among other things, he caused my sister's death," he said, his voice thick.

A shadow flickered across her forehead as if she fought against giving him any slack. In the end, empathy won out and her expressive eyes softened. "I'm so sorry."

She didn't press for details, and for that, he was grateful. "So am I." He backed away from the counter.

"You look like you could use some candy," she said. "It's on the house."

Surprised by her sudden change of heart, he studied her for a moment before lowering his gaze to the tempting display of confectioneries behind the glass counter. "If it's not too much trouble, ma'am. Some caramels would be nice."

She bent down and slid the glass door open. He watched as she carefully arranged the caramels in a paper sack. She then dropped a slip of paper into the sack, folded the top over, and handed it to him.

He reached into his pocket to pay her, but she shook her head.

"Like I said, it's on the house."

He stared at her with knitted brow. "Why would you do such a thing, ma'am? After the trouble I caused?"

She lifted her gaze to his. "A man who cares as deeply for his sister as you seem to can't be all bad."

"Much obliged, ma'am," he said, doffing his hat. "I won't bother you any further."

He made quick strides toward the door before stopping. Glancing over his shoulder, he found her watching him. "Your dress," he said. "I'd feel a whole lot better if you'd let me pay for any damage." He had no idea the cost of a wedding gown, but it couldn't be cheap.

"Go," she said with a beseeching look. "Please. Just…go."

3

DASH IT ALL! KATE FOUGHT THE DESIRE TO SCREAM. HER
aunt had taken it upon herself to interfere yet again
and had arranged a meeting of what she called the
"wounded parties." Kate scoffed. Wounded, indeed.
That didn't even begin to describe how she felt.

At precisely seven o'clock that night, her *former*
fiancé arrived at the house with his adoptive parents.

It was bad enough having to see Frank so soon after
their disastrous non-wedding, and before she'd had
time to calm down, but did Aunt Letty have to invite
his parents as well? Facing them with only her aunt by
her side, Kate felt outnumbered. Trapped.

The five sat as still and upright as pieces on a chess-
board in her aunt's small but tidy parlor, as if waiting for
someone to make the first move. It was a miracle that
any air could circulate amid the tension in the room.

As he sat on the tufted velvet sofa between his
parents, Frank's gaze shifted back and forth, scout-
ing out the room. He needn't have worried, for all
furred and feathered creatures had been relegated to
another room. He couldn't get near an animal without

breaking out in hives, and he looked ready to bolt at the first sign of one.

Finally, Aunt Letty grabbed hold of the arms of her chair and took charge. "I think that before we discuss rescheduling the wedding, we should clear the air. Would you like to start, Kate?"

Kate folded her arms across her chest. "I have nothing to say."

"Well, I do," Frank said. "First, if I ever set eyes on that Texas Ranger again, I'll—"

Sneezing, he pulled out his handkerchief and dabbed at his watery eyes. Already, his sensitivity to fur and cat dander was doing strange things to him. Nonetheless, he continued, his accusations punctuated by fits of sneezing.

Normally, Kate would feel sorry for him, but tonight she was too hurt and angry to give him any sympathy. Out of respect for her aunt, Kate sat primly on her straight-back chair, feet together, hands on her lap, and listened to Frank place blame for the disastrous wedding solely on the Texas Ranger's shoulders. If anything resembling an apology could be found between the sneezes, it escaped Kate's notice.

Even Mr. and Mrs. Foster seemed to have reached the end of their patience. His mother kept looking at the grandfather clock sighing in the corner. His father shifted uneasily and tapped his hand on his lap with the same intensity as a sea captain sending an SOS.

If Frank noticed his adoptive parents' waning interest, he showed no sign. Instead, he called the ranger every unpleasant name under the sun until Kate didn't think she could take it any longer.

"Are you saying that you had no part in ruining our wedding?"

To his credit, Frank looked momentarily fazed, as if it had finally occurred to him that he'd gone too far. "Ah, come on, Kate." He raked his brown hair away from his forehead until it stood up like a picket fence. "What did you expect me to do? *A-a-choo!* Stand by while the man had his way with you?"

Kate clamped her mouth shut, and her nostrils flared. It wasn't the first time Frank had made such an accusation. Not by a long shot. He'd even accused poor Mr. Anderson of flirting with her when all the man had done was brush away an annoying fly.

"His w-way with me?" she stammered when she could find her voice. "Is that what you think?"

"What did you expect me to think?" he asked, his voice filled with accusation.

"I told you, I never saw the man before in my life."

"All I can say is, he looked awfully friendly to me."

She took a seething breath and twisted her handkerchief in her lap. Out of respect for the older folks, she forced herself to calm down. "And that's why you ruined our wedding?" she asked, her quiet voice edged in reproach. "Because he *looked* friendly?"

"He had no business looking at you like that. Far as I'm concerned, he has no business here at all!"

"That's where you're wrong. He's here on special assignment and is looking for the man who caused his sister's death." The poor man had sounded absolutely devastated when he'd spoken of his sister's death.

All eyes turned to her, but only Frank broke the

silence. "How come you know so much about him?" he asked, grinding the words out between wooden lips.

Before she could answer, Mr. Foster threw up his hands. "I thought the purpose of this meeting was to reschedule the wedding."

Ignoring his father, Frank jumped to his feet, his red eyes blazing with jealousy. "I thought you didn't know the man."

"I don't. He came into the shop to apologize. But that's something you know nothing about!"

"I have nothing to apologize for."

Kate shot up from her seat, hands at her waist. "Oh no? How about making us the talk of the town? And what about the time you accused me of flirting with the postmaster? And then there was the time…" On and on she went, naming his offenses one after another. All had to do with his annoying and unwarranted jealousy. Saint Peter at the pearly gates couldn't have produced a more thorough list of offenses.

"That's because I love you," Frank sniffled.

Kate glared at him. "Love has nothing to do with this. This is about trust!"

Frank's mother glanced helplessly at her husband, hands fluttering. "Do something, Howard."

Howard looked like a fish out of water. His door-knocker mustache twitched, and his eyebrows quivered. He crossed and uncrossed his legs. Finally, he cleared his throat and leaned forward, hands spread. "All right. This is getting us nowhere."

"I agree," Aunt Letty said, nodding. "I suggest we put all this behind us and set another date for the wedding. I was thinking about a week from—"

Kate stared at her aunt in total disbelief. The fact that she and Frank stood facing each other like two bulls in a territorial dispute seemed to have escaped her notice. "There isn't going to be another wedding."

Aunt Letty folded her arms across her chest. "Now, Kate, you promised to listen to what Frank had to say."

"I did listen, and nothing he's said so far has changed my mind." She pulled off her ring and tossed it. He caught it midair, his reflexes better than his instincts.

Kate hated disappointing her aunt, but it couldn't be helped. She leveled her angry gaze at Frank and pointed to the door. "This meeting is over!"

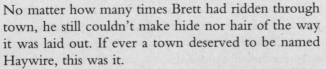

No matter how many times Brett had ridden through town, he still couldn't make hide nor hair of the way it was laid out. If ever a town deserved to be named Haywire, this was it.

Main Street was the only one that made any sort of sense. At least it ran straight—or nearly straight. On one end was Railroad Street. On the other end, the town was split in two by a hundred-foot-wide cross street. Known as the Dead Line, the street separated moral businesses from those beyond the pale.

The street was wide enough so that anyone accidentally venturing into the wrong side of town— occupied by saloons, bordellos, and, inexplicably, the barbershop—could easily turn horse and wagon around. Thus, delicate constitutions were saved and reputations left unharmed.

The other streets curved, made sharp turns, and

then circled back on themselves like pretzels. Brett had passed the same blacksmith shop three times while trying to locate the post office.

Shops and businesses on the streets away from the center of town were laid out willy-nilly, some with entryways facing alleyways. Boardinghouses and private homes were planted on lots in haphazard fashion, as if tossed in place by chance, like dice in a gambler's hand.

The telegraph operator, known as Flash, had explained that the streets followed the original cow paths. All Brett could say was if that were true, then the cows must have been on locoweed.

Haywire wasn't the only town so designed. The idea of building a town on a grid didn't come about until after the war. Prior to that, many towns had been built along bovine trails—even Boston—but none had streets as confusing as those in Haywire.

Reaching his destination, Brett tethered his horse and stomped up the steps of the boardwalk. Overhead, a wooden sign reading SHERIFF swung gently in the breeze.

He doubted cows were to blame for the office, unlike any Brett had ever seen. The jail was upstairs. That meant the office below was privy to the pounding feet of irate prisoners, and today was no different. Brett lifted his gaze to the vibrating ceiling and prayed it didn't collapse.

He moved from beneath the swinging gaslight fixture just in case it should fall. Lowering his gaze, he studied the man behind the weathered oak desk.

Sheriff Keeler stabbed a finger at the newspaper in front of him, his eyes glittering. "I see that your little fiasco landed on the front page." He tutted like an old woman, and the ends of his curling mustache quivered.

Brett had disliked the man the moment they'd first set eyes on each other. Nothing had changed his mind since. Still, he'd done wrong. A Texas Ranger had no business letting his emotions get the best of him, and that he'd done in spades. He deserved a dressing-down.

"I've apologized to the lady for the trouble I caused," he said, lifting his voice to be heard above the sound of pounding feet. "And I apologize to you. Nothing like that will happen again."

The sheriff sat back in his seat and regarded Brett with obvious disdain. Keeler didn't take kindly to having to work with the Texas Rangers—*outsiders*, as he referred to them. He'd made that clear from the start. He viewed Brett's presence as an indictment against him and his office. In that regard, he wasn't alone. Most lawmen felt the same way, but never had one gone to such lengths to show it.

"By right, I should have put you in jail with the bridegroom."

"Why didn't you?"

Keller shrugged. "Well, unfortunately, nothing in the law says you can't stop a wedding. As for the rest, witnesses said you'd acted in self-defense. No law against that either. As for decapitating Jesus… That one's a bit iffy. That could go down as destroying property or even blasphemy."

Brett took that as a warning. The sheriff evidently didn't think he had enough damaging evidence to get Brett removed from his assignment. But he was definitely keeping track, which meant Brett had better watch his step. It seemed like a good time to change the subject.

"Anything new on the Ghost Riders?" The gang of outlaws had been given that name because of their habit of robbing a bank or stage and seemingly disappearing into thin air.

The sheriff reached into a wooden box for a cigar and carefully snipped off the tip. "Do you think I'd tell you if there was?"

Brett was tempted to walk out of the office then and there. Unfortunately, he needed the sheriff as much as the sheriff needed him. "Either we work together peacefully, or we don't. Your choice."

"Let me tell you something, boy." The sheriff stuck the cigar in his mouth and reached for a box of safety matches. "I don't need no Texas Ranger telling me how to do my job. So there's no place here for you or that *cinco peso* badge of yours."

Brett's hands curled into fists by his sides. "Well, it seems like we have ourselves a little problem. Because like it or not, I'm staying until I do what I came here to do." With that, he turned and stalked out of the office.

❧

Kate spotted Frank sitting on the porch steps the moment she arrived home. It had been nearly a week since the disastrous meeting with him and his parents.

Gritting her teeth, she shook the reins and drove her wagon helter-skelter up the long drive and into the barn in back.

Her dogs, Taffy, Blondie, and Mutt, stood at the fence with wagging tails. A red hen scrambled out of the way.

It had been a long, hard day at work. Her disastrous wedding had made the candy shop the center of attention, and business was booming. Her feet were killing her, and her corset poked like steel fingers into her ribs. She was in no mood for another argument.

By the time she'd unhitched her horse, Frank was waiting for her by the barn door. It was as close as he dared come to her horse for fear of breaking out in hives. She turned to him, hands at her waist. "What are you doing here?"

To his credit, Frank looked pathetic. He had bags under his eyes, his hair stood on end, and his wrinkled shirt and trousers looked like they'd been slept in.

He waited for her to put her horse, Cinnamon, into his stall before answering her. "We need to talk."

"We? It seems that the last time we met, you did most of the talking." Stomping past him, she barreled through the yard, past the barking dogs, and into the house. Normally, she would have stopped to pet the dogs, but not today.

Frank followed her through the mudroom and into her aunt's small but adequate kitchen. The fluffy white cat, Gumdrop, stretched her feline limbs and jumped from a chair. From his cage, Blackie fluttered his wings and squawked. Kate had found the raven with a broken wing and had nursed it back to health. As soon as she thought the bird ready, she planned on releasing him back into the wild.

Frank pulled a handkerchief from his pocket and

sneezed. "Okay, this time you talk and I'll listen," he said and sneezed again.

She slammed her purse on the counter and whirled about to face him. Feathers and fur were already starting to do strange things to him, and he stared at her with watery eyes.

"I have nothing to say to you, Frank Foster!"

"That's not like you, Kate. You usually have something to say. Ah-ah-ah-*choo*!"

"Okay, how about this? I'm sick and tired of your jealousy. You're even jealous when I spend time with friends." As a child, he'd complain about his adoptive parents showering more attention onto their other children, though Kate knew that wasn't true.

Since he'd insisted, she let him have it, firing words at him like so many bullets. The knot of hurt and anger inside unraveled like a never-ending ball of yarn.

When she stopped to catch her breath, he interjected, "Man alive. For someone who had nothing to say, it sure took you long enough to say it." He made a face and wiggled his nose. "*Ah-ah-choo!*"

She folded her arms across her chest. "I'm done now, so you can leave."

He dabbed at his watery eyes with his handkerchief. "Ah, come on, Katie. This isn't like you. All I want is a second chance."

"Sorry, you're all out of second chances. Third, fourth, and fifth chances too."

He frowned. "So, what are you saying?"

She sighed. For someone who saw amorous intent in every man's smile or glance, he sure could be thickheaded when it came to his own would-be romance. "I can't go through this anymore, Frank. Your jealousy is driving me crazy."

"You're making a mistake," he said.

"The only mistake I made was believing that you could change and learn to trust me."

"I do trust you. *Ah-choo!*"

"Only when there's no other man in sight!"

A muscle tightened at Frank's jaw. "Okay, so I'm just supposed to ignore it when another man takes a fancy to you. Is that what you want me to do?"

Kate's eyes flashed. There was no getting through to him. "That's it. I've had it! Do you hear me?" She meant business, and by golly, this time he'd better take it to heart. "It's over. We're finished. Done. There's nothing more to talk about."

He sniffled and sneezed. "Does that mean you don't want to see me anymore?"

She threw up her hands. "Not only do I not want to see you, but I don't want to even hear your name."

"Kate—"

"I mean it, Frank. Now go."

"I'll go, *ah-ah-ah-choo*! B-but"—*sniffle*—"I'm not giving up on us. I'll be back." Turning, he stomped through the mudroom.

Bracing herself against the slamming door, Kate squeezed her eyes tight. She and Frank had a long history together, and it was hard ending it like this.

She'd first met Frank on the orphan train that had brought her west from New York. He was nine and she only six. No sooner had they been pushed into the stock car than his face had swollen up like a rubber balloon. Never had she seen anything like it.

It was the cattle, he'd explained. She'd looked around that dark, rank boxcar but hadn't seen any cattle, only the other orphans sobbing quietly in the dark corners or staring into space.

Later, as the train sped away from the city and whizzed through the frozen countryside, he had done something that had scared her more than even his swollen face. He'd slid open the stock-car door. Thinking he'd planned on jumping, she'd cried out in alarm. Instead, he'd lain flat on his stomach and stuck his head outside to breathe fresh air.

Horrified at the thought of him falling from the train, she'd grabbed hold of his legs and refused to let go. The air was frigid, and she'd worn only a thin cotton dress and threadbare cape that had been far too small. Still, she'd held on to him, fearing for his life if she let go. That's how the two of them had traveled across the country. Never once had it occurred to her that had he fallen from the train, he would have taken her with him.

Thus began a bond that had only strengthened through the years. It wasn't an easy bond to break. But what else could she do?

4

THERE WAS A MAN PASSED OUT COLD IN THE DOORWAY of Foster's Saddle and Leather Shop.

The drunk didn't surprise Brett. As in any other western town, Saturday night was the time to press boot to brass and bend the elbow. Already, he'd spotted two men who were three sheets to the wind. By the sound of the off-key singing drifting from the saloons on the opposite side of the Dead Line, others were well on the way to oblivion.

Brett wouldn't have given the drunk a second glance had he not recognized the name on the weathered sign hanging from the building's false front.

A closer look was enough to identify the man slumped in the recessed doorway sawing logs as none other than Frank T. Foster, jilted bridegroom and owner of the shop. Only now he looked as forlorn as a discarded toy, or maybe even something the cat had dragged in. Tonight, the man with steel knuckles sure didn't look like he could harm a fly. Not unless the insect succumbed to the rank smell of whiskey.

Brett hesitated. If he had the sense God gave a

gnat, he'd walk away and never look back. If only he didn't feel responsible for the man's plight! If the town scuttlebutt was right, Miss Denver would have nothing more to do with her former fiancé. Lord knows, had he been in Foster's shoes, he might have been tempted to cozy up to a bottle or two himself. Like it or not, he'd created this mess; it was now up to him to make things right.

Stooping, he gave Foster a good shake. The man kept snoring but otherwise didn't stir. Brett straightened and glanced around. Not a single soul was within shouting distance. At least no one in any condition to help him. Wasn't that just fine and dandy? That meant either leaving Foster where he was or hauling the man up the stairs to the second-floor living quarters himself.

As tempted as Brett was to mind his own business, he couldn't in good conscience do so. Had it not been for him, Foster would be married by now and wouldn't be sleeping off a bender in a crummy doorway.

Recalling the devastated look on Miss Denver's face, Brett clenched his jaw. Like it or not, he felt compelled to do something. To make it up to her. To make it right.

Giving the staircase a measuring glance, he grimaced. Fourteen steps led to the second floor. Fourteen very steep and very narrow steps.

Since there didn't seem to be any way around it, he rolled up his sleeves. Rubbing his hands together, he turned the prone body over. Foster sputtered, and drool dripped from the corner of his mouth.

Wrinkling his nose in disgust, Brett heaved the man off the ground and hoisted him over his shoulder.

Frank's head flopped against Brett's back like that of a rag doll, his arms dangling past Brett's waist.

Knees threatening to buckle beneath the dead-weight, Brett staggered toward the stairs.

By the time he reached the upstairs landing, he was out of breath, his forehead slick with sweat. Fortunately, the door to the apartment was ajar, and he kicked it open with his foot. The room was dark except for the soft glow of gaslight streaming through the dusty windows.

After depositing Frank in a heap on the sofa, Brett fumbled to light the gas lamp on the table in front of the window. The flame sputtered before settling into a steady glow. Two wing chairs flanked a single sofa and a low table piled high with issues of the *Police Gazette*. Clothes were scattered about the room, tossed over the backs of chairs and the sofa and heaped on the floor in little piles.

Brett opened a window, but even the cool night air couldn't erase the stale smell of half-eaten food left on the table to rot.

It hardly seemed like the kind of place a man would bring a bride. But then, maybe the couple hadn't planned on living there after the wedding.

He reached into his pocket for the bag of caramels, hoping the candy would make the sour smell more bearable. Only two were left. Just as he pulled one out of the bag, something floated to the floor. It was a slip of paper. Bending to reach it, he popped the caramel in his mouth.

He unfolded the paper and read the note written in flowery script.

Leaving town would be good for your health.

A vision of flaming-red hair and big, blue eyes came to mind, sparking a smile. Well, now. Either the lady was worried about his safety, or she had a sense of humor. He doubted she meant him any real harm. At least, he hoped not.

Slipping the scrap of paper into his leather vest pocket, he mopped his forehead with a handkerchief and surveyed the room before heading for the kitchen. He struck a match and held it up until he spotted a lamp next to the cookstove. Blowing out the flame before it burned his fingers, he then struck another match and lit the smoke-stained wick.

The kitchen was in no better condition. The sink and counters were piled high with dirty dishes.

He circled the room, opening and shutting cabinet doors. He finally located a package of Arbuckles' Ariosa Coffee in the pantry. He found the coffeepot in a lower cabinet, but no clean cups.

While the coffee perked, he washed out a cup and filled a bowl with cold water. He then walked back into the parlor and splashed water on the man's face, hoping to bring him out of his stupor. "Come on, Foster. Wake up."

Foster groaned and muttered something beneath his breath, showering Brett with the vile smell of whiskey. Wrinkling his nose in disgust, Brett made him sit up. "Yeah, well, same to you, fella."

The sorrowful excuse for a human being in front of him made Brett grimace. It would have been a whole lot easier to let Foster sleep it off, but Brett couldn't bring himself to do that. Somehow, he had to make up to Miss Denver for the terrible wrong he'd done. The only way to make that happen was to get her and Foster back together, and that's what he intended to do.

God help him.

It took nearly two hours and two pots of coffee before Foster could sit unaided. He looked like hell. His eyes were bloodshot and his skin the color of cold ashes.

Groaning, Foster rubbed his forehead. "Leave me alone," he slurred. "Lust leave me alone."

"It's too late for that," Brett said. "Like it or not, you're stuck with me."

Foster squinted through bloodshot eyes. "Why? Whatya want?"

"Two things." Brett dug into his pocket for a photograph mounted on a card. The picture taken at his sister's wedding wasn't a good one, but it was the only one he had of Foster One. "Do you know this man?"

Even though Brett held the photograph no more than a nose-length away, Foster Two still had trouble focusing. "No."

"Are you sure? His name is also Frank Foster. He's not a relative? A cousin? A long-lost brother?"

"Sever naw the man in my life."

Sighing, Brett slipped the photograph back in his pocket. Another dead end.

Foster regarded him like a cat regarding a mouse. "You...you said there were two things you wanted."

"I want to make things right. Between you and Miss Denver, I mean."

Foster's squinty red eyes suddenly flashed in recognition. "Hey, you're the one who caused the problem in the pirst flace. Why, you…" He struggled to get to his feet but was still too drunk to do anything but fall back against the sofa cushions in defeat.

Heaving a sigh, Brett waited until Foster had simmered down. "Word around town is that Miss Denver is finished with you," he said, speaking in a slow, concise voice.

Foster glared at him but said nothing.

Brett moved a ladder-back chair closer to the sofa and sat. "I heard she gave back your ring."

"Yeah, she gave me the mitten, all right. But that don't mean nothin'. So don't go gettin' any ideas."

"Relax. The only thing I'm interested in is getting the two of you back together."

Foster's eyes gleamed with suspicion. "Why? What's in it for you?"

"Nothing but a lot of trouble by the looks of it." Brett bent forward, elbows on his knees, and rubbed his hands together. "I'm the one who stopped the wedding. I figure it's up to me to help make things right." Brett gave Foster a moment to digest this before asking, "So what's the plan?"

Foster pinched the bridge of his nose. "Plan? What plan?"

"The plan to get her back."

Holding his head, Foster rocked back and forth. "Must you shout?"

Brett heaved a sigh. If he spoke any softer, he'd have to whisper. "Have you talked to her? Apologized?"

"She w-won't l-listen. Said…said she's sick and tired of my…jealousy."

Brett leaned back in his chair and rubbed his chin.

"Yeah, well, I'm not crazy about it myself." He thought for a moment. "What about flowers?"

Foster stopped rocking. "Flowers?"

"Yeah, you know. The things that grow in the ground. Did you send her any?"

"I never send flowers."

"Why not? Women love flowers. They convey all sorts of messages that only a woman can understand. If you're smart, you'll buy the store out—the whole kit and caboodle. Just to make sure she gets the right message."

Foster shook his head. "This is Katie we're talking about. She's more the practical type."

"Practical?" Brett blinked back the vision of twirling whirligigs and flashing blue eyes that came to mind. Miss Denver with her spinning earbobs and sign-plastered walls hardly seemed the pragmatic type. Idealistic, maybe. Optimistic. Compassionate. But definitely not practical.

"She doesn't like all that fussy stuff. Besides, flowers die. What kind of message is that?" Foster screwed up his face as if trying to think. "But...but...but I could send her a new jack."

"A jack?"

"Yeah, you know. For changing..." He made a spinning move with his hand as he searched for the right word. "A...a wheel. That's the kind of gift Kate likes."

Brett frowned. How was it possible that two men could look at a single woman and see her completely differently? "You're kidding, right?"

"She's always breakin' tires," Foster slurred. "That's why I make her carry a spare." He squinted. "What's wrong with that?"

"Nothing. It's just—" Holy blazes, where to start? Foster didn't have a clue where women were concerned. Not that Brett was an expert in such matters. He'd never had much luck with the opposite sex, but it wasn't entirely his fault. The life of a Texas Ranger didn't leave much room for romance. Most women soon grew weary of a man whose idea of settling down involved a horse and saddle.

"Forget the jack. If you're serious about winning her back, you'll stick with flowers." Brett thought a moment. "I'll meet you tomorrow at Gordon's. We'll pick out a bouquet, and you can compose a nice note."

Foster narrowed his eyes. "Note?"

"Yeah, you know. The little card that accompanies a bouquet and will say all the right things, like how sorry you are."

"You want me to put that in writing?" Foster looked as if he'd never heard of such a thing.

Brett studied the blurry-eyed man and shook his head. What did Miss Denver ever see in the likes of him? There certainly was no accounting for taste.

"For crying out loud, Foster. It's a simple note. That's all. And it will show her how sorry you are. How much you care. Now, what kind of flowers does she like?"

"How am I s-supposed to know?"

"Okay. Forget about flowers for now." Brett thought for a moment. "What is her favorite color?"

Foster's face went blank for a moment. "Pink, I guess."

"You guess?"

"Maybe it's white." Foster thought for a moment. "Her shop is pink and white."

"White's not a color."

Foster looked surprised. "Is that so? Okay, it's gotta be pink."

Brett rolled his eyes; the man was hopeless. He rubbed his forehead, and a vision of Miss Denver came to mind. He was willing to bet that pink was not her favorite color. Maybe it was the violet-blue of her eyes. Perhaps it was her dazzling red hair or the glow of her smooth ivory skin.

"Forget color. Does she have a special song she likes? A favorite author or poet?"

Frank scratched his temple. "Beats me."

Brett knitted his brow. Maybe he was going about this all wrong. He decided to try a different angle. "What do you two talk about when you're together?"

"The usual. Leather."

Brett stared at him, incredulous. "Leather? You talk about leather?"

"Yeah, so what's the big deal? It costs a bundle to make a saddle these days. The price of leather has gotten outta hand."

Brett sat back in his chair. Great guns; he didn't know which task looked more daunting. Tracking down Foster Number One. Or turning Foster Two into a fine and proper suitor.

5

Kate left for the shop early Monday morning, anxious to work on her uncle's special candy recipe. The candy itself wasn't that difficult to make; adding designs to the center was the tricky part. Only the most skillful confectioners had perfected the art, and she was determined to join their numbers.

She'd been working on perfecting the necessary skills for months and had yet to get it right, but she was close. Oh, so close, and a thrill of excitement coursed through her. Wouldn't Uncle Joe have been proud?

Usually, the town was quiet at that hour, but not today. As she parked her horse and wagon in front of the candy store, she narrowed her gaze on the commotion two doors away. Three barking dogs pulled on leashes while their harried owners struggled to hold them back.

The black-and-white cow dog named Ringo belonged to a faro dealer known only as Lucky Lou.

The snippy tan spaniel baring its teeth was owned by Ironman Watkins, the blacksmith.

Mrs. Tremble, the former schoolmarm, was having

a terrible time holding on to her poodle, Mitzie. Fearing for the older woman's safety, Kate raced to lend her a hand.

"Let me!" Yelling to be heard over the barking dogs, Kate grabbed hold of the poodle's leash with both hands and yanked, but it was no use. The frenzied dogs growled and snapped at each other and resisted all efforts by the handlers to separate them.

A man suddenly appeared at Kate's side. He grabbed the leash out of her hands and jerked the dog back—way back. He then ordered the poodle to sit and, much to Kate's surprise, the dog did as it was told.

Since the poodle had created most of the commotion, its absence calmed the other two dogs, allowing their owners to gain control. As quickly as it had started, the fight ended, and Lucky Lou and Ironman hastened away in opposite directions, dragging their reluctant hounds with them.

Now that Kate had a chance to get a good look at the man who had saved the day, she could hardly hide her annoyance.

As if guessing her thoughts, the Texas Ranger quirked a smile. "Ah, we meet again." He handed the leash to its rightful owner, but his gaze remained on Kate.

Mrs. Tremble couldn't thank him enough. "You saved the day, Mr...."

"Tucker. Brett Tucker."

"Well, thank you, Mr. Tucker." Lifting her dog into her arms, Mrs. Tremble buried her nose in the poodle's coat. The owner and dog had similar white, curly hair and brown eyes. "I don't know what would have happened to my poor Mitzie had it not been for you. Not many people could step in and stop a fight like that."

"That was nothing," Kate said wryly. "You should see how good he is at *starting* a fight."

Tucker cocked his head to the side. "Ah, but you give me too much credit."

Kate scoffed. "You're being far too modest, Mr. Tucker."

"I can assure you that I have many flaws, Miss Denver, but modesty is not one of them." A glint of humor warming his eyes, he tipped his hat and took his leave. "Have a good day, ladies."

Next to her, Mrs. Tremble gave a schoolgirl sigh as she watched him walk away. "Oh, to be forty years younger."

❧

That afternoon, nine-year-old Dusty Campbell stopped at the candy shop on his way home from school, and Kate reached over the counter to hand him a sample.

He eagerly popped the white, spongy confection in his mouth. Behind a curtain of hay-colored hair, his eyes grew round as wagon wheels.

"It feels squishy, like a pillow." He tossed his hair aside with a shake of his head. "Only it tastes better."

Kate laughed. "I should hope so. Actually, that is called a marshmallow."

"Where do marshmallows come from?" Dusty asked, standing on tiptoe to reach the plate for a second one.

"Why from a marshmallow tree, of course," she

said. Actually, that had been true in the past. This latest batch was made from a French recipe that replaced the sweet sap from the mallow tree with gelatin. She'd decided to try out the new recipe on customers to see if they discerned a difference in taste. So far, none had. Though she doubted that gelatin had the same health properties as real mallow.

"Would you like to try a sugarplum next?" she asked. Sugarplums were the most time-consuming candy to make, and she didn't generally give out samples. But work helped keep her mind occupied, and since the wedding fiasco, she had immersed herself in making candy. Lots and lots of candy. The store was now overstocked.

The boy wrinkled his nose. "I don't like plums."

"Oh, but you'll like this," Kate said, holding up a sugarcoated nut confection. "In this case, plum is not a fruit. It's just another word for *good*."

Dusty stood on tiptoes to take the candy. He eyed it suspiciously before taking a cautious bite. A wide smile inched across his freckled face before he popped the rest in his mouth.

Kate smiled back and filled a bag full of the boy's favorite treats, including gumdrops and a lollipop. As much as she enjoyed working in the kitchen in the back of the store, her favorite part of the job was making people smile. The candy store was truly the heart and soul of the town.

When a pretty girl struck a young man's fancy, Kate was the first to know. That's because a shining new love required the biggest box of candy that money could buy. Her sweetmeats helped celebrate births, birthdays, and anniversaries. When Mr. Ain turned ninety, a friend purchased him a glass jar filled with ninety jelly beans, the same kind of candy people once sent to soldiers during the War Between the States.

But her confections didn't just help celebrate happy occasions. They also consoled broken hearts and offered a sweet reprieve when things went wrong. When Mrs. Wheaton scandalized the town by obtaining a divorce, she insisted upon ordering chocolate bonbons, even though it was summer and Kate had warned her that the chocolates would melt.

When Mr. Ellsworth fell off his horse and broke his leg, he comforted himself with a bag of toffee. When little two-year-old Wendy Williams wandered away from home, the frantic search party sucked on peppermint rounds for the calming effect peppermint was known to have. When the child was found safe and sound, the town celebrated with a fondant party.

"How much do I owe you?" Dusty asked, bringing Kate out of her reverie.

"You know I don't charge for samples," she said, though the bag she'd handed him would normally fetch twenty-five cents. He was the youngest of seven children, and the family struggled to make ends meet. He was small for his age, and the older boys tended to pick on him. Today, as always, the candy shop provided a safe place for him until the bullies were gone.

He grinned up at her. "Thank you, Miss Denver."

"You're very welcome." She thought of something. "Oops, almost forgot." She reached into her box of fortunes and picked out the one she'd written especially for him. "Hmm, it says you'll soon make lots of new friends."

Dusty's eyes flickered with hope. "Will they let me play baseball?" He wanted to play ball more than anything in the world, but the older boys refused to allow him on the team.

"I wouldn't be surprised if they do," she said. "Maybe if you——" A loud popping sound made her jump. Shards of glass exploded from the store's front window, bursting through the air like fireworks.

With a cry of alarm, Kate raced around the counter and pulled the boy out of harm's way. "Are you okay?" she asked, frantically checking him for signs of injury.

Clutching his bag of candy, he gaped at her, his lips quivering. Before he could answer, the door sprang open and he flew into her arms.

A man entered the shop, gun in hand and a flour sack over his head. The gunman was halfway through the store before he halted, and Kate's heart practically leaped to her throat. Acting purely by instinct, she yanked Dusty behind the counter, shielding him with her body.

The gunman's gaze zeroed in on Kate for an instant before he rounded the counter. Certain that he meant to do her harm, she pushed Dusty to the floor and grabbed a glass jar for a weapon. Fortunately, she didn't have to use it, because the masked man quickly ducked into the kitchen.

No sooner had his footsteps faded away than the front door flew open again. The flash of a gun made her gasp. Without thinking, she hurled the jar as hard as she could. The jar bounced off the intruder's raised arm, crashing to the floor in a frenzy of jelly beans.

She quickly reached for another jar and was ready to hurl it when a commanding voice shouted, "Stop!"

Her hand froze. In her panic, she'd failed to take a good look at the second man entering her shop. "Mr. Tucker!"

He skidded to a halt in front of her. "Next time I'll announce myself. Where'd he go?"

She pointed to the kitchen. "That way."

Tucker raced past her, spurs jingling and boots pounding the wooden floor. She heard him yell something before the back door slammed shut.

Forcing herself to stay calm for the boy's sake, she set the jar down and helped him off the floor. "You can get up now. It's safe."

Dusty's cheeks were puffed out like a chipmunk's.

"You shouldn't eat all your candy at once," she said and wiped his mouth with a corner of a clean handkerchief. "It could make you sick."

Dusty swallowed hard before replying. "I didn't want that bad man stealing it."

She pulled him into her arms, and his slight body trembled next to hers. Her gaze traveled over his head to the broken window in front. It was a miracle that neither of them had been injured by the glass. She'd told Dusty he would always be safe in her shop. If anyone picked on him or tried to harm him in any way, he had been instructed to come there. The hooded bandit had put the safety of her shop in question.

She held the boy close, stroking his head and murmuring words of comfort. Warmth gradually returned to his thin frame, and he stopped shaking.

Hearing the back door open, she stiffened at the sound of footsteps. Releasing the boy, she grabbed another jar.

A white handkerchief waved in the doorway. "Hold your fire. It's only me."

Relief rushing through her, she lowered the jar to the counter.

Tucker walked out of the kitchen, shoving his handkerchief into his pocket. He looked none too happy. "Lost him," he said. "This maze of a town is an outlaw's paradise." Beneath his wide-brimmed hat, a strand of blond hair had fallen over his furrowed brow. "You okay?" His gazed dropped to the child hiding behind her skirts. "The boy?"

"He's fine. We both are."

Dusty pulled away from her to stare up at the tall ranger. "The bad man didn't get my candy."

"Good to hear," Tucker said.

"What did he do?" Kate asked.

"He attempted to rob the bank. Him and his buddies." Tucker walked around the counter to the shattered window. "Sorry about that. I thought I could nail him before he entered your shop, but my bullet ricocheted." He pushed back his hat and looked at her over his shoulder. "I was just trying to keep you safe."

She bristled. "Like you tried to keep me safe when you stopped my wedding?"

"I don't know what to say, ma'am. 'Cept I'm sorry." She heard his intake of breath. "I'll see to it that the glass is replaced as soon as possible."

His apology sounded sincere, but she wasn't ready to let him off the hook. Not yet.

"I must say, Mr. Tucker, that ever since you arrived in town, it's been one catastrophe after another."

He rubbed his chin. "I was kind of thinking the same thing. Almost seems like Haywire has it in for me."

"Or *you* have it in for Haywire," she said.

"Oh no, ma'am," he said, holding up his hands. "I have nothing against Haywire. And you can rest assured that as soon as I finish my business here, I'll be outta your hair." He backed toward the door and stopped. "Just one thing." He stared at her over the counter. "Did you happen to notice anything strange about the man?"

"Strange? You mean other than the flour sack over his head and the gun in his hand? No."

He shrugged. "Just thought I'd ask. You never know." After a beat, he asked, "Did he say anything?"

"No, nothing."

He tossed a nod at the broken window. "If I can't get anyone to take care of that today, I'll board it up myself."

She shooed away a buzzing fly with the wave of her hand. "Thank you."

He studied her, and she felt oddly self-conscious beneath his steady gaze. "Blue," he said.

At first, she thought she'd heard wrong. "What?"

He gave her a sheepish grin. "I was just taking a guess that your favorite color is blue. Same color as your pretty eyes."

Heat climbed up her neck to her face. Considering what had just happened, it seemed like a strange thing to say. More than that, she wasn't used to men complimenting her on her appearance—or even mentioning it. Except, perhaps, to tease her about her red hair and freckles.

"Am I right?" he queried.

She wiped her damp hands on her apron. "Yes, blue is my favorite color, but what has that got to do with the bank holdup?"

"Not a thing," he said. "I…just wanted to get your mind off what happened. A clear mind is better able to remember details."

A sense of disappointment washed over her. She'd hoped the compliment had been sincere, but it seemed that everything with Tucker was about his job. She only wished he hadn't used the color of her eyes to distract her. All it did was call attention to his own sultry blue eyes.

"So, do you recall anything else about him?" Tucker pressed.

She cleared her throat. "All I remember is that the man was a little shorter than you." Practically every man in Haywire was shorter than the Texas Ranger. "He was also dressed in black."

"And he wore a ring," Dusty added.

Tucker turned to the boy. "That's good, son. Can you tell me what the ring looked like?"

Dusty shrugged. "It was just a ring."

"Do you remember what finger it was on?"

"This finger," Dusty said, pointing to his pinkie.

The corner of the ranger's mouth curved upward in a crooked smile, revealing a flash of white teeth. The smile had been meant for Dusty, but somehow, it managed to steal Kate's breath.

"Okay, then. If you think of anything else, let Miss

Denver know." To Kate, he said, "You can reach me at Mrs. Crowell's boardinghouse." He headed for the door, pieces of glass crunching beneath the soles of his knee-high boots.

With a tip of his hat, he left the shop. Gazing out the broken window, Kate followed his progress as he dodged a horse and wagon and bounded across the street. *I was just taking a guess that your favorite color is blue. Same as your pretty eyes.*

"Can I have another sugar good?" Dusty asked.

"May I, you mean?" Kate said, turning toward the counter. Ah, the resilience of children. She was still shaken, but Dusty was beginning to look like his old self again. "You most certainly may. In fact, I think we both could use a sugar good."

6

LITTLE MORE THAN AN HOUR LATER, A CROWD gathered in front of the candy shop to stare at the broken window. Mr. Williams from the Haywire Sash and Window Shop had removed the fragments of glass and was now priming the frame to get it ready for a shiny new pane.

Though Kate had already told the spectators everything that had happened, the questions kept coming.

Lucky Lou pushed his way through the crowd. For once, he didn't have Ringo with him. "Did you recognize him?" he asked.

Kate shook her head. "No, his head was covered."

"What did the bank robber say?" asked another.

Though Kate had little information to give them, the onlookers hung on her every word. There had been other robberies, of course, but none had ended in a dramatic foot chase down Main. Texas Ranger Tucker was new in town, but already his name was on the tip of everyone's tongue. Some couldn't make up their minds whether to condemn him for stopping Kate's wedding or to praise him for preventing a bank holdup.

Doc Avery shook his grizzled head. "I was sure the ranger would get his man."

Just then, Aunt Letty's horse and wagon came barreling down the street and pulled up in front of the shop. She'd left earlier to purchase flypaper. The broken window had served as an invitation to every winged insect in town.

"Lord have mercy!" she exclaimed upon joining the knot of onlookers in front of the store. "Haven't you folks got anything better to do with your time than stand around gawking?"

"Now, Aunt Letty," Kate whispered. "They're just concerned."

Even as she spoke, the crowd continued to grow. Even Harvey Wells showed up. Never missing an opportunity to demonstrate his latest invention, he immediately set to work.

"Are you tired of walking around with food on your mustache?" he asked of the crowd at large. Without waiting for an answer, he added, "No more, my friends, no more." He whipped out a piece of metal attached to two pieces of string. These he tied around his head. "This is what I call a mustache apron." Showing off the ridiculous-looking piece beneath his nose, he seemed oblivious to the giggles it generated. "Never again will you have egg on your face," he said with a deadpan expression.

"There ought to be a law," Mrs. Cuttwell said, her pointy nose twitching. As the town seamstress, she was as quick with her needle as she was with her tongue.

Harvey blinked. "A law?"

Mrs. Cuttwell gave an impatient flick of her hand.

"I'm talking about thieves shooting out windows and scaring folks."

Next to her, Mr. Bellwether, the former mayor, glared at the sheriff, his ponderous girth shaking like a leaf. "There *is* a law." It was no secret that he blamed the sheriff for not doing something about the crime rate that had caused him to lose the last election. "And if the sheriff would do his job, we could put the criminals in this town where they belong. Behind bars!"

Sheriff Keeler glared back. He didn't take kindly to criticism. No one knew how he'd react to praise, since none had ever been given. "If you could do better…"

Bellwether made a face. "I dare say that even our dear Mrs. Cuttwell here could do better."

Mrs. Cuttwell tittered like a schoolgirl and punched the former mayor playfully on the arm. "Why, Mr. Bellwether. What a nice thing to say."

Mrs. Peters shuddered and directed her question to Kate. "I can't imagine coming face-to-face with an outlaw. Weren't you afraid?"

"Yes," Kate admitted. "Maybe a little."

"I don't know what the world is coming to," Aunt Letty said. "A body's not safe anymore. In my day, I could have put my life's savings on the front porch, and it would have still been there in the morning."

Ironman Watkins shoved his blackened hands into the pockets of his leather apron. "That's because more money could be found in the poorhouse," he said, his comment followed by a ripple of laughter.

Knowing that the blacksmith spoke in jest, Kate joined in the fun, but her laughter died when she spotted Frank shouldering his way through the crowd.

Not wanting to deal with him, she turned her back. Coming face-to-face with an outlaw was enough drama for one day.

"The point I'm trying to make," Aunt Letty said, "is that we were once able to leave our doors unlocked and not have to worry."

"We still leave our doors unlocked," Kate said. Most doors didn't even have locks, and those that did were seldom used.

"Yes, but I no longer feel safe doing it," Aunt Letty said.

The seamstress folded her arms across her ample chest and lifted her pointy nose. "You're a fine one to talk, Letty. You're part of the problem."

Aunt Letty's jaw dropped. "Me? What are you talking about? How could you say such a thing?"

"Now don't go acting all hoity-toity." Mrs. Cuttwell stuck her cone-shaped nose practically in Aunt Letty's face. "You know darn well that those awful books you insist on selling are responsible for leading our youths astray."

Aunt Letty's face turned an alarming shade of red. Hers was the only shop in town selling books, and she took great pride in keeping the latest dime novels in stock. "I know no such thing."

Mrs. Cuttwell glowered. "If you don't, you should. Why just the other day, Johnny Marsh was caught stealing fruit from Gordon's—two apples and an orange," she added for the benefit of the crowd. Receiving the appropriate gasps of disapproval, she continued. "He told the sheriff he had been led down the road of iniquity by dime novels."

Aunt Letty stared daggers at the woman and refused Kate's effort to drag her away. "I've read just about every dime novel that comes through my store, and not one mentioned an apple! You must be thinking of the *Good* Book."

"I most certainly am not!" Mrs. Cuttwell's florid face turned another shade darker. "The very idea! *Your* books are filled with people killing each other and"— she sniffed—"doing other despicable things."

Steam practically escaped from Aunt Letty's ears. "And how would you know that unless you've read them yourself?"

"Ladies, ladies!" Mayor Wrightwood positioned himself between the two glaring women and separated them with the spread of his arms. "I think we should put this topic of conversation to rest until another day."

"I agree," Kate said, pulling her aunt away from her nemesis and into the store. Since half the population of the town was gaping through the window, she led Aunt Letty into the kitchen where they could talk in private.

Her aunt practically shook with rage. "Oh, that woman makes me so mad."

Kate refrained from telling her to calm down. That always made her aunt more intense rather than less so. "She makes a lot of people mad," she said instead.

"It makes me sick to think that she made your wedding dress."

"Now, Aunt Letty. You know she's the only seamstress in town, and you can't deny that she does good work."

"Yes, well, she should stick to sewing and keep her

honker out of everyone's business." A worried frown replaced her aunt's anger, and she quickly changed the subject. "Oh, Kate. I can't stop thinking about what happened. You could have been injured. Or worse. All that glass."

For her aunt's sake, Kate tried to act nonchalant. If her aunt knew how frightened Kate had been, it would only worry her more. "Fortunately, the bullet lodged in a wall by the window, so neither Dusty nor I were in any real danger." She only wished that Dusty hadn't witnessed the whole thing. She wouldn't blame the poor lad if he never set foot in her shop again. "The outlaw's only interest was in making his escape."

Aunt Letty scoffed. "That still doesn't explain why he shot out our window."

Kate didn't dare relieve her aunt of that false notion. If Aunt Letty knew that the same man who had disrupted the wedding was the real culprit, there was no telling what she would do.

"Guess he panicked."

"Hmm." Aunt Letty was about to resume the conversation but then changed her mind. "Do you want me to make the deliveries today? You must still be upset. I know I would be."

"There's no rush. They can wait till tomorrow. It'll give me a chance to stop at Connie's." Kate hadn't seen her best friend since the wedding. Truth was, she hadn't felt much like socializing.

"Good. Maybe Connie will talk some sense into you."

"What's that supposed to mean?"

Her aunt planted her fists on her ample hips. "You know darn well what that means. It's been nearly a month since your disastrous wedding, and you're still brooding."

"It's only been three weeks, and I am *not* brooding," Kate said.

"I saw how you looked at Frank out there," Aunt Letty argued, crossing her arms. The stubborn look on her aunt's face told Kate she had no chance of winning that argument. None.

Fortunately, the bells on the door jingled, giving Kate an excuse to end the conversation.

Seated at Foster's kitchen table, Brett stifled a yawn and debated whether to indulge in another cup of coffee or leave. A glance at his pocket watch told him it was after ten p.m., and he could use some shut-eye.

It had been a frustrating day. If only he hadn't been cursed with such a strong sense of justice and responsibility. He took any burden to bear upon his shoulders. Fool that he was, he always tried to make things right.

In his mind, every wrong had to be remedied. In that regard, his conscience wouldn't let him rest until he'd made amends and brought Kate and Foster back together again.

But that wasn't the only thing weighing him down. He'd failed yet again. Yes, failed with a capital *F*. He'd practically had that would-be bank robber and possible Ghost Rider in his clutches. Had his bullet not ricocheted off the lamppost and into the candy shop window, he might have succeeded.

Instead, the outlaw had vanished somewhere

between Outhouse Alley and the maze of streets running parallel to Main. Had it been Foster One? God, Brett hoped not. It pained him to think that the man he hated more than he'd ever hated anyone might have escaped yet again.

He'd never met Foster One, not personally. No one could have been more shocked than Brett was to learn of his stepsister Alice's marriage to a man she'd known for only a short while. But by the time Brett had taken leave from the Texas Rangers and traveled home to meet his new brother-in-law, it was too late. Foster had already vanished, taking what little money his stepsister had and breaking her heart in the process. Breaking Brett's too.

He'd blamed himself as much for Alice's death as he blamed Foster. He was only sixteen when his parents died. His brother, Paul, was fourteen and Alice only twelve. Being the oldest, Brett took it upon himself to care for both siblings and, working a series of odd jobs, he'd done just that.

When Alice turned eighteen, she'd landed a position as a housekeeper to a cattle baron. That was the year he'd fallen in love with Deborah Freeman. Convinced that Alice had a real home and a secure future, he was ready to ask Deborah to marry him and settle down. His plans came to a screeching halt when he found out that his brother had been seeing her on the sly, and the two had eloped. Heartbroken, Brett had left town and joined the Texas Rangers.

How was he to know that Alice would meet up with the likes of Foster One? Had Brett stayed home and watched over her like he should have, Alice might still be alive.

Now, Foster Two set a fresh cup of coffee in front of him, bringing him out of his reverie and reminding him of the purpose of his visit.

"Her favorite color is blue." Brett was willing to bet it wasn't just any blue Miss Denver liked, but a blue that was brilliant and clear and matched the depths of her eyes.

Foster plopped down in the seat opposite him, his expression grim. It sure looked as though that old monster, jealousy, was about to rear its ugly head again.

"How do you know that? How do you know her favorite color is blue?"

"How do you *not* know it?" Brett shot back. The only way to combat Foster's jealous streak was through guilt. In that regard, Foster gave him much to work with.

Guilt worked this time too. Foster looked like someone had pulled the stuffing out of him. "Why you making such a fuss? I don't even know my own favorite color."

Brett shook his head in disbelief. He'd been in love only that one time, but he still recalled how it felt. He'd wanted to learn everything he could about the woman he'd loved—what she thought about, dreamed about. How she spent her time. No detail had been too small or irrelevant. Love had a way of turning even the smallest details of one's life into something big and magical.

"Is it really that important?" Foster asked. "To know her favorite color, I mean?"

"Of course it's important," Brett said. "The way to a woman's heart is to pay attention to all the little things that make her who she is. Knowing her favorite color might seem trivial to you, but it will tell her how much you care."

Foster set his elbows on the table and raked his hair with both hands. "Cripes! Why am I even listening to you? You're the reason I'm in this mess."

"And I'm trying to help you out of it."

A dubious look crossed Foster's face. "What makes you such an expert on women?"

"Experience," Brett said. Okay, claiming to be experienced where women were concerned was an exaggeration, but it seemed to do the trick. At least Foster looked less resistant.

"Okay, so we know what color she likes." Foster gazed at Brett in despair. "Now what?"

"Now you purchase the biggest bunch of flowers you can find. And don't give me that garbage about flowers dying. Flowers are an expression of love, and that's the language any woman understands." Brett reached into his vest pocket for a small notebook and slid it across the table.

Foster examined the notebook. "What's this for?"

"That, my friend, is the key to success. You will write words so sweet that they will melt your lady's heart." The signs that hung in the candy shop and the books displayed in a corner suggested Miss Denver had a fondness for the written word. Why else would she decorate her shop with sayings by Shakespeare, Tennyson, and Elizabeth Browning?

Foster's forehead creased. "I'm not very good at... you know...putting my feelings on paper."

"That's what you have me for." Brett glanced around. "Where do you keep your writing supplies?"

Foster pointed to the parlor. "In the desk drawer."

Brett left the kitchen. Finding what he was looking for in the rolltop desk, he returned a moment later. He set pen and ink in front of Foster and sat again.

Foster took the pen in hand and stared at the blank sheet of paper in front of him. "I'm not good at expressing my feelings. I don't even know how to start."

"It's customary to start a letter with the word *Dear*, as in *Dear Kate*."

Foster's eyes flashed. "You have no right calling her 'dear.'"

Brett was fast running out of patience. "If you're serious about winning her back, you've got to control your jealousy. Otherwise, you'll drive her further away."

"So, what's a man supposed to do when someone else hankers after his gal?"

"I don't know. Sing. Dance. Think about something else." Brett thought a moment. "Whistle."

Foster frowned. "What?"

"Yeah, that's it. Whistle." Brett demonstrated. "Whenever that green-eyed monster starts to roar, whistle. It'll help you focus on something else." Convinced he'd hit upon the perfect solution to Foster's jealousy problem, Brett tossed a nod at the still-blank paper. "Now write."

When Foster hesitated, Brett pounded his fist on the table. Holding Foster's hand was not what he'd come to Haywire to do. "I said write!"

Surprisingly, Foster did what he was told, this time without argument. He formed each word with slow, careful movements, then stopped. "What should I write next?"

Brett stared at the two-word greeting and sighed. The man was hopeless. "How do you feel about losing her?"

"How do I feel?" Foster's eyes grew as dark as two deep wells. "I'll tell you how I feel," he said, his voice shaking. "I feel like crap. Like rotten eggs. I feel like a big mound of horse—"

"Okay, that's good. *Real* good. Now you just need to find a more…delicate way of putting your feelings into words."

Foster eyed him in bewilderment. "How do you mean?"

Brett thought for a moment, and a vision of Miss Denver on her wedding day popped into his head. No sooner had the vision faded than another took its place. It was all he could do to keep from smiling at the memory of entering her shop following the attempted bank holdup.

She'd been ready to fight him tooth and nail. No soldier in combat could have looked more determined than she had in protecting that little boy. Grateful that the candy jar hadn't hit him in the head, Brett rubbed his still-sore arm.

Later, when he'd stopped by to make sure the window had been replaced to her satisfaction, she'd looked happy to see him. Well, at least she didn't throw anything at him.

He'd found her in the kitchen, cranking hard candies from a press. Her cheeks were flushed a pretty pink, and her lips looked velvety soft. She wore a pink apron over a blue floral dress, and shiny gold globes danced at her ears.

"Well?" Foster said, snapping Brett out of his thoughts. "What should I write next?"

"I'm thinking," Brett said. It had been a long time since he'd written words of love. "Maybe you can say something like 'My heart is broken in a hundred little pieces.'"

Foster dipped the nib of his pen into the bottle of ink. "You want me to write that down?"

"Maybe not in those precise words, but something like it. It's better if the words are your own."

Foster thought for a moment and then brightened. "Kate loves animals. How about 'Losing you is like riding a lame horse.'"

Brett wrinkled his nose. "I don't think that's the image we're looking for."

"A lame mule?"

"Forget 'lame.'"

Frank's mouth drooped for a moment. "Okay, what do you think of this? 'Losing you is like walking around with my head in a bag.'"

Brett made a face. "That'll only make her think of the bank robber. Confound it! Why are you making this so difficult?"

"I'm not making it difficult," Foster said peevishly. "You are."

Brett pinched the bridge of his nose and counted to ten. "Okay, let's start from the beginning. When did you two first meet? When did you first know that you were in love?"

Frank answered the questions in long, rambling

sentences. He and Kate had met as children. "I was nine, and she was six," he said. "We both came out west on an orphan train."

Hearing how the two of them had met under such trying circumstances, how they had protected each other and grown up together, made Brett feel worse for having come between them.

At long last, Foster fell silent, and Brett sat forward, feeling hopeful. Maybe the trip down memory lane had served as inspiration. "You've known her for most of your life. Now think. How does losing her make you feel?"

"Like rotting fish. Like garbage that has been in the sun too long." Brett's spirits sank, but Foster didn't seem to notice. "Hey, that's what I call poetic. I bet what's-his-name Poo couldn't do any better."

Brett slumped in his seat. "Poe. You mean Poe." Pulling the watch out of his vest pocket, he flipped the case open with his thumb. It promised to be a long and torturous night.

7

KATE LEFT THE SHOP EARLY THE NEXT MORNING TO make deliveries. Most of them were to shut-ins. The shop made no money off such deliveries, but the smiles she received were payment enough.

The moment she drove her horse and wagon away from the winding streets of Haywire, she relaxed, and the nagging pain in her neck began to subside. She'd hardly slept the night before. Each time she'd closed her eyes, a vision of the outlaw came to mind.

Not wishing to ruin the day with such dark thoughts, she inhaled the rich fragrance of warm grass and blooming wildflowers. It had rained the night before, but only a few clouds remained. The brief shower had left the air clear and fresh.

This was by far her favorite time of year. That's why she'd chosen to have a spring wedding, rather than waiting for the more traditional month of June. The sun's golden glow spread over the land like warm honey, but that wasn't the only thing that lifted her spirits.

Today, the earth was dressed to the nines in its finest attire. Bluebonnets stretched across the prairie for as far as the eye could see, filling the air with a pleasing, sweet fragrance.

Cattle raised broad white faces as she drove by, ears perked. Birds rose from the tall grass in graceful flights. Butterflies and bees vied for nectar.

The calm, peaceful scenery cleared Kate's head and allowed her time to think. Maybe Aunt Letty was right; maybe she had been too hard on Frank. She'd always known he had a jealous streak. As a young girl, she'd been flattered, but that was before she'd come to know that jealousy had nothing to do with love. Rather, it stemmed from insecurity. Knowing Frank's background, she couldn't blame him for feeling insecure, but that didn't make his possessive nature any easier to bear.

Since the day was too pleasant to dwell on such thoughts, she focused her gaze on the long, narrow dirt road ahead.

After making two stops, one to a Civil War amputee and another to a bedridden grandmother, she reached the small adobe house owned by Old Man Fletcher. His wife had died ten years earlier, and since then, he'd not left his house.

She knocked on the door. It took so long for Fletcher to answer that she feared something might be wrong. Just as she reached for the doorknob, she heard his gruff voice.

"Come in."

She threw the door open and found him sitting in his usual upholstered chair, his well-worn face resembling a peach pit. "Thought you could use something sweet," she said, holding up a basket packed with his favorite treats. He was particularly fond of the candy she'd named Uncle Joe's Licorice Balls, but he also favored peppermint candy.

He grunted and indicated the table next to his chair with a toss of his near-bald head.

She set the basket by his side. "Did I wake you?" she asked.

"Wake me? No, why?"

"When you took so long to answer the door, I thought you were asleep."

"Don't I wish."

She studied him. He didn't look like his usual cheery self. Today, his eyes were dull, and he appeared distracted. "Are you having trouble sleeping?"

"Nope. The trouble is *not* sleeping."

"I could ask Doc Avery to stop by. Maybe he can give you something to help."

Fletcher made a face. "Forget it. The last time that ole sawbones forced me to take that vile poison he calls med'cine, I stayed sick long after I got well."

Kate laughed. "I still think you should have him check you over."

He scoffed, his eyes dark and remote. "Can't a man feel a little under the weather without calling in the cavalry?" He tossed a nod at the basket by his side. "So, what did you bring me today?"

"All your favorites," she said. "I also brought you the latest Mark Twain."

"That'll keep me occupied," he said.

She glanced around the room. Fletcher usually kept his place spotless, so the muddied boots by the door seemed out of place. "Anything else you need?"

"How about a rich woman willing to play nurse-maid to an old man?"

"If I find one, I'll send her your way."

He managed a wan smile. "You do that."

"I better get a move on." She hated to rush away, but she had a lot more deliveries to make and wanted to finish before the heat of the day. "I'll stop by next week."

She left with more than a little concern. Fletcher lacked his usual sparkle. Maybe he was just tired. He did say he was having trouble sleeping. Still, it might not be a bad idea to ask Doc Avery to stop by and have a look.

Leaving Fletcher's house, Kate drove her wagon along the old trail following the river's edge. The route would take her slightly longer to reach her next destination, but the scenery was worth it.

Beneath the bright glare of the sun, the normally muddy water looked like a strip of shiny brown taffy. Had it not been for the deliveries she had to make, she would have been tempted to stop and sink her feet into its murky, cool depths. How she longed to put the fishing pole kept handy in the wagon to good use! She hadn't gone fishing since Uncle Joe died. The shop now took up most of her time.

A movement on the river caught her eye, and she pulled the wagon to the side of the road for a better look. Was that what she thought it was? Squinting against the water's glare, she shaded her eyes with her hand.

At first, she thought it was an alligator. None had been spotted this far north, but that was still a possibility. She narrowed her eyes. The current caused the object to turn slightly, allowing for a better view.

She now saw that it was a log, and clinging to it was a white spotted dog.

Alarm coursed through her, and she gasped, "Oh no!"

Farther downstream, the river dropped into a series of rocky waterfalls. The dog's life was clearly in danger. She must do something, fast!

Setting the wagon brake, she scrambled to the ground and pulled off her shoes and stockings. Quickly unhooking her skirt, she let it drop to her feet. Tugging on the ribbons of her bonnet, she tossed it away and took a running leap into the frigid water.

Her muscles stiffened in response to the cold, and she immediately regretted not removing her petticoat. The buoyant fabric caught the river's undertow and threatened to drag her down. Nonetheless, she kept going. Kicking hard, she sliced her arms through the water. Between the strong current and the weight of her nether garments, she made slow progress.

Surfacing, she treaded water to get her bearings and spotted the log no more than fifteen feet away.

The muscles in her arms and legs burned, and she felt limp with exhaustion. Fearing her ability to keep fighting the strong current, she wiggled out of her petticoat, hoping that would help, and her garment floated away like a giant marshmallow.

The dog let out a whining sound, then wagged its tail and barked as if cheering her on.

"Hold on," she called. Wearing only pantaloons from the waist down, she found it easier to kick now, but the flow of water kept pulling her under. Kicking harder, she lengthened her stroke. Progress was slow, but persistence paid off, and she made it to the middle of the river. The log bobbed up and down just out of reach. Gasping for air, she kicked with all her might, but it was no use. The log drifted away, and the dog howled like a lone wolf.

The canine's safety paramount in her mind, she swam as hard as she could. Just as she was about to reach the log a second time, an excruciating pain shot up her calf.

She threw her head back and tried to float, but the current dragged her under. Breaking through the surface, she spewed water and gasped for air. She tried to flex her foot and kick through the cramp, but the murky depths sucked her in again. Gathering her strength, she shot upward, sputtering.

Taking a moment to catch her breath, she doubled over and stretched her leg until her lungs screamed for air. Popping her head out of the water, she moved her arms as if climbing an invisible ladder but couldn't stay afloat long enough to fill her lungs.

Icy fingers of terror gripped her heart. *No, no, no! This can't be the end. Don't panic! Mustn't panic… God, no!*

She thought of Aunt Letty. Her dear, sweet aunt. What would become of her? Kate had promised her uncle she'd take care of her. *Oh, Uncle Joe, forgive me.* She thought of…of… Her mind went blank.

Darkness closed in on all sides. All at once, she was back on that orphan train. The rank, sour smell of cattle filled her head. Frank was halfway out the open door. She grabbed his feet, but he slipped away from her grasping hands. Helplessly, she watched his body fly out of the train and into the night air like a bat from a cave.

She opened her mouth to scream but instead gulped a mouthful of water. She couldn't move. Her arms, her legs, her body felt stiff as marble. Suddenly, she was five years old again, standing by her mother's bed.

"Wake up, Mama, wake up," she cried. But her mother wouldn't move. Hadn't moved all day.

Desperate now, she shook her mother's lifeless body, sobbing, but no one in that dark, dingy tenement building came to help her. Nor was there anyone to tell her what to do. She was all alone. Fear unlike any she'd ever known washed over her.

She threw herself across her mother's lifeless body. As she lay there, crying her heart out, firm, ironlike fingers reached out to grab her. All at once, she knew how it felt to be in the unrelenting grip of death.

8

"MISS DENVER!"

Startled, Kate gasped for air and battled her way through the darkness. Had she only imagined the voice? Was she dreaming?

She couldn't feel her body. Couldn't feel anything. She was floating. Was this how it felt to die?

The voice again filled her ears, this time louder. Clearer. "Don't move. You're safe."

Safe.

That's what the social worker had said the day Kate had been forced onto the orphan train against her will. That horrid cattle car hadn't made her feel safe then, but for some unknown reason, she felt safe now.

"Miss Denver!"

There it was again, the voice. A velvety-smooth male voice that triggered a distant memory. She groaned and tried to open her eyes, but the light was too bright. She sensed a shadow, a presence, and blinked. Her brain was scrambled. She coughed— coughed so hard that it felt as if her whole body would turn inside out.

Firm hands rolled her on her side and patted her on the back. Water sputtered from her lungs until at last the pain in her chest subsided.

Those same hands turned her over again, and she found herself staring into a deep-blue sea. She fluttered her eyes until her vision cleared. What had looked like the ocean depths turned out to be the sultry blue eyes of her rescuer. His rugged, handsome face looked familiar, and a moment later, her brain clicked in to tell her why.

"It's…it's you," she whispered when she could find her voice.

"'Fraid so." The anxious look left the Texas Ranger's face, and his mouth quirked in a heart-stopping grin. "We've got to stop meeting under such dire circumstances." Cradling her in his arms, he was dripping wet, his blond hair plastered against his head.

A drop of moisture like a pearl held her gaze, and she visually followed it from his forehead to his cheekbone, all the way to his jutting square jaw. Embarrassed to be caught staring, she cleared her throat. "It's…true," she said, her voice still husky.

He lifted his eyebrows. "What's true?"

"Your life really does flash before your eyes when you're drowning."

"In that case, I hope I never have occasion to drown."

"Are you saying you wouldn't want to take another look at your past?"

The corners of his mouth tilted up again, revealing a glimpse of glistening white teeth. "No, ma'am. Once was enough."

The sun felt warm against her flesh, but still she

trembled. Whether from her near brush with death or the crushing memories of the past, she couldn't tell. She didn't want to think that the ranger's arms had anything to do with it.

"You're cold," he said. His brow creased with concern, he pulled her closer.

She pressed her head against his wet shirt and was very much aware of his virile strength. Embracing the power that emanated from him, she sank fully into his protective arms, and her mind floated back to her childhood.

One night, while at the home for orphans, she'd woken to find a rat in her bed. Anxious to escape, she had run outside. In the dark of night, the enormous tree in the yard seemed sturdy and safe—a protective guardian—and she had imagined it was the loving parent she so desperately needed. Hugging that tree with all her might, she'd sobbed her heart out. She would never forget the look of disgust on the other orphans' faces the following morning when they found her with her arms wrapped around that old elm. *What a baby*, they'd taunted. *What a crybaby*.

After that, she'd refused to let anyone see her cry. She'd vowed never again to show weakness or vulnerability, her uncle's death being the one exception.

Now she shamelessly let the ranger hold and comfort her, and it felt…surprisingly good. More than that, it felt right somehow. He felt every bit as mighty and sturdy as that old tree. Every bit as protective.

"I thought I was a goner," she whispered, blinking back tears. "I was so scared."

"I know." He trailed his hands up and down her

spine. "I was scared too. Scared I wouldn't reach you in time."

His response surprised her. Not many men would admit to being scared. Wondering what other surprises lay hidden behind his tough exterior, she dug her fingers into his back and pressed against his strong, lean form. Willing his strength to become her strength, she welcomed the warmth that spread like liquid sunshine through her body.

Once she stopped shaking, she could no longer justify staying in the safe harbor of his arms. Still, it was with great reluctance that she pulled away.

"Take it easy," he said. His hand on her shoulder sent more warm currents rushing through her.

He removed his hand, and she took a quick breath. As the last of the fog cleared from her brain, something suddenly occurred to her. Craning her neck in alarm, she scanned the river.

"The dog…"

Tucker chuckled. "Your yelling and screaming did the trick. You scared it so much, the mutt jumped off the log and swam to shore."

The news made her catch her breath in relief. "I wasn't yelling and screaming."

"Oh no? Well, somebody was." He lifted a hand to his throat and made a gagging sound. "And that same someone almost drowned me."

"I'm sorry, I…" What she'd thought had been the grip of death must have been the ranger's arms around her. She shifted her gaze to the muscular biceps that not even the sleeves of his wet shirt could hide. Feeling her cheeks flush, she bit her lower lip.

His gaze blazed. "No harm done."

Recovered enough to feel naked beneath his probing eyes, she crossed her arms in front of herself. The thin fabric of her pantaloons clung to her waist and hips, leaving little to the imagination.

As if he'd caught himself staring, he stood. Bending, he picked up the skirt she'd dropped earlier and held it out.

Gazing up at him, she took the skirt from him and pulled it to her chest. "I don't know how to thank you," she said. "You saved my life."

"I'd say that was the least I could do for all the trouble I've caused you."

"I hope I didn't make it too difficult for you," she said.

He shrugged. "Nothing I couldn't handle." He tossed a nod at the skirt in her hands. "Better get out of those wet clothes."

He sat on a log, his back toward her, and proceeded to put on his gun belt and boots.

She staggered cautiously to her feet. Other than feeling a bit light-headed—and more than a little foolish—she was okay. At least she was no longer shaking.

Nothing could be done about her shirtwaist, but the light fabric would soon dry in the heat of the sun. She donned her skirt and reached for her bonnet. Her hairpins were missing, and long, soggy strands hung down her back. She bunched her hair on top of her head and pulled on her hat, tying it beneath her chin. Tendrils of wet hair fell about her face, but it was the best she could do.

"Can I look now?" Tucker called after a few minutes.

She jammed her foot into a high-button shoe. "Yes."

He stood and regarded her with questioning eyes. Somehow, he managed to give his wet trousers, shirt, and vest more dignity than they deserved. "You sure you're okay?"

Kate finished buttoning up her shoes and nodded. "I don't know what happened," she said by way of explanation. "I'm actually a pretty good swimmer."

"The water's cold, and the current is strong. It was all I could do to swim against the flow."

Whether that was true or not, she didn't know, but she appreciated him trying to make her feel better.

Studying her, he continued. "You're lucky you didn't meet up with a water moccasin or an alligator." A probing query hovered in the depths of his eyes. "Are you always so impervious to danger?"

"Only when it involves saving an animal."

He looked interested, maybe even impressed. "And how many animals have you saved?"

"I don't know. Dozens, maybe more. Fortunately, most of them were on land. I'm just grateful that you happened to be in the area."

"You have the Ghost Riders to thank for that. The sheriff and his deputy chased them out this way before they disappeared. Thought I'd check the place out."

She tilted her head. "Do you believe in all that ghost stuff?"

"No, and I also don't believe that people vanish into thin air." He glanced at her horse and wagon. "I'd be happy to drive you home. I just need to tie my horse to the back."

"Thank you, but I have deliveries to make."

Concern pooled in his eyes. "I'm not sure that's a good idea. Not after what you went through. You probably should take it easy for the rest of the day."

"I'm fine. Really, I am, thanks to you."

His crooked smile caused her pulse to race again. "I'm glad I was able to do something besides cause you more grief."

She smiled back. After today, how could she still hold a grudge against him? Catching herself staring, she stood and headed for her horse and wagon. Though her legs still felt a little shaky and her throat raw, she was anxious to leave. He was making her nervous. He had a way of looking at her that made her feel like she was more than she was: more attractive, more interesting, more womanly—more something.

She didn't need to rest, and she certainly didn't need to act like a silly schoolgirl who had just caught the eye of her first beau. What she needed was dry clothes.

Climbing into the driver's seat, she felt the heat of the ranger's gaze upon her. She drew in her breath and grabbed hold of the reins. "Thank you again for everything," she called down to him.

"My pleasure."

She flashed him yet another a smile. "I'm glad I didn't drown you."

"Had you done so, I would have had only myself to blame," he said wryly, and she noted a glimmer of humor in his eyes. "I was warned that leaving town would be good for my health," he added and pulled a wet slip of paper from his vest pocket.

It was the strip she'd included in his bag of caramels. "You kept that?" She raised a questioning brow.

"Don't tell me you believe in fortune-telling, Mr. Tucker."

"This actually sounded more like a warning."

"Perhaps you should heed it," she said.

"I'll take my chances." With a tip of his hat, he stepped back, allowing her to pull away.

Brett stood in the middle of the dirt road watching Miss Denver's wagon turn by the grove of oak trees and vanish from sight.

She'd sure given him a scare. He'd been certain she was a goner. Had he not reached her in time…

He shook his head with a shudder. What a woman. She'd put up quite a fight. Fortunately, she was small in stature and no match for a man his size.

He could still recall how she'd felt in his arms after he'd hauled her out of the water, up the riverbank to where she'd left her horse and wagon. The current had carted her a distance away, and he'd had to carry her along the rocky bank in stockinged feet.

He still recalled the relief he'd felt when her eyes flickered open and a smile hovered on her lips. Not until he'd known she was all right did he note the pleasing way her wet clothes hugged the feminine peaks and valleys of her dainty form. But more than anything, he remembered how she'd clung to him, her womanly curves fitting seamlessly next to his own contours. It was as if they had been created from a single mold.

Startled by the direction his thoughts had taken, he

scrubbed his face with his hands. He had no business ruminating on the lady's considerable charms. She and Foster were currently estranged, but if things went according to plan, that would change. The truth was, the lady was already spoken for, and he'd best not forget it.

Besides, he had work to do. Outlaws to catch. His sister's killer to find. He tugged on his hat and checked the guns at his side. His shirt and vest were relatively dry, thanks to the heat of the midday sun, but his trousers were still wet.

He surveyed the area around him. To the west lay the river. Limestone hills rose from the opposite shore, probing the sky with jagged peaks. The wide-open prairie spread eastward, tall grass rippling in the breeze like gently lapping ocean waves. Blocking the view to the south was a grove of oak trees.

Locals referred to the river's sharp turn as the Elbow. The water flowed west for about a quarter of a mile before turning in a southerly direction and making its way to the Gulf.

While he had been busy chasing the third would-be bank robber through town, the sheriff and his deputy had pursued the other two men on horseback, losing them at the Elbow.

Vanished into thin air was how Deputy Sweeney described it. *Never saw anythin' like it in me life.*

Brett mounted his horse and followed the river to the bend. The road rose and fell, giving him a clear view of the church a short distance away. Reaching his destination, he dismounted and tethered his horse to a bush.

The white brick building looked almost picture-perfect in the sun, its tall steeple rising high about the roof. Once again, he was reminded of the wedding he'd ruined. He sure had made a mess of things. The sooner he got the couple back together, the better. It was the right thing to do. Still…

Surprised to catch himself suddenly wishing things could be different—wishing he'd met Kate Denver under very different circumstances—he shook his head. He had no business thinking such things. Nor did he have the time. He had work to do.

The flapping of wings drew his attention to a blue heron at the water's edge.

The upper and river roads flanked a grove of trees before converging into one and allowing a full view of the road ahead. Brett couldn't see Miss Denver for the cloud of dust that churned from beneath her wagon wheels, but he could still envision her smile and the deep blue of her sparkling eyes.

With a quick intake of breath, he pulled his gaze away and concentrated on his immediate surroundings.

He then followed the road a piece by foot, his gaze focused on the mottled ground. The upper road was heavily traveled, so it wasn't surprising to find it covered with both shod and unshod hoofprints. Wagon wheels had cut narrow grooves into the packed clay road. It was also liberally dotted with animal droppings—some fresh, some not.

He returned to the church, walked around it, and rattled the double doors. No doubt the horse tethered in front belonged to the minister. The door flew open, and Brett nodded a greeting.

"Reverend Johnson."

The preacher didn't look especially pleased to see

him. "Oh, it's you." He turned, leaving the door ajar. Brett assumed that was an invitation to follow.

The reverend walked down the aisle to the front of the church and started fiddling with a cloth at the altar. Brett stared up at the damaged ceiling and groaned inwardly. Somehow, it looked even worse today.

"Mrs. Cuttwell did a good job repairing the damage from the fire, don't you think?" the reverend asked.

The altar cloth was actually a quilt. A log cabin had been skillfully stitched to the center of each square. It seemed like a strange choice for the church, especially since everything from the stained-glass windows to the painted ceiling depicted traditional Biblical scenes.

Since Brett didn't think it was his place to say as much, he simply nodded in agreement. Except for a slightly different shade of white on some squares, no one would ever guess the cloth had undergone fire damage. Mrs. Cuttwell, whoever she was, had done a fine job indeed. Too bad she didn't repair ceilings.

The reverend followed Brett's gaze upward. "Don't know anyone who can fix that," he said with a rueful frown. "Do you?"

"'Fraid not," Brett said. "But if you find someone, I'd be happy to foot the bill."

"Hmm. So, what can I do for you?"

"There was an attempted robbery in town. The bank this time."

"That's what I heard."

"Perhaps you also heard that the would-be robbers vanished somewhere in this vicinity."

The reverend nodded. "That's all everyone talked about on Sunday. The Ghost Riders of Haywire."

"Did you see anything suspicious on that day?"

"'Fraid I can't help you there. Thursday is my visitation day. I was visiting the sick and infirm. I wasn't here. Sorry."

It was another dead end, but no more than Brett had expected. Either the citizens really didn't know anything about the robbers, or they were a closed-mouthed group.

"Perhaps you could help with something else." He reached into his pocket and drew out the dog-eared photograph. "Have you seen this man? He was known as Frank Foster, but he might be using another name."

The reverend took the photograph, reached into his pocket for his monocle, and popped it into his eye with a practiced hand. After carefully studying the image, he pulled the eyepiece away and gave Brett a quizzical look. "So, this is the reason you stopped the wedding." He shook his head and handed the photograph back. "I'm sorry, no, I don't recognize him. What makes you think he's in these parts?"

"Just a hunch." It wasn't much of an answer, but Brett didn't want to go into details.

The reverend dropped the monocle back into his coat pocket. "Have you talked to Hoot Owl Pete? He knows just about everything that goes on in Haywire."

"Hoot Owl Pete, eh? Where can I find him?"

"Unless I miss my guess, you'll find him where he's always at. Parked in front of Gordon's general store. Just be ready to get an earful. No one can tell a windy tale like he can."

"Much obliged." Brett slipped the photograph into his vest pocket. "I won't take up any more of your time."

With another rueful glance at the ceiling, he walked out of the church and headed back to where he'd left his horse. This time, he cut through the grove of trees and scoured every square inch of the wooded area. A bear had foraged its way through not long ago. Deer and rabbits had left their tracks, but he could find nothing that indicated the recent presence of man.

He crossed the road and tramped through the tall grass and soon came to a buffalo wallow. The size and depth indicated it had been there for a good long while, probably since before the Alamo. His gaze traveled in a wide arc around him. The prairie wool was tall and thick enough to hide a man, but not a horse. And certainly not three horses.

Spotting a diamondback rattler coiled and hissing in the middle of the road, Brett froze in place. The object of the snake's attention was a squirrel pup that had ventured out of its nest.

The pup was saved by a short, sharp warning from a larger squirrel, probably its mother, and the two rodents ran away, vanishing among the trees.

Giving the snake a wide berth, Brett circled back to his horse. After mounting, he took one last look around. *Vanished into thin air. Never saw anythin' like it in me life.*

With a shake of his head, he tugged on the reins and rode to town.

9

LESS THAN TWENTY MINUTES AFTER LEAVING TEXAS Ranger Tucker, Kate reached the farmhouse where her friend Connie lived with her parents.

Her friend opened the door to her knock. "Kate! What a surprise! I was just—" She took one look at Kate's disheveled appearance and gasped. "Oh my, what happened?"

"Just a little…accident," Kate said, stepping into the cool interior of the house. "Nothing to be concerned about." She dangled a paper sack. "I brought you something."

Connie took the bag and peered inside. "Ah, my favorite lemon drops. Thank you." She pulled out the slip of paper. "'What you're looking for can be found in your own backyard,'" she read aloud and sighed. "I'm afraid the only things that can be found in my backyard are some cows and a bunch of chickens."

"And Harvey Wells," Kate said. Harvey's family owned the adjacent property.

Connie was the oldest of four children, and it bothered her that all her siblings were already married and she had yet to find a beau. With her dark hair and good looks, Connie could probably have most any man she set her cap for.

Unfortunately, the only man she was interested in was Harvey Wells. Connie had carried a torch for him ever since the two had attended grammar school. But Harvey had not shown the slightest interest in Connie, at least not in a romantic sense. His mind was on other things, mainly his many inventions.

"Next subject," Connie said, failing to fall for the bait.

Kate refused to be deterred. "What are you wearing to the spring dance?"

"What makes you think I'm going?"

"You always go," Kate said. "And I have it on good authority that Harvey will be there."

Connie set the bag of candy on the mantel. "Well, I hope he has a good time, but it won't be with me. I have no intention of attending." After a beat, she asked, "Are you going?"

Kate sighed. The spring dance was the social occasion of the year and one of her favorite events. "How can I?"

"Oh, Kate." Connie's face softened in apology. "I'm so sorry. I hoped that by now, you and Frank would have patched things up."

"I don't want to talk about Frank right now," Kate said. Her mind was still in a whirl over her near-drowning. She shuddered to think what would have happened had the Texas Ranger not arrived when he did. *You're safe*, he'd said. *You're safe*.

She shivered at the memory of being in his arms. A strange inner fire flared up, and a rush of heat raced through her body all the way to her toes.

Connie must have noticed something, because she stepped forward, arms extended. "You poor thing." She gave Kate a quick hug before pulling away. "Oh my! Your hair… You're wet. You still haven't told me what happened."

"Long story. Do you mind if I borrow dry clothes?" Fortunately, they were close to the same size and had often swapped clothing in the past.

"Oh yes, of course. Come to my room." Connie turned and led the way upstairs.

"I just need a petticoat, pantaloons, and a dry shirtwaist," Kate said as she stared at the vast assortment of clothing crammed into Connie's wardrobe. There were enough items to dress half the county.

Connie pulled out a blue gingham shirtwaist, a petticoat, and white unmentionables. "Here. You better change your corset too. You don't want to catch your death of cold."

Kate laughed. As if such a thing was possible in the Texas heat. "Now you sound like Aunt Letty." With the dry garments in hand, she took only a few moments to change. She stared at herself in the mirror. "That feels better."

Connie looked over Kate's shoulder. When they were younger, some people mistook them for sisters. That was mostly because of their hair color. Connie's, however, was a rich auburn and lacked the brassy brightness of Kate's.

"You still haven't told me what happened," Connie said.

"If you must know, I spotted a dog floating on a log and was afraid the poor thing would get caught in the rapids." Kate turned away from the mirror and, as quickly as she could, told her friend the rest. Or at least as much as she dared.

Connie's eyes widened in horror. "You could have drowned."

"I'm quite aware of that, but as you see, I'm perfectly all right."

"But had that Texas Ranger not saved you—"

Kate felt her cheeks flare. Saving her was only part of it. He'd then held her in his arms and made her feel safe and protected and…

"I know, I know," she said with a dismissive shrug. "Let's talk about something else."

"Kate, I worry about you." Connie reached for a hairbrush. "It's not the first time you've put yourself in danger. Remember when you saved that lamb from a pack of wolves and almost got mauled yourself?"

Kate took the offered hairbrush and set to work untangling her hair. "Yes, well…"

"And then there was the time you climbed a tree to save Mrs. Watkins's cat and dislodged a beehive and—"

Kate shuddered at the memory. "Don't remind me." Her face and arms had been covered in bee stings. "Can we talk about something else?"

"What I want to talk about is Frank."

Kate set the hairbrush down on the dresser. "Okay, let's go back to the bee stings."

"Oh no. You're not getting out of it that easily," Connie said. "Are you and he…done for good?"

Kate pulled her hair back and worked it into a bun. "Yes."

Connie reached into a drawer for a box of hairpins. "I can't believe that. You have so much history together."

"I know."

Connie finished helping Kate pin her hair in place. "I would give anything to meet a man like Frank. He's handsome and successful and clever. More than anything, he adores you just the way you are and doesn't try to change you."

"But he's also got a terrible jealous streak," Kate said.

"That's because he loves you so much."

"It doesn't feel like love. It feels…like he doesn't trust me." Was it possible to fully and completely love without trust?

"You always said that Frank made you feel safe."

Kate bit her lip. *You're safe now.* Even as she silently recalled those soothing words, she felt a tug in her heart. Unfortunately, the voice in her head belonged to the Texas Ranger, not Frank, and for that, she felt bad. Even guilty.

When Kate failed to respond, Connie persisted. "Isn't feeling safe the same as trust?"

"You don't need another person to make you feel safe," Kate said, checking her hair in the mirror. "Trust is different. It requires at least two people. Just like true love."

Connie patted her on the back. "Oh, Kate…"

Kate held up her hands. "Let's talk about something else. Like what you're going to wear to the dance." She perused the open wardrobe and pulled a yellow dress off the wooden peg. The dress had a low, square neck, elbow-length sleeves, and a draped skirt trimmed in lace.

"Oh, this is perfect! You'll be the belle of the ball."

Connie folded her arms across her chest. "I told you I am *not* going."

Kate held the yellow gown up to herself and glanced in the mirror. "Then I won't tell you my plan for getting Harvey to notice you."

Connie dropped her arms to her side. "You have a plan?"

"Yes, but you have to agree to go to the dance before I tell you what it is. Deal?"

Her friend hesitated before finally giving in, as Kate knew she would. "Deal."

❧

Brett found Hoot Owl Pete seated in a rocking chair in front of the general store.

He greeted Brett with a nod and a flash of large, white teeth. "Come and join us. Sit for a spell."

A sturdy-looking man with wide shoulders and ebony skin, Hoot Owl Pete wore his salted black hair tied at the back of his neck with a piece of rawhide. Dressed in overalls and a red-checkered shirt, he held an unlit corncob pipe in his hand and looked Brett up and down.

"I don't believe we've been formally introduced."

"Brett Tucker, Texas Ranger," Brett said, offering his hand.

Hoot Owl Pete shook it with a firm grip. "Heard about you. You're the one who broke up Kate's wedding."

Brett pulled his hand away. "Right now, I'm hoping to break up a gang of outlaws."

Hoot Owl Pete rocked in his chair. "Well, it's 'bout time someone did." He tossed a nod at the man seated next to him. "You know Lucky Lou? He deals faro at the Golden Nugget."

"Is that so?" Brett asked. That explained the fancy duds. Brett didn't remember the man, but he recalled the black-and-white dog seated by his side. "That your dog?"

"Yeah, that's right. His name is Ringo."

Hearing his name, the dog wagged his tail, and Brett stooped to pet him before taking a seat. "Lucky Lou, eh? How'd you get that moniker?"

Hoot Owl Pete answered for the man. "Show him." Lucky Lou shook his head, but Hoot Owl Pete insisted. "Show him."

Reluctance written across his pockmarked face, Lucky Lou pulled a neck chain from beneath his shirt and held it up for Brett to see. Three spent bullets hung from the chain.

"He almost got hisself killed three times," Hoot Owl Pete said. "Tell him."

Lucky Lou pointed to each silver casing in turn. "This one near got me in the war. This one barely missed me during a stagecoach robbery, and the one here came from the gun of a jealous husband."

With a hearty laugh, Hoot Owl Pete slapped his hand on his thigh. "A jealous husband!" Throwing his head back like the lid of a coffeepot, he laughed harder. "Can you beat that?"

"Nope, sure can't," Brett said. It was hard to believe that a man as homely as Lucky Lou could turn a woman's head, let alone make a husband jealous.

"You said you got shot during a stagecoach robbery? Where was that?"

"Up north somewhere. Guess you could say I was in the wrong place at the wrong time." Lucky Lou replaced his chain. "Well, me and Ringo better get a move on." He stood. "See you around." Tugging on his dog's leash, he left.

"Yeah, see you," Brett said, watching him go.

Hoot Owl Pete struck a wooden match and lit his pipe. Shaking out the flame, he took a long draw on the pipe before removing it from his mouth. "Guess it's safe to say you're here because of the Ghost Riders. Heard you almost caught one the other day."

Brett gave a curt nod. Losing that man in the maze of an alleyway behind the candy shop was still a sore subject. "I was hoping you could help me."

"Don't know how."

"I heard you know practically everything that goes on in Haywire."

"That might have been true in the past, but those days are long gone. Since the railroad came to town, the population has doubled. It also brought a lot of Easterners, and those greenhorns are as closed-mouthed as a bunch of clams."

It wasn't the first time Brett had heard that complaint. Many Texas lawmen had expressed similar grievances. Not only had the population doubled and even tripled in many towns and cities throughout the Lone Star State, but so had crime. That was partly because the railroad made it easy for criminals to escape the clutches of the law.

Hoping the day wasn't a complete loss, Brett reached

into his vest pocket for the dog-eared photograph. "I have reason to believe that this is a member of the gang. Possibly the leader." He handed the photograph to Hoot Owl Pete, who puffed on his pipe while studying it.

He returned the photograph with a shake of his head. After blowing a cloud of smoke, he removed his pipe from his lips. "Whoever he is, he's got himself the perfect face for an outlaw. No distinguishin' features. No pox marks. No scars. No facial hair. Nothing."

"He might have grown a beard since this photograph was taken."

"And he would still look like half the men in the county." Hoot Owl Pete set his pipe on the wicker table by his side. Reaching into his pocket, he pulled out a small bag. "You look like you could use a peppermint," he said.

Brett shook his head. "Thank you, but I'm more of a caramel person."

"Sorry. Can't help you there. But I know a pretty lady who can, and I don't have to tell you her name."

"No. No, you don't," Brett said and cleared his throat. It had only been a couple of hours since he'd held that same pretty lady in his arms. The intensity with which the encounter had affected him was surprising and more than a little worrisome. He'd been able to think of little else since.

Hoot Owl Pete set the paper bag next to his pipe. Reading the slip of paper that had come with the candy, he laughed. "It says here, 'When trouble comes knocking, don't offer it a chair.'" He dropped the slip of paper back into the sack. "Good thing you're already seated."

"I'm only trouble to those who break the law," Brett said.

"Or get married," Hoot Owl Pete added with a laugh.

Brett drew in his breath. He'd hoped to make his mark as a Texas Ranger, not a wedding crasher. "Ever been married?"

Hoot Owl Pete shook his head. "Nope."

"Cold feet?"

"Cool head."

Brett chuckled. "Guess we could all use a cool head where women are concerned." Leaning forward, he rubbed his hands between his knees. "Hope you don't mind me asking, but how did you get the name Hoot Owl Pete?" With his tree-trunk legs and timber-sized arms, the man looked more like a bear than an owl.

In answer, Hoot Owl Pete made a *Whoooo! Whoooooo! Whoooo!* sound. He laughed at Brett's expression. "I was a conductor for the Underground Railroad. Runaways looking for me would listen for the sound of an owl. I'd give them supplies, smear pepper on their feet to confuse the hounds, and send them on their way to the next safe place."

His eyes misted with a faraway look as if reliving those long-ago years. "Thousands of runaways passed through here on the way to Mexico." He focused on something that only he could see. "We done good."

"Yeah, you did," Brett said, standing. "I won't take up any more of your time."

"Good luck with finding the man you're looking for."

"Thanks," Brett said. The way things were going, he'd need all the luck he could get.

Later that afternoon, Kate stared at the sorrowful mess on the marble slab and shook her head. She had been working on her uncle's recipe for months and had yet to get it right. The runny white blob meant there wouldn't be any candy-making history for her today.

Sighing, she scooped up the sugary mass with a spatula and dumped it in the trash. She'd hoped that work would help her relax—or at the very least make her forget being in the arms of the Texas Ranger. But attempting to make something as complicated as Uncle Joe's candy with her mind still awhirl had been a mistake.

Not only was candy making a laborious art, it was also an exacting one and required concentration. Anything that could go wrong often did. Adjustments had to be made for the weather, and that was easier said than done. Texas humidity and heat worked against her at every turn. Candy required a certain ratio of sugar to moisture and was best made in dry climates.

But humidity wasn't the only challenge. Sugar had nine degrees of boiling from thread to hard crack. A degree either way could mean all the difference between success and failure.

Creating colors was even trickier and often took as long to produce as the actual candy. Colors needed to be reasonably permanent and not fade when exposed to light or mixed with other ingredients. They also had to be harmless. She suspected children would balk if it were known that they had spinach to thank for the bright-green color found in her popular tongue slaps and peppermint sticks.

The jangle of bells pulled her out of her thoughts and out of the kitchen.

It was her little friend Dusty. He slammed the door shut and peered through the window before turning.

His pale face made her heart sink. "Oh, Dusty. Are those boys bothering you again?"

Trying to look brave, Dusty gave his shoulders a careless shrug, but his eyes gave him away. He was clearly trying not to cry.

Kate's temper flared. She was tempted to march outside and give those bullies a piece of her mind, but she doubted it would do any good. She'd already talked to their parents, and that had gotten her nowhere.

Dusty's father didn't believe in interfering. He wanted his son to stand up for himself. Given the boy's small size and sweet disposition, that hardly seemed like a viable solution.

As for the bullies…Charley and Spike were brothers, and talking to their father was like talking to a lamppost. Bobby Baker's mother was an overwhelmed widow who had no idea how to control her seven children.

Kate motioned Dusty behind the counter. "Come on back. You can help me mix colors."

That brought the hoped-for smile to his face, though he did glance out the front window again before following her to the kitchen.

Hoping to allay his fears, she quickly tied an apron around him and put him to work, stirring the sugary concoction in a large pot.

His enthusiasm and willingness to help made her smile. If he were older, she would be tempted to hire him on the spot. How anyone could pick on such a sweet child was beyond her comprehension.

Something had to be done about the town bullies, and done soon. The question was what?

10

BRETT LEFT HIS BOARDINGHOUSE EARLY TUESDAY
morning, yawning, and headed straight to the livery.
Already, the sun was bright, promising another warm
day, but his foul mood persisted.

He'd been in town for more than a month and had
little to show for his efforts. He was no closer to finding his former brother-in-law than the day he'd first
ridden into Haywire. The Ghost Riders still hadn't
been captured, and he was making little headway with
Kate's former fiancé. The man didn't have a clue how
to win her back. Not a clue.

But those were the least of his worries. He was fit to
be boiled for glue, and it had nothing to do with work
or even Foster One or Two. He was mad at himself
for letting Kate Denver get under his skin. Heck, she
hadn't just sneaked her way in; she'd practically bur-
rowed a hole right through him all the way to his heart.

And he had no right feeling this way. No right at
all. Had it not been for him, she would now be Mrs.
Foster. A married woman. Out of his reach.

For the love of Pete, what was he thinking? She was

still out of his reach. Just because he'd held her in his arms, just because she'd clung to him as if she'd never let him go, just because she could make his heart sing with a simple smile… None of these was a reason to think things had changed.

Foster Two had many faults, but he didn't deserve to lose the woman he loved. Certainly not to the man responsible for ruining his wedding.

Brett grimaced. Okay, okay, okay, he'd been in binds before. Not romantic binds, but binds. The first step in handling trouble was to state the problem. He blew out his breath and forced himself to put his feelings into words. He was in terrible danger of falling for Kate Denver. There, problem stated.

The next step was to decide on a plan. In this case, the only thing that made sense was to stay away from her. Far, far away. The problem was, that might be easier said than done. That was why it was imperative to get her and Foster back together as soon as possible.

Determined to make that happen, Brett crossed over to the stables as quickly as his troubled thoughts allowed.

He'd paid the young liveryman extra to have his horse, Soldier, saddled and ready to go. The time saved allowed him to catch Deputy Patrick Sweeney before he'd left his house.

The sheriff didn't like Brett questioning his deputy, or even witnesses, and had thwarted his every attempt to do so. But Brett refused to be deterred. Even with the recent population explosion, Haywire was still a relatively small town. A neighbor, a friend, a tradesman—someone—had to have seen or heard something.

To that end, Brett had grilled bartenders, good-time

gals, and coffin drivers, as faro dealers were called. So far, he'd turned up nothing. The Ghost Riders had money to spend, but they sure in blazes weren't spending it in Haywire—or at least not in the expected ways.

He'd questioned businessmen, ranchers, and farmers, young and old, and had nothing to show for his efforts. Either Haywire citizens were strangely unobservant, or the Ghost Riders were especially cunning.

Brett didn't think Deputy Sheriff Sweeney knew any more than he'd already let on, but it wouldn't hurt to question him again. Sweeney was also a witness, and witnesses sometimes forgot things in the heat of the moment, only to recall them later.

The deputy lived with his wife and children in an adobe cabin about a mile out of town. Mrs. Sweeney directed Brett to the barn, where he found the deputy saddling his horse.

If the deputy was surprised by the early-morning visit, he didn't show it. "Got a minute?" Brett asked.

"Not really. The sheriff don't like his men to be late." A compact man with ginger hair and sideburns, he spoke with an Irish brogue.

"I won't keep you. I just need to clarify a couple of things. Been thinking about what you said about the Ghost Riders and wondered if you'd mind going over it again. I want to make sure I've got the facts straight."

Sweeney squinted. "And this couldn't wait till I got to the office?"

Brett shrugged but didn't answer. "I want to go over the part where they left town. You said they headed south."

"That's right," the deputy said, indicating the direction with a nod.

"You and the sheriff followed them. How far behind were you?"

Sweeney thought a moment before answering, his voice drowned out by a bleating goat. At Brett's request, he repeated his answer. "A half mile, maybe."

"And you were able to see both men and their horses clearly?"

Between the bleating goat and the man's burr, Brett had a hard time understanding him. "Would you mind repeating that?"

"Like I said, we could see them until they reached the Elbow."

"And after they vanished, you didn't see or hear anything unusual?"

Sweeney shook his head. "Not a thing."

Brett tossed a nod at the noisy nanny. "What's wrong with your goat?"

"Don't know. She's been making a racket like that for two days nigh."

"Looks like she's limping. You ought to get her checked out." Brett hooked his thumbs into his belt. "Did you say you lost them at the Elbow?"

"Yeah, that's the bend in the river." The Irishman crooked his arm to indicate it. "A grove of trees blocks the view of the road. That's where we lost them."

So far, Sweeney's account matched the sheriff's almost word for word. "Did you check out the area?"

"Combed it from one end to the other. The way I figure it, there are two types of people in the world. There are those who don't believe in ghosts and those of us who've seen them with our own pure eyes. As God is my witness, I'm telling you, those two criminals vanished into thin air. Never saw anythin' like it in me life."

∽

That morning, Kate stopped at Doc Avery's office to ask him to check on Mr. Fletcher. She then walked the short distance to the shop, where she found a basket of flowers on the counter. The size of a bread box, the basket held an abundance of cornflowers and white lilies. A blue satin bow adorned the handle.

"For me?" she asked.

Aunt Letty's mouth curved into a satisfied smile. "That's what the envelope says."

Dazzled by the beautiful arrangement, Kate blinked in disbelief. No one had ever before sent her flowers.

"Well, aren't you gonna find out who they're from?" Aunt Letty asked. The look of innocence on her aunt's face didn't fool Kate one whit. She was willing to bet her aunt had sneaked a peek at the card. Of course, Aunt Letty would never admit to such a thing.

Kate plucked the envelope from the blossoms and pulled out a little white card. "They're from Frank," she said with a puzzled frown. Frank had sent her flowers?

Though she was positive Aunt Letty had already looked at the card, Kate read the handwritten message aloud. "'When I first saw you, I fell in love and knew we were meant to be together.'" She looked up. "I don't believe it. This doesn't sound like something Frank would say."

Aunt Letty shrugged. "Wonders never cease. Read the rest."

Kate continued reading. "'Losing you is like a world without candy. A world without sunshine. A world without laughter.'" Overcome with emotion, she paused a moment before reading the rest. "'My life has no meaning without you. Please come back to me.'"

Hands clutched to her chest, Aunt Letty heaved a dreamy sigh. "Oh, the poor, poor man. He's obviously heartbroken."

Kate stared at the note and didn't know what to think. Had it not been written in Frank's handwriting, she would never have guessed in a million years that the note had come from him. It wasn't like Frank to express his feelings, at least not in such endearing terms.

Just as surprising was the huge bouquet of flowers. She distinctly remembered him saying that buying something doomed to die in a day or two was money down the drain.

Touching one large bloom by the stem, Kate buried her nose in the petals and inhaled the sweet fragrance.

She drew away with a sigh. Did Frank really know that blue was her favorite color, or had it just been a lucky guess? Flowers and flowery prose were not his usual style.

In the past, Frank's idea of a romantic gift had been something far more practical, like a kitchen tool. For her birthday, he'd given her an eggbeater. For Christmas, he'd completely missed the hints she dropped for a new hatpin. Instead, he'd presented her with leather fireplace bellows. The fact that he'd made them himself didn't alleviate her disappointment, but she'd tried her best not to show it.

Not only were the flowers out of character for him, but they further complicated matters and added to her confusion. Since yesterday's near-drowning, Kate had not been able to think of anything but the Texas Ranger. *You're safe*, he'd said. *Safe*. It was the third time she'd heard him use the word *safe*, and each time, he'd struck a chord deep inside her. How could he possibly have known? How could he possibly have guessed how important it was for her to feel safe?

Most orphan-train riders suffered from a deep-seated fear of loss. She suspected it was the reason for Frank's jealousy. That was why she'd put up with it as long as she had. But knowing the root of his jealousy didn't make it any easier to live with.

Now, in view of the flowers and the note, she felt guilty for thinking kinder of the ranger than of Frank.

This…this gesture… She wasn't sure what to call it. A peace offering? An apology? A promise to do better? She hesitated to call it romantic. Frank was far too prosaic for that. Still, this was unlike anything she had come to expect from him. Maybe he really was trying to change.

"Now will you consider giving him a chance to make things right?" Aunt Letty asked.

Kate bit her lip. *A world without candy, a world without sunshine…* Nothing Frank had said or done in the past had touched her as deeply as those few words.

Still, she didn't want to get her aunt's hopes high. She had to make certain that Frank really had conquered his jealousy before deciding whether the two of them had a future together. "I'll think about it."

How could one goat cause so much trouble? Brett battled his way through the door of Foster's saddle shop. The deputy's nanny goat squealed and squirmed in his arms, and it was all Brett could do to hold on to her.

Brett intended to lower the goat to the floor gently so as not to cause further injury to the animal's leg, but the nanny scrambled out of his arms before he had a chance. The goat's rear leg buckled for a moment before she clambered to her feet and careened around the shop.

Brushing goat hair off his vest and trousers, Brett let his gaze wander. The buttery smell of leather mingled with the smoky scent of birch-tar soap. It was the first time he'd set foot in Foster's shop, and he was impressed by the quality of the saddles on display. Some were plain but sturdy with high horns. The latter was designed for the Texas custom of attaching the lariat to the horn before tossing it. Other saddles were intricately carved and trimmed in silver. Most were Mexican-style saddles.

Foster's workbench was situated behind the counter, but he was nowhere in sight. A half-finished stock saddle sat on a wooden frame, surrounded by all manner of hand tools and leather shavings.

As clueless as he was about women in general, and Kate Denver in particular, Foster had his good points and was a fine craftsman. Some might even say he was an artisan.

The door opened, and Foster entered carrying a saddle. Upon seeing the goat, he stopped dead in his tracks. "What the devil?"

The nanny was chewing on a saddle string, and Brett pulled her away. "It's just a goat."

Frank heaved the saddle onto a wooden stand and quickly took refuge behind the counter. "It can't be here. Animals do funny things to me. They make me sneeze and break out in spots. I don't even own a horse."

Brett scratched his temple. "I don't understand how someone allergic to horses can be a saddle maker."

"What's to understand? I work with leather that is tanned and cleaned."

"Okay, that makes sense. But knowing how animals affect you, I still don't understand how you can marry Kate, the Clara Barton of the animal kingdom."

"How do you know that about Kate?" Foster's accusatory tone was tempered by a sneeze.

Brett rubbed his chin and decided not to mention Kate's near-drowning. If she wanted Foster to know, he'd let her deal with it. "It's not exactly a secret." He knitted his brow. "You still haven't answered my question."

Foster threw up his hands. "Okay, if you must know, Kate agreed to keep her menagerie at her aunt's house."

"Menagerie? How many animals does she have?"

"I don't know." Frank sneezed again and this time drew a handkerchief from his pocket. "It changes daily. She has this knack of finding injured animals and nursing them back to health. The wild animals she lets go. The rest she finds homes for. She's kind of like the Children's Aid Society for animals." He sidled to the other end of the counter, putting as much distance between himself and the goat as possible. "So, what's it doing here?"

"That, my dear man, is the key to Kate's heart.

Now that you've paved the way with flowers, you need a reason to see her. That's where the goat comes in. As you can see, something's wrong with her leg, and you need to ask Kate to look at it. Show her how concerned you are about the animal's welfare. How much you appreciate her nursing skills."

Foster stared at him. "Are you out of your cotton-pickin' mind?" He sneezed again and dabbed at his watering eyes with his handkerchief. "I can't walk into her shop with a goat."

"No, but you can take it to her house."

"I can't do that either. I told you I don't own a horse, and she lives at least a mile away."

Brett stared at him. Never had he seen a face swell up so quickly. "How do you normally get there?"

"I generally walk, but there's no way I'm walking all that way carrying a blessed goat!"

Brett rubbed the back of his neck and tried to think. Things kept getting more and more complicated. "Okay, here's what we're gonna do. I'll drive you there with the goat. I'll drop you down the road a piece so that Kate doesn't see me. If she thinks you walked all the way from town to help the poor animal, trust me, she'll melt on the spot."

Foster pointed to his blotchy face. "Do you see what's happening here?"

"How can I miss it? You look horrid. And I couldn't have planned this better had I tried. When Kate sees how you made your life miserable just to save a poor goat, she'll give you another chance."

Foster stared at him through red, watery eyes. "You mean she'll take me back?"

"I wouldn't go quite that far. At least not yet. You said it yourself. She's pretty riled." Brett thought for a moment. "I saw a sign in town about a dance next week."

Foster sneezed into his handkerchief. "Are...*ah-choo!*" He blew his nose before continuing. "Are you talking about the annual spring dance?"

"Yep, that's the one." Brett studied Foster with thoughtful regard. "How do you feel about taking Kate to that dance?"

Foster discounted the idea with a shake of his head. "She won't even talk to me. How am I gonna get her to go to a dance?"

"Trust me. That's where the goat comes in. When Kate sees how you're tryin' to help it, she'll look at you with new eyes. When you see her start to grow soft toward you, that's when you ask her to the dance."

A flicker of hope flared in Foster's red eyes and just as quickly died. "What if she turns me down?"

"If you look as bad as you do now, she won't have the heart to turn you down."

The stubborn look left Foster's face, or at least Brett thought it did. It was hard to know for certain what was going on beneath the swelling and redness.

Frank eyed the goat with a doubtful frown. "Are you sure this is gonna work?"

Brett shrugged. Where Foster was concerned, he wasn't sure of anything. "She liked the flowers, didn't she?"

Frank nodded and reached for a folded piece of paper on the counter next to the money box. "She sent me a thank-you note. Said they were candy for the eyes."

"See? What did I tell you? Women like that kind of stuff. No doubt she also liked what you wrote." The wording on the note had been Brett's idea. He'd also come up with the part about the candy, sunshine, and laughter. It wasn't hard. He loathed filling out reports to ranger headquarters, but where Kate was concerned, the words had flowed. "I haven't led you astray yet, have I?"

Frank's shoulders slumped further. "Okay, okay. You made your point." He studied the goat ruefully. "So you think me showing up on Kate's doorstep with a goat will do the trick?"

"I certainly hope so." Holding Kate in his arms had made one thing all too clear: the sooner he could get Kate and Frank back together again, the better. For his sake as well as theirs.

11

KATE HAD JUST FINISHED CLEARING THE SUPPER DISHES when she heard a sound on the front porch. Drying her hands on her apron, she rushed to open the door and gasped.

The light from the parlor cast a faint yellow glow onto the dark porch, revealing a most startling sight. "Frank!" She squinted for a better look. "Is that you? And what are you doing with that—?"

"Yes, it's me." Frank sounded as miserable as he looked. "Who did you think it was?" Battling to hold on to the squirming animal in his arms, he did a fancy two-step. "Where can I put this thing?" The thing he referred to was a goat. A squirming, bleating goat.

Kate stared at him in bewilderment. Frank stayed away from animals. Far, far away. "Whose goat is that?"

"It belongs to…a friend of a friend. It's…hurt. I—"

Aunt Letty rushed out of the kitchen and squeezed in the doorway next to Kate. "Well, don't bring it in here."

"Take it to the barn." Kate reached for a lantern and lit it before following Frank outside. The goat's bleats set off a chorus of barking dogs from the other side of the fence.

Inside the barn, Kate hung the lantern on a nail and then pointed to a pile of clean straw. "Set her down there."

Frank did as he was told and quickly backed away. Kate dropped to her knees by the animal's side, talking softly. "There now. What's the problem, hmm?"

"She's limping," Frank called from the open door. He sounded like he had a mouth full of pebbles. "*Ah-choo!*"

Kate glanced his way. The flickering lantern light revealed a face covered in hives, and one eye was nearly swollen shut. "Oh, Frank!" she gasped. It seemed like every time he had an attack lately, it was worse than the one before it. "Your poor face. I can't believe you put yourself through this to save an animal."

He dabbed his runny nose with a handkerchief. "I'll be okay," he said and sneezed again. "My misery is a small price to pay. I knew that the only way to… to…save this p-poor animal was to bring it to the best"—he stopped to sneeze—"b-best nurse in town."

Kate gaped at him. *Poor animal? Best nurse in town?* Not only did he not look like himself, but he didn't even sound like himself. Never before had he shown interest in her animal-healing skills. He'd even made her promise not to bring any creatures to his apartment. Now, in spite of everything, she felt a softening in her chest. He really was trying…

"You better go back to the house," she said. "Aunt Letty will take care of you."

After he'd left, Kate turned her attention back to the goat. The problem seemed to be the left rear leg.

She cleaned out the hoof and thoroughly examined it. It had been recently trimmed, and there was no sign of hoof rot.

She worked her fingers up the leg. It didn't appear to be broken and there was no real swelling, but the knee joint felt warm. The goat flinched at her touch and tried to bolt, but Kate held on until the animal had settled down.

Since no visible wounds or bug bites existed, she gently applied a splint and placed the goat in an empty horse stall to limit its movements. After setting out oats and filling the trough with water, she headed back to the house.

She found Frank sitting at the kitchen table drinking coffee. His face was still swollen, and the strong smell of vinegar filled the room. It was Aunt Letty's cure for everything.

"I think it's only a sprain," Kate said, washing her hands in the basin of water kept handy next to the sink.

"I'll leave you two young'uns alone," Aunt Letty said with a meaningful glance at Kate. She reached for a bookmarked dime novel with an amorous couple on the cover and shuffled from the kitchen.

Kate dried her hands and sat across from Frank. He looked so miserable that her heart went out to him. "That was a very kind thing you did," she said.

He shrugged as if to say it was nothing. "I figured that the…the Clara Barton of the animal kingdom would…would know what to do."

"Clara Barton?" Kate blinked to make sure it really was Frank sitting in the room with her. "Are you feeling all right?"

"I am now." He gingerly touched his face with his fingertips. "I think the swelling has gone down."

"That's good," she said, though she saw little if any improvement. He still sounded as if he had a mouthful of pebbles. For a long moment, neither of them spoke. In the past, they had enjoyed an easy rapport, which made their current silence seem awkward and uncomfortable. It was as if she sat across the table from a stranger.

"The flowers… They're beautiful," she said to break the tension. "They're still on display in the shop."

"They're not dead yet?" he asked.

"No…they're still beautiful."

He sniffled and wiped his nose. "T-that's good."

"And the note… It meant a lot."

He raised his eyebrows. "It did?" He looked and sounded surprised. "I didn't think you liked all that mushy stuff."

"I didn't think it was mushy at all. The flowers…the card…that was the nicest gift you've ever given me."

He frowned. "What about the eggbeater?"

"Oh, I liked that just fine."

"And the bellows?"

"Most useful." Kate moistened her lips. "What I meant to say is that the basket of flowers is the nicest gift you've given me when it wasn't my birthday or Christmas."

Frank tried to smile, but his still-swollen face wouldn't let him. Instead, his lips spread in a lopsided grimace. "Glad you liked them. I know how fond you are of blue."

"You do? I didn't think you paid attention to such things."

"'Course I do. Just because I don't talk about them doesn't mean I don't pay attention." When she made no reply, another awkward silence stretched across the table.

Finally, he cleared his voice. "I better be going," he said, rising.

She stood too. "I'll drive you home. I don't want you walking in your condition."

"No, that's okay."

"Are you sure? It'll only take me a couple of minutes to hitch up the wagon."

Frank shook his head. "Your horse will make this worse."

"Maybe if you put a towel over your head or—" She tried to think.

"I…I'd rather not risk it. Besides, the walk will do me good. Nothing like fresh air to cure what ails you."

Kate followed him to the door. "You better leave the goat here overnight. I'll check on her later."

"That's probably a good idea."

"You never did tell me whose goat it is," she said.

He looked momentarily confused. "Like I said, it belongs to a friend of a friend. Don't know his name. I'll have someone stop by and pick her up tomorrow, if that's okay. While you're at the shop."

"I'll be glad to deliver her," Kate said.

Frank shook his head. "My friend's…uh…friend… likes to handle these things himself."

She frowned but said nothing. The hives were sure making Frank act strange. Sound strange too.

He hemmed and hawed and scraped the toe of his boot across the carpet. He then had a sneezing fit. By the time he was through, his face had turned a bright scarlet.

She stared at him in alarm. "Are you all right?"

"I will be. Soon's the swelling goes down." His Adam's apple quivered. "Eh...about the spring dance..." He cleared his voice before continuing. "I was kind of wondering if, you know...you and I... could...you know...go to the dance together."

Kate hesitated, not sure what to say. "Well, I..."

"For old times' sake," he added quickly. When she didn't respond, he pursed his lips. "Unless you're going with someone else." It was impossible to miss the sharp edge of his voice. For a split second, it seemed as if the old Frank was back, but then he quickly added, "I'll understand if you are."

Her eyes widened. Had she heard right? He'd understand if she went with someone else? "I didn't plan on attending this year, but..." She drew in her breath. The poor man looked and sounded utterly miserable. Though she suspected the goat was more at fault for Frank's misery than she was, she still didn't have the heart to turn him down.

"I'd be honored to go to the dance with you, Frank," she said, and because she didn't want him to think that all was forgiven and forgotten, she added, "For old times' sake."

He took her hand in his and shook it like a thirsty man priming a pump. "Whew! That's the best news ever. He sure does know his stuff."

She pulled her hand away and rubbed her shoulder. "Who?"

"What?"

"You said he knows his stuff."

He looked startled. "You! *You* know your stuff. The…the way you took care of the goat, I mean."

"We'll know better about that in a day or two," she said.

Holding his handkerchief over his nose and mouth, he opened the door and stepped outside. "Night, Kate."

"Good night." She watched until he vanished into the folds of darkness before shutting the door with a puzzled frown.

First, he'd sent her a basket of flowers and poetic note. Then he'd appeared on her doorstep with an injured goat and said he'd understand if she went to the dance with someone else.

Frank sure hadn't acted like himself. But if he wasn't acting himself, then who was he?

❧

On Thursday, just as Brett was leaving the sheriff's office, the Butterfield stagecoach came a-skally-hooting into town and pulled up in front with a flurry of dust. The guard riding shotgun jumped to the ground and yelled, "We been robbed!"

The announcement brought the sheriff and his deputy on the run. While the guard and driver gave their reports to the sheriff, Brett cornered the only passenger, a matronly spinster by the name of Miss Dubois. The indignant lady stepped out of the coach and shook her parasol like a chicken shaking out its feathers.

Brett introduced himself. "Wonder if you'd mind answering a few questions, ma'am?" he asked.

Reaching for the gold lorgnette hanging around her neck on a black beaded chain, she lifted it to her eyes and looked him up and down as if trying to decide if he was worthy of her time.

Apparently, he passed her scrutiny, because the probing look left her face. "I'd be happy to answer your questions, but like the driver said, we were robbed. Took my jewelry and money."

"Could you tell me how many there were?"

"A ring, a necklace, and nearly four dollars in cash."

"I meant robbers. How many robbers were there, and can you describe them for me?"

"There were three of them," Miss Dubois said. "One was about your height. The other two were a few inches shorter. They were dressed in black and wore flour sacks over their heads with holes cut out for eyes."

No question. The Ghost Riders had struck yet again. "What about their eyes? Did you notice anything? Color?"

"Oh dear." She thought for a moment. "I'm afraid not."

"Did any of them speak?"

"Just the one."

Brett's gaze sharpened. "Do you remember what he said? What he sounded like?"

"His voice was gruff." She thought for a moment. "Muffled. He told me to take off my ring." She shuddered at the memory.

"I'm sorry to bother you with these questions, but anything you can tell me will be a great help."

She lowered her lorgnette. "Would it recover my belongings?"

"It might. I can't promise. Is there anything else you remember about the three men?"

"Hmm. Let me think. It all happened so quickly."

Brett reached into his vest pocket for the photograph of Frank Foster One. He covered the lower part of the face with his hand so that only the eyes showed. "Is it possible that this is one of the men who robbed you?"

Her gaze dropped to the photograph. "I don't know. It's hard to say. As I told you, their heads were covered."

Brett slipped the photograph back into his pocket. Her answer wasn't any more than what he'd come to expect, but it was still a disappointment. "Anything else you can tell me?"

Her hand fluttered to her chest. "No, it all happened so quickly." She paused for a moment. "I'm sorry."

"That's all right, ma'am. I understand. I'm sure the sheriff will want to talk to you before you leave. He'll also want a list of stolen items."

"Yes, of course." She started toward the door of the sheriff's office and stopped. "Peppermint," she said.

"I'm sorry, ma'am? Did you say something?"

She turned to face him. "The man who took my ring…"

"What about him?" Brett asked.

"When he spoke, I could have sworn I caught a whiff of peppermint candy."

12

ON THE NIGHT OF THE SPRING DANCE, KATE FINISHED putting on her earbobs and checked herself in the cheval mirror with a critical eye.

With Aunt Letty's help, she'd arranged her hair in a French twist, which was all the rage. The fringe of red hair on her forehead had been coaxed into submission with curling tongs and made her look younger than her twenty-two years.

The blue sateen gown had been an extravagance, but worth every penny. The neckline and short sleeves were trimmed with lace and the carefully draped skirt and bustle embellished with white ribbon bows.

She gathered her gloves and purse and left the room. Just as she reached the top of the stairs, she heard her aunt's strident voice—it sounded like she was ordering someone to leave.

What in the world?

Hiking up her skirt with one hand, Kate hastened down the stairs and joined her aunt at the open front door.

"Mr. Tucker!" The last person Kate expected to see

on her doorstep was the Texas Ranger. "What...what are you doing here?"

"He was just leaving," her aunt said and started to close the door.

"Auntie," Kate said beneath her breath. It wasn't like her aunt to be so rude. With a meaningful look at her aunt and a rueful smile at the ranger, she opened the door wider.

Mr. Tucker whipped off his wide-brimmed hat. "I apologize. I didn't mean to cause any trouble."

Aunt Letty glared at him. "That's all you've done is cause trouble. If it wasn't for you, my niece would be happily married by now and—"

"Auntie, please!"

Tucker gave her aunt a beseeching look. "I can't tell you how sorry I am. That's why when Foster asked me to pick up your niece and drive her to the dance, I agreed. I figured it was the least I could do after all the trouble I've caused."

Aunt Letty folded her arms across her chest. "Why didn't he pick her up himself?"

"That was the original plan, ma'am," Tucker said. "He'd hoped to rent a horse and buggy from the stables. But he didn't want to chance another case of hives. He's still recovering from the last bout."

"That makes sense," Kate said, eager to soothe her aunt's ruffled feathers.

Aunt Letty looked like she was about to say something more. Instead, she slammed her mouth shut and walked away.

Tucker looked genuinely sorry. "I didn't mean to upset your aunt. I wish I knew how to make it up to her."

Meeting the ranger's piercing gaze, Kate bit her lower lip. "Are you and Frank now friends?" Given the circumstances, it seemed like an unlikely alliance.

He quirked a smile. "You sound surprised."

"It's just…it wasn't that long ago that he accused you of…having your way with me."

Something flared in his eyes: a light, a flame, a spark. But it was gone so quickly, she wondered if she'd only imagined it.

"He now knows that's not true," Tucker said, breaking eye contact. After a beat, he met her gaze again and added, "I don't think he would have asked me to pick you up if he still believed such a thing."

What Tucker said made sense. Still, it was hard to imagine that Frank had suddenly become so trusting as to allow another man to drive her to a dance. Certainly, Frank would never have agreed to such a thing if he knew how Tucker had cradled her in his arms the day she'd almost drowned.

The thought quickened her pulse, and she forced the memory from her mind. "It's very kind of you to come and get me in his place, but I'm sure you have better things to do than drive me around."

"As it turns out, I don't. I'm still a stranger here in town and don't know that many people. Besides, it'll give us a chance to talk. Something's come up that involves the Ghost Riders. I could use your help."

"My help?"

He shrugged. "If you don't mind."

Her curiosity whetted, she motioned him inside. "Come in while I get my wrap."

"Thank you, ma'am." He stepped inside, filling the

room with his presence, along with a pleasing smell of soap and bay-rum hair tonic. Dressed in his usual dark trousers, plaid shirt, and vest, with his gun holstered at his side, he was mighty pleasing to the eye. She'd always thought him attractive, but now that she knew how it felt to be in his arms, more than just his good looks intrigued her.

Kate set her gloves and purse on the entry table and plucked her blue cape off a wooden peg by the door.

Tucker stepped forward, hand extended. "Permit me."

As he took the cape from her, his gaze traveled the length of her blue gown. This time she didn't imagine the admiration in his eyes, and her cheeks flushed beneath his warm approval.

"I must say, Miss Denver, you look mighty pretty." He locked her in his gaze a moment before looking away and clearing his throat. "I'm…sure Foster will approve."

He shook out her cape before draping it around her shoulders, his hands seeming to linger a moment longer than necessary.

"Thank you," she murmured. Whirling around, she reached for her purse and gloves, surprised to find her hands shaking.

"Ready?" he asked from behind her.

"Y-yes," she stammered. Willing her knees not to buckle, she called to her aunt. "We're leaving."

Tucker opened the door with a flourish, allowing her to exit first.

Outside, he stood ready to help her into the buggy. Not used to such an attentive escort, Kate hesitated before offering her hand.

It wasn't that Frank was completely without

manners, but the first Mrs. Foster had died soon after she and her husband had adopted Frank. His father hadn't remarried until Frank was in his late teens. Having been raised in a masculine household, Frank lacked the usual social skills, but that had never bothered Kate. In fact, she'd never really thought about it.

Until now.

Settling on the leather seat, Kate tucked her skirt around her and clutched her purse in her lap. She wasn't sure how to act in Tucker's presence, and that was odd. In the past, she'd always felt comfortable in male company, but then most men had treated her like a sister or friend. The ranger was different. She wasn't sure how he'd managed it, but she felt very much a woman around him, and was very much aware of his maleness. Sisterhood was the furthest thing from her mind.

He climbed into the driver's seat next to her. They eyed each other for a moment. "Ready?" he asked.

"Ready," she said.

Without another word, he shook the reins and clicked his tongue. The buggy rolled forward, and a gentle breeze cooled her flaming face.

Finding it easier to breathe now, Kate tried to relax. But a moment later, she was distracted by the brush of his leg against hers. If that wasn't worrisome enough, his hands on the reins reminded her of the feel of his hand on her shoulder. It also made her recall the day she'd laid her head on his broad, manly chest.

Confused by such thoughts, she concentrated on the road ahead. What was the matter with her? She had no business dwelling on such things. It wasn't like her to act like a silly schoolgirl with her first crush.

The stress of preparing for the wedding and her subsequent broken betrothal had evidently taken a toll. As for Mr. Brett Tucker…they had nothing in common. Considering the excitement of his job, he probably found her dull and boring.

Satisfied that she now had her thoughts, if not her nervousness, under control, she lifted her gaze. It was a perfect night for a spring dance. The sun had set, and stars began dotting the deep-purple sky.

Kate made a silent wish upon the brightest star. In years past, her wish had always been the same: to provide an infirmary for injured animals. But, Frank's sensitivity to fur and feathers had ended that dream. Now she just wished for a home and family of her own.

"Warm enough?" Tucker asked, breaking into her thoughts.

"Yes, thank you." She studied his profile. "You said earlier that you needed my help."

He glanced at her. "I don't know if you'd heard, but the stagecoach was held up again."

"Yes, I did hear that," she said. That's all the day's customers had talked about.

"I wasn't able to get a very good description of the robbers, but one seems to have a sweet tooth. According to a witness, he smelled of peppermint."

"Peppermint?"

"That's what she said. He was wearing a flour sack over his head, so I don't know if it's possible to smell one's breath through that, but she was adamant. I checked, and you're the only one in town who sells candy."

Kate knitted her brow. "Are you saying that one of my customers robbed a stage?"

"It's a possibility."

Shuddering at the thought, she gripped her purse. She hated the idea that someone she knew, someone who'd patronized her shop, someone with whom she'd exchanged pleasantries and maybe even a laugh, could be an outlaw. Silly as it seemed, she'd always found people with a sweet tooth to be friendlier than those with blander tastes. That was hardly a quality that led to crime.

"I can't imagine any of my customers robbing a stage," she said.

"It's been my experience that most outlaws look like ordinary people. You wouldn't know by looking at them that they lead a double life. My company recently broke up a gang led by a former Methodist preacher. So, you see? You never can tell."

Aware, suddenly, that the ribbon at her cape's neckline had come loose, Kate worked the length of satin into a bow. "It's still hard to believe. I mean... I've known most of my customers for years. Some are even second- and third-generation customers. They're good people."

"I'm sorry, but...I still have to check it out. It's my job."

She sighed. "I know."

"Would it be possible to give me a list of customers who purchased peppermint candy in the last, say, month or so?"

"I'd be happy to draw up such a list, but I'm not sure how complete it would be. Peppermint is one of my most popular candies."

"I'd be obliged for whatever you can do." They

drove in silence for a mile or so before Tucker spoke again. "Being that you agreed to attend the dance with Foster, does that mean you and he are patching things up?"

She turned the question over in her mind before answering. "I don't know. He's trying hard to change his ways, but…"

Kate felt his gaze on her. "But…?"

She hesitated. It seemed odd to be talking to the ranger about something so personal, but he seemed receptive and interested. "Lately, he's like a different person."

"Oh? In what way?"

"In many ways." Strange as it seemed, the changes in Frank had also revealed a new side of herself. Though she'd previously scoffed at such things, she'd discovered she enjoyed being treated like a lady. She'd liked receiving flowers and had reread the note so many times that it felt as if each word had been branded into her heart. She liked even more knowing that Frank appreciated her ability to doctor injured animals.

"He's so much more thoughtful and…caring," she said.

"Is that so bad?"

"No, of course not. It'll just take some getting used to."

"Like you said, he's trying."

"I know." That was one of the reasons Kate felt so torn. It was hard to stay angry at Frank when he was knocking himself out to please her. "What about you?" she asked, anxious to change the subject. "Ever think about settling down?"

"Me?" he asked as if the thought had never occurred to him. "Nah. That would mean giving up my job, and I can't imagine doing anything else. These bones were meant to roam."

His answer was no more than what she had expected. Nevertheless, a sudden crush of disappointment caught her off guard. Keeping her thoughts to herself, she gazed straight ahead.

A soft glow of light revealed the town of Haywire. They rode in silence for a moment before she asked, "Have you had any luck finding the man you're looking for? The other Foster?"

"Not yet," Tucker said, "but I think he might be a member of the Ghost Riders."

"Really? The one who smelled of peppermint?"

"Could be. Him or one of his men." Kate heard his intake of breath before he continued. "There was a similar crime wave a few years back in San Antone. After each robbery, the gang vanished without a trace, and one day, they disappeared altogether."

"And you think this is the same gang?" she asked.

The gas streetlight they passed turned his probing eyes into liquid gold. "There're a lot of similarities. Coincidently, the robberies stopped the day Frank Foster left town."

Kate still couldn't get used to the idea that her Frank shared his name with an outlaw. "You said he was responsible for your sister's death."

"He was her husband. When he took off without a word, he broke her heart. She wouldn't eat. Wouldn't sleep. She finally came down with pneumonia and died. I blame him for her death."

"That's…that's so sad." She studied Tucker's handsome profile. "Why do you suppose he took off?"

"Before Foster left town, there was a robbery that turned bad. Originally, four men were involved. But one of the thieves was shot and captured. We hoped he would give us the names of the other three men. Unfortunately, he died before he had a chance. I think the death explains why there're only three men now. Though I wouldn't be surprised if there was still another one pulling the strings."

"If one of them really is the man you're looking for, he must know you're in town. You haven't exactly been anonymous, you know. Your name was in the paper."

"I wouldn't expect that he'd know my name. I call Alice my sister, but that's only half right. We actually had different fathers and different last names. Foster knew her as Alice Taylor, and he and I never met. I was up north when they got married and missed the wedding." Tucker frowned as he stared at the road ahead. "Sorry to bore you with all my troubles."

"Nothing you say is boring," Kate said.

He caught her gaze with his own. "I wouldn't have told you all this if I didn't trust you to keep a confidence. I don't want Foster getting wind of who I really am."

"Everyone in town knows you're a Texas Ranger," she pointed out. "Your man must know why you're here."

"I don't think the law worries him, but a personal vendetta might. If he knew I was here on my sister's behalf, he might run."

Kate drew in her breath. He had no way of

knowing how much his trust in her meant. Uncle Joe had believed there was no greater compliment than being trusted by another. That was why Frank's unfounded accusations had hurt so much.

"I hope you catch him soon," she said.

"I just hope I catch him before he leaves town." Tucker glanced askance at her. "Or before I cause another couple to break up."

Turning her attention to the distant lights, Kate moistened her lips. "You might have done us a favor."

"Oh?"

She met his questioning gaze. "It's given us a chance to…decide if marriage is right for us."

"He cares for you deeply," Tucker said. "You know that, right?"

She nodded. She *did* know that. He just didn't trust her—or at least hadn't in the past—and trust was vital in keeping the bonds of love strong. "I care for him too."

Sighing, she looked up at the spatter of bright, twinkling stars. Why did it suddenly seem that caring for each other might not be enough?

13

Brett drew his rented horse and buggy behind a long line of wagons, buggies, and carriages and set the brake.

During the last mile or so, he'd sensed a sudden change of mood in Kate. His effort to keep the conversation going had solicited only one-syllable responses. Was she having second thoughts about attending tonight's affair with Foster? Or was it the fact that maybe one or more of her customers might be members of the Ghost Riders?

He jumped to the ground and ran around to the passenger side to help her down, but she had already climbed out of the buggy herself. Avoiding his eyes, she straightened her wrap and fluffed out her skirt.

"Are you okay?" he asked.

This time she did look at him. The rising moon turned her eyes into stars and cast a dewy glow upon her full, moist lips. "Yes," she said. "Thank you for the ride."

Surprised to find himself wishing things were different—wishing he was her escort for real, wishing he could dance the night away with her in his arms—Brett cleared his throat and smoothed down the front of his vest.

"Shall we?" he asked, crooking his elbow.

She hesitated a moment before slipping her arm through his. Together, they walked toward the barn's blazing lights, and he felt like the luckiest man alive. His elation lasted only as long as it took to remind himself once again that he was a temporary escort. The moment they walked through the barn door, he would lose her to Foster.

Fiddle music filled the air, along with the sounds of pounding feet and bursts of laughter.

Just as they reached the barn, she pulled her arm away. It felt all wrong, as if she had taken part of him with her.

Frank met them at the door as they had rehearsed. Dressed in full "war paint," including a red bow tie and matching suspenders, he didn't look half bad. It helped that his eyes were no longer swollen shut, but he'd also slicked down his hair and combed it to the side.

"You look mighty handsome, Kate," Foster said, giving her a playful punch on the arm as though he were greeting a male friend.

Brett grimaced. *Handsome?* Kate was the most beautiful woman in the room, and that was the best Foster could do?

"You don't look so bad yourself," she said, accepting the sorry excuse for a compliment with goodwill.

Brett cleared his throat, and when Foster failed to take the hint, he gave a short cough—an agreed-upon gesture that action was needed. The man's memory was as short as the tail-hold of a bear.

Brett coughed again. Finally, recognition flared in

Foster's eyes, suggesting he'd remembered what they'd practiced.

"Pretty!" Foster exclaimed, making Kate jump. "You look as pretty as…as…as…newly tanned leather."

It wasn't the kind of compliment Brett had in mind, but he let it pass. Pretty was better than handsome, no matter how Foster defined it.

Kate looked surprised, and two spots of red flared on her cheeks. "Why…thank you, Frank." She flashed a smile before asking, "How's the goat?"

Foster looked baffled. "Goat?"

"The one you brought to my house," she said.

"Oh, *that* goat. Uh…" Foster glanced at Brett. "Fine, fine. Completely healed."

The news brought a smile to Kate's face, and Brett felt his heart practically turn over. "That's good to hear," she said.

A young woman rushed over to join them, her sausage curls bouncing up and down like tight little springs. "Oh my," she gushed. Pressing her hands together, she looked at Brett with fluttering eyelashes before turning to Kate. "Does this mean that you and Frank are a couple again?"

Kate looked as though she didn't know how to answer. Perhaps she was having second thoughts after being compared to newly tanned leather. Or maybe she just wasn't ready to forgive and forget.

The fiddler started thumping his strings, a signal that the short break was over and the dancing was about to begin again. Brett rushed to Kate's rescue by directing the woman's attention to himself. "Would you care to dance, Miss—?"

She giggled. "Hopkins," she said. "Cynthia Hopkins."

"Brett Tucker," he said.

He crooked his elbow, and Miss Hopkins shoved her arm through his. "If you'll excuse us," he said. Staring at Foster, he inclined his head ever so slightly toward Kate. When Foster failed to take the hint, Brett coughed again. This time he both nodded his head and rolled his eyes in Kate's direction.

As far as social mores were concerned, Foster was as helpless as a cow in quicksand, but he finally got the message and asked Kate to dance.

Satisfied that things were going as planned, Brett led Miss Hopkins onto the sawdust-covered dance floor. He tried his best to be an attentive partner and make sense of her endless prattle, but his eyes seemed to have a mind of their own. He watched Kate and Frank like an overanxious parent. Though Brett had circled his partner around the dance floor several times, Frank and Kate hadn't moved from the same spot.

Frank's idea of dancing was to sway from side to side and then rock back and forth, barely moving his feet. Brett cringed every time it appeared Frank had stepped on Kate's dainty slippers. He'd been so busy rehearsing Foster on what to say and how to win back Kate's heart that he'd completely forgotten to ask if the man could dance.

"Am I right, Mr. Tucker?"

He drew his gaze back to his partner. "I'm sorry, ma'am." He felt bad for letting his mind wander. "You were saying?"

She frowned. "I know where I saw you before.

You're the man who messed up Kate's wedding. Am I right?"

The reminder made him grimace. "I'm afraid so. It's not something I'm proud of. Let's hope that a happy announcement is in the works."

Miss Hopkins's gaze wandered over to Foster and Kate. "I hope for Kate's sake the announcement includes a promise from Frank to quit dancing."

Brett chuckled. "That's not a bad idea."

The music stopped, and a man with a sweeping mustache clapped his hands and yelled in a leather-lunged voice, "Time to change partners, folks!"

Shuffling feet and swirling skirts followed the command as everyone rushed around to partner up with someone new. It took some fancy footwork on Brett's part to reach Kate's side before anyone else did. He only hoped that Foster would play his part the way they'd practiced.

"May I?" he asked, holding out his hand.

Kate hesitated. Her big, blue eyes said yes, but something held her back. No doubt she was worried that Foster's jealous streak would flare up and he would make a scene.

Brett cleared his throat. *Come on, Foster. This is your big moment. Do it the way we practiced.* It took much in the way of visual prodding and clearing his throat before Foster finally got the hint.

"Sure, go ahead," Frank said, looking like he'd bitten into a lemon. It wasn't how they'd practiced it, but at least Foster got some of it right.

Leading Kate away, Brett glanced over his shoulder at Foster. "Whistle," he mouthed. Instead of showing his jealousy or acting it out, Foster was supposed to whistle. If his tuneless whistles didn't chase the green-eyed monster away, nothing would.

Brett turned back to face Kate, and it suddenly seemed imperative to recall his purpose in asking her to dance. It was the only way he could think to prove to her that Foster had conquered his jealousy or, at least, was trying to.

Brett slipped his arm around her tiny waist and closed his fingers over her dainty, soft hand. She draped her arm over his shoulder and rewarded him with a brilliant smile that made him tingle inside.

Though he was a good head taller than Kate, they seemed perfectly matched as he circled the dance floor effortlessly with her in his arms. His heart pounded, but fortunately the music muffled the sound. So this was how it felt to float on air.

Brett could almost feel Foster's visual daggers as he steered Kate around the other couples. Foster's pursed lips and red face suggested he was whistling up a storm, and the strange looks directed his way seemed to confirm that. Hoping Kate hadn't noticed, Brett led her in such a way as to block Foster from view.

"I'm surprised Frank didn't object to me dancing with you," she said. "He doesn't usually like me dancing with anyone but him. He can be so jealous at times."

Brett gazed into her starry eyes. If she didn't stop looking so utterly fetching, he'd give Foster plenty to be jealous about.

Now was the time to say something positive on Foster's behalf, but he couldn't think much past the present moment.

"As a young child, he was bounced from family to family," she continued, relieving Brett of the need to jump to Foster's defense. "He never had a real home until he came here to Haywire. And even then, he grew up without a mother. Mr. Foster didn't remarry until Frank was in his late teens." Her eyes softened into pools of appeal. "A background like that would make anyone feel anxious. That's why he's…"

"Afraid of losing you?"

She moistened her lips, calling attention to her pretty pink mouth. "Something like that."

Catching himself staring, Brett cleared his throat and gazed over her head. He forced himself to concentrate on the fiddler, the refreshment table, the other dancers. Anything to keep from drowning in the depth of her blue eyes.

"Horehound will help," she said. "Or perhaps you'd prefer peppermint? For your throat, I mean."

His gaze locked with hers. "My throat?"

"I noticed back there that you kept clearing your throat and coughing."

"Oh, that. Yes, you're right. Maybe some…hard candy would help."

She smiled up at him. "You can pick up a bag when you stop by the shop tomorrow for the list."

His mind went blank for a moment until he recalled the list of customers she'd promised him. "I'd be much obliged." He spun her around and then pulled her back. Holding her close, he felt her stiffen in his arms.

"Something the matter?" he asked.

"It's Frank," she said. "Look! He's all red in the face."

Brett followed her gaze. Foster's overwrought

whistling had turned his face as red as an overripe tomato.

Her face lined with worry, Kate pulled away. "I better see what's wrong."

Before he could stop her, she rushed to Foster, in whose arms—Brett told himself—she belonged. But knowing that didn't stop him from wishing things were different. Wishing that the arms she had run to had been his.

Drawing in his breath, he glanced around the dance floor and tried to act as if everything were fine. It would have been fine, if memories of holding her hadn't kept coming to mind.

Contrary to what Kate believed, not a thing was wrong with his throat. But he sure in blazes was worried about the condition of his heart.

❧

"*Psst*, Kate."

Kate whirled around and spotted Connie beckoning from the open barn door.

Using the first opportunity to slip away from Frank's watchful eye, she joined Connie outside. "What are you doing here? Why aren't you inside enjoying the dance?"

Connie looked especially pretty tonight. The bright-yellow dress showed off her small waist and ample bosom. The color complemented her dark hair, which was swept to the crown of her head and cascaded down her back in a mass of shiny curls.

"Is Harvey here?"

Kate took her by the arm. "He is, and it's time to make your grand entrance."

Connie pulled back. "I can't. What if he ignores me?"

"He won't tonight."

"How do you know?"

"Trust me," Kate said.

Connie's eyes narrowed in suspicion. "Did you…?"

"Of course I did. Just like I said I would. He came to the shop, and I slipped a little…advice into his bag of candy."

"Did he read it?"

Kate shrugged. "We'll know soon enough."

Connie continued to fret. "You didn't mention me by name, did you?"

Kate laughed. "Of course not, silly. Don't look so worried. The advice was simply that love comes in all colors, even yellow." Kate gave a satisfied nod. "You'd be amazed at how a mere suggestion can turn a man's head. Now unless there's a run of yellow dresses, Harvey should be all yours."

Connie's mouth rounded in anticipation. "Oh, I do hope you're right."

Kate gave her friend a little nudge. "Go on. Your prince is waiting."

Connie started forward and Kate followed, fingers crossed.

Without warning, Connie halted just inside the barn door, and Kate almost plowed into her. "What's wrong? Why did you stop?"

Connie curled her hands into fists by her side. "Looks like your suggestion turned Harvey's head just fine… In Mary-Ruth's direction!"

Kate followed Connie's gaze and groaned. Harvey was dancing with Mary-Ruth Myers, who just so happened to be dressed to the nines in a bright-yellow gown.

14

THE FOLLOWING MORNING, AUNT LETTY WATCHED Kate pour horehound mixture into the tray of the candy-making machine. "Well? How come you haven't said a word about last night's dance?"

Before answering, Kate picked up a knife and spread the mixture evenly over the tray, releasing a subtle smell of licorice.

She'd managed to avoid her aunt's questions earlier at the house. But there was no escaping them here at the shop. "Not much to say. It was very nice and well attended."

It would have been perfect had Connie not had her heart broken, and Kate blamed herself for that.

"That's not what I mean, and you know it."

Kate sighed. "If this is about the Texas Ranger—"

"I don't know how you can have anything to do with that awful man. Not only did he ruin your wedding, but Hoot Owl Pete said it was the ranger who shot out our window."

Kate set her knife down and turned the crank. Perfect little hard candies popped out of the machine.

If only what she had to tell her aunt would pop out that easily.

She stopped turning the crank and faced her aunt. "There's something you don't know about him."

Aunt Letty frowned. "There's nothing you can tell me that would make me change my mind. He's trouble with a capital *T*." She sniffed. "You know what happened to Cathy Spencer when she got involved with that troublemaking Jeff Parker. She ended up on her very own Wanted poster. And I'll tell you another thing—"

"He saved my life." Kate hadn't wanted to mention her near-drowning, but it was the only way she could think to keep her aunt from being rude to Brett in the future.

Aunt Letty's mouth dropped. "What?"

"I almost drowned." Choosing her words with care, she told her aunt everything—or almost everything— that had happened at the river. Some parts, like the way he'd held her in his arms, seemed best to leave out.

Her aunt's eyes rounded in horror. "Mercy, child. What were you thinking?"

"All I could think about at the time was saving that poor dog."

"Kate, if anything had happened to you..." With her hand on her chest, Aunt Letty gasped for air. "Why didn't you tell me this before?"

"I knew it would only upset you. But after the way you treated Mr. Tucker last night...I thought you should know that he's more than made up for stopping the wedding."

"Harrumph." Aunt Letty folded her arms across chest. "I wouldn't go that far."

"I know you're still upset with him, Auntie, but saving my life counts for something, don't you think?"

Aunt Letty gave a reluctant nod. "Maybe."

"Maybe?"

"All right." Aunt Letty dropped her arms to her sides but didn't look any less stubborn. "I'm grateful to the man, but don't expect me to like him. And that still doesn't let him off the hook. If it wasn't for him, you and Frank would be husband and wife, with maybe a little one on the way."

Unable to have children of her own, her aunt couldn't wait for the day Kate provided her with a little grandniece or grandnephew to spoil.

"Don't look at me like that," her aunt said. "Remember what happened to Claire Nelson?"

"Yes, I remember," Kate said with a sigh. How could she not? At least once a week, Aunt Letty reminded her how Claire's seven *thoughtless* children had failed to present her with grandchildren before the poor woman reached the pearly gates.

"All I ask is that you not be rude to him," Kate said and, on the chance that her aunt needed more persuasion, repeated that the ranger *did* save her life.

"I'm never rude," Aunt Letty said, her voice obstinate. She studied Kate for a long moment. "You've not said a word about Frank. Did the two of you make any headway?"

"Headway?"

"You know what I mean."

"Frank was very…sweet."

"Sweet?" Aunt Letty reached for an empty candy jar and began filling it with the newly pressed horehound candy. "Babies are sweet. Puppies are sweet. That's hardly the way to describe a future husband."

Kate brushed her hair away from her face. "Well, he *was* sweet. And he didn't even get jealous when Brett asked me to dance."

"Oh? So now it's Brett."

Kate bit her lip. His first name had slipped out without conscious thought. Even more surprising, she liked the way her lips parted as she released it, as if she were to throw a kiss. Startled by the thought, she quickly banished it from her head.

"I know you don't want to hear this, but *Mr. Tucker* and I are friends," she said. Or at least she'd thought they were. Now she didn't know what to think. He had been so attentive at the start of the evening and had made her feel like a queen. But as the evening had progressed, he'd become more and more withdrawn until he'd hardly said a word while driving her home.

Aunt Letty shook her head. "I don't know how you can be his friend. Not after what he's done. If it wasn't for him, you'd be..."

"I know, I know. Mrs. Frank Foster." Kate sighed. "Auntie, please. We've been all through this. Brett made a mistake and has tried his best to make up for it ever since."

"All right, all right." Her aunt capped the full jar of candy. "So, did you dance? You and Frank?"

"Yes. Yes, we did." If it could be called that. Dancing with Frank was like dancing with a lamppost. His feet hardly moved. While dancing with Brett was like floating on air. He was at least six inches taller than

Frank, which meant she only came up to his shoulders. Yet they'd glided around the barn floor as if only one.

Oh no, not Brett again. Jolted by the way he commanded her thoughts—he'd been all she'd been able to think about since the dance—Kate slid a second tray into the candy-making machine and turned the crank more vigorously than necessary. The brass rollers pressed the sugary sheet into dozens of perfectly shaped little candies but did nothing to soften her mood or stop her obsessive thoughts.

"Frank even said I looked pretty," she said, knowing that would please her aunt.

"Of course you looked pretty." Her aunt's face softened into a gentle smile. Kate recognized the faraway look in her aunt's eyes and knew it had nothing to do with the present. "I remember when your uncle and I first laid eyes on you."

Kate knew the oft-repeated tale by heart but never tired of hearing it. Her adoptive aunt and uncle had traveled to Missouri to visit Uncle Joe's sick father. While they were there, a train carrying orphans from New York had arrived. It had been the first such train to Missouri, and no one really knew what to expect, least of all the young, frightened passengers, including Kate.

"And there you were," Aunt Letty said. "You were so tiny…"

"I think the word is 'scrawny,'" Kate said.

"And cute as a button."

Kate stopped turning the crank and rolled her eyes. "Homely as a blank wall, more like it. That's why no one wanted to adopt me."

Her aunt began filling a second jar. "No one else

wanted to adopt you for fear you wouldn't be strong enough to do your share of work."

Kate smiled. That was her aunt's version of the story, but Kate suspected that the real reason no one had wanted her was because of her gawky, thin appearance and ginger-red hair.

"Your uncle took one look at you and said, 'She's coming home with us.'"

"I remember," Kate said, her mind traveling back to a memory that in many ways she wished she could forget. She still had nightmares of that awful, smelly orphan train.

Though she had been but six at the time, Kate remembered that long-ago day as if it were only yesterday. When she was two, her father had been killed in the war. Four years later, her mother succumbed to consumption, leaving Kate orphaned. She then became a ward of the Children's Aid Society and was taken to a house with stern caretakers and overrun with vermin.

Not long afterward, Kate and three dozen other children had been transported to Missouri by cattle car. They'd arrived at the station in the middle of the night. She recalled huddling on the platform until a kindly minister arrived to take charge. The minister's wife did her best to make the orphans look more respectable with the aid of a wet sponge and a hairbrush, but not much could be done about the rank smell of cattle.

Soon, the station had been packed with people. Kate and the other orphans were exposed to all manner of probing. Legs and arms squeezed, teeth examined, hair checked for lice. Some orphans were asked to lift heavy boxes. The oldest, strongest, and—in Kate's mind—best-looking children went first. She had been the last one standing.

Just when she'd thought she'd have to go back to that awful house in New York, a tall man with a bushy mustache stepped forward to claim her. His sheer size frightened her at first, but it wasn't long before he'd won her over with his kindness.

"You'll be safe with us," he'd said. *Safe*.

Her aunt said something, breaking into Kate's thoughts. "I'm sorry, Aunt Letty," Kate said, wiping away the tears such memories never failed to produce. "What did you say?"

"I was just saying what a dear, sweet thing you were. You looked like a wounded bird. When we got back to town, we told everyone you were our niece and, strangely enough, no one ever questioned it."

"That's because you treated me as your own," Kate said. Years later, she'd found out that some of the orphans arriving on that same train hadn't been as lucky with their new families as she had been with hers. Some had even been treated like slaves.

Aunt Letty's face melted into a smile. "Since we weren't lucky enough to have a child of our own, we were convinced that you were a gift from heaven."

"You and Uncle Joe were the real gifts," Kate said.

Her aunt finished filling another jar and set it aside. "Lordy, aren't we a fine couple? This is supposed to be a happy place, and here we are, looking like we just lost a best friend."

Kate laughed and glanced at the clock. "Oh my, look at the time." Customers would soon arrive, and she had yet to write out the list Brett had asked for. That thought brought another, whisking her back to how it felt to dance in the arms of the tall and handsome ranger.

15

BRETT LEFT THE BOARDINGHOUSE AS SOON AS HE'D finished breakfast. After saddling his horse, he rode through the tangled streets of Haywire to the telegraph office.

Last night's dance had gone well, and considering Foster's inept wooing skills, that was saying something. Insisting that Foster ask Connie to dance had been brilliant on his part. Kate hadn't appeared jealous, but she did notice, and that was a start. It also helped that later Connie had sung Frank's praises. Kate had seemed impressed that even her best friend had noticed the change in Frank.

It was hard to know what had been more difficult—steering Foster through the intricacies of courtship or containing his own traitorous heart.

His attraction to Kate had almost gotten out of hand, and that had better stop. He had no right, no right at all, to act on his feelings—none! But last night, he'd come mighty close—dangerously close—to doing just that.

If only her lips hadn't looked so tempting. If only

holding her in his arms on the dance floor hadn't made him recall holding her by the river.

Lonely. That's what he was. It was the only way he could explain the intensity of his attraction.

Then too, it had been a long time since he'd been with a woman. For the last three years, he'd spent endless long hours in the saddle with little more than his horse and the bleak Texas landscape to keep him company. He loved his job and couldn't imagine doing anything else, but it did get lonely at times.

No wonder Kate had tangled his spurs and tied his insides in a knot. The very thought made his heart pound, and he shifted his weight in the saddle. The lack of female companionship would drive any man crazy.

A woman. That's what he needed. Someone to love and to cherish. Someone to welcome him home with open arms following a hard day's work. Someone who would get his mind off Kate.

Startled by the unexpected path his thoughts had taken, Brett shook his head. Just because he was lonely was no reason to imagine himself domesticated. He wanted the *company* of a woman; he didn't want to marry her. He liked his job too much. Liked the freedom.

Knowing that his obsessive thoughts were simply the stirrings of a lonely heart, he felt somewhat better. The annoying affliction had a cure; all he had to do was find a woman. Spend some time with her, and his problems would be solved. Easy as that!

But first there was work to be done, outlaws to catch. And, of course, he still felt responsible for getting Kate and Foster back together. The way things were going, that shouldn't take much longer. That is, if Foster didn't mess up.

And that was a very big if.

The telegraph office was located next to the train station. Already, the morning train to Austin had left, and the station was deserted. Dismounting, Brett tied his horse to the hitching rail and stomped up the wooden steps. The sound of angry voices made him pause before entering the building.

The moment Brett opened the door, the voices inside fell silent. Lucky Lou and Flash, the telegrapher, gaped at him. Seemingly oblivious to the tension between the two men, Lucky Lou's dog, Ringo, cocked his ears and wagged his tail.

Brett touched the brim of his hat in greeting, and Lucky Lou responded with a curt nod. Today, he was rigged out in fancy doodads, including a pair of spurs and a silver concho hatband.

Just as Lucky Lou turned from the counter, he dropped a pen. Ringo quickly dashed forward, picked it up, and ran to the door.

"Sit!" Lucky Lou commanded in a firm voice, and the dog did as he was told.

Lucky Lou then attached a braided leather leash to the dog's metal collar and retrieved the pen from his mouth. Tossing it on the counter, he left, slamming the door after him.

Curious as to what the argument had been about, Brett turned his attention to the telegrapher. "Tough customer?"

Flash shrugged and scratched his chin. The speed at which he tapped out dispatches had earned him his moniker. His big ears, razor-thin nose, and lantern jaw were his by chance. "Nah. Just a bad loser. Said I cheated last night at faro." He shrugged again, as if being accused of cheating was of no consequence. "What can I do for you?"

"I need to send a wire."

Flash set paper, pen, and a bottle of ink on the counter and moved a book of riddles, puzzles, and rebuses aside. "Here you go."

Brett glanced at the book. "Like puzzles, eh?"

"Yep. Give me a puzzle to solve, and that's all I can think about." He opened the book. "But I can't figure this one out. What is long when it's young and short when it's old?"

Brett thought for a moment. "That's easy. It's gotta be time."

Flash's eyebrows practically reached his hairline. "Hey, you're good. You should be one of those Pinkerton detectives or something."

"Or something," Brett said under his breath and reached for the pen.

He was required to send weekly accounts to headquarters, but so far, there had been nothing of any significance to report. He was still considering the problem when Foster burst through the door like a man with his pants on fire.

"I need to talk to you," he said.

Guessing what Foster had on his mind, Brett bit back his annoyance. Before the dance, the man had been so anxious, he'd been knocking around like a blind dog in a meat market. Today, he didn't look much better.

"How did you know I was here?"

The question seemed to surprise Foster. "It's a small town. Everyone knows you're here."

"Yeah, just like everyone knows the identities of the Ghost Riders," Brett muttered.

"What?"

"Never mind. What did you want to see me about?"

"I just want to know what Kate said."

Brett raised an eyebrow. "Said?"

"Yeah, you know, about last night's dance."

"She said she had a good time."

Foster rubbed his chin with the back of his hand. "That's it? That's all?"

"What more did you want her to say? It was a dance, not a religious revival."

"She didn't, you know, suspect anything?"

Brett frowned. "Anything? Oh, you mean your red face. No, she blamed it on the heat. Blast it, Foster! What were you thinking?"

"Me? You're the one who told me to whistle."

"Yes, but I didn't tell you to blow up a norther." Brett sighed with exasperation. "You were lucky this time, but you've got to get that jealousy of yours under control."

"I'm working on it." Foster lowered his voice. "Do you think she's ready to take me back?"

"Now slow down. These things take time. Capturing a woman's heart is like fishing. You toss out the bait, and once she bites, you reel her in gently." Brett made a circular motion with his hand to demonstrate. "If you reel her in too fast, you'll lose her."

Following Brett's example, Foster moved his hand as if pulling in a fish.

"That's the way," Brett said. "Courtship requires a series of quiet, thoughtful actions. You don't want to be too obvious, or you'll scare her off. On the other hand, you don't want to be too vague."

Flash, who had been listening to this conversation with great interest, asked, "What do you mean by too vague?"

Before Brett could respond, Foster answered for him. "He means not to compare her to leather."

While Flash puzzled over that, Foster continued, "Okay, so how much longer before I land the fish… uh…Kate?"

Brett rubbed his forehead and rued the day he set to work teaching Foster the fine rules of courtship. "Patience, my friend. Patience."

Following a constant flow of customers, Kate welcomed the afternoon lull. After sending her aunt out for something to eat, she set to work counting money and organizing inventory.

Just as she finished replenishing the penny candy jars, Cassie Decker walked in.

Cassie was a widow with three young children, all under the age of six. Her husband had died the year before. To make ends meet, she took in laundry and mending.

Today was her daughter's birthday. "She's five years old," Cassie said, pulling off her threadbare gloves.

"That calls for a special box," Kate said.

"Oh, I can't afford a box. Just…" Cassie's wistful gaze

traveled along the glass display case. "Two peppermint sticks will do," she said at last. The shrug of her shoulders suggested she was trying to make the best of things.

Kate couldn't help but notice Cassie's dull hair and chapped hands, and her heart went out to her. It couldn't be easy raising three children by herself. "Nonsense," she said. "Birthdays call for something more." Cassie started to protest, but Kate cut her off. "Please, you'll be doing me a favor." She picked up the prettiest box of assorted candy in the shop. "This was left over from last night's dance. Since it was a special order, I can't sell it at the full price."

It was a lie, of course, but Cassie would never accept charity. "It's yours for the same price as I would charge for the sticks of candy."

Cassie hesitated. "Are you sure?"

"As sure as I am that your daughter will love it." Cassie's grateful smile did Kate a world of good. It wasn't often that the young widow smiled.

Kate placed the box of candy in a paper sack and added a slip of paper. Like most of her customers, Cassie couldn't wait to read her fortune and dug it out immediately.

"'The troubles you have will one day be but a memory,'" she read aloud and laughed. "Since I have three children still under the age of six and no husband, I'm afraid my troubles are here to stay. At least into the far future."

"Maybe a rich man will come to town and sweep you off your feet."

Cassie shook her head, but Kate noticed that she carefully tucked the slip of paper into her purse.

No sooner had Cassie left than others began to arrive. Between customers, Kate jotted down the names of people who had recently purchased peppermint candy, though part of her was reluctant to do so. She hated the thought that one of them might be a Ghost Rider.

Tucker entered the shop just after three that afternoon, and it was all Kate could do not to be distracted by him and keep her mind on her work. While she waited on customers, he wandered over to the book section.

Watching him as she filled a paper sack with candy, she noted that he reached for a Thomas Hardy novel over the more popular dime novels. *A reader*, she thought. *Definitely a serious reader.*

"Oh dear." Mrs. Cranston peered into the bag Kate had absentmindedly handed her. "I asked for butterscotch, and I believe you gave me horehound instead."

"Oh, I'm sorry," Kate said, embarrassed to be found remiss. It wasn't like her to mess up orders. She quickly corrected the error and added a few extra pieces of candy to make up for it. "Here you go," she said.

After Mrs. Cranston had left the shop, Kate tucked a stray strand of hair behind her ear and called over to Brett. "We better take advantage of the lull while we can. We have exactly thirty minutes until the next wave of candy lovers walk through that door."

He looked interested. "Oh?"

"As soon as school lets out, the penny-candy gang will be here. I'm known as the candy lady."

"Ah." Brett walked over to the counter and handed her a copy of Mark Twain's *Life on the Mississippi*. "I'd say coming from a small fry, that's quite a compliment."

Smiling up at him, she sensed something intense flare between them before she looked away.

"I heard that Mr. Twain typed that whole book," he said as she wrote out a receipt. "He's the first author to accomplish such a feat."

"That's amazing," she said. "I suggested we purchase a typing machine for the shop, but my aunt said it would never replace the pen."

"I have a similar opinion about the telegraph." His eyes flashed with warm humor. "Mark my words, it will never replace smoke signals," he added, and they both laughed. Only after their laughter died did he slant his head toward the book section. "I must say, you carry quite a selection."

"During the war, soldiers requested books from home, and no one in town carried them. My aunt decided it was her patriotic duty to provide books along with candy to the military." She tossed a nod at the well-stocked shelves. "That's how books ended up in my uncle's candy shop. When Aunt Letty found out that our soldiers needed shoes, she wanted to stock them too, but my uncle put his foot down."

"What a pity, Miss Denver," Brett said with a quick smile. "I could use some new footwear."

She handed him the wrapped book. "Call me Kate," she said.

"All right, Kate."

She liked hearing her name on his tongue. Liked the way he strung out the *A* sound as if his mouth was reluctant to let her name go. *Kaaate.*

"But only if you call me Brett," he added.

"All right, Brett," she said. Since Brett was how

she'd thought of him, it seemed natural to call him that to his face.

After he'd paid for the book, she tore a sheet of paper out of her notebook. "I don't know how complete this list is, but it's a start." She slid the written page across the counter.

He picked it up and quickly scanned the length of the page. "Whew. That's a lot of names."

"Peppermint is one of our most popular candies." She should have stopped there, but didn't. Blaming it on nerves, she babbled on about the health benefits of peppermint.

"Is that right?" he said after a while, sounding more interested than the topic deserved.

"Absolutely. It's also said to cure stomach ailments and headaches." She reached into a jar for a red-and-white peppermint stick and handed it to him. "That'll help your throat."

His fingers touched hers as he took the candy, and she quickly pulled her hand away. To hide her reddening face, she pretended to rearrange the jars on the counter. "Some people prefer the taste of peppermint, but horehound works better. And to my knowledge, no one has ever smiled after popping a horehound candy in the mouth. Not like they do when tasting peppermint."

"You've just cut my workload in half. I can now assume that one of the Ghost Riders suffers bouts of indigestion and looks happy."

Meeting his gaze, she laughed and pointed at the list. "In that case, you can cross off Mr. Thornton. I don't think there's enough peppermint in the world to make him smile."

Brett studied her thoughtfully for a moment. "I noticed earlier that you had your customers' orders memorized. How do you do that? How do you remember what they like?"

"Practice," she said. "Some of my customers have been coming here since the store first opened."

"What about the woman with the doodads on her head? I heard her say she'd never been here before. How did you know she'd like those whatchamacallits?"

Kate laughed. The doodads, as he called them, were feathers. "French kisses," Kate said. She lowered her voice. "The woman had love on her mind. I could tell by the twinkle in her eyes. She had what Aunt Letty calls *the look*."

"The look, eh?" Brett chuckled. "What about her friend? Why those purple thingies?"

"That's easy. She was British and smelled of lavender, so it just stood to reason she would like lavender candy."

Brett's gaze swept over her face. "Chocolate. Pure, rich chocolate with something sweet and soft inside."

"I don't think so," Kate said, meeting his gaze. "You're more of the adventurous type." She tapped her chin. "I think you'd prefer something crunchy. Something you can sink your teeth into, like brittle or pralines."

A faint glimmer of humor returned to his eyes. "I was thinking of you. The candy that suits you."

"Oh." Feeling flustered, she blushed. She regularly analyzed her customers to determine their preferences or needs, but never had anyone turned the tables on her.

"Am I right?" he asked.

"Chocolate melts with the least bit of heat," she

said. Reminded of how the other orphans had taunted her as a child, she wondered if he thought her weak too. After how she'd carried on at the river, she could hardly blame him if he did.

"Ah, but when it melts, it's even more appealing," he said, putting her mind at ease. He tilted his head. "So, am I right?" he asked again.

"Maybe," she said quickly, anxious to change the subject. "Do…do you think the list will help?"

"What? Oh, the list." His gaze traveled down the page still in his hand. "Yes, I'm sure it will. But I don't see Hoot Owl Pete's name here."

"Oh, I forgot about him. Like I said, the list isn't complete. I'll add more names as I think of them." She frowned. "You don't suspect him, do you?"

"Not really. He doesn't fit the Ghost Riders' descriptions, but you never know. Eyewitnesses aren't always reliable."

"Hoot Owl Pete is not an outlaw. He was a friend of my uncle's, and he's a good person." She tilted her head. "How do you know he likes peppermint candy?"

"He offered me one." After a short pause, he added, "Interesting man. He told me he was once a conductor for the Underground Railroad."

She nodded. "That's how he and my uncle became friends." She pointed to a quilt on the wall. "This shop was once an Underground Railroad station."

Brett stared at the quilt she'd indicated. "I saw a similar quilt at the church. Does that mean the church was also a station?"

She nodded. "I don't know how many runaways my uncle helped, but I heard that thousands crossed the Rio Grande into Mexico. That was a great source of pride to my uncle. Hoot Owl Pete too. Occasionally, we receive a letter of gratitude from someone my uncle helped escape. I keep them in a box in the back."

Brett studied her. "You really have a passion for this shop, don't you? Its history."

The question brought a smile to her face. Growing up, she'd spent many happy hours under her uncle's tutelage. He'd taught her more than how to make candy; he'd taught her how to speak to a customer's heart.

"You're right. I do love this shop." She blushed beneath Brett's studied gaze. "I know it sounds crazy. People like you do important work. All I do is make and sell candy."

"Don't say that," he said. "Don't even think it. I've watched you with your customers. It's not just candy you're selling. It's...hope."

His observation surprised her. More than that, it touched her deeply, and she felt a tug on her heart-strings. She'd never thought about the shop's purpose in quite those terms, but it seemed like the perfect way to describe what they did there.

"Everyone can use a little hope." She smiled at the memory that sprang to mind. "My uncle used to say that hope is the glue that keeps a heart from breaking."

Brett nodded in agreement. "You uncle was a wise man."

She smiled. "Yes, he was."

"So...what's my hope for today?"

She thought for a moment, then reached into the box for a prewritten fortune. Rifling through them, she finally found one that seemed to apply. She then dropped it into a bag filled with peppermint candy.

He immediately drew out the slip of paper and read it aloud. "'That which you seek will soon be found.'" He tucked the slip into his pocket. "I certainly hope that's true."

"Oh, it's true," she said and smiled. "Nobody in their right mind would argue with the candy lady."

16

THE GHOST RIDERS STRUCK AGAIN.

And again.

The sudden streak of holdups worried Brett. It worried him a lot.

In the past, the robberies had been separated by weeks and even months. Though his last name was different from his stepsister's, the possibility that Foster One might have figured out who he was worried Brett. Foster could be making a last stand before skipping town.

Of course, the increase in robberies could simply mean that the gang had grown more confident with time and therefore more brazen. If that was the case, it could work in Brett's favor. Confidence bred mistakes, and mistakes led to capture.

It was always the same story—the Ghost Riders robbed, ran, and vanished. There was no way of knowing when or where the gang would strike next.

The county had three main towns, including Haywire. Each town was separated by wild, untamed land that included rugged hills and granite domes.

Rivers and streams were more of a hindrance to a posse than to outlaws, as were the caves and caverns hidden among the hills. It was nearly impossible for a handful of lawmen to cover such a wide and varied range. Just questioning one witness often took a full day in the saddle.

Even more puzzling was the way the Ghost Riders managed to stay one step ahead of the law. They somehow knew when gold would be transported by stage or private company.

So far, the thieves had avoided the traps set by lawmen, and there didn't seem to be a blasted thing the town marshals or the county sheriff could do about it.

Keeler was every bit as frustrated as Brett and made no bones about it. As the county sheriff, he was under the most pressure to bring the outlaws to justice.

That explained why Brett found the sheriff in a foul mood that morning. For once, no pounding feet rattled the ceiling. Even the prisoners seemed reluctant to draw the sheriff's ire.

Lucky Lou wasn't so lucky. The sheriff was reading the riot act while his deputy watched quietly from the sidelines.

"Doggone it!" Keeler yelled, pounding his fist on his desk. "This is the third tag I've given you in less than a month. If I catch your dog running around loose again, it'll be the last time!"

Beneath his fancy duds, Lucky Lou looked like he was sweating bullets. "I can't help it if my dog keeps losing his collar. He hates leashes. And I don't see why I have to pay a licensing fee again. I've already paid twice."

"Don't complain to me. Complain to your dog."

As if he knew the discussion was about him, Ringo cocked an ear and wagged his tail.

Lucky Lou slapped the fee on the sheriff's desk. He then grabbed the disk-shaped metal dog tag and slipped it on his finger. Giving his dog a stern look, he said, "I'm putting you on a bread-and-water diet if you lose this one, you hear?"

"Woof!"

"Nice grappling irons," Brett said, looking down at Lucky Lou's jingle-bob spurs. The nearly three-inch wheels and rowels suggested they were of Mexican descent.

"Thanks."

"Got to git me some of those," Deputy Sweeney said.

Tugging on his dog's leash, Lucky Lou left the office, slamming the door shut behind him.

The sheriff pinched the bridge of his nose. "Okay, where were we?"

Deputy Sweeney drew his chair closer to the sheriff's desk. "We were blatherin' about the Ghost Riders. The only thing they 'aven't robbed is the train, but I wouldn't put it past them."

Brett nodded. "You could be right. That's how the real money is transported these days."

The sheriff shook his head. "Ain't gonna happen. That'll bring the Pinkertons, and no outlaw wants them on his tail." He tapped his fingers on his desk and stared at his deputy. "I want you ridin' herd on the stage that's due in at noon." He stood and reached for his gun belt hanging on the wall. "Meanwhile, I'll ride out to Barterville. The marshal sent me a dispatch sayin' their bank's safe was blown two nights ago."

"I'll ride with you," Brett said.

The sheriff glared at him. "I'm a big boy. I don't need no escort." With that, he shot out the door.

After the two lawmen had left, Brett reached into his pocket for the list Kate had given him. Thirty-nine names were on that list. Thirty-nine people had recently purchased peppermint candy. Thirty-nine potential suspects to check out…including Sheriff Keeler.

❧

Kate filled a box with candy for the women's book club. As she worked, she kept an anxious eye on Connie. It had been nearly a week since the dance, and Connie was obviously still upset.

She paced the floor with a glazed look of despair. "What would it have cost Harvey to ask me to dance at least once?" she railed and popped another chocolate in her mouth.

Kate dropped the last piece of taffy into the box and sealed it. "I'm sorry, Connie. I don't know what to say. Harvey's a fool not to see your fine qualities. But someone will. Trust me. It's just a matter of time."

Connie wiped chocolate from the corner of her mouth with the back of her hand. "That's easy for you to say. You don't have only one man vying for your attention," she said, bursting into tears. "You have two."

Kate stared at her. "What are you talking about? Two?"

"Don't look so innocent. I saw you with that handsome Texas Ranger. What's his name? Tucker?"

"Whatever you *think* you saw is wrong. He's in town on business, nothing more. He has no interest in anything else. Nor do I."

"That's not how it looked to me," Connie argued.

"Come on, Connie," Kate said, feeling oddly defensive. "You know I need stability. That's hardly the kind of life a Texas Ranger can offer. I need someone whose roots run deep. Who loves this town as much as I do. Who understands and knows my history."

Connie took a deep breath. "Like Frank."

"Like Frank," Kate said. "He was there on the orphan train with me. He went through everything I went through. He left a perfectly good home in Missouri to track me down."

No one was more surprised than she was the day he'd shown up on her uncle's doorstep, demanding to know if she was being treated right. She was only seven at the time and Frank nearly ten.

Impressed that the boy had demonstrated such initiative, her uncle had talked Mr. Foster into taking Frank in. That had turned out to be a fortunate choice. Even after his first wife died, Howard Foster had provided Frank with a good home and seen that he stayed in school even while he worked as an apprentice in the leather shop.

"Frank's always been there for me, Connie. He was only a child when he traveled nearly five hundred miles to find me. He walked me to school every day. Fought my battles."

"You fought your own battles. All he did was cheer you on."

"Maybe so," Kate said, "but that was enough."

Growing up, she'd been somewhat of a tomboy. *Don't mess with Kate*, her uncle had said on more than one occasion. What no one knew, certainly not her uncle, was that her rough-and-tumble ways had been little more than bravado. She was like the sweet nougats her aunt made, with the hard crusts and soft centers. Underneath her brave front, she'd never strayed far from the frightened little girl on the orphan train.

Tucker had surprised her when he'd likened her to pure, rich chocolate, sweet and soft through and through. At first, she'd taken offense, but the more she'd thought about it, the more she realized that he'd known something about her that she hadn't even known herself. She was no longer the little orphan with the tough skin, determined not to reveal a soft center.

What she had once mistaken for strength was really a lack of courage. It took mettle to reveal one's vulnerable center.

Aware, suddenly, that Connie was staring at her, Kate shook away her thoughts.

"Kate, has it ever occurred to you that…maybe the man you once needed isn't the same one you need now or will need in the future?"

Kate gaped at her friend and set the box of candy next to the others for delivery. When had Connie become such an expert on love? "I have no idea what you're talking about."

Connie looked like she was searching for words. "I like Frank, I do," she said. "He means well, and he's trying to be what you want him to be, but…"

Kate stiffened. *What she wanted him to be?* "Go on."

"The other night at the dance, you—"

Kate gestured her impatience. "For goodness' sake, Connie. Say what you want to say."

"I don't know how to explain it, but when Frank and I were dancing, I noticed you were dancing with the Texas Ranger."

"So?"

"It's just that…" Connie hesitated. "You seemed… I don't know…more…more—"

Kate tapped her fingers on the counter. "Would you stop beating around the bush? More what?"

Connie chewed on a nail. "More alive, somehow. More carefree. More…you."

Kate stared at her friend, dumbfounded. She had enjoyed dancing with Brett. Enjoyed it more than words could say, but had it really been that obvious? And if so, why hadn't Frank noticed? Or if he had, why hadn't he said something?

"What you saw or *think* you saw was me simply having fun. It's not every day that one gets to dance with a man who actually knows what to do with his feet."

Connie's gaze shot to the ceiling. "If you say so."

"I do say so." For some reason, it seemed imperative to convince Connie of the truth. Or maybe she just needed to convince herself. "Connie, listen to me—"

Before she had a chance to say more, the shop door flew open, and Frank stuck his head inside. "Kate, come quick. The bank. It's your aunt!"

❦

Skirts hiked to her knees, Kate raced down the center of Main and arrived at the bank ahead of Frank and Connie.

It was a madhouse. Aunt Letty was sprawled on the floor, surrounded by a crowd of onlookers, and everyone was talking at once. Doc Avery leaned over her aunt's prone body, listening to her heart through his monaural stethoscope.

Kate dropped to her knees and took her aunt's hand in her own. "What happened?" Aunt Letty looked pale and slightly dazed. Since she looked in no condition to answer, Kate directed her question to the doctor, but Frank answered instead.

"Bank robbery," he said, squatting by her side.

Next to him, Hoot Owl Pete added, "Your aunt walked in just as the thieves ran out."

Ironman Watkins nodded. "Yep, and one knocked her clear off her feet. Saw it with my own eyes."

Kate gasped, her free hand flying to her mouth. "Oh no! Aunt Letty."

"And he looked really mean," a young messenger said, his eyes bulging like a beetle's.

"How could you tell?" Lucky Lou asked, inching his way through the crowd. "He was wearing a flour sack."

"I could tell!" the youth insisted.

"He was mean, all right," a bank clerk concurred. "What kind of man would knock an old lady over and leave her?"

The dazed look suddenly left Aunt Letty's face, and she shot upward like a broken spring. "Watch who you're calling an old lady!"

Kate tried to hold her down. "Auntie, please…"

The doctor reached for his black case. He gave his patient a stern look. "Letty, I want you to take it easy for a day or two. And that's an order."

Aunt Letty brushed off his advice with a wave of her hand. "Nonsense. You know what happened to Abigail Meyers when she decided to take it easy. She fell out of bed and broke her hip." She struggled to stand, and it took Frank and a second man to help her to her feet. "I've got work to do," she said, straightening her skirt. "The church fair is this weekend. Who do you think is gonna make the candy?"

Mrs. Cuttwell crossed her arms and peered down her beak-like nose. "I'm sure we can do without candy this one year. All that sugar is as bad for the body as those awful books of yours are for the mind."

No one could get under her aunt's skin faster than the dressmaker, and today was no different. "Harrumph! I don't see that lack of sugar is doing any favors to *your* body."

The seamstress's face flared. "Is that so?"

"Yes, that's so!"

Not wanting the argument to escalate any further, Kate rested her hand on her aunt's shoulder and glared at Mrs. Cuttwell. Couldn't the woman see that her aunt was still in shock?

"Are you sure my aunt will be all right?" Kate asked the doctor, hoping the dressmaker would take the hint.

Doc Avery tucked his stethoscope into his bag. "She's fine. Just have her get some rest."

Her aunt rolled her eyes. "That's your cure for everything."

"Now, Aunt—"

"Forget it. Soon as I make my deposit, I'll meet you back at the shop."

Brett's voice made Kate turn. He locked her in his gaze for a moment before directing his attention to her aunt. "Excuse me, Mrs. Denver. Do you feel up to answering a few questions? I won't keep you but a moment."

Kate placed her hand on his arm and felt him grow tense beneath her touch. "Perhaps this should wait till later," she said, withdrawing her hand.

Aunt Letty pulled away from Frank and straightened her hat. "Would you all just quit fussing? I'm fine." She turned to Brett. "If there are any questions, the sheriff knows where to find me."

Brett refused to back down. "All I need is a description of the assailant, and I won't bother you any further."

Sensing her aunt's reluctance to talk to Brett, Kate whispered in her aunt's ear. "Remember, he saved my life."

Aunt Letty lifted her chin, a sign Kate recognized as resignation. "All right, if you insist," she said while she took a moment to collect her thoughts. "He stood about this tall." She held her hand a few inches above her head. "He was dressed in black and wore a flour sack over his head."

"Did he say anything?" Brett asked.

"Not a word." Aunt Letty sniffed. "Didn't even apologize for knocking me clear off my feet." She thought for a moment. "All I heard were keys."

Brett eyebrows knitted. "Keys?"

"Yes, you know…" She took her keys from her pocketbook and rattled them.

Kate could tell from Brett's expression that he'd

hoped for more. Nonetheless, he thanked her aunt. "If you don't mind, I'll stop by the shop in a day or two in case anything else occurs to you."

"I'm sure my aunt won't mind," Kate hastened to say, and Brett left to question other witnesses.

Frank said something and, embarrassed to be caught staring after Brett, Kate tried to cover her lapse by pretending to look for someone. "Where's the sheriff? Shouldn't he be here?"

Frank gave her a funny look. "I heard someone say he was out of town. So, do you want me to?"

"Want you to what?"

"Take your aunt home."

"Certainly not!" Aunt Letty said. She opened her purse and pulled out a thick envelope.

"Thank you, Frank," Kate said. "I'll handle it from here." After Frank left, she turned to her aunt. "Give me the money, and I'll make the deposit."

"I can do it." Her aunt started for the teller cage and stopped.

"What is it, Aunt Letty? What's wrong?"

"It's just that there was something familiar about the thief."

Kate frowned. "Familiar? In what way?"

"I'm not sure. It's just…something…" She shook her head. "Why can't I remember?" Gasping, she pressed her hand to her chest. "Oh dear. You don't think I'm losing my mind, do you? You know how Daisy Turnbull kept forgetting things before she was carted off to the loony bin."

"Yes, but she had a history—"

"And Phyllis Moore. Remember her? She almost

got shot when she forgot where she lived and walked into the wrong house."

"There's nothing wrong with your mind, Auntie. We all forget things from time to time. Especially after something as traumatic as a bank robbery."

Aunt Letty's forehead creased. "Are you sure that's all it is?"

"Positive. Now stop worrying. I won't let anyone send you away. I promise."

Aunt Letty forced a wan smile. "I just wish I could remember what it was about the man that makes me think I know him."

"It'll come to you," Kate said. "You just need time."

"I certainly hope you're right. Because if you're not…I have the strangest feeling that something awful will happen."

17

THE FEEDBAG CAFÉ WAS CROWDED, NOISY CONVERSA-
tion clashing with the sounds of silverware and dishes.
Seated at a table by the window, Brett had spent the
last hour and a half perusing his notes.

Sometimes the biggest and most important clues were
the ones most easily missed or overlooked. Criminals
sometimes made stupid or careless mistakes—mistakes
that often escaped notice at first. Then suddenly something came to light. A clue. A lead. A sudden realization.

That's how it was with the Ghost Riders. Their
holdups all seemed to have been done at random. No
one could guess when or where they would strike
next. Brett had searched for a pattern; there was always
a pattern. People, even those outside the law, were
creatures of habit.

Then suddenly, the one thing he'd missed dawned
on him. The one thing they'd all missed was that all
four holdups in and around Haywire had occurred on
a Thursday. The pattern didn't hold true for the robberies throughout the rest of the county, only those
taking place in Haywire.

Maybe it was only a coincidence, but somehow he doubted it. There had to be a reason why the Ghost Riders struck on that particular day of the week and no other.

He checked his watch. It was now one thirty in the afternoon. He had been sitting at the table since nearly noon.

"More coffee?" Mrs. Buffalo asked, filling his cup before he had a chance to reply.

"Much obliged," he said.

She studied him a moment before moving away. A portly woman with frost-white hair, she nonetheless moved like someone half her age. No doubt she was curious why he had occupied a prime window table for so long.

From where he sat, he had a full view of the boot and shoemaker shop directly across the street and two doors from the candy shop. The store's owner, Shoe-Fly Jones, was the sixth person listed on the peppermint list. His real name was Samuel Jones.

The next person on the list owned the tinker shop next door to Jones's place. Adjacent to that was the bakery. All three proprietors had purchased peppermint candy in the last couple of weeks and matched the description of the Ghost Riders. All three men appeared to be upright citizens, and not one seemed to live beyond his means. "Pillars of the community," Reverend Johnson had said when Brett questioned him.

Crossing off their names, Brett zeroed in on the next person listed, former mayor Bellwether. According to local gossip, the mayor hadn't taken kindly to losing the last election. Would that have been reason enough to turn to a life of crime?

Brett was still considering the question when Foster joined him. Without waiting for an invitation, he pulled out a chair and sat.

Brett groaned inwardly. He was in no mood to deal with the man, but with a town this size, it was impossible to hide from him. Accepting his fate, Brett folded the list and tucked it into his vest pocket.

"Now what's the problem?" With Foster, there was always a problem.

Foster rested his arms on the table and leaned forward, looking solemn as a judge. "I'm thinking it's time," he said.

"Time?"

"You know. To ask Kate to marry me. The dance worked like a charm. Connie told me that Kate now knows I'm a changed man."

Brett wasn't so sure about that, but he kept his thoughts to himself. Lord knew he'd worked hard enough coaching Foster on etiquette and the fine art of courtship, so maybe there had been some positive changes. Maybe he *had* impressed Kate. It's what Brett had hoped for. Wanted. Bringing the two of them together was the least he could do after playing havoc with their lives and stopping their wedding. He just wished the thought didn't make him feel like someone had plunged a knife in his heart.

"Have you got a plan?"

Foster sat back. "A plan?"

Brett blew out his breath. *Here we go again.* "You can't just walk up to a woman and ask her to marry you."

Foster frowned in puzzlement. "Why not? It worked last time." He gave his head an emphatic nod. "Walked right up to her in the general store and proposed in front of the pickle barrel." He pulled the ring from his pocket and held it up to the window for Brett to see. The solitaire diamond sparkled in the sun. "It fell in the barrel, and we had to dive for it. We both ended up smelling like vinegar, but it did the trick. She said yes. I told her she didn't have to cry, and she said she wasn't crying. The vinegar made her eyes water."

Brett stared at him incredulous. "You're lucky she didn't pickle *you*."

Foster looked offended. "What's that supposed to mean?"

Brett leaned forward and lowered his voice. "The whole point of our plan so far has been to convince her that you're a changed man. That means putting more thought into the proposal. Make it something she'll remember for the rest of her days. Do you really want your children to know that their father proposed to their mother in front of a pickle barrel?"

"I-I never thought about it that way." Foster scratched his temple. "If you were gonna propose, how would you do it?"

"Me?" Brett cleared his throat. "Well, I would take her out for a nice meal. Maybe at the hotel."

Definitely the hotel. And he'd ask for a cozy corner table for two. He would reach for her hand and gaze into her eyes. With the soft candlelight bringing out the red-gold highlights of her hair, he would focus on her lips—a prelude to the kisses he intended to plant there…

"And then what?" Foster asked, interrupting Brett's thoughts.

Jolted back to reality, Brett reached for his drinking glass. Gulping down a mouthful of water, he tried to recall his purpose in bringing Kate and Foster together. "T-then…I would take her on a hayride—"

"Can't do that," Foster said. "Hay makes me sneeze."

"Oh, right." Brett set his glass down and tried to think. "Okay, then I would take her on a long walk beneath the full moon." The thought brought back memories of how Kate's sweet lips had looked the night he'd driven her home from the dance. The way the nighttime sky had coaxed out the fiery highlights of her hair. "Maybe by the river."

Oh no, not the river. Mustn't think of the river. The river never failed to bring back memories he'd sooner forget. Like how she'd felt in his arms. The way her wet clothes had clung to her gentle curves. Her head on his chest…

"And then I would kiss her," he said quickly. "Kiss her until dawn." Kiss her like she'd never been kissed before. He would run his heated lips over her smooth, creamy skin and kiss her until they were both dizzy with need. "And then as the sun began to rise, I'd fall on my knees and propose."

Shaken by the thoughts…the memories…the heaviness in his heart, he suddenly realized Foster was staring at him all funny-like. "What?"

"You said you would kiss her," Foster said, looking like he wanted to throttle Brett.

"You asked me what I would do, and I told you. It was…just an example."

"Oh, yeah, right. It just sounded so…real. Like you really wanted to do those things yourself."

"That's what makes me a good teacher," Brett said defensively. "I can put myself in your shoes."

"That makes sense, I guess." Foster stared down at the ring in his hands. "So, what do you think about tomorrow? You know, about me popping the question and all?"

Brett's mouth ran dry, and he swallowed hard. "Maybe you should wait till next week. Kate's still upset about what happened to her aunt at the bank."

Foster frowned. "How do you know that?"

"How do you *not* know that?" When Foster failed to respond, Brett blew out his breath. "I stopped by the shop earlier to question her aunt again about the robbery." Unfortunately, Mrs. Denver had nothing more to add to her original statement.

Foster returned the ring to his pocket. "Okay, I'll wait a couple of days."

"Good idea." Brett rubbed his forehead. "So how do you plan to propose?"

"How?"

"Yes. Show me." He meant for Foster to rehearse the words out loud. Instead, Foster took it one step further by dropping to his knee by Brett's chair.

"Kate," Foster began without preamble. "I think it's time that you and me got…you know…hitched."

Brett drew back, appalled. "Great thunder! What kind of proposal is that?"

The corners of Foster's mouth drooped. "What do you mean?"

"What do I mean? A proposal isn't like a cork.

You don't just pop it out. This is the most important question a woman will ever be asked. You must make it special. Memorable." He motioned to Frank's chair. "Get up."

Brett waited for Foster to return to his chair before dropping to his own knee. "First, you take her hand in yours." He took hold of Foster's roughened hand, and suddenly his mind started playing tricks on him. He was back at the barn dance, Kate's small hand in his. Soft as silk it felt. Soft as a rose petal. Shaken by the flushed feeling that came over him, he stared at the poor substitute in his hand. What in blazes was the matter with him?

Foster made an impatient moue. "Well, get on with it."

"All right, don't rush me," Brett muttered. "Proposals can't be rushed." He gazed up at Foster, but the eyes that came to mind were Kate's, so blue that even the sky paled in comparison. And he felt himself sinking into the imagined depths.

Mindful, suddenly, of why he was kneeling in front of Foster, he cleared his throat. "What is her full name?"

"Her real name is Katherine Denver, and her middle name is Anne," Frank told him.

"Okay. Now, what do you love about her?"

Foster eyeballed the ceiling a moment. "I guess I love the way she can change a wagon wheel in record time."

Brett frowned. "Go on."

"She's pretty good at poker and is a fast runner. Sometimes she even beats me in a race."

"What else?"

Foster thought for a moment. "I love how she

wields a hammer." He demonstrated with a thrust of his arm. "Last year, she helped rebuild the Madison barn after the wind blew it down and…"

Foster raved on about Kate's carpentry skills, and Brett could only shake his head in disbelief.

"Hang it, Foster!" Brett said when at last he could get a word in edgewise. "What kind of crazy talk is that? A woman wants to be loved for who she is, not for her prowess with a hammer."

Aware he was still holding Frank's hand, he got down to business. "Now, this is how a man proposes." He cleared his throat. "Katherine Anne Denver… It's important to use her full name. That shows that what you're about to say is special. You know what I mean?"

Foster had a blank look on his face, but he none-theless nodded, and Brett continued. "Next, you say something like…I love everything about you. I love the way you smile, the way you make me smile. I love the way you treat everyone with kindness. I love the way you toss your head when you laugh and wrinkle your nose when—"

Foster yanked his hand away.

Brett knitted his brow. "Now what's the matter?"

"You have no right saying those things about Katie."

Brett rolled his eyes. "I'm giving you examples of what a marriage proposal should sound like."

"I don't want you using Kate as an example. Use someone else."

"Blast it!" Brett grabbed hold of Foster's hand. "How 'bout this? I love the way the hair curls out of your ears. There! Are you satisfied?"

Foster glared back.

Still on bended knee, Brett forced himself to calm down. "Okay, now pay attention. This is important. After you tell her all the things you love about her, you could say something like...I want to spend the rest of my life making you as happy as you make me."

Foster stared down at him but said nothing, and Brett continued. "Okay now, here comes the big moment." He tightened his hold on Kate's...uh... Foster's hand. "Kate, you would make me the happiest man alive if you'd say you'll marry me."

Brett would have said more, but Foster snatched his hand away with a frown. "You make it sound like you...you really mean what you said."

Brett blinked. "What?"

"You made it sound like a real proposal. Like you really want Kate to marry you. Like...like you love her or something."

Realizing with a sense of horror that he could very well be guilty as charged, Brett sat back on his heels. His mind scrambled. He loved Kate? That couldn't be true. Sure, he was attracted to her. Maybe even infatuated with her. But that didn't mean he was in love with her. At least not in the full sense of the word.

Since Foster was staring at him all suspicious-like, Brett fought to pull himself together. "I'm trying to show you the proper way to propose," he blurted. "You're supposed to say yes. Yes, I'll marry you."

"All right, dang it." The volume of Foster's voice would have made an auctioneer proud. "Yes, I'll marry you!"

The sudden silence that filled the dining room gave Brett a bad feeling. Still on his knees, he glanced over his shoulder, only to have his worst fear confirmed. All heads, including that of Kate's friend Connie, were turned to their table, and there he was, still on his knees, holding Foster's hand in his own.

18

NEARLY A WEEK AFTER THE BANK ROBBERY, KATE opened the door to find Frank standing on her porch.

Yesterday, he'd stopped by the shop to ask her to have dinner with him, and she'd agreed. But he was early, which was so unlike him.

His gaze traveled down the length of her. She was wearing a red floral dress with a red waistcoat. "You look hands—uh…mighty pretty."

"Why, thank you, Frank. You don't look so bad yourself." It surprised her to see him dressed in his Sunday best, including his red bow tie.

"Are you ready?" he asked.

She nodded, though she didn't look forward to the mile-long walk ahead of them. "I told you I'd meet you in town." That's what she normally did, but Frank had insisted on coming to the house.

"No need." He stepped aside so she could see the horse and buggy parked in front. "Rented from the stables," he said.

Kate pressed her fingertips to her mouth. "Are you sure you'll be all right?"

For answer, he pulled out a kerchief and tied it over the lower half of his face. "We're hoping that if I don't touch the horse and keep my nose and mouth covered, I'll be okay."

"We?"

"What?"

"You said 'we.'"

"Eh…Doc Avery and me."

"I hope he's right." She would feel awful if Frank had another one of his spells.

"Shall we?" he asked.

Nodding, Kate called to her aunt. "I'm leaving."

Aunt Letty appeared at the kitchen door, a smile of approval on her face. "Have a good time."

"We will, Mrs. Denver," Frank said politely.

He started down the porch ahead of Kate, then stopped and offered his arm. She blinked to make sure it really was Frank and not some impostor.

He seemed unusually quiet as they drove to town, and she knew that was a sign he had something on his mind. He didn't even comment when she told him about providing Brett with a list of customers who had recently purchased peppermints.

"I hate thinking that one of my customers might be a Ghost Rider," she said. The possibility had made her suspicious of everyone walking into the shop. Oh, how she hated that! Hated the questions that popped into her head whenever someone showed up in new clothes or sporting a recently purchased gold watch.

"You don't know that's true," Frank said, his voice muffled by the kerchief. "Maybe the man never stepped foot in your shop. He might have gotten the candy from a family member or a friend."

She let out a sigh. "That doesn't make me feel any better."

"Sorry, Kate. I…I don't want you feeling bad."

She smiled. "I know you don't."

He sneezed, and she gasped in alarm. "Are you all right?"

"Yeah. The kerchief tickles my nose."

She laughed, and he looked at her oddly. "What's so funny?"

"It's just that you look like a bandit with that kerchief over your face."

He laughed too.

Moments later, he surprised her by pulling in front of the hotel and setting the brake. The hotel restaurant was more expensive than the Feedbag Café, but before she could protest, Frank was already on the ground and making a wide circle around the horse to help her down.

He surprised her a second time by offering his arm. Feeling like one of those fancy ladies from the east, she laughed. "Oh my, aren't you the gentleman?" He grinned as she slipped her arm through his. "Maybe you ought to get rid of the kerchief," she said.

"What? Oh." He pulled the kerchief off with his free hand and stuffed it into his pocket.

The noise greeting them in the hotel dining room was deafening. A group of boisterous cattle drivers was whooping it up, and Kate could hardly hear herself think.

The restaurant host greeted them and shrugged an apology. "Sorry," he said, gazing at Kate. Because of the noise, he lowered his head next to hers. "We don't have any tables available."

Frank thrust his hands in his pockets, puckered his lips, and whistled.

Kate glanced at him with a frown before turning her attention back to the host. "When will you have a table available?" she asked, raising her voice to be heard.

The host gave her an apologetic look and said something, but between the noisy guests and Frank's whistling, she had to ask him to repeat it.

"Tomorrow," he said, making wild gestures with his hands. "I can have a table for you tomorrow."

Shaking her head, Kate thanked him, and they left. Frank was still whistling as they stepped outside.

She planted her hands on her hips. "Why are you doing that?"

"Doing what?"

"Whistling."

Frank shrugged. "I don't know. Just a habit, I guess."

"Well, it's annoying," she said and started toward the Feedbag Café.

The proprietor greeted them at the door with narrowed eyes. Pointedly ignoring Frank, she inquired about Kate's aunt. "Has she recovered from her scare at the bank?"

"Yes," Kate replied. "Thank you for asking. But you know Aunt Letty. Nothing will hold her back."

The restaurant owner, Mrs. Buffalo, showed them to a corner table. No bill of fare was necessary. The café's menu hadn't changed in twenty years.

"I'll have the beef stew," Frank said.

Mrs. Buffalo gave him a stern look. "Are you sure you wouldn't want me to throw in some rice with that?"

"No, just the stew will do."

Kate glanced at Frank with a puzzled frown. "Eh…I'll have the chicken and dumplings."

After the café owner left to place their orders, Kate leaned forward. "Mrs. Buffalo seems to be acting rather oddly, don't you think?"

Frank shrugged. "I didn't notice."

Kate raised an eyebrow. "You didn't notice the way she was looking at you all funny? And what did she mean about throwing in rice?"

"Who knows? Maybe she just sees that I'm a changed man."

"That doesn't explain her odd behavior."

"Forget Mrs. Buffalo. Let's talk about something else." After a short pause, he added, "I like the way you do that."

"Do what?" she asked.

"You know, shake out your napkin and put it on your lap."

She frowned. "I don't think I have any special way of doing it."

After several aborted attempts at conversation, their orders arrived, and that's when Frank really started reeling off compliments. He liked the way she held her knife, salted her food, and even buttered her roll.

"So, what's new with leather?" she asked after he'd praised the way she cut her meat.

A look of relief crossed his face, and just like that, the old Frank was back. "You won't believe this," he said, looking as serious as a cocked pistol, "but one of my leather suppliers has upped his price again. Said there was a shortage. Do you believe that?"

Once the floodgates had been opened, there was no stopping him. He talked about leather until Kate's eyes practically crossed with boredom. Through it all, she smiled politely, nodded when appropriate, and managed to ask a halfway intelligent question or two.

After they left the café, Frank covered his mouth and nose with his kerchief and suggested they ride out to the river. Kate was tired and wanted to go home, but since Frank seemed to have his heart set on taking a drive, she agreed.

"All right," she said, stifling a yawn. She hadn't been to the river since her near-drowning and wasn't all that anxious to go back. Just thinking about what had happened there brought back the memory of being in Brett's arms.

But Frank was trying his hardest to please her. The least she could do was meet him halfway.

It was a pleasant night with just a slight breeze. A waning moon held court amid a canopy of glittering stars. "I'm glad you talked me into this," she said, inhaling the sweet air. "It's a beautiful night."

"I hoped you'd think that," Frank said, sounding pleased.

Just before they turned down the road leading to the river, a distant sound made Kate stiffen. Sitting forward, she grabbed hold of Frank's arm. "Stop!"

Frank tugged on the reins. "What's wrong?" he asked, his words muffled by the kerchief.

"Listen." Holding her breath, she strained her ears.

This time, there was no mistaking the low-pitched bawls. "There it goes again." She climbed out of the buggy and lifted the lantern off the side. "It sounds like an animal in trouble."

Holding the lantern aloft, she picked her way through the tall grass growing by the side of the road and stepped close to the fence.

Craning her neck to see over the top rail, she spotted the problem. A calf was stuck in a muddy buffalo wallow, all four of its legs buried. "Oh, Frank, look," she exclaimed.

A short distance from her calf, the mother cow gave Kate the evil eye and made a lowing sound.

"You better get back in the buggy," Frank said. "That looks like one mean mama."

He was right about that, but leaving was out of the question. The calf was still sinking, its head now barely above ground. The long, harrowing cries sent chills down Kate's spine. If she didn't do something, the animal would surely suffocate.

Setting the lantern on the post, she hiked her skirts to her knees and gingerly climbed over the fence.

"Dad-blast it, Kate," Frank called. "What do you think you're doing?"

Reaching for the lantern, she held it high. "I've gotta do something. I can't just leave it."

Keeping a cautious eye on the mother cow, Kate approached the distressed calf with slow, careful steps, speaking in a low voice. The cow lifted her tail and grunted.

"Whoa. I'm just trying to help your little one," Kate murmured.

For answer, the bovine snorted and stomped around the wallow's edge.

Heart pounding, Kate kept moving, the mud squishing beneath her feet. The calf arched its neck and let out a frantic bawl. "There now," she said in a soothing tone.

From the other side of the fence, she could hear Frank cuss. "Hang it, Kate, why do you always do this?"

"Shh. You're scaring it."

The calf whimpered as she neared. Watching her with dark, fluid eyes, the mother cow lowered her horns and pawed the ground.

"It's getting late." Frank's voice grew more insistent. "And it's cold out here."

"I know, but I can't leave."

"So, what do you want me to do?"

She inched closer to the distressed animal. "Drive to the Brandon farm and tell Mr. Brandon that one of his calves is in trouble."

"I'm not leaving you alone out here. Not with the Ghost Riders on the loose and a mean cow about to attack."

The calf let out another harrowing cry that brought a responding howl from its mother.

Kate's mind raced. "I need you to distract her."

"Ah, come on, Katie…"

The calf sank a few inches lower.

"Hurry! I need help," she yelled in alarm.

"Ah, gee. You know what animals do to me. You know how I break out in spots and my eyes swell and my nose gets all red and—"

"Please, Frank. If we don't do something, the poor thing's gonna die."

Frank paced back and forth, his curses rending the air. Finally, he threw up his hands and climbed over the fence. In the dim light, his red kerchief looked like a beard. "Okay, let's get this done."

Before he reached the wallow, the calf's mother snorted and pawed the ground.

Frank pulled off his red kerchief and tossed it. Instead of distracting the cow, it seemed to incense her more, and she charged.

Yelping, Frank turned and ran, the cow at his heels.

While Frank kept the mother cow occupied, Kate quickly plunged into the thick of the wallow and sank to her ankles. Forcing herself to proceed with caution, she tested her footing before each step. The wallow was shallow around the edges but deep in the center.

Moving as close to the calf as she dared, she shoved her hands into the mud and grabbed hold of its front legs. The animal squirmed and fought to pull free, splashing mud everywhere. Face turned, Kate tried holding on, but the calf was as slippery as an eel's tail.

Frank raced by a second time. Breathing down his back, the cow lowered her horns. "Do something. Quick!" he yelled.

"I'm trying, I'm trying!"

Slipping and sliding in the mud, she battled to hold on to the animal. The calf squirmed and bellowed. Tears of frustration sprang to Kate's eyes. Already, she could feel blisters forming on the palms of her muddied hands.

Frank circled the wallow for a third time, gasping for breath.

"I can't hold on!" she cried. Oh God! Unable to

see for the mud in her eyes, she let go of the calf and wiped her face on the sleeve of her dress.

If only she had a rope. The thought gave her an idea and she grabbed her wet, sticky skirt. The fabric was too tough to tear barehanded, but the soft cotton of her petticoat gave way with little effort. Tying the strips of fabric together with muddied hands, she made a loop.

This she worked over the struggling calf's head. Holding on to the end of the makeshift rope, she pulled. The calf was strong enough to pull back but not strong enough to help itself.

Frank jumped into the wallow, and mud shot up like a geyser. Mama cow followed him to the edge of the mudhole and stopped.

"Keep pulling!" Frank bellowed.

"I'm afraid I'll hurt it."

"Keep pulling," he yelled again.

The twisted fabric cutting into her palms, she yanked with all her might, her feet slipping and sliding in the sludge. Gasping for air, she stopped to wipe the mud out of eyes with her sleeve and then gave the rope another hard tug. Just when she thought she could pull no more, Frank lifted the struggling animal out of the mud with both arms.

He had a heck of time holding the calf still so Kate could remove the makeshift rope.

The mama cow stuck a hoof into the wallow, looking mean enough to eat the devil with his horns on. With no time to waste, Frank tossed the calf onto the grass. He then grabbed hold of Kate's hand. "Come on!"

Together, they ran to the fence and scrambled over it. Once they'd reached safety, she looked back.

In the yellow light of the abandoned lantern, the mud-covered calf looked like it had been dipped in chocolate. The two of them were nearly as bad.

She stared down at her clothes in dismay. Her dress, shoes—everything was ruined. Frank's clothes too. But had the mother cow attacked them, it would have been so much worse.

Now, the bovine stood over her young. Sniffing her calf from head to hoof, she set to work licking it clean.

Holding her muddied hands away from her body, Kate couldn't help but smile. "Isn't that the most beautiful sight you ever did see?"

When Frank didn't answer, she turned, and her mouth dropped. Already, his eyes were swollen and his muddied skin covered in bumps. He looked like a warty toad.

"Oh, Frank, I'm so sorry."

"*Aaaa-choo!* Why did I let him talk me into this?" Frank muttered. "Why?"

Him? Him who? "What are you talking about?" she asked. "Who talked you into this?"

He slumped against the fence and slithered slowly to the ground, muttering to himself. She clearly wouldn't get a straight answer out of him tonight.

Kate stared at him in alarm. What had she done to the poor man?

"Come on. I'm taking you home." She grabbed his arm and helped him to his feet. Since his eyes were now swollen shut and he couldn't stop sneezing, getting him into the buggy was the hard part. After he had settled in the passenger seat, she took hold of the reins.

His condition grew steadily worse. By the time they reached town, the poor man was completely out of his head. Doubled over in his seat, he rocked back and forth muttering to himself.

It was hard to make sense of what he was saying, but it sure sounded like he was muttering something about *pickles*.

19

Brett stopped in front of Foster's saddle shop and stooped to pet Ringo. Tied to a post, the dog greeted him with a wagging tail. Warding off the dog's licking tongue, Brett stood and braced himself with an intake of breath.

If everything had gone as planned, Foster should be one happy man. He and Kate might have even settled on a wedding date.

It's what Brett wanted; it's how things were meant to be. Getting the two of them back together had been the right thing to do. It was the only way to make up for stopping their wedding.

Oh sure, he was attracted to Kate, but that's all it was. It couldn't be love. Blast Foster for putting the thought of love in his head in the first place. Once planted, it had been nearly impossible not to imagine such a thing true. Fortunately, he'd had time to think about it and had come to his senses.

Love would only complicate his life. That he knew from experience. He'd been burned once, and once was enough. More than enough. In addition, look what love had done to his sister. To Foster. The poor man had been a wreck these last few weeks.

Nope, love wasn't for him. Brett was perfectly content with his life as a Texas Ranger and had no desire to disrupt it for a woman. What he felt for Kate was simply a case of attraction. Yep, that was it. Attraction.

It hadn't been the first time he'd been drawn to a woman, and he sure in heck hoped it wouldn't be the last.

Now that the couple was back together, he could pour all his energy into doing what he had come to Haywire to do—concentrate on tracking down the Ghost Riders. As soon as Foster One was behind bars, Brett could finally put the past behind him. It wouldn't bring his sister back, nor would it alleviate his guilt for not protecting her, but at least he could rest knowing that justice had been served. If he was lucky, Kate and Frank's wedding would take place after he had finished his business and left town.

He flung the door open and stepped inside the shop. Lucky Lou greeted him with a nod, but it was Foster who made Brett's jaw drop. "What happened to you?"

If the bloated face did indeed belong to Foster, he looked like he'd been run over by a herd of cattle. If that wasn't shocking enough, Foster's eyes were practically swollen shut and resembled two narrow buttonholes.

Foster looked and sounded fit to be tied, but the only words Brett could make out were *pickles* and *cow*.

Cow?

Standing in front of the counter, Lucky Lou shrugged.

"That's all I've been able to get out of him." He tossed a nod at his dog, who was peering through the shop's glass door. "Dang dog keeps chewing through his collar. This is the third one I've purchased this year." He paid Foster and left just as Kate entered the shop.

With a quick glance at Brett, she greeted her fiancé with a worried expression and set a basket on the counter.

"Aunt Letty sent more vinegar," she said, pulling a bottle out of the basket. "And here's some licorice. It's supposed to help with the swelling." She placed both on the counter.

Foster made a funny sound. "Grg go, blok, grin."

"What happened to him?" Brett asked.

Kate's large, liquid eyes met his, forcing him to remind himself that it wasn't love. Mustn't be love. Couldn't be love.

"We pulled a calf out of a buffalo wallow," she said. "And you know how he is around animals."

Brett scratched his temple. "I don't understand. I thought you and he... What were you doing at a buffalo wallow?"

She quickly explained. "We couldn't let the poor thing die." She pressed her hands to her chest. "He helped me save that little calf's life."

"That's...that's great to hear," Brett said. "Does that mean that you and he...?"

"What?"

Brett's gaze dropped to the hand at her chest. She wasn't wearing Frank's engagement ring. Not knowing what to think, he stared at her bare finger. He'd hoped that seeing a band on her finger would erase any lingering doubts about his true feelings. It was the only way he could think to put Kate out of his mind and concentrate on the job at hand.

Helping the couple reconcile was the right thing to do. No question. Yet he couldn't deny that a small—okay, large—traitorous part of himself took pleasure in seeing her finger bare. It wasn't something he was proud of. It wasn't even a part he could control. But it was there nonetheless, and for that, he felt guilty.

He met her blue-eyed gaze. "Can we safely assume you are now in the cow-rescuing business?"

She tried to suppress a giggle, but that only made her laugh more. "I hardly think so," she said.

Her infectious laughter brought a grin to his face, and for a moment—a very brief moment—it felt as if only the two of them existed.

Brett didn't realize he was staring until he heard a strange sound coming from the other side of the counter. A quick glance told him that Foster was trying to whistle.

Brett's smile wavered. "I'm just glad it was a calf the two of you saved and not a bear or wolf."

Foster's face grew even redder around his puckered lips, but Kate didn't seem to notice. She was too busy describing all that had happened. "You should have seen it," she said, her face aglow. "The sweet little thing looked like he was covered in chocolate."

She giggled, and Brett's heart jolted. Held captive by the play of emotions on her face, he couldn't take his eyes off her.

"Sounds like that calf was lucky you happened to be in the area," he said, adding in a louder voice, "you and Foster."

She smiled up at him, and it was as if there wasn't enough air in the room. "Frank wanted to take a ride by the river."

Forcing himself to breathe, Brett glanced at Foster. The man had managed a low hissing sound in place of a whistle. He looked so bad that it was hard not to feel sorry for him. This time, he had every right to be jealous, and for that, Brett felt bad.

Kate lifted her shoulders in a regretful shrug. "I'm afraid we never made it there."

"There'll be another time," he said, as much for Foster's sake as for hers.

"Yes, I'm sure." She brightened. "Oh, by the way, I thought of a couple more names to add to the list of peppermint buyers."

"That's…that's good. I'll stop by later, if that's okay." After a beat, he asked, "How's your aunt? Has she fully recovered from her ordeal?"

"Yes, she has. Nothing's gonna keep Aunt Letty down for long. Did you find what you were looking for from the names I gave you?"

"No," he said. "But I've only interviewed half the people on it."

"No suspects, then?" she asked.

He shook his head. "Not yet."

"Grip a con a maya."

This time, Kate turned to Frank, her expression soft and tender. "What did you say, dear?"

Brett felt something snap inside, like someone had torn away a piece of his heart. She'd called Foster *dear*. But that was the least of it. Her gentle voice and the concern on her face made one thing abundantly clear:

no matter the difficulties between them, Kate still cared deeply for Frank.

Brett cleared his throat. "I–I better get a move on."

Kate's eyes rounded. "I hope you're not leaving on my account."

"No, no. I just stopped by to say…hello." Touching his finger to the brim of his hat, he spun around and quickly left the shop.

20

KATE WORKED LATE THAT NIGHT. TAKING CARE OF Frank had put her behind on her orders, and she had yet to make the taffy she'd promised Mr. Turner. It was his wife's favorite candy, and tomorrow was her birthday.

Fortunately, Frank's swelling had gone down, and he'd looked more like himself again, though his good humor had yet to return.

Stifling a yawn, she set to work. Taffy was best made with two people, but tonight was choir practice, and her aunt had already left for church.

Kate mixed sorghum molasses, sugar, and vinegar in a large copper kettle and placed it on the stove to heat, stirring it with a long-handled wooden paddle. When she thought the time was right, she dropped a small piece of the mixture into a bowl of water. The resulting hard ball confirmed it was ready.

Uncle Joe had preferred testing candy the old-fashioned way—with only his finger. First, he'd dip his finger into cold water, then thrust it into the boiling-hot syrup, then back into cold water again. Kate had watched him do it numerous times but still hadn't worked up the nerve to try it herself.

Removing the pot from the stove, she added baking soda. After letting it cool, she poured the glistening brown mass onto the marble slab.

A sudden banging on the front door startled her. Working alone at night had never bothered her before. It did now, thanks to that outlaw running into her shop. With more than a little apprehension, she left the kitchen.

Spotting Brett's tall form through the window, she let out a sigh of relief and rushed to let him in.

"I saw the light," he said, stepping inside and seeming all at once to fill every square inch of her shop. "I stopped by for that other list you mentioned. Hope that's okay."

"Yes, of course. I'm just making taffy," she said.

"Taffy, eh? It that what smells so good?"

"Probably." She turned the lock on the door. "If you have time, I could sure use another pair of hands."

He cocked his head to the side. "Oh?"

"Come on, I'll show you." She turned and led the way to the kitchen. Plucking a pink apron off a wooden peg, she held it out to him.

"You want me to wear that?" he asked.

She laughed at his expression. Nothing put a look of panic on a man's face quicker than asking him to don an apron. "Required uniform," she said.

His gaze flickered over the apron in her hand. "I think I should warn you. When I was a teen, I took a job as a wrangler on a ranch. One of my duties was to help the cook. I lasted for exactly one meal."

"Are you trying to scare me?"

He quirked an eyebrow. "Is it working?"

"Not on your life." She gave the apron a shake, and after a slight hesitation, he tossed his hat on a chair and shoved his arms through the ruffled sleeves.

She tied the apron strings around his back and regarded him with a smile. The apron that reached all the way to her ankles didn't even touch his knees.

"Wash up, and we'll get started," she said, tossing a nod at the basin of soap and water.

After he'd washed and dried his hands, she told him to hold out his palms. She then rubbed lard on them. He had large hands, nicely shaped, with long, tapering fingers and neatly trimmed nails.

Feeling his gaze on her, she had the strangest urge to jump back. Instead, she forced herself to calmly move away. Heart fluttering, she turned to wash and grease her own hands. Even with her back toward him, she was aware of his eyes on her, and that only quickened her pulse.

Moments later, they took their places on opposite sides of the counter, the taffy mixture mounded on the marble slab between them.

"It's easy," she said. "You just pinch out a piece like this." She demonstrated with two fingers. "Then all you have to do is twist and pull. Twist and pull."

With a boyish grin that made her heart do flip-flops, he set to work following her example. "This is pretty easy," he said after a while.

His infectious smile making her tingle inside, she quickly cast her eyes downward. "Just wait. It'll get harder." Pulling taffy never failed to bring back pleasant memories, and tonight was no different. "When I was a little girl, I used to help my uncle make taffy, and I'd get blisters on my hands."

His gaze met hers. "Sounds like you miss your uncle a lot."

"I do. He taught me everything I know about running this shop. He and my aunt."

Brett glanced around. "Speaking of your aunt, where is she? I was hoping to talk to her."

"Sorry. Tonight's choir practice," Kate said, furrowing her forehead. "Is there a problem?"

"Problem? No. I just want to go over her statement again. She still insists that the man who knocked her down seemed familiar in some way. I keep hoping that maybe something more has occurred to her."

Kate knitted her brows. "I know something's been bothering her. But…I don't think she's figured out what it is. I'll tell her you stopped by." She raised her eyes to find him watching her, and her cheeks flared.

"I know, I know," he said and laughed. "Twist and pull, twist and pull." They worked in silence for a moment before he asked, "How do you manage this by yourself?"

"When I'm here alone, I hang the taffy from that hook." She drew his attention to the brass hook on the wall. "But it goes faster with two people." She flashed a smile. "It's also more fun."

He grinned back. "Glad I could oblige." Holding her gaze, he changed the subject. "How's…uh… Foster doing?"

"Improving," she said. "The swelling is down."

"He's lucky he has you to take care of him." The

tone of his voice sent a ripple of awareness rushing through her.

"I'm not so certain about that," she said. "I'm the one who caused the problem."

He quirked an eyebrow. "I don't think he sees it that way."

She drew in her breath, but the air seemed almost too thick to breathe. For several moments, they lifted and pulled in silence. Looping the taffy back, her fingers brushed against his. Their gazes met for an instant before she looked away.

The taffy suddenly became a lifeline, demanding her full attention. When at last it had been pulled into long, narrow ropes, Kate carefully avoided his eyes and showed him what to do next.

"Fold it over like this. Then twist and pull again."

"How do you know when it's done?" he asked, following her lead.

"Oh, you'll know," she said. "You'll know."

Gradually, the appearance and feel of the taffy changed. It now felt more solid, and the color was almost as blond as the hair on Brett's head.

When their glossy ropes measured a couple of feet long and a quarter of an inch thick, she gave the final instructions. "Okay, you can stop pulling now. Just overlap it and twist."

After a moment, he said, "I can't get it to budge."

"That means it's ready." She reached for a knife, cut off a piece, and handed it to him.

Brett popped the taffy in his mouth. "Hmm. Now that's what I call good."

"Of course it's good," she said and, feeling

self-conscious beneath his approving gaze, added, "Thanks to your help, all I have to do is cut the rest and wrap it for tomorrow's pickup."

They both turned to the sink at the same time and stopped.

"Sorry," he said, pulling off his apron. "After you."

Kate plunged her hands in the water and scrubbed them with soap. Brett handed her a towel when she was done, their fingers briefly making contact.

Fortunately, he then turned his back to wash his own hands, missing the flare of her cheeks.

After he dried his hands, his gaze found hers. "You have a speck of sugar on your face," he said, stepping closer.

Something passed between them. A light. A silent message. The sharing of a single heartbeat. It wasn't the first time she'd sensed something—a connection—between them, but never had it felt so strong.

She lifted her hand to her heated cheek.

Shaking his head, he stepped closer and ever so gently ran his finger over the tip of her nose. "Here."

But he didn't stop there. Instead, he drew an imaginary line from her nose along the side of her face to her chin, his gentle touch sending pleasant sensations rushing through her.

"And here," he said softly. Tenderly, he traced the fullness of her lips, forcing them to part with a burning need that was all at once exciting and frightening.

His eyes searched hers, the questioning depths demanding an answer. Her mind said she mustn't, but somehow, he knew the desires of her heart, because he did exactly what she wanted and captured her lips with his own.

When she offered no resistance, he took her fully in his arms and kissed her with an urgency that shattered her defenses. Clinging to him, she kissed him back, savoring the sweetness of his probing mouth. Relishing the willingness of her own.

By the time their lips parted, they were both breathing hard.

Momentarily dazed by what had just happened, it was all Kate could do to pull away from his arms. The air still sizzling with the heat of their embrace, she ignored the temptation to fan her hot face. Instead, she ran her damp hands down her apron.

His kiss had been unexpected, as had her own eager response. But nothing surprised her more than the disappointment she felt now that it was over.

A shadow flitted across his face. "I...better go."

There it was again, the question. Only this time it was in his voice as well as his eyes. *Do you want me to stay?*

Her heart said yes, but some niggling voice in her head said no. No, she mustn't do this. No, this was wrong. Looking for something to do with her hands, she grabbed a wet sponge and wiped down the counter as if her life depended on it.

"Th-thanks for your help," she stammered, keeping her gaze focused on the task at hand. "You made my work so much easier."

"My pleasure."

He stared at her from beneath a furrowed brow, his eyes dark with apology and something else she couldn't decipher. Her hand stilled, and her heart sank.

"That shouldn't have happened." He took a deep breath, and his voice broke. "I don't know what got into me... I had no right. You and Foster—"

Oh God, Frank! How could she have forgotten him, even for a second? True, things were still up in the air between them, but he was trying hard to mend his ways, and for that, he deserved her fidelity, at least until things were settled one way or another. Turning so soon to another man's arms was unforgivable. And this time, she couldn't blame it on her near-drowning.

"It was just...a mistake," she said, more to appease her guilty conscience than to relieve Brett's mind. She moistened her lips, only to find that the taste of him still lingered there, making her want more. "Let's... let's just forget it." As if she could.

"It won't happen again." His emphatic voice left no doubt of his sincerity. "You can put your mind at ease. You don't have to worry about me taking further advantage."

She stared at him, not knowing what to think. Surely, he wasn't oblivious to how much she'd wanted his kiss? Welcomed it. Hated for it to end. Hated herself for feeling that way.

"You...you didn't take advantage," she said, her voice wavering. Why had Brett's single kiss seemed so much deeper, fuller, and more memorable than all the kisses exchanged with Frank?

"Thank you for saying that, but after everything that's happened..." He shook his head. "I'm afraid none of us are quite ourselves."

She swallowed hard. While in his arms, she'd felt more like herself than she had in a very long time.

His jaw grew taut, and the lines deepened around his eyes. "If you can give me that list, I'll be out of your hair."

Her mind went blank for a moment until her brain clicked in. "Oh! The list." Flustered, she tossed the sponge in the sink. Reaching for her notebook, she tore out a sheet of paper. He took it from her. Their fingers touched briefly before she snatched her hand away.

Following another physical jolt, she backed away and reached for her knife. While he studied the list of names, she chopped up the rest of the taffy. The banging of her knife echoed her frenzied heartbeats.

After the candy had been cut into one-inch pieces, she asked, "Anything wrong? With the list, I mean."

"No, it's just that something you said earlier got me thinking. About your aunt at choir practice. It reminded me of a conversation I had with Reverend Johnson."

He sounded so businesslike, so distant, so impersonal, it was hard to believe she had been in his arms moments earlier. The tenderness of his voice was now but a memory, but the feel of his lips lingered on.

"Oh?"

He folded the list and tucked it into his vest pocket. "It's been my experience that criminals work in patterns. Maybe not at first, but after a few holdups, they know what works. What feels comfortable. It doesn't take long before their methods become habit."

She set her knife down. "You're not suggesting that the Ghost Riders are choir members, are you?"

He shrugged. "You never can tell, but it occurred to me that the church might be more involved than I'd originally thought."

She frowned. "You don't think that Reverend—"

"No, no, nothing like that," he hastened to assure her. "But that's all I can tell you." He reached for his hat and stood looking down at it, the air between them rife with unspoken words and barely contained emotions.

"I'll walk you to the door," she said, breaking the awkward silence.

He lifted his gaze to hers and rocked back on his heels. His eyes were dark, making it hard to read his thoughts. His demeanor, however, was apologetic.

Fearing he might once again express regret for having kissed her, she quickly added, "Thank you for your help. I'll make a candy maker of you yet."

They walked side by side through the dimly lit shop, maintaining a safe distance.

Hesitating at the door, he studied her face as if trying to memorize it. "Kate, I…" He cleared his voice, and her stomach clenched. "I enjoyed tonight. It was fun."

She moistened her lips—a mistake, for it drew his gaze to her mouth. "You can now officially call yourself a taffy puller," she said, the calmness of her voice belying the confusing mess inside.

He chuckled. "A skill like that might come in handy someday." They stared at each other for a heartbeat before he turned and yanked the door open. "Good night," he said brusquely, and just like that, he was gone.

She closed the door after him and turned the lock. Forehead pressed against the cool, smooth glass, she forced herself to breathe. Despite the confusion in her head, one thing was abundantly clear—things had just gotten a whole lot more complicated.

21

THE FOLLOWING MORNING, KATE WALKED OUT OF THE house and into the backyard, carrying the birdcage with both hands. It was time.

The raven's wing was healed, and there was no reason to keep the bird caged up any longer. She set the cage on the ground next to the large sycamore where she'd found the injured bird.

From behind the fence, Taffy, Blondie, and Mutt watched her with wagging tails, no doubt hoping for a treat.

Dropping to her knees, she unlatched the steel door. Perched on the wooden bar, the raven cocked its head but made no effort to escape.

"You aren't making it any easier on me." Once she had taken someone or something under her wing, it was hard to let go. This wasn't only true of animals and people. She also held on to past hurts and losses. Now, she had something else to hold on to—the memory of Brett's kiss.

It wasn't just that he'd kissed her. Nor that she had willingly kissed him back. No, it was far more worrisome than that. She felt that something had shifted inside her. The protective shell around her heart—so carefully cultivated in early childhood—had cracked open and was in terrible danger of falling away altogether.

Frank wasn't one to dig beneath the surface. He took everything at face value. Never once had he pressed her to bare her soul or reveal the secret depths of her heart.

She'd sensed that wouldn't be true of Brett. At times, she felt like his probing eyes could see right through her, and that's what worried her. Having lost both parents at a tender age, she lived in fear of losing those closest to her. That's why she always kept a part of herself in reserve—locked away. A part she hoped to protect from pain or loss. A part that no one had been allowed to touch.

Until now.

Until Brett.

And that scared her. Scared her more than words could say.

Her thoughts were interrupted by a distant squawk, and she shaded her eyes and looked up. A black bird circled overhead. Wings spread wide, its shadow flitted over the ground.

Blackie responded with caws of his own and hopped down from the perch.

She tapped the side of the cage. "That a friend of yours?" Blackie fluttered his wings. It took several more taps before the raven flew out of the cage and landed on the grass a short distance away.

The bird in the sky kept circling, its cries growing more insistent. At long last, Blackie lifted his wings and flew to the top of the tree. He then rose into the sky to join the other raven, and the two flew off together.

Hating to see the raven go, Kate watched until the winged duo was out of sight. Sighing, she stood and reached for the empty cage. If only the memory of Brett's kiss could be so easily released.

Following a restless night, Brett mounted his horse and headed in the direction of the church. He hardly noticed the brightly shining sun, the vivid blue sky, the splash of bright colors spilling out of resident flower boxes.

He felt like a cad. A despicable, two-timing cad. What had he been thinking? It was bad enough that he had crazy, mixed-up feelings for Kate Denver, but to act on them was inexcusable.

If only she'd not looked so beguiling last night, so absolutely enticing. So utterly fetching. So completely desirable. He'd watched her pull the taffy into long strings and imagined how those same fingers would feel in his hair. On his skin.

The sugar on her lips had nearly driven him wild with wanting to know if her mouth tasted as sweet. The blazing-red color of her tangled locks had made him long to run his hands through every shiny strand.

Never had he fought so hard to resist temptation. Never had he failed so miserably.

God forgive me. Stealing someone away from another was wrong. That he knew from personal experience. His brother had stolen Deborah Freeman from him.

Snatched her right from beneath his nose. Never would he forget the pain of rejection and betrayal. Never could he do to another what his brother had done to him.

Foster, even with all his faults, was basically a good man. A hard-working man. He didn't deserve that kind of fate.

Brett's only hope was to finish his business in Haywire as quickly as possible and leave town. That might not be such a far-fetched idea. If he was right about why the local robberies occurred only on Thursdays, the Ghost Riders' days could be numbered.

If he was wrong, it was back to square one, and that's what worried him. He couldn't afford to stay in Haywire a moment longer than necessary. Not after what had happened last night. What was bound to happen again if he didn't watch his step.

Groaning, he pressed his heels against his horse's flanks, but trying to outrun the memory of Kate's sweet lips was a losing battle.

It was with great relief that he reached the church. Maybe now he could concentrate on work. After dismounting and tethering his horse, he checked the church doors. They were locked, and there was no sign of the minister. Brett circled the building and found nothing that indicated a basement or cellar, and that was a puzzle. If the church had been used as an Underground Railroad station, where had the fugitive slaves hidden?

He walked around the church a second time, poking the ground with a stick on the chance he'd missed a cellar door hidden by foliage or soil. But there was nothing.

Turning with a sigh, Brett walked back to his horse. A low birdcall drew his gaze skyward. A buzzard flew in ever-widening circles overhead, wings raised in a V, its lonely cry spreading across the land. Oddly, it sounded like the cry of his lonely heart.

After watching the bird for a moment, something occurred to him, and he ran back to hunt for the stick he'd tossed away. Finding it, he proceeded to walk around the church. With each completed circle, he moved outward a couple of feet at a time. He was a good twenty or thirty feet from the church when the probing tip of his stick hit something hollow.

He dropped to his haunches and brushed away the foliage, revealing a wooden door. He lifted the rusty handle, and the heavy hatch door opened with a squeak of its hinges. He gaped at the hole in the ground. A ramp led downward.

"Well, what do you know?" Buzzards were thought to be a bad omen, but in this case, Lady Luck seemed to be smiling down on him.

Brett could think of only one reason for the lack of stairs: horses.

He started down the ramp. Reaching the bottom, he pulled out a box of safety matches. Striking one, he spotted a lantern hanging from a granite wall and lit it.

The light revealed a large underground room, the ceiling reinforced with rafters and the walls with chicken wire. So this was where the fugitive slaves had found shelter.

Unless he missed his guess, it was also where the Ghost Riders hid out. To those giving chase, it would indeed seem as if the outlaws had vanished in midair. The cavern door was well hidden and hard to find. A closer look at the ground revealed bristle marks from a

broom used to hide tracks. Even he had walked right
by the hatch door and failed to notice it on his earlier
visit to the church.

He checked all four dirt walls. It turned out that
the only way in and out of the room was by the ramp.

The grotto was void of anything except the
trash littering the floor. The empty whiskey bottles,
cigarette butts, and a playing card suggested how the
outlaws kept themselves occupied while waiting for
the coast to clear.

The cavern solved one problem but not the other. He
now knew how the outlaw gang had managed to escape
capture, but he was no closer to knowing their identities. That meant having to wait until the next holdup.

Just as he turned to leave, something caught his
eye. A slip of paper. He stooped to pick it up and
immediately recognized Kate's flowery script. It read:

He who knows the road can ride at full trot.

Arching an eyebrow, he tucked the scrap of paper
into his vest pocket. It seemed that all roads led back
to the candy shop, and that worried him.

22

By eleven o'clock the next morning, it was
already hot, and Kate longed to go to the old swimming hole and cool down. Unfortunately, there was
too much work to be done.

She had just finished replenishing the display cabinet when Harvey Wells walked in. He greeted Kate
with a silly grin. Despite his buckteeth and gangly
appearance, Harvey was considered a catch by mothers
of marriage-aged daughters. He'd earned the honor
mainly through his rich uncle, who owned one of the
largest cattle ranches in the Texas Hill Country.

"Coming here that last time was the luckiest day
of my life," he announced, reaching for a free sample.

"Oh?" Kate asked. "How so?"

His grin grew wider. "I would never have asked
Mary-Ruth to dance with me, had it not been for
the fortune that said 'Love comes in all colors, even
yellow.'"

To hide her irritation, Kate rearranged the jars on
the counter. "I'm not sure what you mean."

"When I got to the dance, who should be dressed

in yellow but Mary-Ruth. That's when I knew what fate had in store."

"How did you know that? There were other women in yellow," she said. Connie, for one.

"Yeah, but once me and Mary-Ruth started kicking up our heels, I knew she was the only one for me."

That wasn't what Kate had wanted to hear. How she hated knowing the part she'd played in breaking her friend's heart!

"Do you want your usual two-timing…uh, two-flavored stick candy?"

Her slip of the tongue seemed to go unnoticed, as did the coolness of her voice. "Not today," he said with a lopsided grin. "Today, I want the biggest, fanciest box of candy money can buy." He puffed out his chest. "Nothing but the best for my girl."

Kate tried not to let her annoyance show. He definitely had what Aunt Letty called "the look," so it was probably unfair to blame him for how he felt. Sometimes the heart had a mind of its own, and there wasn't much a person could do but obey its command.

"I can't put it together right now." She tossed a nod at the stack of orders. "I can have it ready later this afternoon."

"That's fine," he said, reaching into his pocket for his money clip. "Would it be possible to have it delivered to Mary-Ruth's house?"

"Yes, but it will cost you extra." She slid a pencil and paper across the counter. "Write down what you want the card to say."

Harvey scrawled out his message and slid the paper back to her. The word *love* was printed in big, bold letters. "Want to see something?" he asked, pulling out what had looked like a steel rod from his pocket.

"Don't tell me that's another one of your"—she'd almost said *crazy*—"inventions." Most of his inventions had no real value. Like the baby sling that worked on a series of cables to lift an infant from its cradle across the room and into its mother's arms. She was annoyed with him for hurting her friend, but she would never willingly hurt his feelings.

He grinned. "Yeah, and this one's gonna make me rich and famous. This here is what I call a marriage saver," he said.

Kate eyed the steel rod with curiosity. "How's that going to save a marriage?"

"I'll show you." With a quick motion, he secured a previously rolled cigarette to one end and extended the rod until it was a good ten or fifteen feet long. "If a man's wife doesn't approve of him smoking in the house, all he has to do is attach his cigarette in the little clip at the end and poke the rod out the window. He can sit inside talking to the missus while the cigarette he's smoking hangs outside."

Kate laughed. She couldn't help it. "I think that might have a better chance of success than your rocking bathtub," she said. "Or even your baby sling."

He looked pleased. "I hope you're right. But if you're not, I've got an idea for a device that could save your life if you're ever accidentally buried alive."

Kate shuddered at the thought. "Good luck with your…uh…marriage saver."

"Thanks."

No sooner had he left than Mr. Thornton walked

in the door. Resigning herself to another frustrating encounter, Kate greeted him with a forced smile. Two unwanted customers back to back.

She'd first met him ten years ago when she was a young girl, and her unfavorable opinion of him had not changed. Having the misfortune of being born and raised in Massachusetts, Mr. Thornton had all the Eastern eccentricities of dress and speech but none of the charm.

Today, his striped trousers were secured by red suspenders and his shoes protected by pearl-gray spats.

Not once in all the years she'd known him had he smiled, nor had he ever bothered to say *please* or *thank you*. "What a crank," she'd said after meeting him for the first time. Her uncle had looked appalled. "Well, he is," she'd insisted.

Uncle Joe had made no effort to hide his disappointment in her. But instead of scolding her, he'd reached beneath the counter for a gumdrop and held it up. "People are like candy," he'd said. "Some are all sparkly like gumdrops. Others, like Mr. Thornton, are like lemon drops. You have to dig deep to find the soft centers."

Out of respect for her uncle's memory, Kate still kept digging. She always greeted Mr. Thornton with a smile, though it was never returned. In addition, she never failed to add a little something extra to his order and enclosed a fortune she hoped would lift his spirits. To her knowledge, none ever had.

Today, as always, he silently perused the candy displayed behind the glass and ordered his usual butterscotch candy. She was running out of fortunes and would have to make more. She finally settled on the one that read:

Life is like a cup of tea. It's all in how you make it.

He slapped a coin on the counter, snatched up the bag of candy, and headed for the door without so much as a goodbye.

Just as he left the shop, Kate made a face and stuck out her tongue. Before the door closed, Brett breezed in, catching her in the act.

He laughed. "That bad, eh?"

Blushing, she placed her elbows on the counter and rubbed her temples. "In the ten years I've known that man, not once has he ever smiled or said a civil word."

Brett's amused expression melted into sympathy. "He must be related to the sheriff."

Dropping her hands, she smiled, her irritation forgotten. "I didn't expect to see you again after—" Heat rose up her neck, and she fell silent.

He stiffened and squared his jaw. "Something came up," he said. He seemed to be avoiding her eyes, and his voice was as formidable as his expression.

Not sure what to think, Kate waited for him to explain. Instead, he pulled a strip of paper out of his vest pocket and laid it on the counter. Recognizing her own handwriting, she raised her eyebrows in question.

"'He who knows the road can ride at full trot,'" he read out loud. His gaze dipped to her pursed lips before he quickly looked away. "Do you remember who you might have given that to?"

She thought for a moment before shaking her head. "I'm sorry. Is it important?"

"Could be." Still avoiding her gaze, he moved the paper a tad closer to her with the tip of his finger. "Do you notice anything odd about it?" he asked.

"Odd?" She shook her head. "No, why?"

"See that crease?" He pointed. "Someone took the time to carefully fold it in half. I noticed that most people read their fortunes and toss them aside. But this person folded his, which means he meant to keep it. And if that's true, it could mean that he takes these things seriously."

"You kept the one I gave you," she said, watching his face carefully. "The day at the river, you showed it to me. Does that mean you take such things seriously?"

This time his gaze met hers. "I always take warnings seriously," he said. Something in his eyes suggested he wasn't as immune to her as he tried to let on. That maybe their kiss had affected him as much as it had affected her. In a flash, the look was gone, making her doubt her own eyes.

"I believe I found a Ghost Riders' hideout," he said, changing the subject.

"You found it?"

He nodded. "Not far from the church."

"Oh, Brett, that's wonderful! It means you're getting close to catching them."

"I hope so," he said, though there was no gratification in his voice. "Then my work here will be done." He glanced at her as if expecting some sort of objection. When none came, he said, "Think again. Who might you have given that particular maxim to?"

She pressed a hand to her forehead. "It might have been someone going on a trip," she said and brightened. "Like Mrs. Ambrose. Oh, yes, now I remember. She was planning a trip abroad. And that seemed to fit the occasion."

"Anyone else?"

"Let me think." After a beat, something occurred to her. "I also gave that same fortune to Mrs. Applegate before she delivered her second child." She thought a moment. "Oh yes. I also added it to Mrs. Cambridge's order. She's been widowed twice and was trying to decide whether to take another chance on love. And then there was..." She cited several other customers, all of whom she'd hoped had benefitted from that particular maxim.

He waited for her to finish before shaking his head with warm approval. "That's amazing, You're amaz..." He coughed and looked away. "A...a magician."

She blushed. "It's just something I learned from my uncle. He was a big believer in the power of suggestion." She sighed. "I wish I was more help, but..." She shrugged.

"So far, you've named a few women." Now he was serious again. "Can you think of any men who might have received that particular saying?"

Hitting a blank, she shook her head. "I'm sorry. I'll ask my aunt if she remembers anyone."

"That would be a big help."

"Is...is there anything else I can do for you? How about some rock candy?"

"Maybe later." He started to leave but then changed his mind. "Maybe there is something you can do."

"Oh?"

Rubbing the back of his neck, he hesitated a moment before asking, "How would you feel about helping me catch a couple of real, live ghosts?"

23

ALL DURING THE FOLLOWING WEEK, KATE INCLUDED the same fortune in every bag of candy, per Brett's instructions. It read:

> On the day of the next full moon, your
> path will be bathed in gold.

Most of her customers would probably not give the handwritten fortune a second thought. But if Brett was right and one of her regulars was a Ghost Rider—and took such things to heart—the fortune might force him into action.

Nothing, of course, had been left to chance. Brett had personally seen to it that word had discreetly filtered out about a big shipment of gold coins heading for Haywire by stage on Thursday. Not only did that day correlate with Reverend Johnson's visitations, but also with the full moon. Even nature seemed to be working in their favor.

Now all that was left to do was wait.

Kate felt honored to have such an important task to

do. But even as she dutifully played her part, she hoped and prayed that none of her customers were involved.

That included Mr. Thornton, who'd entered the shop that morning with his usual grim-faced expression just as Harvey Wells was unveiling his latest invention to a curious crowd.

Hoot Owl Pete moved to make a spot for Thornton. Next to them, Mrs. Tremble watched with her poodle cradled in her arms. Mitzie's sharp-eyed gaze was fixed on Ringo happily chewing on a dog cake. Standing between former mayor Bellwether and Reverend Johnson, Lucky Lou switched the dog leash from his right hand to his left and helped himself to the plate of candy Kate had set out. The cinnamon candy was new, and she wanted to test it before offering it for sale.

Harvey pointed to the strange-looking contraption on the counter that resembled a paddlewheel. "This here is every candy-maker's dream," he said with a flourish.

Mrs. Cuttwell made a face. "I certainly hope it works better than the dressmaker's dream you invented," she said with a haughty shake of her head. She turned to the crowd. "He said his mechanical scissors would take the drudgery out of cutting, but all they did was fray the fabric."

"Anything's gotta be better than that danged horse-shoeing machine." The blacksmith imitated Harvey's high-pitched voice. "Just put the horse's hoof in the hole, and the machine will do the rest." Ironman returned to his normal voice. "It did the rest, all right. The horse jumped sky-high and never did come back down."

Harvey cleared his throat, "Yes, well, even the greatest inventors experience a setback or two."

"Or three or four," Hoot Owl Pete said and then promptly reminded Harvey about the mannerly hat that automatically raised in polite salutation. "It raised, all right, along with half the scalp."

Ignoring his critics, Harvey drew everyone's attention back to his current invention and continued. "The moment of greatest achievement has finally arrived." He proceeded to demonstrate. "This is what I call a taffy puller," he explained. "It's easy to use. All you do is wrap the taffy mixture around these paddles here, like this." He pulled a mass of sticky, boiled sugar out of a bowl and demonstrated. "Ladies and gentlemen," he said, "you are about to witness candy-making history." He then turned the crank.

The glossy ribbon of sugar twisted and turned.

Kate clapped her hands. "Oh, Harvey, that's amazing. That'll save us so much time."

Even Aunt Letty seemed impressed. "I'll say."

Looking pleased, Harvey turned the crank faster.

A strand of taffy broke loose and flew across the shop, hitting the dressmaker square in the face. All heads swiveled in her direction and, for a long moment, no one uttered a word.

Then all at once, the most amazing thing happened. The man who hadn't cracked a smile in all the years Kate had known him suddenly doubled over in laughter, tears running down his cheeks.

One by one, the others joined in until the shop rang out with howls of delight.

Aunt Letty rushed to the dressmaker's side, her eyes flashing angry sparks. "It's not funny!" she said, her sharp voice stifling all but a few titters. She tugged on Mrs. Cuttwell's arm. "Come on, Helen, let's get you cleaned up." She coaxed her nemesis around the counter and into the kitchen.

Looking sheepish, Harvey gathered up his machine. "Back to the drawing board," he said with a nervous titter. With that, he slithered out of the shop.

Kate waited for the others to leave before dropping on hands and knees to scrape the taffy off the floor.

She was still on bent knees when her aunt walked out of the kitchen, her voice preceding her. "Oh good, they're gone."

Kate stood. "Where's Mrs. Cuttwell?"

"She snuck out the back, poor woman."

Kate raised an eyebrow. *Poor woman?* She wrapped the glob of taffy in paper and dumped it into the wastepaper basket. "That was a very kind thing you did. Can I assume that the two of you have put your differences aside?"

When her aunt said nothing, Kate studied her vacant expression. "Aunt Letty?"

This time her aunt jumped. "Hmm?"

"I said that was a kind thing you did. Taking care of Mrs. Cuttwell like that. I know she's not your favorite person." When her aunt failed to respond yet a second time, Kate joined her behind the counter. "Is something wrong?"

"I was just thinking about Priscilla Manning."

Kate arched an eyebrow. "What about her?"

"Remember how she told us she had a terrible premonition that something awful was going to happen? Then a day later, a blue norther blew down her house."

"That happened years ago, Aunt Letty. Why are you thinking about it now?"

"I have a similar feeling."

Kate glanced out the window at the clear blue sky. "You think our house is going to blow down?"

"No, no, no. This has nothing to do with the house. It's about the man who knocked me down at the bank. Remember I told you I heard his keys rattle?"

Kate nodded. "Yes."

"I heard those same keys today. Here in the shop."

Foster gaped at Brett and waved the stitching awl in his hand. "Shakespeare? Is that what you said? Man alive, you're out of your cotton-pickin' mind!"

Brett grunted. No truer words had ever been spoken. Ever since he and Kate had kissed, he'd been half out of his mind with crazy thoughts. Thoughts he had no business entertaining. Thoughts that were tying him up in knots.

As a ranger, he needed a clear, focused mind. That's how crimes got solved. The muddled mess inside his head was not helping. His thoughts were as jumbled as straw in a mattress. If Foster One got away this time, Brett would have only himself to blame.

As for Shakespeare, he'd known it wouldn't be an easy idea to sell. Nothing with Foster Two ever was.

"Kate likes Shakespeare." At least Brett assumed she did based on the number of Shakespeare's quotes on her store walls. "You need to come up with a way to make up for the mess you made last week. Taking her to Austin to see one of his plays is just the thing."

"Mess?" Foster slammed the awl on his workbench. "Everything was going just fine and dandy until that blasted calf showed up. You're the one who suggested I take Kate for a ride by the river."

"Okay, so things didn't go as planned," Brett conceded.

He had no desire to argue. There was too much work left to be done. His latest plan to catch the Ghost Riders had to be foremost in his mind. That's all he could think about now. Nothing could be left to chance.

He'd purposely avoided the candy shop these past couple of days, as much for Kate's sake as for his own. He'd told himself that nothing had changed after their kiss, but that wasn't true. Their kiss hadn't just left its mark; it had been a source of guilt, not just for him, but for her as well. He'd witnessed it in her eyes, heard it in her voice, and for that he felt bad. Really bad. Obviously, she still had feelings for Foster and was just as anxious as he was to forget what had happened.

"Tell me, Foster. Do you love her?" The question was not his to ask, but he had to know the depth of Foster's feelings. Had to know that bringing them together really was the right thing to do.

"What?"

"I said, do you love her?" *Do you dream of her at night? Do you ache to hold her in your arms? Does each second away from her seem like hours?*

Foster frowned. "What kind of question is that? 'Course I do. Do you think I'd go to all this trouble if I didn't?"

Brett sucked in his breath. "What about Kate?"

He hated himself for asking. Hated himself for hoping the question brought doubt to Foster's eyes. The Tucker blood ran thick through his veins, and he was no better than his brother. God help him. "Is there any doubt that she might not share your feelings?"

Foster looked affronted. "She's got as many locks on her heart as she has in her hair, but that's about to change. After what happened with that cow, she's been real nice to me."

"All right then, so what's the problem?"

"I have a business to run," Foster said, indicating the still-unfinished saddle. "I can't just close up shop."

"It's only for a day. And it's time to put your ring back on her finger where it belongs."

He couldn't tell Foster that the real reason he wanted Kate out of town was so she would be safe. If one or more of the Ghost Riders got wind that she had played a part in trapping them, there was no telling what might happen.

"A day in Austin should do the trick."

Foster didn't look convinced. "It sounds like another one of your harebrained schemes."

"Trust me on this, it's not."

"Trust you!" Foster's lip curled. "Kiss her till dawn, you said. Heck, after rescuing that blasted calf, I couldn't even get near Kate with my swollen face, let alone kiss her."

A pain shot through Brett's middle. Foster would have to mention kissing her. He cleared his throat. "There are no cows in a Shakespearean play."

"That doesn't mean the plays don't stink!"

"Come on, Foster. Think about it. Kate likes the Bard. She even adds his quotes to the candy she sells."

Foster scoffed. "Easier to quote Shakespeare than to sit through one of his plays."

"Trust me, it'll be the perfect day."

"Yeah, like the drive by the river was supposed to be perfect. Like the dinner at the hotel was supposed to be perfect. Like—"

"This time will be different, I swear. You take the train to Austin. Go to the theater. On the train ride back, just as the sun is setting in the west, you propose. No cows. Guaranteed."

Foster scowled. "What's with you and the sun?"

Brett's casual shrug belied the seriousness of his thoughts. He couldn't admit the truth. That the golden rays of the sun set Kate's hair on fire and made her eyes sparkle like blue glass. Nor dare he say how the sun's warmth was a reminder of her brilliant smile.

"The sun stands for…consistency, like love."

How he came up with that explanation on such short notice, he had no idea. But it did the trick. The stubborn look on Foster's face was now tempered with hope.

"You think this plan will work?"

"Of course it will work. Just act like you're enjoying the play. It's a comedy, so laugh when others laugh and clap when they do."

Foster still didn't look fully convinced. "I don't know…"

"Kate will love it. You know she will. And what better way to prove that you're a changed man?"

He felt bad for forcing Foster into something he didn't want to do, but it was for his own good. With a little luck, the plan to capture the Ghost Riders would succeed, but there was always the possibility that something could go wrong, prolonging Brett's time in Haywire.

When Kate returned from Austin, the ring had better be on her finger. Because if it wasn't, there was no telling how much longer he could keep his feelings to himself.

"You can do it," he said. "Shakespeare is a small price to pay for spending the day with the woman I… uh…you love." He hated pleading with the man, but desperate times called for desperate measures.

When Foster still hesitated, Brett sighed with impatience. "Come on, Foster. Think about it. A whole day alone with Kate." He spaced each word for emphasis. "What could possibly go wrong?"

24

Spending time locked up in an underground cavern with the sheriff was Brett's idea of hell, but he was determined to make the best of it.

That was more than the sheriff tried to do. Instead, Keeler spent his time pacing the cavern and staring daggers at him.

"So, where are they?" he asked for perhaps the hundredth time in the last two hours.

Seated on the ground, Brett held his pocket watch close to the lantern light and checked the time. It was just a little after one p.m. "The stage should be arriving any minute now."

That meant that in less than an hour, this should all be over and the Ghost Riders would be wearing steel bracelets. He hoped and prayed that Foster One was among them.

The scene was set. Deputy Sweeney was now in position. His job was to give chase. Once the Ghost Riders entered the underground cave, Brett and the sheriff would take over. Brett anticipated no problems. The element of surprise was on their side.

The hardest part was waiting. Not only did he have to ignore the sheriff's caustic remarks, but he also had to keep pulling his thoughts away from Kate. Even in the dark gloom, he could picture her big, blue eyes and brilliant smile. At times, he even imagined her laughter and visualized the way she…

He groaned inwardly. *Oh, no, you don't. You're not going there. Never again.*

It was over. Whatever hold she had on him had to stop. By now, she and Foster should be at the theater. If Foster played his part as they'd rehearsed, Kate would soon be wearing his ring.

Over.

Grimacing, Brett shifted his weight. The ground was hard and seemed to grow harder with each passing moment.

The sheriff continued pacing. "What if they don't show?"

"They'll show," Brett said, sounding more confident than he felt.

This time, the sheriff stopped pacing, a derisive look on his face. "And if they don't?"

"Then we have a problem."

The sheriff's eyes filled with contempt. "What's that supposed to mean?"

"It means our plan wasn't as foolproof as we thought." Brett let that sink in a moment before adding, "You sure the telegraph sent to the express company was in code?"

"'Course I'm sure. What do you think I am? An idiot?"

"Okay, then. There's no way that the Ghost Riders

can suspect a trap." Even the stagecoach driver didn't know that the strongbox he was transporting was filled with rocks instead of gold coins. "Only you, me, and Sweeney know the full plan. If something goes wrong…"

The sheriff narrowed his eyes. "Go on."

"Then one of us had to have spilled the beans. And I know it wasn't me."

"Are you suggesting that I—?"

Brett shrugged. "It had crossed my mind."

Keeler frowned. "Had?"

"The other day when I told you to meet me here at this cavern, I found you wandering around looking for it. You had no idea where this hideout was. That seems to put you in the clear."

Keeler greeted this news with a tight-lipped smile that failed to reach his eyes. "You aren't suggesting that Sweeney—"

"You trust him?"

"Yeah, I trust him."

Since they depended on Sweeney for backup, trust was good. "Okay then. We have nothing to worry about."

The sheriff continued his pacing. After a long silence, he said, "I still think we should have tried to capture them during the actual robbery."

"It's easier this way," Brett said. "And a whole lot safer." This way, there was little chance of any passengers getting hurt.

He checked his watch again. If his calculations were right, three or maybe even four horsemen should come sweeping down the ramp in less than twenty minutes.

Kate boarded the homebound train from Austin ahead of Frank. Knowing how much he liked sitting next to the window, she chose the aisle seat. As much as she'd enjoyed the play, she was happy they were heading home.

She'd been frantic all day with worry, though she'd done her best to hide it from Frank.

If things had gone as planned, the Ghost Riders could very well be behind bars right now, and the citizens of Haywire would once again be able to rest easy.

She chewed on a nail. But what if something had gone wrong? Brett and the sheriff weren't on the best of terms. And what if the Ghost Riders suspected a trap?

She prayed now as she'd prayed all day. *Oh God, please keep Brett safe.*

"Whew," Frank said after settling in his seat and adjusting the window shade. "I thought all those curtain calls would make us miss the train."

"See? I told you not to worry. We made it with time to spare."

Resting her head on the back of her seat, she closed her eyes. It had been an excellent production of *A Midsummer Night's Dream,* the best she'd ever seen, and some of her favorite quotes from the play were still ringing in her head. One line especially kept running through her mind: *The course of true love never did run smooth.* She let out a long sigh. No truer words had ever been spoken.

The whistle blew, startling her back to the present. The train rolled forward with a jerk before gradually picking up speed. Soon, the scenery whizzed by in a blur outside the dusty windows.

She nudged Frank's shoulder with the tip of her folded fan. "Thank you for everything," she said. It had been obvious how much Frank hated the play, but he'd been a good sport and hadn't complained. He'd even managed to laugh and clap at the right times, though she could tell his heart wasn't in it.

When he failed to respond, she asked, "You okay?" He'd hardly spoken a word since leaving the theater.

"Yeah, sure, I'm fine."

"It wasn't *too* awful for you? The play?"

"It was worth it, knowing how much you enjoyed it."

"I did enjoy it," she said, but the theme of appearances versus reality had hit close to home. As much as she'd enjoyed the play, it'd had an unsettling effect. She pulled her fan away and tucked it in her purse. "Lately, you've said the nicest things. It's almost as if…"

His gaze sharpened. "What?" he asked. "It's almost as if what?"

She tried putting her thoughts into words. "Like you're…two different people, and I don't know which one is real."

His eyebrows rose like half-moons. "I'm real," he said, pinching his arm through the sleeve of his shirt to demonstrate. "See?"

"You're completely missing the point," she said with a sigh.

"Don't you like this new me?" he asked.

"Yes, of course. But it takes some getting used to," she admitted.

She kept waiting for him to fall back into his old

ways, but he hadn't even gotten jealous when the conductor smiled at her. Or at least not that he'd let on. He'd simply shoved his hands in his pockets and whistled like he hadn't a care in the world. Though to be honest, his annoying new habit of whistling was beginning to get on her nerves.

Kate shifted her gaze to the window. She'd accused him of not trusting her; now she was the one unable to trust him—or at least the *new* him—and for that, she felt bad.

They rode in silence for several minutes, each lost in their own thoughts. Next to her, Frank kept checking his watch.

The crimson sun slowly sank, staining the western sky a vivid red. Shadows yawned and stretched over hill and dale. Frank seemed to grow more restless with each passing moment. He jiggled his leg, tapped his fingers on the armrest, and kept looking out the window.

The gentle motion of the train had put the baby across the aisle to sleep on her mother's lap. Now, the only sounds were the murmur of low voices and the *clickety-clack* of train wheels against iron rails.

Kate's eyes drifted downward. She was about to sink into slumber when something startled her. Her eyes flew open. Much to her surprise, Frank had left his seat and was kneeling on the floor in front of her, a serious look on his face.

Thinking something was wrong, she sat forward. "Frank, what is it?"

Seeing the ring in his hand, her mouth dropped open. Was he really going to propose to her here? On a crowded train?

Glancing at the other passengers, she whispered, "Frank, I don't think this is a good idea." She wasn't even sure she was ready to give him an answer. At least not the one he obviously expected.

Ignoring her concerns, he pulled off his hat and set it on his empty seat. "Katie…" He cleared his throat and pulled a scrap of paper from his shirt pocket. He quickly scanned it before beginning again.

"Katherine Anne Denver," he began, surprising her. She couldn't remember him ever saying her full name.

Looking as serious as an old cat, he continued, "I love everything about you. I love the way you smile, the way you make me smile. I love the kindness you show to others—"

Touched by his words, Kate covered her mouth with her hand and gazed at him through misty eyes.

Frank's eyes widened in alarm. "What's wrong?"

"Nothing, it's just"—she brushed away her tears—"you've never said anything that nice to me before."

He jerked his head back. "Sure, I have. What about the time you changed the wagon wheel? I told you that a man couldn't have done it any quicker."

"Well, yes, there was that."

"And I praised you to high heaven when you caught that twelve-pound bass."

"Yes, yes, you did."

"And don't forget how I complimented you for winning the yodeling contest at last year's county fair."

She leaned forward. "What I meant to say is that I didn't expect you to say such nice things here. On the train."

He pulled out his handkerchief and mopped his brow. "Is it okay if I continue?"

"Well..." She glanced around, but the other passengers were either sleeping or had their heads buried behind newspapers. She looked back at him. He looked so earnest, so hopeful, that she didn't have the heart to tell him no. Yet neither could she tell him yes. Not while the memory of another man's kiss was still so fresh in her mind.

Evidently taking her silence as acquiescence, Frank replaced his handkerchief and studied the scrap of paper in his hand. "Katherine Anne Denver, I love..."

Kate listened in disbelief as Frank cited everything about her from her hair to the way she wrinkled her nose. Never had she imagined that he could be so sensitive. He made her brassy-red hair sound like gold, and her freckles... Oh my, he even had something nice to say about those.

How could she not have known that he thought this deeply? Cared this much. "Oh, Frank," she whispered.

"Wait. I'm not done yet." He held up the ring. The setting sun turned the diamond into a flash of white fire.

"Katie. I mean Katherine Anne Denver..."

Someone shouted, drowning out his next words. Kate craned her neck to see over the heads of the other passengers. At first, she didn't see anything, but then everything changed. Three men with flour sacks over their heads ran down the aisle, brandishing guns.

Watching in horror, Kate drew back, hand on her mouth. Still kneeling in front of her, Frank asked what was wrong, but before she could answer, one of the bandits stopped by her seat. He pointed his weapon straight at Frank's head.

Kate gasped, and a shiver of panic raced through her. "Oh, please, don't hurt him!"

"I'll take that," the bandit said, voice muffled, and just like that, he snatched the diamond ring clear out of Frank's hand.

25

NEWS OF THE TRAIN ROBBERY RACED THROUGH TOWN like wildfire. It reached Brett as he was having supper at the boardinghouse where he was staying.

One of the other boarders had burst into the house yelling, "The train has been robbed."

The words were hardly out of the man's mouth before Brett was on his feet. He shot up with such force that his chair went flying across the floor.

Not wanting to take the time to saddle his horse, he ran the half mile to the train station.

He had been so certain—so absolutely certain—that his trap would work. He and Sheriff Keeler had stayed hidden in the underground cavern nearly all afternoon waiting for the Ghost Riders, but they'd failed to show.

Instead, Sweeney arrived by his lonesome with the unwelcomed news that the stage had reached town unmolested.

Now more bad news. Something had gone terribly wrong. Was Kate all right? Why had he talked Foster into taking her to Austin? It had never occurred to him that the trip would place her right in the heart of danger. That his carefully laid plans would go astray.

He reached the train station out of breath. Others had raced to the station upon hearing the news, and mass confusion reigned. The sheriff and his deputy had already arrived, and everyone was talking at once.

"Plumb stole my watch," a male passenger yelled.

Not to be outdone, a woman shouted, "That's nothing. They stole my purse."

Brett almost bumped into Lucky Lou. For once, he didn't have his dog. "Have you seen Kate?" Brett asked.

"No, can't say that I have. Was she on the train?"

"Yes, yes, she was." Or at least she would have been had Foster played his cards right.

With growing anxiety, Brett moved through the crowd. At last, he spotted Kate, and relief washed over him like a tidal wave. At that moment, it seemed that no one else existed. Elbowing his way to her side, he unthinkingly took her by the arm.

"Are you all right?"

She whirled about, startled. "Oh, Brett, it's you. Yes, yes, I'm fine. We both are."

Drawing a blank, he released her, and only then did his brain begin to function. "Oh, you mean Foster. What happened?"

She gazed at him with quivering lips, her blue traveling suit emphasizing the color of her eyes. "Oh, Brett, I was so afraid. A man held a gun to Frank's head." Her voice wavered as she spoke, and she looked like she was on the verge of tears. As she recounted the chain of events, her expression reflected horror and disbelief.

Taking her hands in both of his, Brett squeezed them tight. "You're safe now," he said. "I won't let anyone hurt you."

He heard her intake of air. "Frank too," she said, beseeching him. "Please, don't let anyone hurt him either."

"I…I won't."

"Had something happened to him…" She shook her head. "I can't bear to think about it."

Brett watched her intently as she spoke. If he hadn't known it before, he knew it now. Kate's feelings for Foster ran deep. He could see it in her eyes, her face, hear it in the tremble of her voice.

Not wanting to dwell on how he felt about that, he got down to business. "Was it the Ghost Riders? Were they the ones who robbed the train?" He already suspected the answer, but he needed confirmation.

"Looked like it," she said. Her forehead creased. "There were three men, and they wore flour sacks over their heads. And one of them was shot."

"Shot?"

She nodded. "Somehow they got the train to stop before reaching town. As they were making their escape, a passenger pulled out a gun and fired out the window. I saw one of the bandits grab his shoulder and fall to his knees."

That was encouraging news. In a town this size, it shouldn't be that hard to find an injured man. "What happened then?"

"I don't know. The train took off."

With a jolt, Brett realized he was still holding her hands. That's because he had suddenly noticed her ringless finger. Releasing her, he glanced around at the still-milling crowd.

"Where's Foster?"

"He's talking to the sheriff." Kate's gaze softened, and she touched his arm. "I don't understand, Brett. Why would they hold up the train?"

He grimaced. He'd told her some of the plan, but not all. "Somehow they must have found out that the gold was not on the stage. We made a last-minute switch to the train."

Her eyes softened in sympathy. "That means your plan didn't work."

He drew in his breath. The feel of her hand threatened to burn a hole through his sleeve. Her touch was pure torture, and the only way he could think straight was to pull his arm away.

Through the crowd, Brett spotted the sheriff talking to Lucky Lou and Hoot Owl Pete while Deputy Sweeney questioned a woman holding an infant.

He'd previously discounted the idea that the sheriff or his deputy was involved, but now he had second thoughts. Only the three of them had known that the shipment of gold had been sent on a circuitous route to Haywire by train. That certainly pointed the finger of suspicion at the two lawmen. One or even both of them could very well be a Ghost Rider. But how was that possible?

The sheriff had been with him all day, and the deputy's whereabouts were accounted for. How could Keeler and Sweeney be in two places at once?

But if it wasn't them, who else knew of the switch?

Dear God, who else?

26

After tossing and turning all night, Kate rose just as the silver fingers of dawn crept along her windowsill. Already, the air blowing through her open window was warm, promising another hot day. It felt more like summer than spring.

She quickly dressed, and after fixing herself a hasty breakfast of coffee, cold bread, and jam, she headed for the shop. Instead of waiting to ride to town with her aunt, she walked the mile, hoping to clear her head.

It wasn't just the holdup that had been on her mind all night; it was Frank.

Dear, sweet Frank. She still couldn't believe the nice things he'd said. He'd touched her deeply, maybe more deeply than he ever had.

So why the confusion? It wasn't like her not to know her own mind, but her emotions were so tied up in knots that she couldn't begin to unravel them.

Frank had been about to propose. He'd been on his knees, ring in hand. Had it not been for the holdup, he would have asked her to marry him, and she had no idea how she would have answered him.

It was true he had changed. She'd had to keep blinking to make sure it really was him and not another man who had taken over his body. He'd been so sweet and thoughtful in recent weeks and seemed to have his jealousy under control. There really wasn't any reason not to marry him. What woman wouldn't want a husband like him? The mind was certainly willing, but the heart held back, and she had no idea why.

Was it Brett Tucker? No, no, no, that wasn't it. There was no denying that she found him attractive. What woman wouldn't? The combination of blond hair, blue eyes, and winning smile made him the most attractive man she had ever set eyes on. But that didn't make him suitable as a husband.

In any case, he wasn't interested in her. He wouldn't be so eager to leave town if he were. At heart, he was a roamer and had even said as much. Men like him could never settle down. He'd also made it clear how much he regretted his part in stopping her wedding.

He never missed a chance to put in a good word for Frank and try to convince her to take him back. He'd also told her in every way possible that their kiss had meant nothing and would never happen again. What more proof could she possibly want?

Maybe knowing that he wasn't interested—knowing he was out of bounds, knowing that he would soon leave Haywire behind—maybe that's what made him so attractive. Wasn't it the forbidden fruit that people found most tempting? Every day, she watched her customers try to resist the mouthwatering display of confections in her shop. Few, if any, succeeded.

So, was that the answer? Was knowing that Brett was out of reach the real attraction?

Whatever the reason, she owed it to Frank to be honest with him. It wasn't fair to let him go on thinking things could go back to the way they were before their disastrous wedding. She loved Frank, she did, but not in the way he deserved to be loved. She knew that now. The question was what to do about it.

Pushing her thoughts aside, she inhaled the fresh morning air. Since it was still early, the town was relatively quiet. She waved at Old Man Gordon, who was erecting a sign in front of the general store announcing that day's specials. Already, Hoot Owl Pete had taken up residence in front of the shop, next to the carefully arranged pyramid of plump peaches.

The window of Frank's saddle and leather shop still displayed a closed sign. From the door of the boot and shoemaker shop, Shoe-Fly Jones waved, and she waved back. The tantalizing scent of fresh bread wafted from the bakery, and two horses were already tethered in front of the Feedbag Café.

Arriving at her own shop, she turned the key in the lock and entered. The sweet smell of caramel and cinnamon greeted her like an old friend. Today, she would master her uncle's recipe if it killed her. Losing herself to the task of candy making was the only way to take her mind off things she'd rather not think about.

Donning her apron, she immediately set to work. Tossing sugar and water into the large copper pot, she placed it on the stove and stirred the mixture with a wooden paddle until the sugar reached the hard crack state.

No sooner had she poured the mass onto the cold slab and set it aside to cool than her aunt entered the kitchen, complaining about the high price of molasses. "Sixty-seven cents a gallon, can you believe it?" Dumping her bag on the counter by the sink, she glanced at the white, misshapen glob on the counter and shook her head.

"Land sakes, I should have known. You're at it again. Whenever something happens to you, out comes your uncle's hard candy recipe."

Kate poked a finger into the sugary mass to see if it was cool enough to pull. "Uncle Joe said that only a true artisan can make this right."

Aunt Letty rolled her eyes. "There's no money in that. It takes too long to make. You can make a week's supply of toffee in the time it takes to make a small batch of that stuff."

"This isn't about money," Kate said. "It's about art."

Aunt Letty shook her head. She was far too practical to worry about art. In that regard, Kate took after her uncle.

Transferring the sugar mixture to a heated plank to keep it pliable, Kate pinched out a strand and blocked out the design, using a strip of green dough. Later, she hoped to master a more complex design, but for now she would keep it simple. She wrapped the strand in a length of white sugar mixture. To this, she added a layer of red and rolled the mass into a strip several inches thick.

She stretched and pulled at the strips until at last she had a thin, narrow rope. She then cut off an inch. Holding her breath, she picked up the piece and yelped with joy. "Look! I did it, I did it!"

Dancing around the room, she held the piece so that her aunt could see the design in the center.

Her aunt's eyes narrowed. "What is it?"

"What? Oh, it's a leaf."

"It looks like a vase."

Kate examined the piece in her fingers and turned it. "That's because you were looking at it upside down."

Aunt Letty squinted for a closer look. "A leaf, eh?"

Kate shrugged. "Okay, the design still needs work. But it's a start."

"Yes, it is." Aunt Letty shook her head, but she looked pleased. "If I didn't know better, I'd say that you and your uncle were blood relatives."

At the mention of her dear adoptive uncle, Kate sighed. "I just wish he were here."

Her aunt's face softened. "I have a feeling he's looking down on us this very minute."

Kate set the piece on a plate. "And probably laughing at my leaf."

"Vase," Aunt Letty said, and they both laughed.

"Oh my, look at the time," her aunt exclaimed. "I'll open the shop while you finish up here."

By the time Kate had cut up the rest of the candy and cleaned the kitchen, the store was filled with customers. Unfortunately, Kate's candy got nowhere near as much attention as yesterday's train robbery.

Brett walked in, and Kate's heart skipped a beat.

"Just wanted to make sure you're okay," he said.

Touched by his concern, she drew in her breath. "Thank you, I'm fine." The candy shop was her refuge, and no matter what happened, she always found comfort there.

Lucky Lou pulled his dog away from the display case and tutted. "Honestly, I don't know what the world is coming to. It's getting so you can't leave the house for fear of being robbed."

"Ah, but I have just the solution for that," Harvey Wells said and held up what looked like a woman's purse. He waited until he had everyone's attention. "Let's say you're out shopping. Suddenly, a man comes up to you and points a gun at your head." He indicated that with a pointed finger to his temple.

A couple of women gasped and, reminded of the holdup, Kate ran her hands up and down her arms.

"Ah, but not to fear, ladies," Harvey said in his best peddler voice. "When he tells you to hand over your purse, simply pull the string that's attached to the handle, and there you have it!" He yanked on the string and the bottom of the purse opened, allowing the contents to drop to the floor. "The thief won't want to stick around long enough to pick things off the ground. He'll take off, and your valuables will be safe."

As he was explaining his invention, Ringo pulled his leash out of Lucky Lou's hand, snatched the roll of money that had fallen from the purse, and ran.

"Hey, come back with that!" Harvey yelled.

Lucky Lou and the other men tried to corner the dog, but when another customer walked into the shop, Ringo escaped through the open door.

Harvey chased the dog outside, waving his hands and yelling at the top of his lungs, "Stop, thief!" The other customers spilled out of the shop like ants scrambling out of a nest, all of them shouting. Even Aunt Letty joined the pursuit.

Kate burst into laughter. She couldn't help it. All those people running after a single dog was just too funny for words. Brett, however, didn't seem to see the humor. Instead, he stood watching Lucky Lou through the window.

"What's he doing?" he asked.

Kate walked around the counter to join him. "He's trying to call Ringo back. That's a dog whistle he's blowing."

"Dog whistle?"

"It's another one of Harvey's inventions," she said. "But this one seems to work."

"Work how?"

"Harvey said that dogs can hear the high-pitched sound, even though we can't."

Brett met her gaze, a faint light twinkling in their depths. "You mean Wells actually came up with an invention that works?"

"Hard to believe, isn't it?" Kate bent over to pick up the keys and other things that had fallen out of Harvey's purse. "Of course, it wasn't his idea," she added, placing the objects on the counter. "But the original whistle is too bulky to carry around. Harvey took that same idea and created a whistle that fits in a pocket."

Just then, Ringo returned. Tail wagging, the dog bounced around the wooden sidewalk before standing on hind legs to greet his owner.

"See?" Kate said. "Works every time."

But Brett was no longer watching Harvey; his gaze was fixed solely on her.

"Kate…" He cleared his throat. "I'm sorry for putting you in danger. I would never have suggested

Foster take you to Austin if I thought something would happen."

She blinked. "It was your idea?"

A pained expression crossed his face. "I wanted you out of town. I worried that the Ghost Riders would figure out the part you'd played in their capture. I also knew that Foster planned to propose. It seemed like a good idea on both accounts." He splayed his hands. "I'm sorry it didn't work out."

She stared at him. He had known Frank would propose? Fighting the hurt inside, she lashed out. "Oh, I'm sure you are. Then you would no longer have to feel guilty for breaking us up!"

Leaning back as if he'd been slapped, he gave her a puzzled look. "I…I thought that's what you wanted. You and Foster."

For some reason, she couldn't admit to having feelings for a man who didn't return the favor. Maybe it was pride. Or maybe she was simply trying to protect herself. In any case, she hid her true feelings behind a mask of indifference.

"Of course it's what we want," she said, the words feeling like acid on her lips.

Before Brett could respond, the door to the shop flew open, and Aunt Letty returned, shaking her head. "That darn dog's back, but we don't know what he did with the money."

Kate struggled for control. "Oh dear."

Brett backed toward the door. "I…I better be going." Bidding her aunt a brusque goodbye, he left.

Aunt Letty studied Kate with a suspicious gleam in her eyes. "Did I interrupt something?"

."What?"

"You and the cowboy looked mighty serious when I walked in. Did I interrupt something?"

Kate glanced out the window, but Brett had already vanished from sight. Ignoring the squeezing pain inside, she shook her head. "No, not a thing."

✤

After shooting out of the candy shop like a rattler out of a box, Brett headed for Foster's Saddle and Leather Shop.

He'd been so close, so very, very close, to asking Kate if she really meant what she'd said about wanting to marry Foster. Had her aunt not walked in, he would have done just that.

Did she love him with her whole heart and soul? Did she count the days, the minutes, the seconds until Foster's ring would be back on her finger? Did she want to spend the rest of her life as Mrs. Frank Foster?

Foster was convinced that she did. Had told Brett as much.

But sometimes when Brett looked deep into her eyes, he could swear he saw flames of desire directed at him. He even caught glimpses of what looked suspiciously like the stirrings of something deeper for him and him alone.

Was it only wishful thinking on his part? Was he only seeing what he wanted to see? Probably.

Thank God, her aunt had arrived in time. She'd saved him from being a bigger fool than he already was. But he still wasn't out of danger. Not yet.

Foster had sent a note to the boardinghouse saying

he wanted to see him. He'd made it sound urgent. Brett walked up the steps of the boardwalk. It'd better be about the train robbery. Maybe Foster had recalled some vital clue. Just don't let it be about Kate.

Any hope that Foster had summoned him to talk about the holdup died the moment Brett walked through the door. Foster greeted him with a wild look, waving his arms like a madman.

"Take her to a play, you said. Propose to her as the sun goes done, you said." Foster's eyes blazed with fury. "What could possibly go wrong?"

"Okay, now calm down—"

"Calm down!" Foster stared at him from behind a half-finished saddle. He didn't have any welts or spots, but his face was purple with rage. "Is that all you can say? Don't you understand? They stole my ring."

"So you said." Brett rubbed the back of his neck and tried to think. "You have the worst luck of anyone I've ever known."

"Yeah, and it all started the day you blew into town. That's it. I'm not listening to you anymore." He motioned with his hand. "We're done. Finished."

Brett couldn't blame him for feeling as he did. Not one bit. He had made a mess of things. But stopping Foster's wedding was the least of it. Brett's feelings for Kate had now reached mammoth proportions. He'd tried fighting them, ignoring them, and denying them, but it was no use.

He lowered his voice, hoping Foster would do likewise. "Okay, forget the ring for a second. Do you think Kate was going to...you know...say yes?"

Foster looked at him as if he were out of his mind.

"Of course she would have said yes. How could she not? I sat through the worst jibber-jabber known to mankind." He raised his eyes to the ceiling. "If I never hear another word of Shakespeare, it will be too soon."

Brett's spirits sank. He hated the part of him that wanted—hoped—to hear doubt in Foster's voice. See doubt on his face. In his eyes. Instead, Foster sounded completely confident. "Are...are you sure?"

"Sure, I'm sure. A man knows these things. Had it not been for the holdup—"

"I know, I know." Brett rubbed his head. Was it possible to feel any worse? Any lower as a human being? Any more disgusted with himself for wanting Kate to himself?

Foster let out a long moan. "I can't propose till I order a new ring." He tossed a nod at the mail-order catalog on the counter. "And that could take weeks."

Brett picked up the catalog and thumbed through the pages. Something tiptoed on the edge of his consciousness, a memory that continued to tease even as it refused to materialize.

Shrugging the thought away, he studied each ring in turn. Solitary diamond rings were interspersed with elaborate filigree rings embedded with rubies, emeralds, and sapphires. It wasn't hard to envision how each ring would look on Kate's dainty hand. One particular ring caught his attention. The rose-gold ring held a solitary diamond surrounded by little pieces of sapphire the exact color of Kate's eyes.

Brett abruptly closed the catalog and tossed it aside. The last thing he wanted was to help Foster pick out a ring for Kate. He pulled out his money clip and peeled off several bills.

"Here." He slapped the money on the counter.

Foster frowned. "What's that for?"

"I'm partly to blame for the theft of the ring. The least I can do is help you pay for a new one." With that, he stalked out of the shop.

He'd hoped that paying for the ring would relieve him of his responsibility and he could put the matter out of his mind. But the truth was, it only made matters worse. For now, he would have to live with the fact that he had helped pay to put another man's ring on Kate's finger.

27

Kate took a big breath and walked into Frank's leather shop with a feeling of dread. It was late, and most of the other shops in town were closed.

Frank looked up as she entered and quickly walked around the counter to greet her. "Katie. I didn't expect to see you tonight."

Kate moistened her lips. "We need to talk."

He frowned. "Are you okay? You're not still upset over what happened on the train, are you? The ring…"

"That's what I need to talk to you about." She hesitated. The words she'd rehearsed all day now seemed inadequate. Cold, even. Still, beating around the bush wouldn't do either of them any good.

"I…I don't think we should get married, Frank."

The words hung between them for a moment before Frank jerked back as if she'd slapped him. "What are you saying?"

She sighed. "Frank, I love you. You're a good friend. But I'm not sure that what we have is…real enough for marriage."

His eyes widened. "How can you say that? Is…is it because of my jealousy?"

She shook her head. "That no longer seems to be a problem."

He brightened. "See? I can change. I am changing."

"I know, Frank, and I appreciate how hard you've been trying. But—"

He took both her hands in his. "I know what the problem is."

Her eyes widened. "You do?"

"I've been rushing you. You've had two run-ins with the Ghost Riders, and your aunt was knocked down by one. You're upset. Who can blame you? No wonder your head's messed up."

Kate drew in her breath. Frank spoke the truth. Things had been crazy of late, and her nerves were still in a jangle. Maybe she wasn't thinking right.

"Give me another chance, Kate. Things were good between us before, and they can be good again. Please, say you will. I swear you won't be sorry."

She pulled her hands away. "Frank, listen to me—"

"A month. That's all I'm askin' for. No, make it sixty days. By then, if you'd have forgotten about the train robbery and—"

"I'll never forget the train robbery!"

"Maybe not, but at least you'll be able to think clearer. Just give me till…till July…to the Independence Day dance to prove that what we have is real." When she hesitated, he added, "I'll bet you'll feel a whole lot different by then."

"I-I don't know…"

"Ah, come on, Katie. What can it hurt to take more

time to think about this? I'll do anything you want me to. Just tell me."

Frank looked so desperate to please that Kate felt her resolve crumble. "I don't know that sixty days will make all that much difference."

"I'll take my chances."

"All right," she said, though everything inside her screamed no. "Sixty days. But I don't want you getting your hopes up."

A look of relief crossed his face and, like the Frank of old, he grabbed her hand and shook it as if pumping water from a well. "You won't be sorry, Kate."

She pulled her hand away. "Frank, I can't promise."

"I know, I know." He studied her with knitted brow. "Could we not tell anyone that things are still up in the air between us? If your aunt gets wind of this, you know she'll interfere. She means well, but somehow she always makes things worse."

As much as she loved her aunt, Kate knew he spoke the truth. Though in the case of marriage, Aunt Letty always took Frank's side. "I won't say anything."

Since there didn't seem to be anything more to be said, she pleaded exhaustion and left, her mind in a muddle.

Outside his shop, she took a gulp of the cool night air and tried to shake off her uneasy thoughts. Frank had asked her to wait till July before making a final decision, and that seemed reasonable enough. Still, pouring out her heart tonight had been hard. How much harder would it be two months from now should her feelings not change?

Last night's encounter with Frank was very much on Kate's mind the following morning as she prepared the last of the orders for delivery.

Loud voices from outside drew her gaze to the window. The bullies were at it again and now surrounded Dusty. As she watched, one of the boys shoved him, and her temper flared.

Wait till she got her hands on those hooligans! Just as she started for the door, she recalled something Uncle Joe had once said about catching more flies with sugar than vinegar. Stopping short of rushing out to the fray, she tried to think. Warning the boys hadn't worked in the past. Neither had talking to their parents. Maybe it was time to try her uncle's remedy.

She reached for the plate of candy she'd made that morning. So far, no one had appreciated the effort that had gone into adding a leaf to the center, but maybe not all was lost.

"Okay, Uncle Joe. We'll try it your way." Flinging the door open, she walked outside, forcing a smile. "Hello, gentlemen," she called, keeping her voice light and friendly.

The mocking voices stopped, and the boys turned to face her. The leader's name was Charley. Though only sixteen, he stood nearly six feet tall and was as thin as a broomstick. Next to him was his brother Bobby, younger by two years. The third boy was known simply as Spike, probably because of the way his cowlick stood straight up.

"Would you boys like to try some new candy? I just

made it this morning, and I'm calling them…Dusty…Dusty Drops."

Dusty's eyes widened. "Did you really name them after me?" he asked.

His enthusiastic response not only made her smile but gave her an idea on how to turn the bullies into Dusty's friends. "Absolutely," she said. "Try one."

The older boys glanced at one another before staring at the plate she held out to them.

Bobby was the first to reach for a candy. He studied the green design in the center of the creamy white filling. "What is that?" he asked.

Spike looked over Bobby's shoulder. "You dummy," he said. "Anyone can see it's a beetle."

"It's not a beetle," Dusty said, studying the candy in his hand. "It's a mushroom."

With a shrug of his shoulders, Bobby popped it into his mouth. "Hmm." He nodded. "S'good."

Encouraged by his approval, the other boys reached for a piece.

"How did you get the mushroom in the center?" Dusty asked.

She gave him a mysterious smile. "Oh, I can't tell you that. It's a trade secret. Do you like the name? I thought it would be fun to name my new candy after one of my friends. And that's you."

Dusty beamed. "I like it a lot," he said, popping the candy in his mouth.

"Here, have some more," Kate said. The boys didn't have to be asked twice. Each of them eagerly grabbed another piece.

"Next time, I want to put a different design in the

middle," she said. "Maybe a sailing ship or an animal. Of course, a new design will need a new name. What name should I use?" She pretended to think. "How about Charley Chunks or Bobby Bars?" She cast a glance at Spike. "Hmm. What do you think about... Sugar Spikes?"

Charley made a face. "That's dumb. Who ever heard of naming candy after people?"

"Why, it's done all the time," Kate assured him. "Mr. Whitman named his chocolate after himself. And overseas, there's a famous candy company named Cadbury, after its founder."

Spike's eyes shone with interest. "Okay, then, name it after me."

She studied him. "What design should I add?" she asked and brightened. "I know. You like to play baseball. What do you think about a ball or bat?" *Those designs should be easy enough to master.*

"I like it," Spike said and grinned. "I like it a lot!"

Bobby elbowed his friend. "Spike's a dumb name for a candy. A Bobby Bar sounds better."

"It's not how a name sounds," Kate said gently. "What matters is what people think when they hear it. The name Dusty, for example, makes me think of the person it's named after, and that makes me think of goodness. I just know that when I pop that candy into my mouth, it'll taste delicious."

The boys didn't say anything, but she had their attention. "I'll tell you what. I won't be making another batch until the end of the month. I'm making Dusty my official candy helper. And so it'll be up to him to name the next candy."

All three boys turned their attention to Dusty, but he was too busy watching Brett across the street to notice. "Hey, Mr. Ranger," he called before she could stop him. "Come and see what Miss Denver made."

"I'll be right there," Brett called back.

Kate swallowed hard. Oh no. She wasn't ready to face him. Not after their last conversation. Still, there was nothing she could do but make the best of it. "His name is Mr. Tucker," she said gently.

Brett put something in his horse's saddlebag and then darted across the street to join them.

Dusty held up a piece of candy in greeting. "Look, Mr. Tucker. They're called Dusty Drops. And they have a mushroom in the center, but Miss Denver won't tell us how it got there."

"It's a trade secret," Charley added. "But it's not a mushroom; it's a beetle."

Brett's gaze met Kate's. "Well, what do you know? A trade secret, eh?" He popped a piece in his mouth and gave it his full consideration. She distinctly remembered him sampling the same type of candy the day before and knew he was putting on a show for the boys. "Hmm, not bad."

Dusty looked pleased. "And I get to name the next candy."

"Choose me," the three boys said in unison.

"I'm the oldest," Charley said. "The candy should be named after me."

"Oh, you can't rush him," Kate cautioned. "Naming candy is a very important task. Only the most special people get to have a candy named after them. People who we don't want to forget and who we love or admire. So, you see? He'll have to think about it for a while."

Spike turned to Dusty. "Wanna play baseball?"

Dusty's face lit up. "Yeah!" he said, barely able to contain his excitement.

"Come on, then. You be the catcher."

The four of them ran off.

Brett helped himself to another Dusty Drop. "I have to say, taming those boys was a brilliant piece of work."

"I'm afraid I can't take all the credit," she said, blushing. "I got the idea from something my uncle once said."

He stared at the piece of candy in his hand.

"Is something wrong?" she asked.

"I was just thinking that the beetle, mushroom— whatever—actually looks like a key."

She frowned. "That's a funny-looking key," she said, trying not to take offense.

"I'm talking a telegraph key," he said. "See?"

He held it up in such a way that it did indeed look like a telegraph key. She sighed. "I meant it to be a leaf."

"A leaf?"

She shrugged. "What can I say? I'm a better candy maker than I am an artist."

"Well, if I'm right, you could add detective to your list of talents."

She angled her head. "What do you mean, detective?"

He gave her a heart-stopping smile. "Kate Denver, I do believe you helped me solve the Ghost Rider case. At least partially." Without explanation, he dashed across the street to his tethered horse, leaving her to watch him in bewilderment.

Brett woke that night with a start. Not only did he have the telegraph operator, Flash, on his mind, but he couldn't stop thinking about rings. Diamond rings. Engagement rings. Wedding rings.

Irritated at himself, he raised his head, slammed a fist into his pillow, and rolled over. It was no time to be thinking about rings. Or Kate. Definitely not Kate. That only took him to places of the heart where he didn't want to go.

It was far better, safer, and more productive to concentrate on his reason for coming to Haywire. He was getting closer to identifying the Ghost Riders and maybe even tracking down Foster One. He felt it in his bones.

And he had Kate to thank for that. The candy design sure had looked like a telegraph key, and that had gotten him thinking. Maybe he'd been wrong. Maybe someone else had known that the shipment of gold would be transported by train.

Maybe Flash had known.

The sheriff said he'd sent the telegram with transport instructions to Austin in cipher. But what if Flash had done more than tap out the message? What if he had decrypted it? It was possible. If he enjoyed riddles, he probably liked solving other puzzles. Deciphering secret messages was a popular pastime. Even Edgar Allan Poe was said to have enjoyed the challenge of cracking messages in code.

Flash was the right height to be a Ghost Rider, but so were most of the men in Haywire. And his candy of choice was licorice, not peppermint. Still…

Perhaps the most critical evidence was his work schedule. Flash hadn't worked the afternoon of the holdup, but coincidentally, Thursday was his normal day off. According to his landlady, Flash was a fairly new resident and had only moved into the boarding-house eight months ago. That was around the time the Ghost Riders had started operating in the county.

Oh yes, now that Brett had thought about it, there were reasons aplenty to suspect Flash. Still, suspicion wasn't proof, and he needed more. A lot more.

He tried thinking of the other clues he had, but his mind kept going back to rings. He was just about to banish the thought when something occurred to him.

Sitting up in bed, he scrubbed his face with his hands. *And he wore a ring.* That's what the boy, Dusty, had said. *And he wore a ring.*

And it had been on his pinkie finger.

Seeing Dusty yesterday must have triggered something in his subconscious. Brett hadn't given Dusty's observation a second thought before, but there was good reason for that. Pinkie rings weren't all that unusual. Probably half the men in town wore such rings. Often they were signet rings with a Masonic or Odd Fellows insignia, but the boy hadn't recalled any special design.

During the War Between the States, a soldier would sometimes wear his wife's ring, the small size necessitating the need to wear it on a pinkie.

He tried to think. Flash didn't wear a ring. At least not as far as Brett could recall. So where did that leave him? A pinkie ring, peppermint candy, and a scrap of paper in Kate's handwriting were all he had to show for nearly two months of work, and that sure in blazes wasn't much to go on.

He lay his head back on his pillow and stared up at the dark ceiling. He couldn't seem to get the ring out of his mind. None of the other witnesses had mentioned any such jewelry. Why was that?

Had the boy been mistaken or...?

His thoughts sifted through his mind like grains of sand. What if it hadn't been a ring the boy had spotted, but something else? But what? A key, maybe. Some people slipped a key ring over a finger, a temporary action that could explain why Dusty was the only one to have noticed it.

Brett groaned. Maybe he was just grasping at straws. Or perhaps he'd been going about this all wrong. The clues were there; he was sure of it. He just couldn't put them together.

He punched his pillow again and rolled over. He tried turning off his brain, but his mind refused to cooperate. Again, he ticked off the few clues he had: a pinkie ring, peppermint candy, and a handwritten fortune...

The ring haunted him for the rest of the night and all the following day. He'd left Haywire early that morning to check out the series of caves outside Barterville. The trip turned out to be a waste of time. Nothing in the caves indicated they had been used as a hideout. The cold ashes of a campfire could have been left by anyone.

Late that afternoon, he rode into the town of Barterville. After getting something to eat at the hotel, he stopped at the marshal's office. Unlike the reception he'd gotten from the sheriff of Haywire, Deputy Marshal Bradshaw looked pleased to see him.

An affable man with a deep voice and a balding head, the marshal invited him to sit. "What can I do for you?"

Brett stepped around the hound dog sleeping on the floor and seated himself in the ladder-back chair. "Just want to ask a couple of questions," he said. "Any leads to the bank holdup?"

"Not a one," Bradshaw said with a rueful shake of his head. "They blew up the safe, grabbed the money, and vanished"—he snapped his fingers—"just like that." The dog lifted his head. With a shake of his collar, he gave his owner a sleepy-eyed gaze and then rested his head on his crossed paws.

"What about you?" the marshal asked. "Any luck with the train robbery?"

Brett pulled his gaze away from the sleeping dog. "Not yet." He reached for the photograph in his vest pocket and slid it across the desk. "Do you recognize that man?"

The marshal picked up the photograph and studied it. "Can't say that I do. Who is he?"

"Don't know what he calls himself now, but he was using the name Frank Foster. I have reason to believe he's a member of the Ghost Riders."

"Is that so?" The marshal slid the photograph back to Brett. "What makes you think that?"

"A couple of years ago, there was a similar string of robberies in San Antone. The robberies stopped when Foster left town."

"And you think this same man is behind the hold-ups here in the county."

"If it's not the same man, then it's a copycat."

The marshal stroked his chin. "But you don't believe that, right?"

"Not for a second," Brett said, staring at the piece of string tied to the marshal's finger.

Bradshaw drew his hand away from his chin and held it out in front of himself. "Just a reminder to stop and get flowers for the wife's birthday."

"Yeah, you don't want to forget that," Brett said. For some reason, the string triggered a half-forgotten memory.

The marshal folded his hands on his desk. "Something wrong?"

Anxious to return to Haywire, Brett rose to his feet. "Not a thing," he said. His mind in a whirl, he almost tripped over the sleeping dog, and the rest of the memory materialized.

Could it be? Was it possible?

"Not a thing," he repeated. Thanking the marshal for his time, he left.

And he wore a ring.

Crazy as it sounded, the piece of string tied to the marshal's fingers might both save a marriage and help solve a case. That and Kate's beetle…mushroom…key!

28

THAT NIGHT, KATE STIFLED A YAWN AND POKED THE brown mass of taffy on the marble slab with a finger to see if it had cooled enough to pull. "I think it's ready."

Aunt Letty laughed.

"What's so funny?"

"I was just thinking of your uncle. Remember how he'd insist on making taffy over an open fire?"

"Yes, and he had a fit when you ordered the cook-stove. Said it didn't belong in a candy kitchen." The memory brought a smile to Kate's face. "I wonder what he'd say about the talking machine they call a telephone." Haywire didn't have telephone service, but the mayor insisted that was about to change.

Aunt Letty rolled her eyes. "Lord have mercy. I shudder to think. Remember how he carried on when they first laid the railroad tracks here?" She oiled her hands and wiped the excess off with a towel. "Your uncle said progress was the exchange of one nuisance for another." She plunged both hands into the sugary mound before her, adding, "That reminds me. I've been meaning to talk to you about something."

Kate pulled a ribbon of brown taffy and folded the ends together. Thanks to the sudden turn of mild weather, the taffy was the perfect consistency. "Oh?"

"What do you think about hiring someone to help out around here?"

Kate's hands paused. "Whenever I suggested such a thing in the past, you rejected it. What made you change your mind?"

Her aunt paused before answering. "The town is growing by leaps and bounds. Business has almost doubled this past year. As a result, we've both been putting in long hours. I mean, look at us. It's almost eight o'clock, and we're still here. Lawdy, we should have been home hours ago."

Kate couldn't argue with her aunt in that regard. The arrival of the railroad had changed the community in many ways. There was even talk about building an opera house, which meant no more having to travel to Austin to see a play.

Aunt Letty pinned Kate with a meaningful look. "Unless I miss my guess, you'll soon be busy setting up your own household."

Kate snapped the taffy ribbon in half. "Things between Frank and me are still up in the air." She hated not being completely honest with her aunt, but she had promised Frank to keep their arrangement secret.

"You can't keep him on the hook forever. Either you're going to have to reel him in or let him go."

"These things can't be rushed."

"Rushed? Mercy, child!" Her aunt held her hands in midair for a moment. "You've known him since you were six. That's a whole lot longer than I knew your uncle before I married him."

"Some people take longer to get to know," Kate said. "Others you know immediately, like…" Surprised to find Brett's name on the tip of her tongue, she quickly searched for a substitute. "Like…like Uncle Joe."

"Frank's a pretty open book. I can't imagine what more there is to learn about him."

"I didn't know that Frank had a romantic side."

Her aunt pursed her lips. "Come to think of it, I didn't know either. Not till he sent those flowers and that note."

"See what I mean?" This new tender side of Frank not only surprised her; it taught her something about herself. She liked being treated like a lady. Liked it a lot. It made her feel special, and Frank had never before made her feel that way. Perhaps the problem wasn't so much that Frank had changed. Maybe the change had come in her.

Aunt Letty's lips puckered. "Are you sure that's all it is?"

Kate frowned. "What do you mean?"

"Has anyone else caught your fancy?"

Kate sucked in her breath. Leave it to her aunt to ask the question she hadn't dared ask herself. "You mean other than the two different Franks?" she asked, biding for time.

"I just want you to be happy. And if I thought for one moment that Frank wasn't the right man for you, I wouldn't push so hard."

"I know that, Aunt Letty. It's just…so much has happened in recent weeks. It's hard to think."

"Maybe you're thinking too much," Aunt Letty said. "Sometimes, it's better to just let yourself feel."

Kate nodded. "Maybe you're right."

"'Course I'm right." Aunt Letty bent a ribbon of taffy in two. "You know, Charley Watts is into that thinking stuff too. By the time he made up his mind who to vote for, it was too late. The election was over."

Kate couldn't help but laugh. Only her aunt could compare picking out a husband to voting for a candidate.

"So," Aunt Letty continued, "how do you feel about hiring someone?"

Kate welcomed the idea but still couldn't help but worry. It was true that business had doubled. And they had put in a lot of long hours of late. But was that the only reason for her aunt's change of heart? Or was something else going on? Aunt Letty had seemed distracted recently and lacked her usual spunk.

"Is there something you're not telling me? You're not ill, are you?"

Her aunt drew back in surprise. "Ill? Certainly not. Who has time to be ill? It's just... I'm not getting any younger, and neither are you. I think we could both use some time to ourselves. Maybe if you hadn't been so tied down here, you and Frank would have resolved your problems by now."

Kate's heart sank. Back to Frank again. Fortunately, the jingling bells signaled that someone had entered the shop, effectively stopping further discussion.

"Who could that be at this late hour?" Kate asked. Whoever it was deserved a hug—or, at the very least, extra sweets—for the timely arrival.

"Probably someone picking up an order," Aunt

Letty said, stifling a yawn. Wiping her greasy hands on a towel, she started for the door. "I'll take care of it."

Her aunt's cheery voice wafted from the front of the shop. "Oh, I didn't expect to see you tonight. Don't tell me. The usual, right?"

A man's low, rumbling voice wafted into the kitchen, but Kate couldn't make out who it was. Her main thought was to finish up so she and her aunt could call it a night.

Just as she reached for a sponge, her aunt's voice stopped her. Puzzled, Kate frowned. It sure did sound like her aunt had said she'd gone home.

That couldn't be right; she must have heard wrong. What possible reason would her aunt have for saying something that wasn't true?

Still, the oddly disturbing tone of her aunt's voice raised the hairs on the back of Kate's neck. Wiping her greasy hands on her apron, Kate tiptoed to the door. The mirror on the far wall allowed her to view part of the counter area unseen.

She spotted Ringo in front of the counter. Head tilted, ears cocked, the dog appeared to be waiting for his treat. Sighing in relief, she forced herself to relax. It was only Lucky Lou.

Obviously, she'd heard wrong.

Maybe her aunt was right; she had been working hard. They both had been. The train robbery hadn't helped, and now she was imagining danger where none existed.

Hiring an employee was definitely a good idea. She was about to go back to work when once again, her aunt's voice made her pause. "You'll never get away with this."

Puzzled, Kate shifted slightly to the right to gain a wider view in the mirror on the far wall, and her jaw dropped. Was that a gun in Lucky Lou's hand?

She pulled away from the doorway in disbelief. Back against the wall, she pressed her hands on her chest to calm her racing heart. What was Lucky Lou doing holding a gun on her aunt? Not sure she could believe her eyes, she braced herself with a deep breath and chanced another quick glance. There was no mistake. She couldn't see Lucky Lou's face, only the hand holding the weapon.

Confusion spurting through her, Kate pulled back. What was the matter with him? Was this some sort of joke? Had he lost his mind?

Fearing for her aunt's safety, she considered her options. She could sneak out the back door and race up Outhouse Alley for help, but she didn't want to leave her aunt alone.

Another quick peek told her things had taken a turn for the worse.

Her aunt was moving ever so slowly around the counter, hands held above her shoulders. Lucky Lou was now in full view, and Kate hardly recognized him. Face dark as night, he didn't look like himself. The wild look in his eyes was even more worrisome than the gun. He turned his head, and Kate ducked out of sight.

After a moment, she looked again. This time, her aunt was heading for the door, the gun pointed at her back. Kate's mind scrambled. Where could he be taking her? It was late, and most of the shops and businesses were closed. Anything that happened after dark took place beyond the Dead Line, and that was three blocks away. There was a good chance that no one would see them.

Forcing herself to remain calm, Kate curled her hands at her side. This was no time to panic. *Think!* She glanced about the kitchen in search of a weapon.

Grabbing hold of a sturdy pot, she braced herself with a deep breath and slipped off her shoes. Bent at the waist, she left the kitchen on stockinged feet. She ducked behind the counter, keeping her head low. Her heart thumped against her ribs, and she feared the sound would give her away.

Her aunt was clearly stalling for time. "I-I won't tell anyone that you're a bank robber."

Kate stiffened and almost dropped the pan. Lucky Lou a bank robber? That could mean but one thing—he was a Ghost Rider.

"I-I won't say a word to anyone," Aunt Letty stammered.

"Shut your mouth and move!"

Crouching behind the counter, Kate prayed her pounding heart couldn't be heard. *Oh God.* As incredible as it sounded, it all began to make sense. Now that she thought about it, Lucky Lou had been at the bank the day it was robbed. He'd also been at the station after the train robbery, questioning her and others as to what they might have seen. She'd thought it was just curiosity on his part, but now she suspected an ulterior motive. He'd wanted to make sure that no one had recognized him beneath the flour-sack hood.

It sickened her to think that all this time, a Ghost Rider had been under their very noses.

"I said move it!" Lucky Lou's harsh voice made Kate jump.

"I'm going, I'm going," Aunt Letty muttered.

Kate gulped and tried to think. She needed to create a distraction. She glanced around and spotted a box of doggie cakes. Reaching for one, she dropped all the way to the floor and crawled crablike toward the end of the counter.

Catching Ringo's eye, she waved and pulled back. Ringo barked.

"Hush, boy," his owner rasped.

Kate held the doggie cake out again, and this time, Ringo tried pulling loose. Jerking on the leash, Lucky Lou turned his head—a mistake. Because Aunt Letty grabbed hold of the gun, and a tug-of-war ensued.

With no time to spare, Kate leaped to her feet and raced to her aunt's defense. Fortunately, Lucky Lou was too occupied to notice her.

"Why, you…" Letting go of the leash, Lucky Lou yanked the gun out of Aunt Letty's hands.

Sneaking up from behind, Kate raised the pan and whacked him good and hard over the head.

He stiffened, and Kate held her breath. She was just about to hit him again when the gun fell from his hand and he crashed to the floor.

She dropped the pan as if it were on fire, and Ringo jumped back. Rushing to her aunt's side, Kate checked her up and down. "Are you all right?"

Aunt Letty leaned against the counter, her hand on her chest. "I'm fine. Just a bit shaken," she said, staring down at Lucky Lou's prone body.

Ringo sniffed at his owner and whined.

"It's okay, boy," Kate said, stooping to run her hand along the dog's back.

She picked up the gun and pointed it at Lucky Lou. A spot of red blood oozed from the back of his head where she'd hit him. "I heard you say he robbed the bank."

"That's right. He…he's the man who knocked me over."

"Thank God you're all right." Kate looked around the shop. "I need to tie him up." She undid the ties around her waist. "Where's your apron?"

"I took it home with the others to wash."

Kate pulled off her apron and dropped to her knees. She wrapped her apron strings around Lucky Lou's hands, testing the knot to make sure it was tight. "Let me have Ringo's leash."

Aunt Letty tried to grab hold of the leash, but suddenly, the dog wanted to play and ran around the room like a kid out of school.

After her aunt had made several unsuccessful attempts to unhook the leash, Kate said, "Maybe there's rope or something in the kitchen."

"I'll see if I can find some." Looking winded, Aunt Letty hurried to the back room. What seemed to take forever but was probably only seconds later, she returned with ribbons of taffy draped over her arms. "Couldn't find any rope. This will have to do."

Kate stared at her in disbelief. "Taffy. You want me to tie him up with taffy?"

Aunt Letty shrugged. "It's the only thing I could find. Maybe it'll sweeten his disposition."

"I sincerely doubt that." Kate swiped a stray strand

of hair away from her face. "I'm not tying him up with that."

"Well, we better tie him up with something. You know what happened to Mr. Benson when he forgot to tie up his bull and—"

"Aunt Letty, please! I'm trying to think." If only Brett were there; he'd know what to do. "I'll watch him while you go for help."

Lucky Lou groaned, and both women jumped.

"Oh God. Hold this." Kate shoved the gun in Aunt Letty's unwilling hands and lifted a long length of taffy off her arm. *I must be out of my mind!*

She wrapped the sugary rope around Lucky Lou's ankles, careful to avoid the sharp-edged wheels of his spurs. Ringo sniffed at the candy rope, and Kate had to keep pushing the dog's cold nose out of the way.

Holding the gun in one hand, Aunt Letty picked up the leash with the other and pulled the dog to her side. "Sit!"

Kate worked quickly. Not only was she worried about Lucky Lou gaining consciousness, but the taffy was hardening fast, and it took quite a bit of pulling and tugging to wind it around his leg all the way to his knees. She overlapped the edges to make it as strong as possible.

She sat back on her haunches with a worried frown. "That's not going to hold him for long." The taffy would crumble into pieces with the least little pressure. She only hoped that if Lucky Lou came to, he would be too dazed to figure that out. As much as she hated to think so, it might be necessary to give him another whack.

Standing, she took the gun out of her aunt's hand, careful to keep it pointed at Lucky Lou. She wasn't about to take chances. "How do you know he's the one who knocked you down?"

"I knew there was something familiar about the man. I just couldn't put my finger on it." Her aunt tossed a nod at him. "Until tonight. You know how he's always bragging about being shot at three times?"

Kate nodded. "Yes, and he wears the bullets around his neck."

"That's how I knew it was him," Aunt Letty explained. "If he moves a certain way, the bullets knock against each other and make a rattling sound. I thought it was keys I heard that day in the bank." The corners of her aunt's mouth drooped. "When he walked in tonight, that's when it hit me. It wasn't keys. It was his bullets."

"Oh, Aunt Letty, you could have been killed."

"You're telling me!" A rueful expression crossed Aunt Letty's face. "I just wish we didn't have to waste good taffy on the likes of him. I dread the thought of staying up all night to make another batch."

"We'll worry about that later. Right now, I need you to fetch the sheriff. I'll stay here. Take Ringo with you."

Aunt Letty frowned. "Are…are you sure you'll be all right?"

"I've got a gun, and I know how to use it."

Aunt Letty rolled her eyes. "That's what scares me."

Brett raced back to town as quickly as his horse could carry him. Even so, it was dark by the time he arrived, and the main part of town was deserted as he urged his horse along Main Street.

He hoped to find the sheriff still at the office. Otherwise, he'd have to bother him at home. Neither prospect appealed to him, but he was obliged to keep the sheriff informed of any new leads.

The light from the candy shop window fanned over the wooden sidewalk. Kate was working late again, and the thought made him ache inside. He envisioned her as she'd looked the night they'd pulled taffy together. Recalled in worrisome detail the way her eyes had sparkled as they'd worked, the way her smile had brightened the room. The way her lips…

Grimacing, he forced the memories away. He had no business dwelling on such thoughts. No business at all. Not while the man he blamed for his sister's death still roamed free. He had work to do, and there was no time to waste. Before the night was over, he hoped to escort one, if not more, of the Ghost Riders to the hoosegow.

Drawing closer to the shop, he willed himself to keep going with nary a glance in the shop's direction. He might have succeeded had he not recognized the horse tethered in front. The horse belonged to Lucky Lou, and knowing that made Brett's mouth run dry.

What in blazes is he doing at the candy shop this time of night?

Reining in his horse, Brett quickly dismounted and wrapped the reins around the hitching rail. The curtains were drawn, which was odd. The shop's curtains were always left open, day or night.

A chilling possibility ran through his mind, and a cold sweat washed over him. Kate was in danger!

With a hand on the butt of his Colt, Brett ran up the steps to the boardwalk. Whipping his gun out of its holster, he burst through the door.

And found himself staring at the business end of a pistol.

29

BRETT TOOK IN THE SCENE BEFORE HIM AND HOLSTERED his Colt. "It's just me," he said, relief washing over him. "You can put that thing away."

Kate dropped the gun to her side. Rounded eyes stared at him from a pale face. "Oh, Brett, thank God you're here!"

Only sheer willpower prevented him from taking her in his arms and holding her close.

Instead, he extended a steadying hand to Kate's aunt, who looked about to faint.

With a grateful smile, she slumped against the counter. "I never thought I'd say this, cowboy, but am I ever glad to see you."

Ringo barked and wagged his tail. "Sit!" Kate said, and the dog sat, his tail thumping against the wood floor.

"It looks like you have everything under control," Brett said, still fighting the urge to take Kate in his arms. She sure did look like she could use some comforting. Instead, he took the gun out of her trembling hand and set it on the counter. "You okay?"

She nodded, her lips curving upward. "I am now."

The look on her face made his knees feel weak, and he immediately drew his gaze away. Reminding himself that he was there in an official capacity, he focused on Lucky Lou's prone body. "What happened?"

"Kate bashed him over the head," Aunt Letty said.

Not sure he could believe what he was seeing, Brett dropped on his haunches for a closer look. Narrowing his eyes, he probed the man's arms and legs with a finger. "Is that…taffy?"

"Yep," Aunt Letty said proudly. "Made fresh tonight."

"It was the closest thing we had to a rope," Kate explained.

Brett lifted his gaze to hers. "How did you know… I mean…why did you knock him out?"

Both Kate and her aunt started talking at once. Unable to make hide or hair of what they were saying, Brett held up his hands. "Whoa. One at a time."

"He's one of the Ghost Riders," Kate said.

"How do you know?" He'd only that day figured it out himself, though he still had no proof. All he had was suspicion, and that wouldn't stand up in a court of law.

Aunt Letty folded her arms across her chest with a disgusted frown. "He's the one who knocked me down at the bank."

"Are you sure?" Brett asked.

"'Course I'm sure." Aunt Letty gave her head an emphatic nod. "Remember I told you I thought there was something familiar about him? It was the bullet casings."

"What?"

"You know," Aunt Letty said. "The ones he wears

around his neck for good luck. If he moves a certain way, they make a tinny sound, like keys. Only they sound hollow." Arms folded, she gave a nod of satisfaction. "Soon as he pulled his gun out, I knew I was right."

Brett quirked a smile. Talk about irony. "Well now. I'd say his luck has finally run out."

He patted Lucky Lou down as much as the taffy allowed, but found no weapons. Only a money clip and what he now knew was a dog whistle. He examined the metal loop on one end and slipped it onto his little finger. Sure enough, if held the right way, it did look like a ring. Could that be what Dusty had seen?

"You don't seem particularly surprised that Lucky Lou robbed the bank." Kate studied him. "Did you suspect him?"

Brett stood. "Not until today."

"Was it the bullets?" Aunt Letty asked.

"It was the peppermint candy, right?" Kate said.

"Neither. It was Kate's telegraph key—"

"Leaf," Kate said with a sniff.

"Sorry," he said. "But you have to admit it did look a little like a telegraph key, and that's what got me thinking. I couldn't figure out how the Ghost Riders were always one step ahead of the law. But your candy reminded me of something. I once walked into the telegraph office and found Lucky Lou and Flash arguing. Didn't think much of it at the time. But then I realized that if anyone was in a position to decipher the sheriff's encrypted notes, it was Flash."

Kate's eyes widened. "You think Flash—?"

"That's what I hope to find out."

"What about Lucky Lou?" Aunt Letty asked. "Was it the argument that made you suspect him?"

"Not at first," Brett said. "The problem was I couldn't figure out how our friend here robbed the bank and managed to be on the scene afterward." He held up the silent whistle. "This might be our answer." He indicated the dog with a nod. "Let go of the leash, Kate." She did as he asked, and he let the money clip fall to the floor. The dog immediate grabbed it with his teeth and ran to the door.

Kate's forehead furrowed. "I'm not sure I understand."

"Ringo is the fourth Ghost Rider."

"What?" Both Kate and her aunt exclaimed in unison.

"That's right." Brett said. "I suspected there were four, but I never imagined one was a dog. After Lucky Lou knocked your aunt down, his buddies took off. Since he tends to be a nervous type, he worried that your aunt might have recognized him. So he ran to the alley, pulled off the flour sack, and used the silent whistle to call his dog. Once Ringo took off with the loot, Lucky Lou then returned to the bank as a spectator. I guess he wanted to make sure your aunt couldn't identify him as a Ghost Rider."

Aunt Letty scoffed. "We should have known. Remember the day they replaced our window? Lucky Lou kept asking if you'd recognized the man who ran into the shop. I thought he was just curious. Now I know he wanted to make sure his identity was safe."

Kate frowned. "So, what you're saying is that he just hid in plain sight while his poor dog did the dirty work."

Brett nodded. "That's what the mutt has been trained to do. He grabs any booty dropped in front of him and runs. Probably hides things somewhere that Lucky Lou finds later."

Aunt Letty brightened. "I just thought of something. Remember when Harvey Wells showed us that silly purse he invented?"

"And Ringo ran out the door with the roll of money that dropped to the floor," Kate added.

"And Lucky Lou called his dog back with this," Brett said, holding up the silent whistle.

"I can't believe you were able to figure all this out," Kate said. Her face softened in admiration, and his heart skipped a beat.

"Me neither," Aunt Letty added. "I would never have put all those pieces together."

"But what about the other one?" Katie asked. "You said there were four. But Lucky Lou, Flash, and Ringo only add up to three."

"Thanks to you ladies, my job just got a whole lot easier. You two are experts at pulling taffy." He tossed a nod at the unconscious man on the floor. "Me? I'm pretty good at pulling out information. As soon as Sleeping Beauty here wakes up, he's going to tell me the name of the fourth Ghost Rider. Least he will if he knows what's good for him."

❧

Brett sat Lucky Lou against the wall and slapped his face gently to bring him around. He then escorted his prisoner to the jailhouse. Lucky Lou did more groaning than talking, and Brett got nowhere with his questions.

Still, he kept hammering. There was no time to lose. Should Foster get wind that one of his men had been caught, he would take off, sure as shootin'.

"Got hisself a good bump on the head," the sheriff said, yawning. "I say we get some shut-eye and try again tomorrow."

Though it was well after midnight by the time Brett returned to the boardinghouse, he could hardly sleep. *God, don't let Foster slip through my fingers yet again.*

At the first crack of dawn, Brett jumped out of bed and quickly dressed. In short order, he left the boardinghouse and raced to the sheriff's office.

It wasn't often that he got a warm welcome from Keeler, but today he did. The generous bonus the sheriff stood to gain for the Ghost Riders' capture had done wonders for his disposition.

"Any luck getting him to talk?" Brett asked, indicating the upstairs jail cells with a nod.

Keeler shook his head. "Haven't had time. Just got here."

The sheriff said more, but Brett didn't wait to see what it was. Instead, he took the stairs two at a time. Only two of the four cells were occupied. One cell contained a man curled up on the floor, snoring.

By the looks of it, Brett wasn't the only one who hadn't gotten any shut-eye. Lucky Lou didn't look so good that morning, but Brett suspected it had more to do with the lump on his head than a lack of sleep.

Lucky Lou sat on a cot, back propped against the wall. He yawned and knuckled his droopy, red eyes.

Ringo suddenly appeared by Brett's side. After

sniffing the cell of the snoring man, the dog plopped on the floor and crossed his paws.

For several moments, Brett said nothing. He had no proof that Flash was involved, only suspicion. Without Lucky Lou's cooperation, he didn't trust the sheriff to arrest Flash with so little evidence. And even if he did, it would be too late. It was only a matter of time before news of Lucky Lou's arrest leaked out. As soon as Foster One heard that his partner had been caught, he'd take off, and Brett could lose him for good. Without Lucky Lou's confession, he had nothing.

Lucky Lou scratched his belly and cast a disapproving glance at the snoring man in the next cell before addressing Brett. "If you think you'll get me to confess to somethin' I didn't do, you're plumb loco." He yawned. "Right now, I just want to sleep."

"You tell me what I want to know, and I'll sing you a lullaby."

"Like I told the sheriff, I don't know nothing." He felt the back of his head and winced. "I didn't rob no bank, and I don't know no Ghost Riders. The old lady's brain is addled."

Brett hung his thumbs from his vest pockets. Nothing was wrong with Mrs. Denver's brain; of that he was certain. By the looks of the egg-sized bump on Lucky Lou's head, there was nothing wrong with Kate's arm either.

The problem was how to get Lucky Lou to talk. Maybe it was time for a bluff. If his hunch was right about Flash, his bluff would work. If he was wrong, Lucky Lou could clam up for good.

"That's not what your buddy said."

That got Lucky Lou's attention, or at least he looked more alert. "What are you talkin' about?"

"I'm talking about Flash. He's downstairs now. Soon as the sheriff's done questioning him, he'll be occupying the cell right next to yours."

Lucky Lou made a face. "So why should I care?"

"Thought you might be interested in knowing what he's told the sheriff so far. Said you were the brains behind the whole operation."

Lucky Lou sat up straight. "The brains?"

"That's what he said. Said he and the other fella took orders from you."

A gleam of suspicion shot from Lucky Lou's eyes. "Why would he say such thing?"

"I don't know." Brett's gaze fell on Lucky Lou's hand-tooled boots and fancy Mexican spurs. "Maybe he's getting back at you for spending the stolen loot before it's time." Flash could have lied about arguing with Lucky Lou about faro. The argument in the telegraph office could well have been about Lucky Lou's spending habits.

"Maybe it was to save his own skin. The sheriff agreed to forego the necktie party in his honor if he named the leader of the gang. He named you."

"Why, that danged fool. He's lying through his teeth!"

Brett shrugged. "That may be true. But unless we locate the real leader, everything falls on your shoulders. Been my experience that juries favor hanging gang leaders. The same could be said about judges." He let that sink in for a moment before adding, "Swing or sing. That's your choice."

Lucky Lou reached for the chain around his neck. Brett had never noticed it before, but Mrs. Denver was right; the bullets rattling together did make a jangling sound. A person not paying close attention could mistake the sound for keys.

Brett studied the man with narrowed eyes. "Tell me something. The bullet that almost hit you during that stagecoach robbery… Were you a passenger or a thief?"

Lucky Lou didn't answer. He didn't have to; his expression said it all. Kicking himself mentally for not figuring that out sooner, Brett shook his head. "Well, I'll be a son of a gun." Like everyone else, he'd assumed Lucky Lou had been an innocent bystander. Instead, he'd been the bad guy.

"Would it be safe to say that you lied about the robbery taking place up north? That it took place in San Antone instead?"

A flash of surprise crossed Lucky Lou's face. "How'd you know that?"

"Let's just say it was a lucky guess. So, what's it gonna be? Sing or swing?"

"That sure ain't much of a choice."

"Maybe not, but your best bet is to tell me everything you know about the man who gave the orders. I knew him as Frank Foster. I need to know his current name and location."

Lucky Lou dropped the chain. "You're wasting your time. I don't know nothin.' I'm innocent as a newborn babe." His ardent denial might have worked had it not been for the beads of sweat on his forehead and the shifty look in his eyes.

"Sorry to hear that," Brett said casually. "Not much

I can do for an innocent man, but I sure in blazes can help a cooperative one." With that, he turned and walked toward the stairwell, Ringo at his heel. "If I were you, I'd make out my last will and testament."

"Wait."

Brett turned. Lucky Lou was now standing, hands wrapped around the iron bars.

He narrowed his eyes. "I told ya, I don't know no Foster fella."

"Oh, you know him all right. Maybe not by that name, but you know him. While you're hanging from the gallows, he'll be living high on the hog with the money you stole. Stick to your story and…" Brett shrugged. "Nothing I can do to help you." He let Lucky Lou gnaw on that for a moment before adding, "So what's it gonna be?"

Lucky Lou's grip tightened until his knuckles turned white. Perspiration now ran down the side of his face. "I'm thinking."

"Well, think faster."

Lucky Lou groaned. "Okay, okay. I'll tell you what you want to know. On one condition."

Brett hesitated. He was in no position to make deals. That was up to the prosecutor. "What?"

"While I'm in prison, you promise to take care of my dog."

30

STILL SHAKEN BY HER ENCOUNTER WITH LUCKY LOU the night before, Aunt Letty arrived at the shop that morning wielding a shotgun.

"Auntie!" Kate gasped. "What are you doing with that?"

"It was your uncle's. After everything that's happened, I decided we could use a little protection around here."

Kate frowned. "But you don't even know how to use a gun."

"What's to know? You point and shoot."

Kate grabbed the shotgun before her aunt could demonstrate. "I think we'd better hide this before our customers arrive."

No sooner had Kate stashed the shotgun in the kitchen than Frank ran into the shop, looking like he'd seen a ghost.

"Katie, I heard what happened. Are you okay?"

Aunt Letty answered for her. "She's fine. We both are."

Frank looked like he wanted to say more, but

curious customers began storming into the shop, demanding to hear all about the previous night's events, and he finally gave up and left. News of Lucky Lou's arrest was already the talk of the town.

Aunt Letty was in her glory and held her audience captive with her stirring account. Encouraged by the gasps of shock and dismay, she made her story more elaborate and outrageous with each retelling.

"I can't believe Lucky Lou is one of them," Mrs. Tremble said, holding Mitzie in her arms. Shuddering, she buried her nose in the poodle's topknot. "I mean, him being a dog lover and all. You just never know what's going through a person's mind, do you?"

Mrs. Cuttwell sniffed. "I knew there was a reason his dog was always trying to escape. Poor thing."

It seemed that everyone had an opinion on Lucky Lou's arrest and was determined to express it. Even Hoot Owl Pete and grumpy Mr. Thornton.

The shop was still packed when Kate slipped out to make deliveries. All she'd been able to think about was the memory of Lucky Lou holding her aunt at gunpoint. She hoped the ride would help clear her head.

Oh, how she wanted this whole thing to be over. As far as she knew, only the one Ghost Rider had been arrested, but Brett seemed confident that another arrest would soon follow. That meant his job here would soon be done.

Not wanting to dwell on the thought, she urged Cinnamon to go faster, and the wagon dipped and bumped along the rutted dirt road. Less than a half hour after leaving town, she pulled up in front of the Fletcher place.

She knocked on the door, surprised to see a Saratoga trunk on the front porch.

Hearing him say "Come in," she opened the door. He greeted her from his chair with a nod. "Well, don't just stand there. Come in, come in."

Stepping inside, she closed the door. "Are you going somewhere?"

"What?"

"I noticed the trunk on your porch."

"No, just...organizing. Want some coffee? I made it fresh last Friday."

"No, thank you. I had a big breakfast." She handed him the basket of candy she'd put together especially for him. "All your favorites."

The hoped-for smile failed to light up his face. Instead, he set the basket on the table and rubbed his hip. He didn't look any better today than he had the last time she'd visited. His skin was ash-colored and his eyes skirted with purple shadows.

"Are you all right?" she asked.

"Yeah, except for this dang rheumatism."

"Would you like me to send the doctor?"

He rolled his eyes. "Heck no! Why do you always insist on sending that ole sawbones out here?"

"Because I'm concerned about you," Kate said.

Scoffing, he reached for the box and pulled out a peppermint candy. "This is all the medicine I need," he said and popped it in his mouth.

His childlike enthusiasm made her smile. "Made fresh first thing this morning."

"Mmm. Tastes good."

"Would you like some coffee to go with that?"

He nodded. "That would be nice."

"I'll get it." She walked into the small, cluttered kitchen. Finding a clean cup in the cupboard, she poured coffee from the coffeepot on the cookstove. The coffee looked strong enough to float a horseshoe. Smelled strong too. Fletcher might not have been kidding when he said he made it five days ago.

Just as she was about to leave the kitchen, she noticed a supply of gauze and tape on the kitchen table, along with a bottle of iodine. Had Mr. Fletcher injured himself? Was that why he looked under the weather?

She carried the cup of coffee into the parlor and set it on the table by his side. "I have some good news that should cheer you," she announced.

"Oh?"

"Yes, it's about the Ghost Riders. Last night—"

Just then, the door burst open, followed by the presence of a compact man dressed in black. Kate was sure she had never seen him before. Even so, there was something about him that looked vaguely familiar. She glanced at Fletcher, but his dark expression was as puzzling as it was worrisome.

Scowling at her, the stranger slammed the door shut with a raised foot. "What's she doing here?"

"This is Miss Kate Denver," Fletcher said. "She and her aunt own the candy store in town, and she brought me a box of my favorite sweets." He hesitated a moment before adding, "Kate, meet my son."

The tense undercurrents in the room made her nervous, and Kate arched an eyebrow. During the many conversations she'd had with Fletcher, never once had he mentioned a son.

"How do you do?" she said. When the younger man failed to return her greeting, she turned to his father. "I'd best be going."

"Before my son arrived, you were saying something about the Ghost Riders."

Kate glanced at the younger man before answering. "Only that one of them has been arrested."

Fletcher reached for another piece of candy. "Is that so?"

Kate nodded. Sensing the tension in the room was about to snap, she gestured toward the door. "I'd better get a move on. I have more deliveries to make."

Fletcher made a face. "I meant what I said. I don't need no doctor poking around and pretending to know what ails me."

Kate knew better than to argue with him. "As you wish," she said. "Enjoy your candy."

"I intend to."

She started for the door, anxious to make her escape. The younger man moved aside to let her pass. "See you next week," she called over her shoulder. Grateful for the fresh air that greeted her when she opened the door, she stepped outside and took a deep breath.

Much to her annoyance, the younger Fletcher followed her out of the house, closing the door behind them. "Pa meant what he said. No doctor."

Noting that the Saratoga trunk had vanished, she turned with a frown. "I'm worried about him. He doesn't look like himself."

"That's for me to worry about, not you." He waved his hands in dismissal, and she caught a glimpse of a bandage inside his open collar.

The bandage made her think of the gauze and iodine on the kitchen table, and her mind raced with fearful clarity. One of the train robbers had been shot! Coincidence? Somehow she didn't think so.

Startled by the thought and what it might mean, Kate recalled the look on Mr. Fletcher's face when his son had walked in. She couldn't make up her mind whether it had been fear or worry on the old man's face, but it sure hadn't been the look of a loving father.

As she met the younger Fletcher's gaze, a horrifying thought occurred to her. Now that she had a closer look at him, she was almost positive he was the man in Brett's photograph. The man he called Foster One.

A sick feeling washed over her. "Like…like I told your f-father," she stammered. "N-no doctor."

Kate turned to make her escape, but he was too quick for her. He grabbed her by the arm, his hand darting out like a snake's tongue. "Now where would you be going in such a hurry?" he asked, his rough voice grating in her ears.

"Ow!" Shock turned to anger, and she jerked back, but he held on tight, his fingers digging into her flesh. "Let go!" she cried. "You're hurting me!"

Twisting her body, she kicked him hard in the leg and tried kneeing him between the thighs. Her small frame was no match for his as he yanked her closer, his face dark with fury.

Pulling out a gun with his free hand, he pointed it at her. "Shut up and do as I say!"

Freezing in place, Kate stared at his weapon with rounded eyes. "You w-won't get away with this," she stammered.

His mouth twisted into a mirthless smile. "You'd be amazed at what I've gotten away with. Now start walking. My rig's in back of the house. You and me are gonna take a little ride."

She dug in her heels and refused to move. With a flash of impatience, he practically pulled her arm from its socket. He spun her around and shoved the barrel of his gun into her back. "I said walk!"

Rubbing her sore arm, Kate walked down the porch steps on wooden legs. *Oh God…*

"Let her go, Fletcher."

Her relief at hearing Brett's voice lasted for only as long as it took Fletcher to wrap his arm around her neck and press his gun to her temple. The deadly click of the hammer sounded like an explosion in her head, and she didn't dare move.

"Who…who are you, and what do you want?" Fletcher called.

"Name's Brett Tucker, Texas Ranger."

"Oh yeah, heard there was a ranger in town looking for me. Didn't bother me none. I've outfoxed more than one lawman in my day."

"If me being a Texas Ranger doesn't bother you, maybe this will. My sister's name was Alice Taylor."

Kate felt Fletcher stiffen behind her. Tightening his hold on her like a vise, he kept the weapon pressed hard against the side of her head. "Don't know why I'd care about your sister."

"I think you do," Brett said. "But either way, you're under arrest."

"Like hell I am."

"If it's hell you want, I'd be happy to accommodate

you." Brett stepped out from where he'd hidden behind a tree, and his voice grew more insistent. "You should hang for breaking my sister's heart, but unfortunately, that's not a crime. For now, we'll just have to charge you with holding up the bank. You can also add stage and train robberies to the list. Should I go on?"

"If you know what's good for the lady here," Fletcher said, his harsh, raw voice grating in her ear, "you'll back off."

"You can't keep running, Fletcher. Sooner or later, I'm gonna catch you. Count on it."

"I guess you have a problem then," Fletcher sneered. "'Cause I don't aim on gettin' caught."

A movement on the porch was followed by a gruff voice. "You're the one with the problem, Son."

"Stay outta this, Pa!"

The distraction caused her assailant to momentarily loosen his grip, and Kate sprang into action. Kicking him hard, she thrust up her arm and elbowed his wounded shoulder.

"Ow!" he yelped.

Moving quickly, she grabbed the barrel of the gun, but he soon overpowered her.

"Why, you little—" He dragged her back against his hard body. His hold around her neck cut off her breathing. She thrashed and dug her fingers into his powerful arm, but it refused to budge.

Brett's voice broke through the darkness. "Let her go, Fletcher. It's over."

For answer, Fletcher tightened his grip. Her lungs screaming for air, Kate swung her leg back, kicking him hard on the shin. Just as she tried kicking him again, a black wall closed in on all sides.

She wasn't sure what happened next, but suddenly, she was free. Gasping for air, she tried to make sense of the scene in front of her. This time, Brett held the gun, and Fletcher's hands were raised shoulder-high. Behind them, Old Man Fletcher pointed a shotgun at his son, his face as dark as a midnight sky.

Brett's gaze met hers. "You okay?" he asked, his voice mirroring the concern on his face.

Hand on her sore arm, she nodded. "How…how did you know?"

"It took a while, but Lucky Lou finally sang." Brett frowned. "I sure didn't expect to meet up with you here."

"I didn't expect to meet up with another Ghost Rider," she said.

"Keep this up"—Brett pulled the man's hands behind his back and snapped on a pair of handcuffs—"and we're going to have to deputize you."

"Thank you, but I think I'll stick to candy making," Kate said. "Less dangerous."

Before Brett hauled his prisoner away, Mr. Fletcher hobbled up to them, shotgun still in hand. The man looked like he had aged ten years in the last few minutes. He glared at his son. "I knew when you came back that you were up to no good, but never did I guess how bad it was."

The mask of his son's face revealed no emotion.

"I'm only glad your mother isn't alive to see this day." With that, the old man turned and hobbled back to the porch.

Kate ran after him. "Mr. Fletcher," she called. "I'm so sorry. If there's anything I can do…"

Fletcher stopped upon reaching the porch. Steadying himself with a hand on the railing, he looked over his shoulder as Brett hauled his son away. "There's nothing you can do. Nothing."

31

LATER THAT AFTERNOON, MAIN STREET WAS PACKED with revelers celebrating the capture of the Ghost Riders.

Standing outside the shop with her aunt, Kate jumped at the sound of a firecracker. Flash, Foster/ Fletcher, and Lucky Lou were all in jail, and there was nothing more to fear. But after everything that had happened, her nerves were still on edge.

"You okay?" Aunt Letty asked, raising her voice to be heard over the noise of the crowd.

"I'm fine," Kate said, craning her neck.

"Who are you looking for?"

Kate hesitated. If her aunt knew she was looking for Brett, she might get the wrong idea. Or maybe even the right one. "Uh…Frank."

"I think I see him." Aunt Letty raised her arm. "Yoo-hoo! Frank. Over here."

Frank waved back and quickly joined them. "What a celebration, huh?"

Aunt Letty nodded. "I'll say. The town hasn't seen anything like it since that wagonload of stolen whiskey was recovered."

After Kate's ordeal at the Fletcher house, Frank had raced to the shop to see if she was all right. Now he queried her with a raised eyebrow. "What do you say we mosey on over to the Feedbag Café for some grub? My stomach thinks my throat's been cut."

Aunt Letty answered for her. "Good idea. You two go ahead. I'll join you after I lock up."

Frank led the way through the crowd of revelers to the café. No sooner had they been seated than Connie came rushing over to their table.

"Oh, there you are, Kate," she said, pulling out a chair. "I've been looking all over for you. I was visiting my grandparents in Austin, and I only just now heard what happened." She sat down and folded her arms on the table. "You're lucky you weren't killed."

Kate shook out her napkin and placed it on her lap. "Well, as you can see, I'm perfectly fine, so you don't have to worry. Now that all four of the Ghost Riders are out of business, we can relax."

Connie blinked. "Four? I only heard of three, counting Flash."

Frank sat back in his chair. "That's all I heard about. Who was the fourth one?"

"Ringo," Kate said and went on to explain.

"That's terrible!" Connie exclaimed. "That poor dog. To be used like that. What's to become of him?"

"Brett is the new owner," Kate said. "From now on, Ringo will be working on the right side of the law."

Frank looked like he was about to give her an affectionate punch on the arm but then changed his mind and squeezed her hand instead. "All I can say is that I'm glad it's over."

Connie concurred with a nod. "Yes, and that means Ranger Tucker will soon be leaving town." She sniffed. "If you ask me, it's not a moment too soon. There's been nothing but trouble since he arrived."

Kate frowned. "I don't know how you can say that. If it wasn't for Brett, the Ghost Riders would still be on the loose."

Connie watched her with narrowed eyes. "I was referring to the way he ruined your wedding."

Frank pulled his hand away from Kate's and raised his glass. "That's all water under the bridge," he said, surprising her with his magnanimous response. "I'll just be happy when things get back to normal."

The hopeful look in his eyes made Kate's stomach knot, and she raised her glass to his. "I doubt that things will ever go back to the way they were."

Connie set her glass down. "Speaking of normal, when are my two dear friends going to set a wedding date?"

Frank took a quick gulp of water before answering. "Uh…we decided to wait until July before setting a date."

Kate twisted her napkin on her lap. "After everything that's happened," she said, choosing her words with care, "I think we could all use a breather."

As if sensing the sudden strain in the air, Connie looked from one to the other with a puzzled look on her face. "Just as long as it's a short breather," she said.

Two days later, Brett entered the candy shop holding Ringo by the leash. Something in his manner told Kate that this wasn't just a casual visit. She sensed a finality in the tenseness of his shoulders, saw it in his eyes. He'd come to say goodbye.

The thought made her emotions teeter between relief and dismay. Dismay because it brought back the usual hollow feeling that every departure left behind. Only this time, it felt like a big, gaping hole about to rip her apart.

Still, if he was no longer in town, she could forget the feel of his lips, the feel of his arms; forget the way he made her traitorous heart do flip-flops. For that, she felt relief.

Kate walked around the counter, holding a doggie cake in her palm. Concentrating on the dog helped her keep her tears at bay. Tail wagging, Ringo barked once and grabbed the treat out of her hand.

She heard Brett's intake of breath. "Fletcher, alias Frank Foster, confessed to everything, or almost everything. He'd heard about Lucky Lou's arrest and was about to leave town. He, Flash, and Lucky Lou won't be causing any more trouble."

Kate straightened. "You must be tremendously relieved."

A muscle quivered in his jaw. "Not as much as you might think. It doesn't bring my sister back."

"No, but…at least you know that justice will be served."

His gaze burned into hers, and the air seemed fraught with tension. To fill in the strained silence, she asked, "What will you do now?"

The question seemed to surprise him. "My job here is done. The rest is up to the sheriff." After a beat, he added, "I need to return to my company."

"I…I wish you didn't have to go." She bit her lip. Oh God, now she'd done it. Said what she had no business saying. No business thinking. Still, she studied him intently, hoping to see something in his eyes, his face, his demeanor that would tell her that parting was as hard for him as it was for her.

Instead, he reared back as if she'd struck him, and her heart sank. "It's time," he said. "I've been away too long, and there's still work to be done. Crime knows no holiday."

"I know…"

He studied her briefly as if to weigh the truth of her statement. "Foster's a good man. He'll do right by you."

She swallowed the sob that rose to her throat. He'd told her in a dozen different ways that their kiss had meant nothing to him. That she meant nothing to him. She needed to accept that. Had accepted it. Still, it hurt. She didn't want it to, but it did. Hurt more than she'd ever thought possible.

"Kate…" Something in his voice made her hold her breath, but whatever he had been about to say fell away unspoken. Instead, he heaved a sigh. "Had I not stopped the wedding…" He shook his head. "You and Foster would be long married by now. I can't tell you how much I regret what I did to you both."

"But it was a good thing," she said, not wanting him to feel bad. "It's given me a chance to appreciate Frank on a whole different level." She forced herself to keep going. "These last few weeks, I've discovered a side to Frank I hadn't known existed. A gentle, more caring side."

"That's…that's good," he said. His gaze penetrated her as if trying to see inside her head. "So…you've made up your mind?"

She blinked. "What?"

"To marry him."

"Well, I…" Her mind scrambled. "I…I'm not sure." She longed to tell him her true feelings, but she'd promised Frank to wait till July before making a firm decision. "We haven't made any plans. So much has happened."

"It'll make your aunt very happy," he said.

And you? Will it make you happy too?

Fearing her fragile shell of control was about to shatter, she turned and walked behind the counter. "Would…would you like some candy for the road?" she asked, reaching for a paper bag. "I just made a couple of batches of Bobby Bars and Charley Drops. And these I'm calling Sugar Spikes." She held up a piece so he could see the baseball in the center. "I'm getting better at the designs. Now they actually look like what they're supposed to look like." She forced a smile. "No more telegraph keys or mushrooms."

His gaze lit on the display. "So I see."

She picked up a scoop and proceeded to fill a bag. Desperate to avoid any pause in the conversation that would allow her to dwell on his leaving, she rattled on. "Dusty couldn't make up his mind which new friend to name them after. So he named them after all three."

She handed the bag of candy over the counter. Their fingers touched, and she quickly pulled away.

If he noticed, he kept it to himself. Instead, he

looked inside the paper bag as eagerly as a child. "What? No hope?" he asked.

"Oh, sorry." She rifled through the slips of paper and debated about giving him the one that read *Parting is such sweet sorrow*. She decided against it. Nothing sweet about saying goodbye.

"Wait here a moment," she said.

She ran into the back and picked up paper and pencil. Her heart was beating so fast, she could hardly think. Now that he was leaving, her feelings suddenly became clear. She loved him. Oh God, how she loved him! She knew that now, and the enormity of it took her breath away.

She loved him not as a friend but as someone with whom she wanted to spend the rest of her life. He'd given her no reason to believe he shared her feelings—none. Still, she felt compelled to tell him. Only not here, not now.

Better for him to find out later, when he was far away. That way, she would not have to see the rejection on his face. Nor embarrass him with her tears.

Gathering her thoughts and using Elizabeth Barrett Browning for inspiration, she wrote:

> Before I met you, I thought I knew how it felt to be in love, but you taught me I was wrong. The depth and width of my feelings for you know no end.

She folded the paper in half with shaky fingers and then lost her nerve. Writing words of love to a man not her husband was not right.

"That for me?"

At the sound of Brett's voice, she glanced up to see him lounging in the doorway.

"Eh, yes," she said.

He walked toward her, holding out his hand. "Can't wait to read it."

She tried to think of some excuse not to give it to him, but couldn't. "You...you can't read this till later," she said.

"Okay," he said. With a look of curiosity, he slipped the paper into his vest pocket, unread. It felt like he was tucking part of her heart next to his.

He hesitated, his piercing eyes impaling her. "Take care of yourself, Kate." Turning, he tugged on Ringo's leash. "Come on, boy."

"I-I don't want you to go," she called after him.

His back stiffened. "It's time for me to hit the trail. My job is done here. A ranger gets rusty staying in one place too long."

Look at me, she screamed in silence. *Look me in the eye and tell me again that our kiss meant nothing to you. That I meant nothing to you.*

But he didn't look at her, and the words she ached to hear never came. Keeping his back toward her, he walked out of the kitchen. "Say goodbye to your aunt for me."

The jingle of bells on the shop's front door told her he was gone.

Brett checked his room at the boardinghouse to make sure he'd left nothing behind. Sensing that they were leaving, Ringo's tail flopped back and forth.

"Ready to hit the trail, boy?"

Ringo perked up his ears. "Woof."

Brett picked up his blanket roll just as someone knocked on the door.

His heart jolted against his ribs. Dare he hope that it was Kate? Come to beg him not to leave? She'd said she didn't want him to go. But then again, even the sheriff had said as much. Even the owner of the boardinghouse.

Still…

He set his bedroll on the bed and pulled Ringo away from the door. "Sit!"

Inhaling, he flung the door open, and the last of his hopes crashed to the floor. Foster!

"What are you doing here?" Brett asked, trying not to let his disappointment show.

Foster took one look at Ringo and backed away, hands extended. "I need to talk to you."

Heaving a sigh, Brett let himself out of the room. He pointed a finger at Ringo. "Stay," he said and shut the door. "Make it quick." He was in no mood to deal with Foster—or anyone else, for that matter.

Ringo whined and scratched at the door. Foster moved as far away from the room as the narrow hall allowed. "Heard you were leaving," he said.

"My work is done here."

"What about me and Kate?"

Brett frowned. "What about you?"

Foster grimaced. "How am I gonna win her back with you gone?"

"You said you didn't want anything more to do with me. Now you're getting your wish."

"Yeah, but courting a woman is too much for one man. I can't do it alone."

Brett gritted his teeth. The man was even more hopeless than he'd thought. "Trust me," he said, his voice edged with exasperation. "Courting is a one-man operation. It's done all the time."

Foster looked surprised. "Is that right?"

"Just keep doing what you've been doing. You know, flowers, Shakespeare. The works."

Foster grimaced as if in pain. "I didn't think getting hitched would be so much work."

He sounded so dejected that Brett almost felt sorry for him. If Foster thought courting was tough, wait till he got a taste of marriage. "You messed up with your jealousy. So now you've got to make things right."

"Is there a way I can contact you? You know, if I need help?"

"No!" The word exploded from Brett with such force that Foster took a step back. Brett curled his hands by his sides and lowered his voice. "I never know where I'll be from day to day. My job—"

"I guess you won't be attending the wedding, then."

A pain shot through Brett's chest. "Sorry."

Ringo's whines had turned into loud barks. Brett tossed a nod in the direction of his room. "I better go."

"Oh, yeah, sure." Foster turned and headed for the stairs, muttering to himself.

32

Four weeks later

KATE WATCHED THE TWO TEXAS RANGERS WALK OUT of the shop, her misery like a steel weight in her heart. What a fool she had been. What an utter, utter fool.

Telling Brett in writing how she'd felt hadn't worked. She'd heard nothing from him. Not a word. She'd all but given up hope, but then an amazing thing had happened. Fletcher had escaped during transport to federal prison. At the time, it had seemed like an act of providence designed to bring Brett back. It was like they had been given a second chance to make things right. A second chance at love.

In anticipation of his arrival, she'd whipped up a special batch of Uncle Joe's candy she had named Tucker Sweets. After much practice, she'd even managed to create a design resembling his badge and anticipated the smile on his face when he saw what she'd done. But nothing had worked out as she'd hoped.

She couldn't get over the shock she'd felt when two other Texas Rangers had arrived in his stead. That told her more than words could say. If he didn't come back for Fletcher, he would never come back for her.

Blinking back the burning sensation in her eyes, she glanced around the shop. The latest delivery of flowers had arrived that morning. As much as she liked receiving flowers, it really was possible to have too much of a good thing. Thanks to Frank, the shop now looked like a funeral parlor.

She sighed. *Oh God, Frank.* He couldn't be sweeter or more thoughtful. In return, he only asked for one thing: her hand in marriage. And that had been the one thing she hadn't been able to give him.

She dumped the last of the Tucker Sweets in the trash and stared at the calendar on the wall. It had been four weeks and three days since Brett had last walked out the door, and still it hurt. She didn't want it to, but it did.

She pounded a fist into her palm. Pining for a man who wasn't interested in her was insane. He'd made it perfectly clear how much he regretted stopping her wedding, how much he wanted to make things right. Wanted her and Frank back together. *Frank's a good man*, he'd insisted. *He'll do right by you.*

Oh yes. He'd made his feelings clear, all right.

So why did memories of him continue to haunt her? Why did they pop into her head when least expected? Why couldn't she just forget him like he had obviously forgotten her?

It wasn't as if anything significant had happened between them. Oh sure, there was the kiss. But he'd apologized for that and had insisted it meant nothing. Apparently, he was more experienced in such things than she was. The chaste kisses exchanged with Frank had left her ill-prepared for the deeper, fuller, more passionate kiss she'd shared with Brett.

If she'd had more than one beau—had kissed dozens of other men—maybe she would be able to disregard their kiss as easily as he had.

Maybe.

Right now, she hated the way he commanded her thoughts. Hated even more the way her heart lurched whenever the bells on the shop door jingled. Hated hoping in vain that he had come back.

Well, fudge. Enough was enough! This senseless holding on was making her tense and miserable. She couldn't go on like this. Wouldn't!

She ripped the calendar off the wall and dumped it into the wastepaper basket. Brett was gone, and that was that. It was time to let go and move on. Time to turn her back on the past and face the future.

A future without Brett.

Three days later, Kate walked into the kitchen to find her aunt cooking breakfast.

Kate poured herself a cup of coffee. "I heard you pacing the floor last night. Is everything okay?"

Aunt Letty turned the flapjacks with a spatula. "What? I can't have a sleepless night if I want to?"

"I worry about you."

Aunt Letty made a face. "It's my job to worry about you. Not the other way around."

"There's no reason to worry about me," Kate said.

Aunt Letty grew serious. "Those rangers in town

brought back everything that happened, and it occurred to me that my plan to live forever might not be as foolproof as I'd thought."

Kate sighed. Her aunt wasn't the only one disturbed by the rangers' presence. They were a constant reminder of all that she'd lost, and she couldn't wait till they left.

Her aunt's voice grew husky. "I worry about something happening to me and you being left all alone in the world."

"You know that's not going to happen. Number one, nothing's going to happen to you. And number two, we have many good friends and neighbors."

Her aunt laid her spatula down and turned from the stove. "After your uncle died, our friends gathered around, and I'll always be grateful for their help and support. But when I woke in the middle of the night and couldn't sleep, it was you who was there to comfort me. It was you who wiped my tears after everyone had gone home. It was you who gave me a reason to go on living. That's what family does."

"So, what are you saying, Aunt Letty?"

Aunt Letty reached in the cupboard for two plates. "I just want to know that no matter what happens, you will always have someone to comfort you in the middle of the night. Someone who will wipe your tears and see that you're never alone."

Kate drew in her breath. She hated knowing she was the root of her aunt's distress, and it only confirmed what she already knew. Though she still had two weeks till the Independence Day dance, it was time to give Frank the answer he'd so patiently been waiting for. Had worked so hard for.

What she had with Frank was the real thing. Whatever she'd felt for Brett hadn't been real. It had been crazy and confusing and, more than anything, unnerving. No one could possibly live in such an unsettled state. Love based on friendship seemed far more stable, and that's what she needed right now.

That's why Frank was the better choice. He never made her feel flustered or unsure of herself. Marrying him meant having to make allowances, of course. She'd have to keep her animals at the house, but it was a small price to pay for her aunt's peace of mind.

Delaying the inevitable was no longer an option, not just for her aunt's sake, but for her own.

Three days later, Aunt Letty stood by the shop window ready to turn the sign to open. "Ready?" she asked, a look of uncertainty on her face.

Kate glanced at the ring on her finger and forced herself to breathe. This ring had a larger stone than the previous one. Was that why it felt so strange?

Since her aunt was looking at her funny, Kate forced a smile. Her engagement to Frank had seemed to take a weight off her aunt's shoulders. She even looked better. More rested.

"Ready," she said.

"You don't sound ready. And what's with the glum face? A bride-to-be is supposed to have the look." Aunt Letty motioned with her hands. "You know, that special glow of happiness that spells love."

"You said I had the look," Kate said.

"That was before your last wedding. I'm talking about now." Aunt Letty tilted her head. "You're not worried about something going wrong again, are you? Someone stopping the wedding? If you are, you can put your mind at ease. I'll have my shotgun with me, and if anyone tries anything, he'll have to deal with me."

Kate sighed. If she was worried about anything, it was Aunt Letty and her shotgun. But since all the trouble in town, her aunt didn't go anywhere without it. "Nothing's going to happen."

"It better not."

Since her aunt was staring at her, Kate tried to emulate the look. Whether she succeeded or not, she didn't know, but her aunt turned to the window to switch the sign. She then unlocked the door. Almost instantly, people flooded the store, led by Mrs. Tremble and her dog, Mitzie.

"Is it true, is it true?" Cassie asked. Today, the young widow had her two-year-old son with her, and she jiggled him up and down in her arms.

Aunt Letty gave a smug smile. "It's true. The wedding is officially on. At long last, Kate and Frank are getting married. Kate, show them your ring."

Kate held her hand over the counter and wiggled her fingers. The sparkling diamond garnered the appropriate oohs and aahs from the crowd.

Connie practically swooned. "Oh, it's beautiful. It's even more beautiful than the ring that was stolen."

Kate smiled and withdrew her hand.

Mrs. Cuttwell exchanged a knowing look with Aunt Letty. Since the incident with the taffy-making machine, the two former foes had become the best of friends. "Well, all I can say is it's about time you and Frank were wed."

"You simply must tell us how he proposed," Mrs. Tremble added, pulling her poodle away from the counter.

"And don't tell us it was in front of the pickle barrel," Cassie added, drawing a laugh from the others.

"No, actually, it was very romantic," Kate said.

"Very," Aunt Letty added with a nod of approval.

"We drove to the river, and Frank recited Shakespeare." Unfortunately, the few lines he'd quoted had been lifted from *Hamlet*. It was probably the first time a suicide speech had been the basis of a marriage proposal, but she didn't have the heart to tell him that. Not when he had tried so hard to please her.

"You're so lucky," Connie said, a touch of envy in her voice.

"So, when's the wedding?" Mrs. Cuttwell asked.

"Saturday," Aunt Letty said.

The dressmaker frowned. "Oh my, that doesn't give us much time. Does your dress need alterations?"

Kate shook her head. "Thank you, but no. The dress fits just fine." If anything, it was a tad loose. Mainly because she hadn't felt much like eating in recent weeks.

Connie heaved a sigh, followed by a sheepish smile. "My maid-of-honor dress needs to be taken out a tad."

Kate shot a look of sympathy at her friend. Connie had insisted she was over Harvey Wells, but there had to be a reason for her continued obsession with chocolate bonbons.

Mrs. Cuttwell gave Connie's waist a pointed

appraisal. "Bring your dress to the shop later, and we'll see what we can do."

After satisfying their curiosity, customers left with bags of candy, anxious to spread the news.

Connie remained after the others had left. "Oh, Kate, I'm so envious. What I wouldn't give to wed someone like Frank." She glanced around the shop. "Though I could do without all the flowers," she said and hastened to add, "Not that there's anything wrong with it. It just seems that some people get so caught up in the romance that they lose sight of what's really important."

Kate frowned. "Is that what you think Frank is doing?"

"Oh no, I wasn't talking about… I mean…you've been friends forever. It's just that you and Frank used to have so much fun together."

"Used to?"

"With the wedding and all that's happened, you have to admit it's been pretty tense around here."

Kate gave her friend a loving pat on the cheek. "I know. But all that's behind us, and from now on, all I want you to think about is finding your own special someone."

The corners of Connie's mouth turned down. "That's easier said than done. I'm not getting any younger."

"What are you talking about? You make yourself sound ancient."

"I'll be twenty-two in June. Everyone I know that age is married and has a slew of children."

"I don't."

"But you will soon." Glancing in the direction of the kitchen where Aunt Letty was unpacking the latest shipment of books, Connie lowered her voice. "I was afraid you had fallen for that Texas Ranger."

Kate stiffened. She didn't want to talk about Brett. "Not the dance again. I explained about that. What you saw that night, or think you saw, was me enjoying dancing with someone who didn't have two left feet."

Connie looked unconvinced. "It's not just the dance. I could see that you found him attractive." A knowing look crossed Connie's face. "Admit it."

Kate bit her lip. "Maybe." There was no sense denying it. Connie wouldn't believe her if she did. "Didn't you?" she asked, feeling defensive.

Connie studied her with narrowed eyes. "Maybe a little." She hesitated. "But I can't help but wonder if you stayed with Frank because he's the needier of the two."

Kate stared at her. "The needier?"

"Now don't get all in a huff. It's just... You know how you're always trying to fix things? If ever an animal or person is sick or in trouble, you immediately try to make things right. You dole out candy and fortunes like a doctor dispenses medicine, and it almost always makes a person feel better. It's one of the things I love about you."

"So, what are you saying?"

Connie grimaced as if searching for the right words. "I can't help but wonder if the ranger had been needy in some way, you might have chosen him over Frank."

Kate gasped. "That's...that's...crazy."

"Is it?"

"There was no choosing. Brett and I had nothing in common. He wasn't even interested in me." Belatedly, she added, "Nor I in him."

"If you say so," Connie said, sounding as doubtful as she looked. "Still…you haven't been yourself since he left town, and that has me worried." Her expression softened. "Oh, Kate, I'm sorry. I shouldn't have said anything. You know I think the world of you and Frank. I just want you both to be happy."

"I do know that," Kate said. "And I feel the same about you. Now will you stop worrying? There's nothing the matter with me. I've just been busy. You know we're breaking in a new employee." The woman's name was Janet Mason. She'd never worked outside the home before, but now that her children were grown, she had been looking for something to do. "It's not easy teaching someone the art of making candy."

Connie's forehead creased. "Are you sure that's all it is?"

"Absolutely." Kate picked up a paper bag. "Now, how about some bonbons?"

"I better not," Connie said with a wistful sigh. "I'll never fit into my bridesmaid dress. But I'll take one of your fortunes. And it better be a good one."

"How about this one?" Kate asked, pulling a slip of paper out the box. "'Love is just around the corner.'"

Her good humor restored, Connie laughed. "I just hope that corner is on planet earth."

33

Brett stared at his dog, fists planted firmly at his waist. "Okay, where's the boot?"

For an answer, Ringo slanted his head and cocked an ear.

The boot in question belonged to the ranger captain.

Brett was already in hock for two pairs of boots, a gun belt, a metal flask, and a sheathed knife. Not good. So far, no amount of training had convinced Ringo to give up his outlaw ways. Nothing on the ground was safe. Training an old dog to paw the straight and narrow was hard, but so was trying to convince a bunch of men of the virtue of neatness. They were just as much to blame for Ringo's constant fall from grace. If they would stop leaving their belongings around, the problem would be solved.

Next to Brett, the man everyone called Cannonball Charlie laughed. "Do you think he's gonna tell you?"

Brett let go of Ringo's collar. "If he knows what's good for him, he will."

Okay, so he was talking through his hat. It would be easier to find the Lost Dutchman's Mine than

Ringo's hiding place. He had tried tricking the dog into showing him, to no avail. Ringo was as fast as he was smart and could vanish in the chaparral quicker than a flea could hop on fur.

Since nothing could be done till morning, Brett joined the company of men around the campfire. Ringo sprawled next to him, head resting on his paws, looking as innocent as a newborn babe.

Brett pulled out the letter in his vest pocket—a letter addressed to his brother.

He hadn't fully forgiven Paul for stealing away Deborah, but he no longer had the heart to carry a grudge. He also better understood the difficulty in walking away from a woman you loved. He couldn't blame Paul for his inability to do what he had hardly been able to do himself.

Walking away from Kate had been the most difficult thing he'd ever done. He'd been so close, so very, very close to telling her how he felt. *Oh, Kate… Kate!*

He replaced the letter and reached into his vest pocket for the little slip of paper that Kate had given him. He'd held on to it all this time and still hadn't been able to bring himself to read it.

It had been more than a month since he'd said goodbye to Kate, and it still hurt. Hurt like hell. No woman he'd loved and lost in the past had affected him as deeply as she had. He thought of her day and night. Everything from the blue of the sky to the stars and moon reminded him of her. He heard her name in the call of every bird, in the whisper of every breeze, in the buzz of every insect.

Adding to his misery, he no longer derived satisfaction from his job. He'd counted on work to heal his broken heart as it had in the past, but he was no longer driven to right the wrongs of the world.

Instead, the long hours of relentless pursuit left him feeling restless and impatient. Last week, his company had broken up a ring of cattle rustlers, yet he'd felt no pleasure.

The nights spent in his bedroll were even worse. That's when he found himself hankering for things he'd never thought to hanker for: home, family, wife.

Kate.

A burst of laughter broke into his thoughts. Next to him, Ringo lifted his head, glanced at the revelers, and then promptly went back to sleep.

The laughter stopped, and the men continued playing the "Can you top this?" game. The stakes were high, and for that reason, the game was taken seriously. The one telling the biggest or most outrageous tall tale was relieved from camp detail the following day.

"Hey, Tucker. It's your turn," one of the men called.

Brett declined with a raise of his hand. He wasn't in the mood for fun or camaraderie and hadn't been since rejoining his company.

"Another time," he said.

"Ah, shucks. You ain't no fun anymore."

"Leave him alone," the man they called Smoky said. "Since he got hisself a case of lovesick, he ain't been worth a bucket of shucks."

The men went back to their game, leaving Brett to his troubled thoughts. *Lovesick? Is that what's wrong with me?* He lifted his gaze to the sky and wondered if he would ever again be able to look at the stars without thinking of Kate.

But that wasn't the only thing on his mind. While Sheriff Keeler had been transporting the Ghost Riders to federal prison, Foster/Fletcher had escaped.

He should have been the one to track Fletcher down, but by the time he'd heard the news, the captain had already assigned two other rangers. That had been more than a week ago, and Brett hadn't heard a word since.

Fletcher better not have gotten away. If he had, then everything Brett had gone through in Haywire—all the pain and heartache that followed—had been for naught.

He stared at the little slip of paper in his hand, debating whether to replace it in his pocket or toss it in the fire unread. For several long moments, he stared at it, then slowly, with trembling fingers, unfolded it.

Just the sight of Kate's flowery handwriting was like a stab to his heart, and he had to read the words several times before he could grasp their meaning. He sat upright and moved closer to the light of the fire to read it again.

Before I met you, I thought I knew how it felt to be in love, but you taught me I was wrong. The depth and width of my feelings for you know no end.

Brett sucked in his breath, and his gaze kept going back to the word *love*. She loved him? Was he reading that right? Kate often quoted poetry, and something about those words did sound familiar. Still, she was so careful about picking out the exact right words.

His mouth ran dry. She would never write the word *love* unless she meant it! Again, raucous laughter interrupted his thoughts. Standing, Smoky stretched his arms, ready to call it a night. One by one, the others stood, some yawning.

But before anyone hit the tents, they were stopped by the sound of galloping hooves. All hands flew to the guns at their sides, and Ringo jumped up, ears perked.

Brett slipped Kate's note into his pocket and reached for his weapon.

"It's just us," a voice called out of the darkness. Ringo barked and wagged his tail as Texas Ranger Collier rode up to camp and dismounted. "We got him," he said.

Brett moved his hand away from his gun. That was a relief. Fletcher was behind bars where he belonged. Hopefully, precautions would be taken this time to make sure he didn't escape again.

The man they called Happy swung off his horse and reached into his saddlebags. "Brought you all back a treat," he said, pulling out a white paper sack. "Anyone want some candy?" He walked around the campfire, offering it to the others.

Cannonball Charlie stuck his hand in the bag. "Where'd you get it?"

"There's this candy shop in Haywire. You won't believe this. They even sell a candy called Tucker Sweets. That's the green one in your hand."

Brett's heart practically leaped to his throat. Had he heard right? Kate had named a candy after him? He'd once heard her say that only the most special people had a candy named after them. People she loved and didn't want to forget. That made the words of love on the note seem more real. Oh God…

Tucker reached into the offered bag and pulled out a piece. He held it closer to the fire and studied the badge in the center that resembled his own. "Who sold you this?" he asked, his voice ragged.

Happy shrugged. "Don't know her name. All I can tell you is that she had the reddest hair I ever saw on a dame."

Collier nodded in agreement. "And she asked about you."

"She…she did?"

"Yep," Happy said. "Told us she understood about all the ranger stuff and why it was so important to us men."

Brett drew in a sharp breath. "She said that?"

"She sure enough did," Happy assured him. "Said she knew you'd understand why she was getting married."

Brett stared at him. "She's getting married."

Happy gave him a funny look. "That's what she said. She's getting married on Saturday."

Brett stiffened. "Saturday?" he asked, his tone sharper than he meant. "This Saturday?" He had been so certain that she and Foster were already wed.

"That's what she said."

Brett's mouth went dry. "That's tomorrow."

Happy shrugged. "I guess it is." His eyebrows arched. "What's it to you, anyway?"

Cannonball Charlie held up a Tucker Sweet. "If I was a bettin' man, I'd say the answer lies with this here candy." He shifted his gaze to Brett. "Am I right, or am I right?"

Had he expected an answer, he would have been sorely disappointed. Brett was already running to his horse, Ringo by his side.

34

ON THE DAY OF HER WEDDING, KATE STOOD IN THE church anteroom staring in the mirror.

Connie circled around her like a nervous hen, fluffing out the skirt of her satin gown and straightening the bow on her bustle. Beneath her fingertip veil, Kate wore her hair in a braided twist with wispy tendril bangs.

She forced herself to breathe. The sick feeling inside was due to her tightly laced corset. Had to be. *Please, don't let it be a sign of cold feet. Or...*

She clamped down on her thoughts. *Oh God, not Brett again.* She had put him out of her mind. Okay, maybe not entirely. She gave herself an impatient shake. Oh, fudge, what was she thinking? He still had a way of springing into her head when she least expected it. But that had to stop. Brett was gone, and he wasn't coming back. She'd finally accepted that.

Gone.

If only he hadn't been so anxious to bring her and Frank together, then maybe...

Gone.

She gave herself a mental shake. *Stop it!* Balling her

hands at her sides, she hardened her resolve. From this moment on, Brett Tucker would be dead to her. Whatever hold he had on her would have to stop. She planned on devoting her life to being the best wife possible to Frank. He deserved no less.

Connie finished fiddling with Kate's gown and stepped back. "You look beautiful," she said, clasping her hands to her chest.

Kate heaved the deepest breath her corset allowed and turned with a smile. "You do too." Her maid of honor's pink gown gave Connie's complexion a rosy glow.

Connie searched Kate's face, her eyes filled with worry. "Oh, Kate, all I want is for you to be happy. You deserve it. After what happened at your first wedding—"

"Nothing like that will happen again," Kate said. "Frank's a changed man. His jealousy is no longer a problem. So, you see? Everything worked out for the best."

Instead of looking relieved or happy for her, Connie's mouth twisted downward.

Kate frowned. "Are you okay?"

"Yes, of course," Connie said, seeming to avoid Kate's eyes. "Why wouldn't I be?"

"You're not still upset about Harvey, are you?"

Connie reached out to adjust Kate's veil. "Nope, he's completely out of my mind. I honestly don't know what I ever saw in him."

"Oh, Connie, are you sure?"

"Yes. Now will you quit worrying?"

"I can't help but worry about you." So, if it wasn't Harvey on Connie's mind, it had to be something else. Connie had been acting strangely of late. "You know that even when I'm married, we'll still be friends. Nothing will change that."

This time Connie did meet Kate's gaze. "I know that."

"Then say what's on your mind. And don't tell me it's nothing. I know you too well, and something is definitely bothering you."

A shadow of indecision flitted across Connie's forehead. "We don't have time for this right now." She glanced at the door as if willing an usher to knock and say it was time to start down the aisle. "Your wedding…"

Kate folded her arms across her lace bodice. "I'm not leaving this room till you fess up."

"Oh, Kate. Don't make me do this. I'm afraid we'll both regret it if I do."

Kate frowned. Now she really was worried. "I mean it, Connie. I'm not leaving this room until I know what's on your mind."

Connie lifted her gaze to the ceiling and let out a sigh. "I didn't want to tell you this…"

Kate felt a jolt of alarm. "Tell…tell me what?"

Dark, misty eyes met Kate's. "I promised Frank I wouldn't say anything, but you and I have been best friends for a long time…"

"Go on."

"The Texas Ranger—Mr. Tucker—tutored Frank on how to win you back."

Surprised to hear Brett's name, Kate frowned. "What do you mean by 'tutored'?"

"I saw them in the Feedbag Café practicing marriage proposals. I later confronted Frank, and he confessed. It was like he was attending some sort of male charm school or something. The flowers, the note, the lame goat, even the purchase of your ring were all Mr. Tucker's doings. Frank told me that Mr. Tucker even taught him how to hide his jealousy."

"Hide his jealousy?"

Connie nodded. "Whenever he feels jealous, he's supposed to whistle until the feeling is gone."

Kate reared back, momentarily speechless. So that explained Frank's annoying habit of whistling whenever they were in public. When she finally found her voice, she squeaked out, "Brett did that?"

He'd made no secret of how much he'd wanted her and Frank back together, but never had she imagined he would go to such lengths. She inhaled. Now it all made sense. The sudden change in Frank had seemed so out of character. So…unreal.

Her temper snapped. "And you waited until now to tell me this?"

Connie wrung her hands together. "I shouldn't have said anything. I promised Frank I wouldn't say a word. But…I'm just so afraid he hasn't changed as much as you might think."

Kate didn't know what to say. All this time, she'd thought that Frank was being thoughtful and sweet, but it was really Brett pulling the strings. It had been Brett all along. She had been nothing but a pawn in the game of love.

A tap sounded at the door, followed by an usher's voice. "It's time."

It was time, all right. Past time.

"Here, don't forget your bouquet," Connie said.

Kate glanced at the carefully arranged spray of red roses. Her aunt had gone to such lengths to make sure that every detail of her wedding was perfect. That made what she had to do so much harder.

Declining to take the posy with a shake of her head, she flung the door open. Hands curled at her sides, she forced a ragged breath and stomped by the usher.

Connie ran after her. "Kate, wait!"

She didn't wait, nor did she slow down. Instead, she stormed outside to the front of the church. Pushing the heavy doors open, she rushed inside. Too angry to think or even care that she was making a scene, she stormed down the aisle to the altar, mindless of the filled pews on either side. The organist picked up speed as if trying to keep up with her.

Connie's words still ringing in her head, Kate barreled toward Frank, eyes flashing. Tilting his head with a frown, he looked like he didn't know whether to run or duck.

Startled, the minister quickly thumbed through his little black book and cleared his throat.

Ignoring him, Kate glared daggers at Frank. "'Losing you is like a world without candy,'" she muttered beneath her breath.

"Dearly beloved," Reverend Johnson began in a ponderous, yet hesitant voice.

"Not now," Kate said and lowered her voice for Frank's ears only. "'A world without sunshine. A world without laughter.'" How foolish of her to think that Frank had suddenly turned into some sort of poet, able to pour his heart out on paper. "I should have known you never wrote those words!"

Frank gulped and ran a finger along his collar. "Ah, come on, Kate," he whispered back. "What was I supposed to do? You know I'm lousy at expressing myself."

"At least then I knew what you said was honest and true. Using someone else's words..." She shook her head. "How can I believe anything you say?"

He grimaced. "Okay, so Tucker helped me. He taught me what to say, what to do, and how to act."

"And how to hide your jealousy!" she said, forgetting to keep her voice down. A gasp from one of the wedding guests reminded her they weren't alone. "Don't forget that!" she said in a quieter but no less passionate voice.

"I'm still working on that part," Frank admitted.

The minister mopped his forehead with a handkerchief and tried again. "Dearly beloved..."

"Not now," Kate and Frank said in unison.

Frank shook his head. "Ah, gee, Katie. Don't look at me like that. I can't help it if I get all tangled up inside if another man looks at you."

She snapped her mouth shut. As a child, she'd grabbed hold of him to keep him from falling from the train. In some ways, she'd been holding on to him ever since. Now to save them both from what would surely be a terrible mistake, she had to let him go. It was the only way.

"I can't do this, Frank. I can't marry you."

He frowned. "Because I let Tucker help me win you back?"

"No. It's because...I agreed to marry a man who doesn't exist."

The problem was, she had liked that man. Liked

him more than she'd ever thought possible. That was one of the reasons she had agreed to go through with the wedding. She had honestly and truly thought Frank had changed. Had believed it with all her heart.

"Tucker's gone," he said. "So you don't have to worry about me doing any more of that dumb stuff."

Kate took a step back. "But...but I liked that dumb stuff."

Reverend Johnson opened his mouth to say something, but before he had the chance, Frank cut him off. "Not now," he said, saving her the trouble.

The minister looked affronted. "I was just going to suggest that we adjourn to my office."

Ignoring him, Frank gaped at her. "So...so what you're saying is you like the flowers that Tucker made me send. You liked them more than you liked my other gifts."

"I liked all your gifts," Kate said, not wanting to hurt him more than necessary.

"The eggbeater?"

She nodded. "I use it every day." She ran her sweaty hands down the satin skirt. This was a nightmare. Here she was, standing at the altar in her wedding gown, discussing a blasted eggbeater.

"But you liked Tucker's ideas better."

Before she could respond, her aunt bustled up to the altar, wielding her shotgun. "What's the matter? What's going on?"

"Please, Aunt. I need to talk to Frank alone."

Aunt Letty scoffed. "Well, you sure chose a funny place to do it. What is so important that it can't wait till later?"

"I can't tell you right now." She gave her aunt's arm a reassuring squeeze. "Please, please go to your seat."

Her aunt looked about to argue, but instead returned to the front pew.

Kate turned to Frank. "I'm so sorry," she whispered. "I…I want you to know I still love you as a friend. I wanted it to be more. There was a time when I thought it was more. But"—she shook her head—"I guess in a way, we've both been pretending to be something we're not."

For a long moment, neither of them spoke, and an uneasy buzz of whispers filled the silence.

Frank heaved a sigh and grimaced as if in pain. "Maybe it's for the best," he said, his shoulders slumped. The whispers stopped, and the guests leaned forward, trying to catch his every word. "If…if it's this hard to get married, I don't want to think about what lies ahead."

She felt terrible. Was it possible to feel any worse? He had tried to change for her and maybe had lost a bit of himself in the process. "I really appreciate how hard you tried, and…I wish it didn't have to end like this."

The initial sadness on his face changed to a look of relief. "I wish it didn't either. But getting married and all that courting stuff is just"—he gazed at her as if seeing her for the very first time—"it's just not for me, and I'm glad to be done with it."

"So am I," she said. "I kinda miss the old Frank."

"I miss him too," Frank said. "And I miss the way we were before all that courting stuff got in the way. We used to have fun together. Laugh."

"That's because we were friends," she said. "Good friends. Maybe that's all we were ever meant to be."

He nodded. "Maybe so," he said. "Maybe so." With an apologetic glance at the minister, he turned and walked away.

Shocked guests swiveled their heads to follow his progress up the aisle. After he'd left the church, the heavy wood door banging shut behind him, all eyes turned to Kate.

Aunt Letty jumped up from her seat. The shotgun she'd brought to the church to prevent another wedding disaster fell to the floor with a clatter.

"Kate, you can't just let him leave like that. Go after him."

Kate blinked back tears. "Forget it, Aunt Letty. The wedding is off."

35

"GIDDUP!"

Brett raced up the hill, his horse's hooves pounding the ground like the rapid beat of tom-toms. Birds circled overhead, protesting the intrusion with loud caws. Cows lifted their heads with swishing tails and blank stares.

He crested the hill, and the church came into view. The carriages parked outside gave him small comfort.

His body was stiff from riding, and he'd lost valuable time in town changing horses. But Soldier was tired, as was Ringo, and he'd left them both at the stables.

He'd hoped to catch Kate before she left for the church, but when he reached town, he found businesses already closed so that their owners could attend the wedding.

At any minute, the church doors could swing open. The thought of Kate and Foster emerging from the church as husband and wife made Brett feel sick.

Snapping the reins, he urged his mount to go faster. Every step carried him closer to her; every second seemed to carry her farther away.

This was crazy. Insane. He had no right, no right

at all. Still, she had given him that note, and the word *love* still rang in his heart. Then there was the candy… Why would she go to so much trouble if he meant nothing to her? Why?

God forgive him, but he had to know. Did thoughts of him fill her every waking hour like she filled his? Did visions of him rob her of sleep? Did the memory of his lips torment her?

He toyed with the idea of slipping into the church unseen. He would know at a glance if she was happy or sad. If she was happy, he would leave and never bother her again. But if she was the least bit unhappy, he would know that too.

Oh God! He'd stopped her wedding once; how could he possibly justify stopping it a second time?

Reaching the church, he quickly dismounted. But before he could race inside, the door burst open and Kate ran down the steps in her wedding gown.

Alone.

She kept running as if she hadn't seen him.

"Kate?" he called after her. "What's wrong? What happened?"

She whirled about, and her jaw dropped. "Brett? What…what are you doing here?"

He held his hands shoulder high. "I'm not here to cause you any trouble. It's just… When I read your note, I knew I had to see you."

She frowned. "I wrote that weeks ago."

"I know." He took a big breath. "I couldn't bring myself to read it till last night, and I've been nearly out of my mind ever since. When I heard about the wedding, I had to know if you were happy—"

"Happy?" she choked out. Before he could explain, something seemed to snap inside her, and she rushed at him with pummeling fists. "Happy? No, I'm not happy. I just found out that this...that everything I believed about Frank was a lie."

"Kate, stop!" He caught her by the wrists. "I don't know what you mean. What's a lie?"

"All of it!" She yanked her arms away from him, her eyes flashing. "I know about the flowers...the note...the goat. It was all your idea."

His jaw tightened, but he didn't deny it. How could he? Everything she said was true. "I was only trying to help."

"You think that was a help? Making me believe that it all came from Frank? Trying to make me fall in love with a man who doesn't exist?"

"Kate, look at me."

She shook her head. "Just go. Leave me alone."

This time he grabbed her by the shoulders. "Look at me," he said, louder this time, his voice full of entreaty. "That man *does* exist, and you're looking at him," he said, his earnest eyes seeking hers.

She tried to pull away, but he tightened his hold and his voice grew husky.

"It took me a while to figure out what you meant to me. At first, all I wanted was to right the wrong I'd done. I honestly thought you loved Frank, and all I wanted was for you to be happy. When I finally realized my true feelings for you, I didn't know what to do. Kate, I love you. I love you more than I thought it possible to love anyone. Maybe that scared me, I don't know. All I know is that you mean everything to me, and I hope you feel the same about me."

For a moment, it seemed as if the earth had stopped turning and the world stood still. All Kate could do was stare at him.

Finally, she found her voice. "You…you love me?" she stammered.

His eyes answered her first, with a light burning so brightly that it took her breath away.

"Every word I told Frank to say came from the heart. *My* heart. They were things I wanted to say to you, but I didn't think I had the right. When I read your note and heard you'd named a candy after me, I had to come back and find out for sure what it meant. Yes, I love you, Kate Denver. I think I loved you from the first moment I set eyes on you. If that's not what you want to hear, then say so. I'll leave and never come back."

Her breath caught in her lungs. Try as she might to resist the appeal in his eyes, it was no use. She felt the shield around her heart fall away, revealing not the grief and sadness she'd walled inside but something far more fluid and beautiful, something that seemed so right.

It was as if a bright light had suddenly illuminated the darkest corners of her mind, making everything crystal clear. She now knew that the reason she hadn't admitted her true feelings for Brett had been fear.

Fear that he would strip away her defenses. Fear

that such a thing would open her up to future losses, future hurts, future heartache.

That had never been a worry with Frank. Maybe it was because he held part of himself back too. Hiding behind a protective shield was the lingering curse of childhood grief, of loving and losing at a young age. She'd accused Frank of not trusting her, but the truth was that, in turn, she hadn't trusted him enough to give him her whole heart.

Somehow, she'd known—sensed—that holding back would not be possible with this man. Once she admitted her true feelings, Brett would demand everything she had to give.

And more.

"I...I don't know what to say," she whispered.

"You can start by saying you forgive me for trying to marry you off to someone else. For taking so long to know my own mind. For leaving without telling you how I felt. For—"

"Taking so long to read my love note to you?" she asked.

He gave her a sheepish smile. "Yeah, that too."

Just then, Aunt Letty crashed through the double doors, brandishing her shotgun. "Oh, no, you don't, Kate Denver. Don't you go believing a word this man has to say!"

"Aunt Letty!" Kate gasped. "Put that gun down!"

"I most certainly will not. I mean it! Had it not been for this man, you and Frank would have been married by now."

"Auntie, please. Put the gun down before someone gets hurt."

"Not till he leaves." Glaring at Brett, she waved the shotgun back and forth for emphasis. "So what's it gonna be, cowboy?"

Releasing Kate's arm, Brett held up his hands, palms out. "Mrs. Denver, I wish I could apologize for all the trouble I've caused, but the truth is, I believe that marrying Foster would be the worst mistake your niece could make."

"I don't recall asking your opinion, Mr. Tucker!"

Kate stepped toward her aunt, hand extended. "It's true, Aunt Letty. Marrying Frank would have been a terrible mistake. I know that now."

Aunt Letty lowered her shotgun with narrowed eyes. "Does...does this mean there's not going to be a wedding? Ever?"

"Oh, there's going to be a wedding, Mrs. Denver," Brett said, locking Kate in his gaze. "Just as soon as your niece here agrees to marry me."

Kate's heart pounded. "Is...is that a proposal?"

"No, but this is." He dropped to one knee and took her hand in his. He gazed deep into her eyes, the tenderness in their depths stealing away her breath.

"Katherine Anne Denver, I never thought I could love a woman the way I love you." His voice thick with emotion, he continued. "I want you in my life now and forevermore. I want our children to have red hair and freckles, same as you. I want to look at them and see your blue eyes and big, bright smile. I want your face to be the last thing I see at night, the first thing I see in the morning. Marry me, and you'll make me the happiest man alive."

Kate let out her breath. *Oh, please don't let this be*

a dream. "What…what about your job? You said you could never settle down. You said—"

"I know what I said, and none of it turned out to be true. Without you, nothing else matters."

"Oh, Brett," she whispered, the last of her reservations falling away. She pressed her free hand against his cheek, tears welling in her eyes. Something broke loose inside, and all the feelings she'd tried to deny rushed through her. "I love you too. I didn't want to…I honestly didn't want to, but there was no helping myself."

His face lit up with a joy that matched her own. "Oh God, Kate! You don't know how much I wanted to hear you say those words aloud. I guess we were both fighting a losing battle. I know I was." He beseeched her. "Does that mean you forgive me for trying to marry you off to someone else?"

Her mouth curved in a smile. "I forgive you," she said.

"What about the rest?"

"The rest?"

"I asked you to marry me."

"Oh!" Kate clutched her hand to her chest, and happiness unlike any she'd ever known bubbled up inside. "Oh, Brett. Yes, yes, yes, I'll marry you!"

Jumping to his feet, Brett took her in his arms and brushed his lips against her forehead. "Oh God, Kate!"

Behind him, Aunt Letty lowered her weapon. "There it is," she said. "There it is."

Surprised that she had forgotten her aunt's presence, Kate pulled out of Brett's arms. "There what is?"

"The look that every bride should have on her face.

The look of a woman in love." Aunt Letty turned her gaze to Brett. "The look of a man in love."

Kate wasn't sure she'd heard right. "You mean… you're not mad that I ruined the wedding?"

Aunt Letty lifted her shoulders. "Who said anything about a ruined wedding?" She gave her shotgun an emphatic shake. "Get a move on. Both of you. We can't keep the minister waiting any longer."

Brett exchanged a glance with Kate. "You want us to get married now? But I don't have a ring."

Aunt Letty's gaze traveled back and forth between the two of them. "Do you swear you'll love my niece to the end of your born days, no matter what?"

"Yes," Brett said, looking deep into Kate's eyes. "And if it's possible to love beyond the grave, I swear I'll do that too."

"In that case, you can borrow my ring until you have time to purchase another." To Kate, she added, "It's the one your uncle gave me on our wedding day."

Her aunt's offer only added to Kate's joy. "Oh, Auntie, thank you."

Juggling the shotgun in her arms, Aunt Letty pulled off her wedding ring and handed it to Brett.

He studied the simple gold band before slipping it into his vest pocket. "I've already picked out a ring for you," he said quietly to Kate. "It has stones that match the color of your eyes, and as soon as I have the chance, I will order it."

Still unable to believe the amazing turn of events, Kate gazed up at him. "You already picked out a ring. But how did you know?"

He laughed at her expression. "A man can dream, can't he?"

Kate felt her heart swell. "Oh, Brett. I just hope I can make you as happy as you make me."

Brett started to say something, but Aunt Letty stopped him with a poke of her shotgun.

"You two will have time for all that jibber-jabber later. Right now, we have a wedding to attend to." She scanned Brett up and down from the top of his Stetson to the toes of his dusty boots. "As for the groom…I guess you'll have to do." She indicated the church steps with a toss of her head and pointed her shotgun at them. "Now git in that church, both of you. Your guests are waiting. And this time, I aim to see that nothing stops this wedding."

Epilogue

One Year Later

"GIDDUP!"

Pressing his heels against his horse's ribs, Brett urged his steed to go faster. Each thunderous pound of his horse's hooves rumbled through him; each moment of delay felt like a nail to his heart. *Oh God! What if I'm too late? What if something went wrong and I'm not there to save her?*

At long last, he spotted the horse and buggy on the road ahead. Waving his hat like a madman, he yelled, "Stop!"

The vehicle pulled to the side of the road. The derby-hatted driver leaned over the side of his wagon. "Confound it, Tucker. The way you were carrying on, I thought you were a highwayman."

"Sorry, Doctor. Your wife told me you were on your way to check on Old Man Fletcher." Brett's horse did a fancy dance beneath him. "It's Kate!"

The doctor gave a solemn nod. "Well, what are we waiting for?" With a shake of his reins, he pulled his buggy forward and made a wide circle in the middle of the road.

After waiting for the doctor to turn, Brett led the way, his heart in his throat. *Hold on, Kate. Hold on.*

Some twenty minutes later, he raced past the sign reading KATE'S ANIMAL INFIRMARY and reached the house ahead of the doctor amid a chorus of barks, bleats, and neighs. Quickly tethering his horse, he raced up the porch. Ringo greeted him as he burst through the door. "Down, boy!"

Racing through the parlor, he came to a sliding halt at the bedroom threshold, the strong smell of vinegar watering his eyes.

Kate was sitting up in bed. He'd left her writhing in pain and swearing like a sailor, and here she was upon his return, with a sweet smile on her face. *What the…?*

And then he saw the bundle cradled in her arms, and he practically fell to his knees in relief.

Connie was the first to speak. "Congratulations. It's a boy."

Aunt Letty ran an arm over her damp forehead. "A big, beautiful boy," she added with a wide grin. "And he's gonna drive the girls wild. I can tell. He's got the look."

"The look, eh?" Brett said and laughed. Pulling off his hat, he walked to the bed, his eyes misty. "Well, what do you know?" Awed and humbled by the sight in front of him, he felt more than anything grateful. The baby hadn't been due for another two weeks. When the first pains came, he'd been so afraid for Kate, so afraid for their baby. Afraid of losing them. Losing the two people who meant more to him than anything in the world.

Kate moved the blanket away from the baby's downy head. "Isn't he the sweetest thing you ever did see?"

He peered at his son's tiny red face and thought his heart would burst with joy. Paternal love bubbled up inside him like hot lava. How was it possible for something so small to command so much love?

"What did I ever do to deserve such a precious child? Such an amazing wife?"

"And an outlaw dog," Kate added. "Don't forget that."

He chuckled and tenderly cupped his son's head. "He has your red hair," he said, his voice choked.

"It looks kind of blondish to me." She smiled up at him. "And he definitely has your eyes."

The doctor rushed into the room, black bag in hand, and skidded to a stop at the foot of the bed. "Good God, Letty. You've been at the vinegar again, haven't you?"

Aunt Letty crossed her arms and raked him over with a disapproving look. "Somebody's got to practice medicine around here! Since you're never around when we need you."

"Sorry. Got here soon as I could." He set his bag on a chair. "Well? Are you gonna introduce me to my new little patient?"

Brett proudly gathered his son in his arms and held him so the doctor could see. "Dr. Avery, meet our son, Joseph." With a loving glance at his wife, he added, "We named him after Kate's uncle."

"For now, we're calling him Joey," Kate said.

Upon hearing the news, Aunt Letty clasped her hands to her chest and promptly got all teary-eyed. "Oh my! Your uncle would have been so proud."

"That's a mighty fine name," the doctor said with a hearty nod of approval. "Let's have a look." As he moved toward the bed, he got his foot tangled in a bunch of cords. "Oh no, don't tell me," he said, untangling himself.

"Harvey's baby sling," Aunt Letty said, rolling her eyes to the contraption on the ceiling holding the thing up.

"Don't worry, Aunt Letty," Brett said. "Long as Kate has me, she won't be needing any baby sling." He laid his son at the foot of the bed with a chuckle.

"What's so funny?" Kate asked.

"I was just thinking of the candy I plan on making in his honor. What should we call it? Joey Chews? Joey Pops? Joey—" He tilted his head. "You laugh?"

"I can't help it," she said. Though her face still looked strained with exertion, her eyes shone with an inner glow. "My husband, the candy maker."

He couldn't blame her for laughing. In one short year, he had gone from Texas Ranger to confectioner and had loved every minute of it. While Kate was in confinement and with Aunt Letty having retired, it had been up to him to run the shop with only the one employee. If his idea for expansion worked as he'd hoped, he would soon have to hire more.

"What about Joey Almond Bits?" he asked.

Kate's smile filled her whole face. "I like it."

While the doctor examined little Joey, Connie walked to Kate's side and patted her on the shoulder. "Since you're now in good hands, do you mind if I leave? I believe I have a date with a pickle."

"No, you go ahead," Kate said, squeezing her friend's hand. "And, Connie, thank you."

"A pickle?" Brett asked after Connie had left the room.

Lowering her voice, Kate explained. "She thinks Frank is about to propose marriage."

Brett frowned. "You mean after all my tutoring, Foster's still…"

"Being Frank, and that's just how she likes it," Kate said and laughed. "Frank and Connie. Who would have thought such a thing possible?"

"Who indeed?" Sitting on the edge of the bed, Brett tilted her chin upward and kissed her tenderly on the lips.

With a happy sigh, she clung to him. "Oh, Brett," she whispered. "Don't stop. Don't ever, ever stop."

Laughter rumbled in the back of his throat. "I have a feeling that my *stopping* days are over," he said. And with that, he kissed her again.

*Read on for a sneak peek at the next book
in the charming Haywire Brides series*

Chapter 1

Haywire, Texas
1886

THE MOMENT EMILY ROSE STEPPED OFF THE TRAIN, SHE
knew she'd made a terrible mistake. It wasn't just the
heat pressing down on her like a thick, wet blanket.
Nor the dust that clogged her throat and stung her
eyes. It wasn't even the relentless flies.

Rather, it was the feeling of dread that settled like a
lead weight in the pit of her stomach. One look at the
sorrowful excuse for a town and the trouble she'd left
back in Boston seemed like a tea party in comparison.

The driver set to work tossing her baggage into the
rear of the hotel omnibus with reckless abandon.

"Oh, do be careful with that," she cried, grabbing
her bandbox out of his hand.

Shooting her an exasperated look, the driver reached
for her carpetbag and hurled it into the compartment
with the rest of her baggage. Since her belongings
commanded all available space, the other passengers
were forced to carry their travel gear on board.

One matronly woman glared at Emily, the nostrils of her beaklike nose flaring. "Some people have no consideration for others," she grumbled, her voice loud enough to gain the attention of those still standing in line.

Emily apologized and offered to help the passenger with her valise, but the woman would have none of it. Instead, she made quite a show of lugging her single satchel up the steps of the omnibus, grunting and groaning and complaining like an old crow.

Emily disregarded the woman's theatrics, but it was harder to ignore the curious stares directed at her stylish blue traveling suit. She had been so anxious to make her escape, she'd not thought about clothes. The last thing she needed was to call attention to herself. Had she been thinking straight, she would have purchased something more sedate. Perhaps a simple gingham or calico dress, though she doubted such a thing could have been found in all of Boston.

The same was true of the plain cloth bonnets locals seemed to favor. Her own felt hat, stylishly trimmed with feathers, now seemed hopelessly out of place.

Sidestepping a pile of horse manure, Emily boarded the omnibus, her bandbox in hand. She pulled a handkerchief out of her sleeve and wiped off the dusty leather seat before adjusting her bustle and sitting.

The driver took his seat and waited until the last of his passengers had boarded before shaking the reins and clicking his tongue. As if to protest the heavy load, the two roans snorted as they plodded forward, scattering more dust with their heavy hooves.

Emily fanned her heated face with the soiled

handkerchief and gazed out the glassless window. Compared to Boston's sturdy red brick buildings, the adobe shops with their false fronts and rough-hewn signs looked like they could be blown away with one good gust of wind.

No cobblestones lined the thoroughfare. Instead a bumpy dirt road wound through town, flanked by wooden sidewalks.

She looked for the drugstore owned by the man she'd traveled all this way to marry, but didn't see it. Instead, they passed a general store, bank, gunsmith, and leather shop, but no ladies hat or dress emporiums. A sign reading *The Haywire Book and Sweet Shop* gave her a flicker of hope. The selling of books suggested that maybe the town wasn't as primitive as it appeared.

She reached into her purse and pulled out the dog-eared letter that had been carefully tucked inside. Unfolding it, she reread the simple instructions written in bold handwriting. She was supposed to check in to the hotel. A driver would pick her up at four o'clock sharp and take her to the courthouse. Her betrothed would meet her there to exchange vows.

She chewed on her lower lip and forced herself to breathe. Never had she imagined herself a mail-order bride. But then neither had she dreamt she would be forced to leave Boston in shame, with hardly a penny to her name.

Her only hope was that her soon-to-be husband was as kind and caring in person as he appeared to be in his letters.

She checked her pendant watch, grateful that she'd remembered to adjust it to local time at the train station.

The omnibus turned onto a bewildering series of winding pretzel-like streets before pulling up the drive leading to the Haywire Grande Hotel.

Judging by the weathered facade, the only thing grand about the hotel was its size.

Her stomach knotted. Whatever fate had in store for her couldn't be any worse than what she'd left behind. While the thought did nothing to lift her spirits, it did help calm her pounding heart. Refolding the letter, she returned it to her purse. Moments later, she stood in the blazing sun and waited for the driver to unload her luggage.

"Will that be all, ma'am?" he asked. His sudden politeness could only mean he expected a generous gratuity.

"Yes, thank you." She handed him twice the number of coins she normally would, more out of guilt for commanding so much space than gratitude.

While a bellhop arranged her luggage onto a wooden handcart, she glanced again at her watch. In two short hours, she would be married to a man she had never set eyes on—a total stranger.

Now, having seen the town, it seemed she was about to exchange one prison for another.

❧

Chase McKnight paced the floor of the judge's chambers. *Where is she?* His bride should have been here by now.

The dark wood paneling along with the teak desk reflected his gloomy thoughts. Never had he imagined a wedding day as bleak and unsettling as this.

There were three men in the room, counting Chase. Judge Gray sat behind the desk waiting to perform the wedding ceremony. Chase's uncle occupied the single chair in front of the desk, ready to serve as a witness. With their dark suits and serious expressions, they could just as easily be attending a funeral.

Chase wished to God he'd never agreed to this marriage. He'd met the bride-to-be but once, years ago when they were both in their early teens. Still, what choice did he have? What choice, for that matter, did the lady have?

Now a widow with three small children—two boys and a girl—she lived in the next county. Not that there was anything wrong with the woman. He'd heard that she regularly attended church, was a hard worker, and had accepted her lot in life with grace and goodwill. If his memory served him right, she wasn't that bad to look at, either. But that wasn't the point.

He glanced at his uncle. "Maybe she's not comin'." It would be disastrous if she didn't show, but who could blame her? He was as much a stranger to her as she was to him, with less than a stellar reputation.

"Relax. She'll be here," his uncle said, though his drumming fingers belied the calmness of his voice. Uncle Baxter was a large, pompous man who resembled his brother—Chase's father—in size, but not disposition. Chase's father was much more easygoing, a trait that turned out to be more of a curse than a gift. In contrast, his uncle was a hard-nosed businessman whose relentless ambition had driven more than one woman away. "She needs this marriage as much as you do."

Chase sincerely doubted that, but now was no time to argue.

Judge Gray reached into his vest pocket for his watch and flipped the case open with his thumb. As round as he was tall, the judge had a long white beard and white hair. Faded gray eyes peered from behind tortoiseshell spectacles. "She better come soon. I've got another wedding in fifteen minutes."

Chase balled his hands at his sides. He longed to shrug off the frock coat and boiled shirt. As a cattle rancher, he wasn't used to such formal attire. Why weddings required such a getup was one of the mysteries of life.

Discomfort turning to \irritation, he glared at his uncle. "I don't know why I let you talk me into this." There had to be another way.

Uncle Baxter leaned forward and snubbed his cigar in the copper ashtray on the judge's desk. "You know what your father's will said. The first son to marry gets the ranch. Do you want your brother claiming what's yours?"

"*Step*brother," Chase gritted out through wooden lips.

The mere thought of losing the ranch was like a knife to his heart. It wasn't just a spread; it was a family legacy. The Rocking M Ranch had been founded by his Scottish grandparents. It was Grandpapa McKnight who had taught Chase everything he knew about cattle and ranching. By the age of twelve, Chase could ride, rope, and shoot as good or better than any man.

The judge checked his watch again. His uncle's

gaze sharpened, and his mustache twitched, but he said nothing.

Chase paced the floor and punched his fist into his left palm. When his uncle first approached him with the idea of marrying the widow, it had sounded like the perfect plan. It wasn't easy being a rancher's wife, and few women could handle the demands. Cassie had grown up around cattle. That alone would make her an asset.

Chase stopped pacing and tossed a nod at the shotgun in his uncle's hand. "Why'd you bring that? I said no violence."

His uncle left his chair. At six feet, he was almost as tall as Chase. "Think of this as insurance." His uncle tapped the floor with the gunstock. "If your stepbrother gets wind that you're here, there could be trouble. I don't aim on letting anything go wrong."

Chase pinched the bridge of his nose. Already something had gone wrong. The bride-to-be had apparently suffered a case of cold feet. "Maybe I can get a bank loan." He resented having to pay his stepbrother to save the ranch. But, if his bride didn't show, he might not have a choice.

His uncle discounted this idea with a shake of his head. "No bank is gonna give you a loan and you know it. Not with the economy the way it is."

"I'll think of somethin'."

"If there was another solution, we'd have thought of it by now." His uncle slipped a hand in his waistcoat pocket and pulled out his gold watch. "You better start praying that the lady shows."

The judge's unkempt bushy eyebrows rose and fell. "You have ten minutes."

Chase took a seething breath and continued pacing while his uncle kept checking the time.

After another couple of minutes, Chase stopped. "Whether she shows or not, I'm not givin' up."

Uncle Baxter grimaced. "You may have to," he said, surprising Chase. It wasn't like his uncle to admit defeat. "It's a shame for it to end this way. The ranch meant everything to your father."

Chase's nostrils flared. "If it meant so much to him, then why did he put such a stipulation in the will?"

How his father's second wife had persuaded him to write such a will was a puzzle that continued to haunt him. Her son, Royce, had never put in an honest day's work in his life. Drinking, gambling, and womanizing were more his style.

"There're some things that are out of a person's control," his uncle said, cryptically.

Chase's gaze sharpened. "What things?"

A look of uncertainty crept into his uncle's expression. "Just…things."

There was something his uncle wasn't saying, but Chase was too incensed to pursue it.

The judge's voice floated across the room. "If your bride doesn't show in the next couple of minutes, I won't have time to marry you. The next wedding party is due to arrive momentarily."

Chase sucked in his breath and started for the door.

"Where are you going?" his uncle asked. "There's still time."

Chase whirled around. "Marrying the lady was your idea and I should never have agreed to it." Lord knew he had enough on his plate without taking on an unwilling bride.

"Now listen to me—"

"No, you listen to me." Chase was shouting now but didn't care. "If I lose the ranch, I lose the ranch. But at least I won't be tied to a loveless marriage!"

He turned toward the door just as it flew open. The widow had finally arrived, and she was decked from head to toe in full bridal regalia.

Author's Note

Dear Readers,

I hope you enjoyed Kate and Brett's story as much as I enjoyed writing it.

While doing the research for my book, I turned up some fun and interesting facts about candy. For example, we can blame our sweet tooth on our cave-men ancestors and their fondness for honey.

I also learned that during the Middle Ages, the price of sugar was so high that only the rich could afford a sweet treat. In fact, candy was such a rarity that the most children could expect was an occasional sugarplum at Christmas.

This changed during the early nineteenth century with the discovery of sugar-beet juice and the invention of mechanical candy-making machines. Many of today's candy favorites, including conversation hearts and Twizzlers, were first produced during this period.

Few people voiced concerns about the candy mania that had swept the country. Sugar candy was touted as a health food that would cure anything from the flu to heart disease.

Soon, jars of colorful penny candy could be found in every trading post and general store in the country. It took almost four hundred candy manufacturing companies to keep up with the demand.

Penny candy changed the market considerably. Children as young as four or five were able to make purchases independent of their parents.

Children weren't the only ones enjoying the availability of cheap candy. Civil War soldiers favored gumdrops, jelly beans, and hub wafers (now known as Necco Wafers).

Never one to miss a trend, John Arbuckle noted the sugar craze that had swept the country and decided to use it as marketing tool. He included a peppermint stick in each one-pound bag of Arbuckles' Coffee to encourage sales.

"Who wants the peppermint?" was a familiar cry around chuck wagons. This call to grind the coffee beans got a rash of volunteers. No rough-and-tumble cowboy worth his salt would turn down a stick of peppermint candy, especially when out on the trail.

Arbuckle wasn't the only one to see gold in candy. Outlaw Doc Scurlock, friend of Billy the Kid and participant in the bloody Lincoln County War, retired from crime in 1880. Though he was still a wanted man, he moved to Texas and opened—what else? A candy shop.

Cadbury, Mars, and Hershey rode herd on the chocolate boom of the late eighteen hundreds and early nineteen hundreds. Penny candy still made up 18 percent of candy sales, but by this time, some merchants had refused to sell it. Profits were thin, and selling such small amounts to children was time-consuming. Chocolate was more profitable. The penny candy market vanished altogether during World War II when sugar was rationed, though it did make a minor comeback in the fifties. Fortunately, no war could do away with chocolate.

As for Haywire, Texas, there're still stories to be told, and you won't want to miss the next book in the series.

Meanwhile, you can reach me through my website: margaret-brownley.com.

Until next time,
Margaret

Acknowledgments

My deepest thanks go to the great Sourcebooks team for the work they put into my books. From editing to marketing and everything in between, I couldn't ask for a more dedicated and talented group.

I'm especially thankful for my editor, Mary Altman, whose insightful comments help make my stories stronger. Sometimes she knows what I'm trying to say in my stories even before I do!

There are no words to express my gratitude to my agent, mentor, sounding board, and all-'round good friend, Natasha Kern. No matter what happens, I always feel better after talking to her.

As always, I can't say enough good things about my family and friends, who never complain when I ramble on about people who exist only in my head.

Finally, thanks to you, my dear readers, for making the journey worthwhile.

TRAILBLAZER

A brand-new series from award-winning
author Anna Schmidt

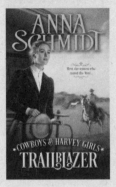

Grace Rogers is ready for an adventure—and to support her
struggling family—so she heads west with the prestigious Fred
Harvey Company. There, a handsome cowboy quickly turns
her head. Too bad the Harvey Girls are forbidden to marry…

Nick Hopkins doesn't plan on falling in love. But after
meeting Grace, he can't keep away. They plan to marry in
secret… But a powerful new rival soon pursues Grace and
won't take no for an answer. Can Nick and Grace save their
happily ever after?

"Western fans rejoice!"
—RT Book Reviews, 4 stars
for *Last Chance Cowboys: The Rancher*

For more Anna Schmidt, visit:
sourcebooks.com

LEFT AT THE ALTAR

From *New York Times* bestseller Margaret Brownley

After she's left at the altar, Meg Lockwood knows she can't show her face in town again. After all, her marriage was supposed to end a bitter feud between rival jewelers, who both keep time in Two-Time, Texas.

Handsome lawyer Grant Garrison is hired to defend the groom in a breach of promise suit—but he instead finds himself developing undeniable feelings for the jilted bride. When the former groom decides to make good on his promise, Meg realizes that her ex-fiancé is no longer who she wants.

Does Meg have enough time to marry the man of her dreams?

"A great story by a wonderful author."
—**Debbie Macomber, #1 *New York Times* bestselling author, for *Left at the Altar***

For more Margaret Brownley, visit:
sourcebooks.com

CHRISTMAS IN A COWBOY'S ARMS

Stay toasty this holiday season with heartwarming tales from bestselling authors

Whether it's a lonely spinster finding passion, an infamous outlaw-turned-lawman reaffirming the love that keeps him whole, a broken drifter discovering family in unlikely places, a Texas Ranger risking it all for one remarkable woman, two lovers bringing together a family ripped apart by prejudice, or reunited lovers given a second chance…a Christmas spent in a cowboy's arms is full of hope, laughter, and—most of all—love.

"Everyone will be uplifted and believe in the joy and wonder of the season through these wonderful novellas."
—RT Book Reviews

For more from these authors, visit:
sourcebooks.com